No one would blame Julian Hickock for bending the law to save his son.

Not Jean Pomeroy, a woman too young to be Hickock's wife but old enough to be his mistress.

Not Wanda Usher, a hard-as-nails hooker who had used her yielding flesh to entrap Hickock's son.

Not Boris Estervan, the porno king who knew every trick of the trade to make a mockery of the law.

Not Martin Delgado, the sleek lawyer whose Harvard tie and ruthless mind were for sale to the highest bidder.

No one would judge Julian Hickock guilty—except himself.

"An old-fashioned, can't-put-it-down book!"
—AMERICAN LIBRARY ASSOCIATION

Also by Ernest K. Gann from Jove

SONG OF THE SIRENS
IN THE COMPANY OF EAGLES
ISLAND IN THE SKY
MASADA (Originally published as *The Antagonists*)

The Magistrate

ERNEST K. GANN

A JOVE BOOK

This Jove book contains the complete
text of the original hardcover edition.
It has been completely reset in a typeface
designed for easy reading, and was printed
from new film.

THE MAGISTRATE

A Jove Book / published by arrangement with
Arbor House Publishing Company

PRINTING HISTORY
Arbor House edition / June 1982
Jove edition / October 1983

ISBN: 0-515-07364-4

Jove books are published by The Berkley Publishing Group,
200 Madison Avenue, New York, N.Y. 10016.
The words "A JOVE BOOK" and the "J" with sunburst
are trademarks belonging to Jove Publications, Inc.

PRINTED IN THE UNITED STATES OF AMERICA

". . . I have heard of a thousand judges, I have seen a thousand before me and I have been able to observe the work of a thousand, and it is always the same thing.

". . . Judge! That formerly had high meaning. The highest in human society. I have known people who have told me that at every trial they have the same horrible feeling in their testicles that one has if one suddenly stands over a deep abyss. . . .

". . . It all comes to the fact that those who live in heaven have no conception of hell, even if one tells them about it for days. There all fantasy fails. Only he can understand who is in it."

—from *The Maurizius Case*, by Jacob Wasserman

ACKNOWLEDGMENTS

For their invaluable cooperation in the writing of this book I am most grateful to Judge, the Honorable Donald Voorhees, John McGovern, Barbara Rothstein and Magistrate John Weinburg of the Federal Courts, Seattle.

My thanks also to the Honorable Anthony Wartnick, and especially for the encouragement and invaluable assistance rendered so willingly by Judge John Vercimak and Judge Barbara Yanick who happen to be man and wife. They took me into their rare combination of a judicial family.

My additional thanks to Judge Steve Schaefer of the Municipal Courts and Judge Solie Ringold of the Appeals Court.

Countless other individuals contributed to this work. Public Defender Irving Paul Jr. was particularly sympathetic to the project as was Sue Clark, Superintendent of the Treatment Center for Women at Purdy, Washington. Her many charges are best left unidentified along with a multitude of individuals luckless against the law. Those on the side of the law, particularly members of the San Francisco Police Department, contributed just as anonymously.

Lawyer Bob Mucklestone was always a skillful white hunter through the unfamiliar areas of the legal jungle. Likewise was Lynn Squires of the University of Washington.

Dr. Jennifer James, also of that institution, offered me constant access to her remarkable research on "the life" and arranged for my counsel with Margo St. James whose personal crusade has at least caused the establishment to occasionally sit up and take notice.

Finally, my thanks to Lois Holub whose unflagging and alert devotion to this work contributed so much.

AUTHOR'S NOTE

The titles *Magistrate* and *Judge* are synonymous. The latter may also be used as a verb and in a casual way has become common usage in addressing certain public officers charged with high legal authority.

The title of *Magistrate* is gradually falling into disuse partly because some elements in judges' organizations seem to feel it lacks dignity or signifies a lesser status.

The author disagrees. There is a noble sound to the word *Magistrate* which seems lacking in *Judge*. For that reason and because with all its flaws it is still a noble profession I have called this work *The Magistrate*.

The Magistrate

Chapter One

Somewhere from the depths of the city there came a brutish cry. It began as a howl and ended in a whimpering—a sound which reverberated through the nearly empty streets.

It was repeated once then fell away and was not heard again. At least on this day. The not quite human sound came from an elderly building now surrounded by tremendous structures of glass and steel. Those who understood the city knew that it came from the county jail, where despair and defiance had been partners for nearly fifty years.

It was early morning in the city. The rumble of the metropolis coming alive was not yet dominant and so it was possible to hear such things. And to view an old moon swimming between the clouds. Its presence at this early hour of the morning seemed incongruous, as if it was something unwanted and left abandoned by the storm of the night. Now the streets of the city were still a such polished black from the rains they reflected the first light in the east. Some of those who were early drivers to work allowed their attention to be diverted from their car radios long enough to assess the eerie mixture of moon and dawn light, and wondered if they were witnessing a rare phenomenon.

They thought, "What the hell is going on," and "Well well, it might turn out to be a beautiful day after all," and some of them made conjectures like "Which half of the moon is cut away when it's old and what in the name of God Almighty am I doing here fighting traffic, I should have been an astronaut? Or at least stayed in bed."

Soon the spectacle was erased by cloud, and most commuters returned to the familiar shelters of their domestic thoughts. Eventually they were swallowed by the central city where the great glass buildings that would serve as air-conditioned wombs for their day projected toward the still rambunctious sky.

These city workers came like bees to the hive and they were only vaguely conscious of the overall rising decibel level; the admixture of sirens, jackhammers, back-firing motorcycles, heel-clickings, tire screeches, and compressor pump engines all combined to create a low vibrato of energy which would become a more intense and overwhelming bedlam as the day progressed and would not diminish until most of the workers were returned to their homes.

Those who worked for the government made their way with a notable lack of enthusiasm to the Federal Building, while the somewhat more primly attired headed for the starkly tall buildings of which various banks and insurance companies were the landlords. As the city shook itself and came to life the jewelers unlocked their doors and decorated the empty green felt of their night windows with sparkling temptations for passers-by, the photographic shops returned their more expensive cameras to their windows, and young lawyers in uniform tan raincoats and carrying briefcases which were often pure show marched resolutely in all directions. It was too early for the opening of the larger department stores so the clerks were not yet in evidence except in the nearby dingy-windowed eating places, where coffee and what the regular customers thought of as breakfast had been available since long before the rain ceased.

The accountants and the computer analysts aimed toward the newest office buildings and the municipal employees toward the oldest.

A young woman named Jean Pomeroy was a part of this mass movement although she drove her car by a circuitous route to avoid both the center city traffic and the freeways, and thus managed to arrive slightly ahead of time at the shipyard where she was employed.

A plump middle-aged woman, one Lucinda Morrow, secretary to the Honorable Judge Julian Hickock, took the bus to the State Building where the superior courts were located.

A man long and lean of bone, a Mr. Exeter, who was so called by all the poor and troubled that he seemed to have no real given name, made his way on foot to the same building; for as always his services as a lawyer were needed by several inmates of the city's jail which was located on the seventeenth floor.

On this same morning a fat-figured, double-jowled man known as Boris Estervan would not trouble himself going to the central city. He rarely did since most of his business was conducted during the afternoons and nights. He lived in a middle-priced suburban development and preferred to start his day in a leisurely fashion with a cup of espresso and one egg boiled precisely three minutes by his wife Rosa. Now she expressed her devotion by staring out the window of their breakfast nook and warning him to take an umbrella if he was going to step outside.

Also rising with this morning's sun was Martin Delgado, a houndlike fellow who had just eased his weekly lust while in the arms of his nubile wife. Preparing for his day in the city he now took extra care with the knotting of his Harvard tie. As citizen Estervan's confidant and attorney, Delgado was anticipating a meeting with the Honorable Judge Julian Hickock and he wanted old-school integrity written across his personage in neat yet bold letters. He knew he must be extremely careful of his words and even gestures when he saw Judge Hickock. At best, his mission was going to be dicey, and it would be well to remind himself constantly that Hickock was an extraordinarily perceptive man.

Lying in one of the city's better hospitals was Nellie-Mae Proctor, a black woman of mighty proportions. She also anticipated a meeting with Judge Hickock, who had always referred to her as his "High Factotum," while she called herself his housekeeper. Now Nellie-Mae worried about what was left of the white family which time, geography, and unpredictable circumstances had somehow made closer to her than her own. No matter how much propaganda people laid on a person these days it was hard not to feel close to a man who shared his troubles and his very few triumphs. Especially when so much of Judge Julian Hickock's family history had been happening right there in front of your eyes, and when your heart ached like a sore tooth for a lonely man who needed Nellie for a lot more than just keeping things straight around the house.

Some thirty miles from the city in a place known as the Clark Treatment Center for Women, resident Wanda Usher stood in the middle of her room and counted slowly to three hundred. It was a trick she had learned early in her three years as a "resident," and she employed it whenever her inner passions threatened to cut loose and betray her.

Since the very first days of her incarceration Wanda had realized that the real smart ones of the world playacted just like they believed in whatever rules were around.

You could not buck the system even on the last day, even on the last hour, even to the very last minute and second. The system was the hands-off winner until all the papers were stamped and the counselors had their say and the superintendent had smiled her silly smile and the jerks who opened the electric doors had made their dumb cracks. Even when Mrs. Millington your sponsor came and drove you away you better keep playing the system or it was sure to turn around and bite you.

All right? All right little Wanda who is not so little any more by ten too many pounds? All right? *Now* is *it,* and this is the real now. Two hundred and fifty-three . . . You cannot even for one second let things hang out and spit right into all their faces, and give them the message about your real feelings. Never never no matter how they tried to make things up to you there was absolutely nothing they could do or anyone else could do now to fix the damage. Like the brain cells were just pounded into so much hominy.

Like once upon a time Wanda Usher was a ordinary human being with feelings and such which were all very normal, like even on gloomy days Wanda used to wake up liking everybody and everything. Sentimental, know what I mean? I liked to touch people. I liked the feel of their skin and the sound of their voices and when a man would take me in his arms I sort of melted from my own inner heat. You could say little Wanda was a hot one all right and be telling the truth, but then, I got a charge out of flowers, and the sun in the trees, and a big open meadow was worth standing and staring at. Blue skies? I could get so grooved on a blue sky with a few white clouds drifting by in ten seconds I could forget where I was. I even wrote poetry about such things.

And the same thing right here at Clark's college for wayward women. Good little ol' Wanda. All the time good little girl with never a complaint from nobody about nothin'. Wanda a model resident, never once had to be put in maximum. From the very first days just pleased us all by going through her Phase A orientation, then as time went by Phase 4, Phase 5.

Rehabilitated.

Good little ol' Wanda. Give the psychiatrists and the counselors all the garbage they wanted to hear, their special flavor day after day, month after month, year after year. No infractions, even minor. Room perfect *all* the time, bed never rumpled, floor spotless—right away it was obvious that was how among other things you could have a radio in your room and finally a little TV set.

No escape tries. For what? To climb all over some bedroom jock for one or two nights before they caught up with you? Dumb unless you liked living in maximum with nothing but you and four bare walls and food shoved in to you like you were some animal.

None of that "Structure Phase" stuff for Wanda Usher. The dumb women who fell into that got themselves a nine P.M. curfew and lights out by ten. Which is what kind of a life? You could spend sixty days in "Structured" before the classification committee met to discuss if you now understood the responsibilities of confinement and all for maybe some dumbass remark, or you missed a count because you were sitting on the pot or something else which was also dumb. Not Wanda. And the same for clothes. Some residents insisted on wearing any old thing when they went for a stroll on the campus. Some *campus* if you didn't mind viewing the woods through a high steel fence . . .

Wanda studied her new wristwatch which she had asked Mrs. Millington to buy for her on the outside as a sort of going away present from Wanda Usher to herself. And out of money earned right here at the center, all right? Wanda Usher, girl draftsman with T-square to go. A free education given by the state and even paid while still in the joint. God's little angel named Wanda who in thirty minutes give or take would be on the outside if the creeps had everything in order like Wanda had.

And who else had better have his affairs in order? Let us say a certain judge whose name will not be mentioned in case anybody is listening even in your sleep, let us say that certain judge had surely better sign his will. Because the days of his ass are numbered and he is going to burn as sure as little ol' Wanda is alive. When everything is finally set up he is going to be told that he is a murderer because he killed you. He is going to learn that you can make a person die without ever touching their body. Then *he* is going to do the dying right in front of your eyes.

Now Wanda looked around her room as if she did not know every minute detail better than anything she had ever known in her whole life including that beat-up human junk shop in Tennessee which had been the only real home she had ever known. It was never a real officiallike *bordello*. It was one of those in-town-for-long? places where dudes came by only if they knew Aunt Louise and where girls who worked on the outside at other jobs came to make a little extra bread. For new coats and dresses and things like that. And Aunt Louise who was really only an aunt by marriage was just the very nicest mother a little girl could have all through the years until she got so sick, and she took care of Wanda and saw she went almost all the way through highschool which was why learning drafting here at the center was most of the time plain easy.

Aunt Louise did a good job except *personally* she was so uptight all the time about men and what they did to women . . . she ought to know . . . she was the original ERA booster, can you stand it? She would not let any man young or old go near her Wanda and so little ol' Wanda did not know, believe it or not, a steer from a bull when Aunt Louise died. Which is no way to start out life.

The macrame hanger with the plant in it which was still hanging in the tiny window always reminded Wanda of Aunt Louise's place which was like a jungle on the lower floor there was so much foliage around. "Kills the stink of tobacco!" Aunt Louise used to yell. She almost never just spoke but always hollered like she was calling hogs and she hated smokers.

Now Wanda brushed the fern gently with her newly manicured fingertips and she thought for a moment that she was going to cry, not so much because the macrame hanger resurrected the vision of Aunt Louise but because the plant would be the only thing left here of resident Wanda Usher after three long years of her life. Three long years with one rug which conformed to the State Fire Code which said it could not exceed three by five feet. Everybody was so uptight about the joint burning down because some poor resident was smoking maybe in bed trying to forget her family or her husband or her kids or whatever the hell life was like before they sent her away. *They* were the power and the glory, not any of that Bible stuff, and the sooner a person realized *that* the easier life could be. It was not some Russian or some oil man or some pimp who took your Deidre away. It was *they* in the person of a certain Judge Hickock . . . whisper the name.

Oh he was a special one he was, and all these three years he had been a real inspiration. If he only knew . . . Which he soon would . . .

At first it had seemed like the sort of thing a human being just could not handle, but when the calendar started looking like a game of tic-tac-toe you found out a human being can handle anything—so long as you had something to keep you going like a fixed target. Long ago, it seemed now more like ten years than three, that certain judge looked down from on high and said, Die Wanda. Maybe he didn't say it in those exact words but he might as well have. Hickock . . . whisper the name.

Says he, I am going to take Deidre away from you and give her to a good home where she can grow up properly. And that ain't all. I am declaring you an unfit mother and I'm not going to give you any more chances to even see her—ever. And what is more, you are going away for a minimum of three years . . .

Die, Wanda. Go away and die while the rest of the world goes on and Deidre grows up without a real mother just like you did. Of course the judge did not say all those things in just those exact words, but he might as well have because what he did say was branded on your brain like a Tennessee song. A good one like "Rasslin' with Ida" or "Come Pick a Cherry with Me."

Well little ol' Wanda refused to die, Your Honor, and now you are the one who is going to find out what hell is all about. Ten seconds after I leave this joint I'm going to crank up the old Wanda computer and feed in the word "vegetable" beside the name Hickock. Then I'm going to ask it what is the best way to make you one—because plain killing is too good for you. It may take some time, but nothing is going to stop me, judge. Nothing.

In the dignified old frame house standing at 1011 Maple Avenue Julian Hickock swore softly. He had made "bride eggs" again, a culinary catastrophe which had occurred too many times since Nellie-Mae had presided over this same stove, using the same frying pan, the same amount of butter melted in exactly the same way and cooked precisely the same amount of time. The tortured mess he now frowned upon bore no resemblance to what he had intended to create. Judges, he had at last decided, were inherently unstable when faced with the heavy decision as to whether something on, in, or about a stove was done or not. Damnit, there was no time to deliberate. Hickock thought that if there had been a jury obliged to survive on his cooking efforts during the past three weeks, their verdict could only have been that he had been guilty of at least a misdemeanor and possibly a felony.

Hickock surrounded his overcooked eggs with four pieces of burnt toast, and took the assembly into the dining room. They said charcoal was good for the complexion, in which case, Hickock mused, he should soon look twenty-five even if he was pushing sixty.

He smiled now at a sudden vision of himself at twenty-five. Then he was known to his law school classmates as "Elephant Ears." He was similarly endowed with a prominent nose, the kind Stuart preferred to paint on his portraits of colonial gentlemen. Given a wig and a stock, Hickock realized, he could easily pass for John Adams at the crucial signing of Philadelphia. Yet his physique would certainly give him away if Adams had been portrayed accurately. For Hickock was lean with his weight distributed evenly about his lanky frame.

Now his weight remained the same as it was during his later student years—proof positive, he was willing to concede, that perhaps the brain did not pick up any weight on the long journey between twenty-five and fifty-nine.

No one had called him Elephant Ears for too many years. How unfortunate, he thought; what a loss of distinctive identity. Now he was known only as the Honorable Judge Julian Hickock.

As he slid into his chair Hickock said, "Good morning, son," to the youth who sat at the far end of the table. It was a long table, gummy from lack of recent polishing, a relic of those now distant times when Dolores Hickock was alive and they entertained regularly. Here the Hickock family had gathered daily: Dolores, who was a good mother and a gracious hostess when she was sober, and daughter Sally, who was now away at Georgetown University studying to be a foreign service officer. The family knew a sense of completion when Nellie-Mae left her apron in the kitchen and took her place at the table.

Hickock now wondered at the unforeseen absences of his troops. Nellie-Mae was in the hospital, another victim of the American calamity known as the crime wave. She had been shopping for a special kind of sausage they all liked, when the proprietor of the delicatessen was held up and pistol-whipped. As the rcbber fled he encountered Nellie-Mae who was determinedly blocking the exit to the street. The robber knocked her down and the fall broke her hip. The damage to Nellie-Mae had been almost as severe emotionally as it had been physically. Why the vicious pistol-whipping of an innocent little man who had turned over what money he had without protest? Nellie-Mae said that even if the robber was the poorest kind of black trash there was no need for him to behave that way.

And Hickock had wondered himself. The robber had been only an individual of course, but what he represented was a boundless ocean of human antagonisms. Who could have foreseen such a national scene in the relatively stable fifties or even in the early sixties when Nellie-Mae had adopted the Hickocks?

And then there had been Dolores. Until her own catastrophe, Dolores seemed oblivious to the growing instability of her fellow citizens. Little by little the old standards had been eroded and sent the people of Dolores's world scurrying for shelter. The frightful crimes she read about happened to people of a different class. Nice people had divorces and that was all. Once Hickock had told her about a young mother he had felt obliged to separate from her child. The woman was a prostitute, he recalled . . . he could remember her face but not her name . . .

"You took the child away forever?" Dolores had asked incredulously.

"Yes. For the child's sake, its safety, I felt it was necessary—"

"How could you do that? That's not good law. It's a violation of the law of nature."

She had been very angry with him and he had wanted to tell her please not to confuse motherhood and the American flag with outright child abuse. But he had kept his peace. Tigers and their cubs, he reminded himself, were as potentially dangerous as hand grenades. Sometimes Hickock wondered if at last Dolores realized she herself had been guilty of a violent crime.

Yet how could the one-time sweetheart of Sigma Nu, the charity worker, the churchgoer, the reader-for-the-blind and the chairperson of the local Republican committee foresee the culmination of her love affair with alcohol? Dolores collided with a certain Mr. Henry Frick; her blood alcohol content at point 14 percent. Vodka, as she so often declared, was not detectable on your breath. She simply would not concede that the game was to keep breathing, a function which Dolores had lost instantly when she met another middle-class citizen, the unforeseen Mr. Frick, at the intersection of Ninth Avenue and Peach Street. In the past three years since that tragic rendezvous it had been little consolation to reflect that Mr. Frick's body contained an almost identical amount of alcohol, which meant that he was quite as intoxicated as Dolores. Hickock had often wondered if anyone at all gave a damn that the number of Americans who killed each other in the same violent way might be a reflection of a new national philosophy which seemed to hold life very cheaply. He or she is dead. He or she was driving a Chevrolet, a Datsun, a Ford, a Volkswagen. It was a more acceptable American way to die than from cancer.

Now Dolores was departed permanently and daughter Sally was unlikely to return to 1011 Maple Avenue on any kind of a permanent basis. Sally had always been daddy's little girl—"daddi*o*" as she preferred to call him. Sally had all her mother's beauty plus brains she must have inherited from her grandmother who had graduated magna cum laude from Vassar in the dark ages of feminine achievement.

All of which Hickock knew had to be very hard on son Victor, whose deep-rooted attachment for the house he was born in was understandable. Unlike Sally he was mainly interested in local events and he resisted all attempts to enlarge his horizons.

Now he had mumbled something that sounded like it might have been a "good morning" but Hickock was not at all sure it had been anything so significant. Was it mandatory, was there some unseen American law that insisted nineteen-year-olds mumble?

Victor had been his mother's boy and in many striking ways he resembled her. He had the same high forehead and long neck, and the same compelling eyes that often brought the ghost of his mother into the house again. His nose was more like his father's, although in much better proportion to the rest of his face, and his hair was the same tawny blond as his mother's. There were even little intonations of speech, ways of phrasing things when he chose to communicate that were identical to the way Dolores had expressed herself. Victor's mother continued to live vividly in her son, and Hickock continued trying to persuade himself that was a good thing.

"I did my usual superb job with these eggs," Hickock said easily. "And how are you faring?"

"I miss Nellie-Mae."

"We are badly spoiled."

Hickock waited for some further comment from his son although he doubted if he would hear anything which might open the morning on a cheery note. Like his mother, Victor had a way of vanishing while still being present. It seemed they were capable of responding to some outer self; the call would come and away they would go, Victor retreating into his shell or gone somewhere in a young man's dream land—a troubled region, Hickock thought, because Victor's mood never improved when he was there. Another heritage from Dolores, Hickock remembered, was that same haste to blame before the facts were known, coupled with a strange reluctance to praise.

There had been times when Dolores's self-deprecating moods had nearly driven her husband to despair, but she had been also quick to turn on the charm when she was so disposed and almost instantly capture the devotion of everyone around her. She had been Public Angel Number One, and Hickock had long been resigned to the fact that a beautiful woman playing that role to the hilt was bound to make her partner appear either insufferably dull or at least a part-time villain. If only she had not somehow bequeathed that ability to her son.

These days, it seemed Victor rarely bothered with charm, and lately his sourness had taken on a new and even more acid note. Hickock cautioned himself that their present relation might be considered as in the best international tradition. The father could do nothing right. The son knew all there was to know about everything.

Straight scripture so why fret? At least once a morning

Hickock found it convenient to remind himself that at nineteen he had also been churning with rebellion.

"It might be a nice thing to do," Hickock said, "if you would stop by the hospital on your way to school and see Nellie-Mae."

"I have."

"Oh? She didn't tell me. That was very thoughtful of you. By the way, how is school?"

"It's still there."

Hickock let the silence fall again and put away the urge to advise Victor that the information he had just passed on was hardly illuminating since if the rather large university which he attended at a considerable cost to his father had burned down during the night, he would undoubtedly have learned about it on the morning radio news. And he might have added that the question, "How is school?" when uttered by an adult did not necessarily refer to its structural status but was standard phraseology indicating an interest in the student's personal welfare, his social life, his grades, and anything else which might provide some crumb of satisfaction to the questioner.

Why was it that every morning seemed to be starting in just this way? When Nellie-Mae was present, maneuvering her bulk with incredible grace between kitchen and table, there was always a certain badinage between the three of them and of course it took an even faster pace when daughter Sally was home. For Nellie-Mae spared no one in the Hickock family.

"You listen to me," she would say to Victor if he complained that his student work load was more than he could hope to conquer. "You get in there with the wisdom right where it hides in little dark places and you say to yourself there will be no place in this whole warehouse where I'm not going to look and maybe swipe a little something and take it away with me. You're so lucky, man, you should get down on your knees every morning and say thanks be to God. Now shut up and eat your cereal."

Nellie-Mae, who had graduated with honors from Tuskegee Institute, knew how to humble others better than any individual Hickock had ever known. She was a powerhouse of mental energies and could have had any number of jobs were it not for her passionate hatred of offices.

"What would I do?" she responded when Hickock had once

suggested she might find work more suitable to her education and talents.

"You want me to sit behind some desk shuffling papers, *government* papers like most black people, sit there until the sweep second hand comes on to five o'clock even when I finished everything there is to do and all the papers are in the right pigeonholes by two o'clock, and you want me to just sit there pretending, or listening to some two-bit honky bureaucrat carry on about his opinion of the international monetary situation because he has a captive audience . . . man that's slavery and I don't intend to go back to it. Here if I feel like reading a book or listening to a good concert I can put my feet up any time I want, and do what I have to do later when I damn well please. If I want to take the afternoon off and go to a movie I can, and considering I don't have to commute to work or lay out half my wages for a dinky little apartment with seventeen locks on the door and a German shepherd to protect me, I make out much better financially. If this kind of work is supposed to be demeaning I just don't agree. I'm proud of the job I do here and most of the time of myself and the people in it. Of course I'm not going to take any sass from any of you, but then you got better sense than to try . . . and that's a lot more than I could expect from some government bureaucrat."

To tease her Hickock had countered, "I should like to point out to you, Nellie, that *I* might be considered a bureaucrat. After all, the state does pay my salary."

"Don't argue with me, Your Honor. Nellie-Mae is speaking of Nellie-Mae, and we should always have different harps for different angels."

Now Hickock wondered why Nellie-Mae had not told him that Victor had been by to see her. Or could it be that they might have discussed Jean Pomeroy? Which brought up the matter of this very evening.

"What are your plans for tonight, Vic?"

"Study. Is there anything else in this world?"

"I mean about dinner. I won't be here."

Hickock saw his son reach very deliberately for his coffee cup, take a sip, and then set the cup down again.

"So? I can take care of myself. I'll take some hamburger out of the freezer."

"You are welcome to join Jean and myself. She is a wizard cook."

"I concede the former. I don't care about the latter."

"Just what do you mean by that?" Hickock felt his face flushing. It always did when he was in danger of losing his patience. Smart lawyers who frequented his court were alert for the warning signal to be seen about his prominent cheekbones and immediately took a different approach to their proceedings.

Victor kept his silence for what seemed to Hickock like a very long time. As his impatience faded Hickock found himself returning to an all too familiar theme. What in God's name could he do about Victor's continuing resentment?

He saw Victor try to smile.

"Well, just to make things perfectly clear because you are accustomed to people haggling over things hour by hour until you finally look down and give your learned opinion, just to lay it on you straight out which is the way you say you like things to be said . . . well, it will hardly be news to you that there are wizards in all kinds of activities. . . ."

"I'm still not quite following you." But he was, Hickock realized; he was following his son with absolute clarity.

"It will hardly be news to you that I am just not at all infatuated with one Jean Pomeroy."

"No one asked you to be infatuated. She kindly offered you an invitation to join us for dinner."

"No thanks. I doubt if I could handle that wine and candlelight scene. This place may be a mess, but it does grow on a guy."

"It has been growing on you for nineteen years, and if I may suggest, nothing is permanent. A young man should not live in the past. There's a whole damn wonderful world out there—"

"There was a whole damn wonderful world right here—"

"I know, but we can't bring those times back."

"We don't have to insult them."

Very well, Hickock decided, let it come out. If that was a risk then so be it.

"I assume," he said carefully, "that you are referring to my friendship with that certain very fine lady."

"Oh, come off it. Those old nineteenth-century phrases just won't fly. Aren't you supposed to be Moses with the tablets standing up on some mountain laying down the law? Your problem is when somewhere in the crowd you hear the sweet voice of that woman and right away get yourself an identity problem. Before you met your friend Jean there were pictures of mom all over the house. Nellie-Mae used to put flowers under that big photograph of you two skiing at Sun Valley. All gone now. Not a sign that mom was ever in this house . . . except in my room and a little bit in Sally's. Here today and gone tomorrow seems to be the drill around here. I think it's time someone reminded you that mom did exist."

"Do you now? That was quite a speech." Hickock struggled to keep his voice easy, but he knew he was losing the fight.

"I was not aware that college sophomores now become instant psychology majors. I had forgotten that a young man of your age is bound to have all the answers, or I would have consulted with you regarding my problem. Perhaps you would care to comment on the fact that your mother and I were married for twenty-three years which is not too tawdry a record in these times, and that for most of those years we lived together about as happily as any man and woman can expect. A part of that contentment and satisfaction with each other resulted in *your* existence, and I am reasonably sure your mother would join me now in wondering if, presently at least, the result is not somewhat of a mixed blessing."

"Do you want me to move out? Are you in a never-darken-my-door-again syndrome?"

"Syndrome, my foot. No, I do not want you to move out. This is as much your home as it is mine, but that does not give you the right to tell me how to live in it or out of it. What I would very much prefer if it is at all possible for you to reflect on what seems to be your estimation of me, is that you recognize it just might be that I have more experience in life than you do, and as a consequence may have picked up a morsel of knowledge here and there. What I would much prefer is what I like to think of as a pleasant father-son relationship between us for the few years we are still assigned to sharing the same dwelling. I think it might be very pleasant for you and for me to have someone we can confide in and trust and hope to find sympathy in . . . and perhaps such a harmonious, mutual respect might lead to a better understanding of each other and the very problem you seem to find so irritating. Now, son, is that too much to ask?"

During the silence that followed, Hickock wondered if Victor had heard a word he had said. For obviously he had gone away again; there was that same faraway look in his eyes, the same mental hat-trick that somehow transported Victor to another world. Come in, Victor, he thought. Earth calling.

Hickock watched anxiously as he saw his son push back his chair and take up his plate and coffee cup. He saw him start for the kitchen and he wondered what he could do to stop him without capitulating entirely. How was he going to make Victor understand that three years was a long enough mourning period, and probably too long? How could he be made to see that Jean Pomeroy was not the origin of the problem, but a come-lately result of an event which could not be reversed?

Victor put his shoulder to the swinging door which led to the kitchen. He pushed it partly open, and then hesitated. He looked over his shoulder and to his amazement, Hickock saw him smile. That warm and winning smile which Dolores had employed so successfully.

"Okay, I read you. I'm willing to give it a try, but as part of our confiding in each other, you should know right now that it is going to be a long never before I agree Jean Pomeroy is a good influence around here. And now," he added, still smiling, "would you do me a favor and cease and desist all galley work? Every time you load the dishwasher or even pass by it, something goes wrong. Just stick with the law and leave things in the galley to me until Nellie-Mae comes home. You are not set up to deal with these matters, and I want to avoid a real disaster. And I thank you very much, sir."

Victor pushed the door fully open and it swung shut behind him before Hickock could be sure he was not being humored. Patronized? At least one thing was apparent, he thought. The kid was not lazy, and he was his own stubborn man. Not so bad . . . not really so bad at all.

Chapter Two

Wanda Usher looked down at the single suitcase which contained the total of her possessions. All the government-issue stuff was turned in and accounted for. All the goodbyes up and down the unit were done with. Goodbye to Agnes who was here for life because she and her boyfriend decided to murder her husband and made a mess of it. And goodbye to Natalie whose boyfriend got her in deep by talking her into helping him rob a bank. And goodbye to Pearl and Joanne and Mildred who were convicted of being pushers even though they said they had the junk only for their own use. They had trouble explaining why there was enough to make them all Queen of the May forever and ever. And goodbye Joyce the whistler who still said there was not one thing in any store that she could not liberate if she really wanted it—except she got greedy and got caught with six tins of caviar in between her boobs. Goodbye to Margie Wing-feather who claimed to be an Indian princess. Well she was a genuine Indian, probably the first and only American Indian dyke in the world who got herself busted at the same time for interference with a fire alarm system and resisting arrest while beating her lady friend with a leather boot.

It was a menagerie all right. Every woman had her story and almost all of them were in for what they said were bum raps and maybe they were considering the way *they* stacked the cards against ordinary people.

Wanda remembered how she had tried for a little sympathy during her first weeks in the admission/diagnostic unit. The shrink in charge was a female and she was full of nosy questions. "Wanda will you tell me now what you're doing with a rap sheet like this? You have been busted seven times for prostitution, four for soliciting, and once before for child abuse. What gets into you? You're not unintelligent, and at least you had a little education. Is that the kind of thing they teach you in Tennessee?"

Wanda remembered she had wanted to tell the psychiatrist to shove it and where did she get off making smartass cracks about Tennessee, especially when she was being paid by *this* dumb ol' state to supposedly help women.

Wanda smiled. Looking back to those early times was easy now. Like it was easier sitting there in the shrink's office than passing the same time in your own tiny "room." Room? It was a cell. Even then she had known the right and the wrong kind of music to play for the creeps who were running this so-called institution. There was a time for harps and a time for organs.

Wanda could see herself in those days, sitting there head bowed, fingers twisting all the time like she was trying to unravel some terrible puzzle. She set the story down slowly while keeping her voice low so in case she forgot some details her listener would ask her to repeat what she said and that would give her time to think up a good answer. "Well I was an orphan, you know what I mean? I was taken in by this family who were in Winthrop and I stayed there until I was about fourteen . . . going on fifteen." Then the story would sort of go on by itself . . . blah-blah-blah—until, "Well there was this man who was my foster father who said he wanted to show me his penis one afternoon down in the basement and he raped me, y'know, and I had my first baby when I was fifteen, a boy . . . named Gary . . . y'know, and when the social workers took him away . . . and all right I guess I flipped because I was so young, sort of forgot about Gary which of course I would never do today, and I bummed a ride up to San Francisco first and I worked at a Colonel Saunders Fried Chicken, and then at a hospital for a while and then I just sort of got lost with some hippies in Mendocino County for a while which I know now was a God-awful waste of time. Well then I went up to Reno for a while and worked the spots *not* as any prostitute but as a waitress, all night work because that's the way people live when there's gambling. But I never did one thing wrong for those couple of years, just little ol' Wanda scratchin' for her living and what with tips and all I made out okay, you know what I mean? That is I rented a cheap little trailer out on the edge of town and I tell you the truth I did once in a while invite some guy out there when I would get horny which was not very often. A girl who has been raped and treated like me don't ever really care for that sort of thing. I didn't get no real charge out of it and I decided gee what am I doing under these circumstances giving it away? So the next guy I decided would have to pay for it and he turned out to be a police officer and there I was busted for the first time in my whole life and we didn't really *do* anything . . ."

A story about little Gary who was really just kind of a wish could take up a whole morning in the shrink's office and sometimes it seemed as if he actually had been a real baby. Blue eyes and red hair.

Of course it paid to be careful and keep some truth in all the stories because the shrinks and the counselors and whoever wanted to stick their nose in a private citizen's business had the rap sheet right in front of them all the time.

What they could not gather from such a list of sins was the real Wanda Usher. Like who could whistle any better? Real classical tunes like the "Anvil Chorus" and "Greensleeves" and "Madame Butterfly." No rap sheet was ever going to tell them how much you liked music or that the one thing in life Wanda had always wanted was a good man in a good home with kids all around and just domesticating all over the place and the hell with the female liberation stuff. Just give me a house with some ivy, a cook-stove, and a half-decent bathroom with the toilet inside and the pigs outside. You better believe Wanda would make the best and truest wife in the whole world. Honest she would . . .

A person could do just about anything they set their minds to. Like here at Clark. It took a little time, but finally the whole scene got changed around to suit Wanda about as well as could be under the circumstances. From the library to goal setting, from arts and crafts to recreation activities, little ol' Wanda was the star. Nobody, but nobody ever before in the whole history of this cruddy institution got the management on their side without the other residents calling her an asskisser or worse. Even the blacks, who knew there was nothing they could do to improve their status, thought Wanda Usher was a neat person. They were just nigras, but being right next to them in the same sort of stuff proved that at least *some* of them could be okay.

But none of this got Deidre back. She was no Gary. She was the real thing. She was now six and God knows where she lived. Those poems you wrote told all about how soft her skin was and how she blew up her cheeks before she laughed . . . Hey, I didn't know what I was *doing!* I was zonked out of my gourd! . . .

Wanda pressed her lips together so hard they became almost invisible. Watch it! Now was no time to get all out of shape about that New Year's Eve which was a long long time ago. It was another life, okay? And you *got* to forget about it. Most of that night was a blank just like you told Judge Hickock in the first place. Well, that man was going to learn a thing or two. Better believe it.

Somehow the prosecutor found Sam, which was never easy to do if he didn't want to be found, and brought him into court and Sam sat right there near the judge and told the whole story—*his* story. Your very own man telling things that had to be lies right up to the time the police came and then telling how everything happened at seven-thirty on that New Year's morning. Your very own pimp saying what a lousy way it was to say Happy New Year. Ratting, so maybe the judge would not bear down too hard on him . . . saying it was all little ol' Wanda's fault and nothin' serious would have happened if it had not been for her bad temper which everyone who knew her was supposed to know about! Sam, the Judas.

Well, Sam was dead now. The only thing left of him was sometimes in the way you talked. You couldn't live with a black man for two going on three years without mimicking him. Sometimes just to hear yourself was like listening to an echo. Some switch for a body that should have been a southern lady. He got himself killed for doing just what he did to you—snitching. He broke the code and opened his bit mouth on some of the other characters at Walla Walla where they put him away for five years. There was some kind of a riot and the first place his neighbors headed for was Sam's cell. They cut off his tongue and let him drown in his own blood and nobody cried . . .

She heard a key slither into the door lock and took a deep breath. She thought, "For a five-foot-six-inch gal I feel twenty feet tall."

She glanced with approval at the mirror above her desk. There was not too much make-up anywhere, just a touch around her large brown eyes. Her eyebrows remained almost natural and she had put just nothing at all on her full lips. Now that there was some reason to think about things like that she remembered her mouth and lips were two of her best points and were best left alone—the kind of lips Sam used to say gave him a super charge even when he was laid back and just looking at them. And you better believe as soon as she could get to a real hairdresser she was going to blow herself to the works and it was not going to be one of those cheap ten cent store clerk weirdo coiffures like was in the cheap magazines. It was going to be just like the ones in *Cosmopolitan,* cut maybe on the more severe side.

The door opened and there was Miss Pope the superintendent. Right in little ol' Wanda's doorway was standing Miss Pope herself who never came near any of the units in person unless it was a super occasion which you better believe this had to be.

"Good morning to you, Wanda. This is your day."

Miss Pope was smiling which was an occasion in itself and there she was wearing a black pantsuit and now that it was this special morning she turned out to be a pretty good-looking woman without that bitchy look she seemed to have had for the past three years. So what the hell give her a farewell smile and say back, "Good morning." Sincerelike and for real this time.

"Mrs. Millington is already waiting outside for you. She even brought an umbrella for you so you don't have to worry about the rain."

They walked out of the room and Wanda did not look back.

"I'm not worrying about a little thing like rain today," she said.

They made their way along the covered sidewalk which served Wanda's unit and then turned into a hallway where they paused before an electric door. Miss Pope handed Wanda a manila envelope.

"Here are all your papers. Take them to your parole officer. And keep your nose clean, Wanda. We never want to see you back here again . . . of course, if you're in the neighborhood and just want to drop by to say hello—"

Don't hold your breath, Miss Pope. Wanda has been her own woman all this time and to this day you're not the only one who just don't have a clue as to what kind of a person I am. Will the real Wanda please stand up? Well, not just yet.

Wanda saw the guard behind the glass screen smile at her and waggle his fingers in a goodbye gesture. Was the creep *ever* going to press the button? A click and a buzzing as the door opened. They passed Miss Pope's office and Wanda waved goodbye to June, her secretary, a one-time forger who had served out her time and when it was up damned if she didn't apply and win her secretarial job right here in this same place.

"Goodbye, Miss Pope. I can't say it's been nice knowing you." There goes that tongue again! Who needs it, right now?

Miss Pope smiled, patted Wanda on her shoulder, then turned back into the building. Wanda walked to the blue Chevrolet. She saw that the windshield wipers were working, but she did not feel rain. She saw Mrs. Millington smiling behind the windshield and she thought it was like seeing the sun break through on a gloomy day. And as she threw her suitcase on the back seat and slipped in beside Mrs. Millington she thought there would always be women like her who played angel, and she thought that maybe some day she would be able to do the same sort of thing, but right now first things first. *Hickock* . . . whisper the name.

By twisting slightly in his chair, Hickock could just see the enormous grandfather clock in the front hallway of the old house at 1011 Maple Avenue. It was the wedding gift from his own father, who could ill afford such a lavish expenditure. As a portrait photographer working in a small studio, he hardly made enough to live on, much less buy grandfather clocks with a fine set of chimes. Hickock heard it now, bonging the count for eight o'clock, and he knew he had an hour before he must leave for his chambers.

Hickock liked to think his father was actually responsible for Jean Pomeroy's entry into his life since that extraordinarily humble and honest man had labored for ten years of his spare time to build a small catboat and left it to his only son.

Beautifully crafted in the finest maritime traditions, the little *Freedom* displayed a saucy stern, a fat beam, and just the right amount of tumble-home in her lovely hull. Others were welcome to their plastic racers of ultra-modern design, Hickock thought. *Freedom* to him meant just that; aboard her was the one place he had known absolute contentment and he was proud of the way she caught every knowing eye when he found time to go sailing.

One pair of eyes had belonged to Jean Pomeroy, who had stood waiting on the dock when, as it usually pleased him,

Hickock had disdained *Freedom*'s little auxiliary engine and sailed her into the slip. As *Freedom* slid home easily, he was so busy dousing the big mainsail and picking up the stern mooring line that he hardly noticed the woman on the dock. He became aware of her as he made up the sail and threw a proper lashing around the boom and gaff. There were often men who paused to look at *Freedom* and Hickock had found it difficult not to invite them aboard for a closer look. Damn selfish to have a boat like this, he thought, and keep her all to oneself. But *Freedom* was not of the style that interested most women. There were no curtains or even windows in her cabin, just plain old-fashioned bronze portholes. There was no sparkling chromium, and he thought it would be difficult, at least for the kind of women he knew, to visualize themselves sunbathing on her cramped deck. Which had been one of the reasons Dolores had ignored *Freedom*. She had claimed the boat gave her a choice, and neither one was her idea of freedom. She could stay below and become seasick while bumping her head here and there, or she could be up on deck and be sure that sooner or later she was going to receive an ice-cold shower bath. Fortunately, both son Victor and daughter Sally thought *Freedom* was a family treasure, and their many sails together were among their father's most delightful memories.

It had now been almost two years since that rainy Sunday afternoon when Hickock had looked up from coiling the peak halliard and saw the woman on the dock was still absorbed in studying *Freedom*.

"Like her?" he asked, wondering if she was the wife of someone he knew, or should know. He had always been ashamed of his inability to recall names on sight, even of people he knew better than casually. It always took too many seconds for his recognition switch to close and associate the face with a title, and he had tried all kinds of experiments to cure the fault. Without the slightest success, he thought, although now he was at least fairly well-convinced he had never seen the woman before.

"She's really quite beautiful," she said.

"I'm afraid she is looking a little seedy right now."

Freedom certainly could use some paint. Her brass binnacle was covered with verdigris, and her door and hatch were peeling varnish. "You either work on a boat or sail her," he said apologetically, "and I just don't have time for both."

"I like her proportions," the woman said. "Too many catboats are compromises these days. They cut down their mast and boom for easy handling, and depend on the engine. I think they look dumpy."

"Do you now?"

Silently Hickock muttered to himself that he would be damned. What kind of woman knew that much about boats, let alone catboats? He sighed. One-time male chauvinists were like fallen-away Catholics. It was getting harder and harder to know just where to take a stand. Now Dolores, there was a woman a man could understand. Like *Freedom,* she was built and performed according to the best traditions. She would never think of wearing slacks, neglecting her nails, or missing a hairdressing appointment. If everything else was right, she might have exposed her beautiful legs for a light tanning, but otherwise she was careful to avoid the sun.

"How come you know so much about catboats?"

"My father had one. We used to sail a lot out of Lake Michigan. I saw you heading in and I couldn't resist."

Hickock wiped away a raindrop from the end of his great nose and continued to make up the main sheet. When it was evenly coiled, he threw a hitch around it and hung it from the boom. He knew exactly what he was doing and he knew the way he tidied up *Freedom* after a sail made a good little show for the minuscule number of people who cared about such things. And he had often thought that had it not been for his overwhelming absorption in the law, he might have been just as devoted to the life of a sailor.

Until he had finished he pretended to have forgotten the woman, a damn subterfuge, he thought, while I play sailor for an audience of one . . . which was at least one better than average. Was she going to stand there in the rain for the rest of the afternoon?

"Do you have a boat of your own?" he asked, ". . . or your family?" That was better. Let's get back to basics here, keep at least one last tradition. Women did not own boats.

"I'm working on one. A little cutter."

"You're building one?"

"Not yet. I'm still in the design stage." She smiled. "When the plans are perfect then I'll have to draw a super-perfect financial plan."

Hickock told himself that he had just been guilty of some

Neanderthal thinking. Why was it that the moment the woman on the dock mentioned she might build a boat he instantly visualized her trying to plank a hull all out of shape, using the wrong kind of wood, nails and hammer? It was a wrong image, he knew, and yet he could not seem to erase it without a conscious effort. Since Dolores's death he had been strangely uncomfortable in the presence of any woman he had not known for a long time, even somewhat frightened of them. And he had found it not at all inspiring when he finally realized he had known very few women. There was Dolores, Nellie-Mae, his secretary Lucinda, and daughter Sally. There had been the wives of a few colleagues whom he rarely saw any longer, and he had never known them well.

Such was the extent of his acquaintance except for the figurines who made their pathetic way through his courtroom. Almost all of them were in serious trouble or they would not have been there; consequently, he knew they behaved in ways that were unnatural to themselves. They were performers on a tricky stage, sometimes remorseful, sometimes defiant, and always to be pitied. The majority of these women revealed that devotion to a man, in one form or another, was responsible for their woes. That fact alone prejudiced a male judge no matter how he tried to avoid it. And that influence was bound to introduce at least some suspicion that women did not really know what the hell they were doing most of the time. There had been times when Hickock had wondered if he would ever learn to separate those women who sat weeping and lying in the witness box from the rest of the female population. He always had to remind himself that bitterness could be the enemy of justice too.

These days Hickock realized that in spite of Dolores's drunken later years, an important part of his own life had perished with her. Left for him was his other devotion, the law. He had never understood why it had been his passion since youth. Brandeis, Learned Hand, Cardozo and Jerome were still his heroes. He simply was convinced the law was the key factor in the health of any society, and in time that belief had become like a separate being within himself. He was proud of the fact that he knew his state's law better than any lawyers who were obliged to practice before him—and they knew it as well, which kept them on their no-nonsense legal toes.

There were few places where Hickock could leave the law

behind him. There was the jazz combo he played in once a month, yet by far his most complete escape was aboard his little boat. By God, he had vowed, if any lawyer, or even a judge came within hailing distance he would torpedo him. No shop-talk here. Seventeen people could be murdered right on the boat in the next slip and he, the *dis*honorable Julian Hickock, would not be interested. Or so he said.

Looking up at the woman on the dock, he saw that she was dark-haired, rather plain, and of medium height. He saw nothing more, probably, he thought, because he was just not interested. The same applied during the various dinner parties he had felt obligated to attend because they were arranged by Dolores's old friends. They seemed to be of a unanimous opinion that a widower was in dire need of something that might be provided by their unattached female friends. He was grateful that after the first few months of negative results the invitations had tapered off, but then how healthy was the resulting social isolation? At least the general knowledge that Nellie-Mae kept a firm hand on the household discouraged the occasional overly solicitous female from charging into his kitchen.

He found it impossible to place the woman on the dock.

"Have we met someplace before?" Did that corny old query sound like he was on the make?

"Not unless it was in another life." She smiled again and he thought it a strangely pleasing smile.

"If you don't mind my saying so, it's always been my opinion that the design of boats should be left to experts."

"I'm delighted you would say so. I agree." She reached in the pocket of her shirt, took out a card, and handed it down to him.

Jean Pomeroy
Marine Architect
Moran Shipyards

Hickock held his free hand over the card to protect it from the rain. He read it a second time, then looked up at the woman.

"Don't you know you can catch cold just standing around in the rain?"

"Are you inviting me to come aboard?"

"Sure."

"I thought you would never ask."

Before he could extend his hand to offer her some stability in descending, she had caught hold of the port shroud and swung easily down to the deck. He noted with approval that even as her feet touched she made the traditionally formal request.

"Permission to come aboard?"

Someone, Hickock knew, had taught her proper nautical etiquette.

"Granted," he said, and introduced himself as Julian Hickock.

They stood looking at each other in the rain for a long moment, and months later they had argued about exactly where on the deck they were standing when the first subtle signals of special empathy passed between them. Jean insisted they were still by the port shroud, and yet it seemed to Hickock they had been farther aft by the hatch when he held out his hand and said it was the kind of weather for hot grog and if she was interested he had a stove and all the ingredients.

That afternoon with the rain peckling on the cabin roof and the steam rising from their glasses launched a new pattern in the life of Julian Hickock. They sailed together, they talked boats and ships and the law together, and took long walks together. He found himself welcome and extraordinarily comfortable in Jean Pomeroy's tiny house where little by little they discovered each other. It was not until more than two months had passed that he realized he had fallen in love with her.

Hickock also discovered two sharp thorns in his new euphoria. The first was Jean's age—good God, she was not much older than Sally! The second was Victor, who from the beginning had shown his resentment toward their relationship.

"I would think a man of your age would know better," he had once said. "At best, you're just a father image, and at worst she wants something . . . probably your money."

"Between one thing and another," Hickock said, reaching desperately for his sense of humor, "I have very little in my financial portfolio to interest anyone. Any halfway smart lawyer who settles for a judgeship is a born financial loser. You and Sally are receiving your inheritance now . . . in your education . . ."

Hickock paused and eyed his son carefully. He yearned for

his understanding and he thought that perhaps he should reach out more and make a firm effort to shed his black-robe manner. Victor deserved a father who lived in his immediate world.

"Of course I might become a dishonest judge and get rich," he chuckled, "but do you know what Cambysis did to dishonest judges?"

"Somewhere I've heard the name but I can't remember him coming to 1011."

"Only in spirit and I do not intend a pun. Cambysis had a punishment for dishonest judges that might interest you. He would skin him alive and upholster a judicial chair in the resulting epidermis. Then he would appoint his son to sit in it."

There followed a long pause then Victor said, "Not very funny."

"Neither is your attitude," Hickock replied more sharply than he intended.

At another time Victor had said that in some ways he could understand his father's need for feminine companionship, but why get serious? Why not find someone his own age before he got hurt?

"How are you going to feel five or ten years from now when she starts making eyes at some young stud? I'm trying to protect you, that's all . . ."

Now that he had finished his unsatisfying breakfast, Hickock sat motionless for a moment. He could hear the clicking of the grandfather clock, and it suddenly struck him that it was an overly pompous sound, a solemn measurement of his life these days. Lonely days, when he was honest enough to face the truth. How much longer was he going to listen to that steady tick-tock while he was really wishing he was elsewhere? Where was the rebellious, nonconforming young Julian Hickock who had spawned a hardline, conforming son? Obviously, Hickock the elder was sitting on his tail comfortably counting pompous tick-tocks while the rest of the world throbbed with life. Here, amid his comfortable middle-class serenity, in what was considered a "nice" residential neighborhood, a clock chimed a certain number of times, and off went Hickock the elder to the fringes of a jungle where all was uncertainty except the continuation of anguish.

Enough, he thought. Enough of this petty brooding about the state of the world and thus betraying your age. And forget that

"Hickock-the-elder" handle. Instead turn you thoughts toward your day's work, focusing once again on one Boris Estervan whose immediate future, perhaps even his life, now rests in your hands.

There was something very frightening about one human with so much power over another. And yet there was no other way. At least it was a full jury that had found Estervan guilty of employing underage females in the making of a porno film. Two counts—a felony in this state. Of course Estervan was a rat, but there were so many mitigating circumstances to the case it had become far more vexing than its importance deserved. There was just no clear solution to the problem, not the least of which was Estervan's age. He was sixty-eight years old and not in the best of health. A sentence based entirely on the book might kill him, and despite his contempt for the law, he did not deserve a death sentence.

Such is my learned, pompous opinion, Hickock whispered as he pushed away the last of his burnt toast . . . at least for the moment.

Chapter Three

Wanda Usher rolled down the car window and breathed deeply of the morning air.

"Do you mind?" she asked Mrs. Millington. "The world is so fresh after a rain. I throw my arms around it, know what I mean?"

Mrs. Millington allowed her eyes to stray from the heavy freeway traffic just long enough to smile at Wanda.

"What a lovely idea, Wanda. Like a poet."

"How did you guess? I mean I do write poetry. What I like is to feel things. Like when I was in the center—that I do not consider living, okay? You are like a vegetable that it says here put in the pot and cook for so many years and then serve and see what you got. I'm me. I'm the same body and the same person inside me so for what am I spending three years of my life like in a vegetable pot? And there's another word I could use for vegetable."

Mrs. Millington kept her eyes on the traffic while she expressed the hope that Wanda would never have to return to the treatment center and that from now on she should think about being very careful. "I do hope you're going to avoid some of your old friends," she added.

"My old friends are all gone now . . . gone with the wind, Mrs. Millington, like in that book. You're right on I should stay away from them." Little ol' Wanda was going to avoid all those people she and Sam had known and that whole bunch of weirdos who frequented the area down by the city market and all along First Avenue who were always in some sort of mess. There were much more important things to do. Are you listening, judge?

Wanda squirmed slightly as if making a personal impression in the plush velour of the seat. She allowed her voice to become casual as she inquired, "Mrs. Millington? Do you happen to know where Maple Avenue is?"

"Of course. It runs right through my neighborhood."

"Well . . . would you know about where 1011 is?"

"That would be in the ten-hundred block . . . not far from my place . . . maybe a twenty-minute walk. Do you have a friend who lives there?"

"Oh don't worry! It's not one of my old troublemaker friends—"

Wanda wished she had not asked about the address. Long ago when she was first sent away to Clark she had searched the telephone book until she found Julian K. Hickock's address and it had been engraved on her thoughts ever since. The house soon became a vivid set piece in her imagination and she used it frequently as the locale for certain events she envisioned for its occupants. And the less Mrs. Millington knew about *that* the better.

"I hope you're going to like your room," Mrs. Millington said. "It's very simple, but you'll only be there a little while."

"Mrs. Millington, I have to tell you that it will be like a palace to me. I will call the fairies in to decorate it and that room will glow like some phosphorescent thing . . . just vibrate with beautiful feelings, you know what I mean? Just to think I can walk in and out of it anytime I feel like it will be like having wings on my shoes. You better believe little ol' Wanda will be living a real genuine fairytale right there in your house."

Wanda saw that Mrs. Millington was smiling and she was pleased because that was what she wanted her to do, and she was smiling herself and, she thought, feeling very very super indeed.

"You certainly have an interesting way of putting things, Wanda."

"I never got to highschool, see? Once upon a time my family had this big plantation down south. The place was called Usher House and my granddaddy, he lost it. And my father died and my mother disappeared when I was little and so I never got the education like I should. Now the very first thing I'm going to do this very day is buy a newspaper and look for the kind of job that will be sort of part time, y'know . . . so when I'm finished working I can take some of those adult education courses they told me about at the center and pretty soon little ol' Wanda is going to read as good as anybody."

Wanda was surprised how distinctly her Tennessee accent came forward the very minute she had mentioned the old plantation. She could even hear it herself, and what was more she could just see that plantation with its big house and Spanish moss hanging from the trees around it and all, and she hoped Mrs. Millington could too.

"Well, Wanda, here we are," said Mrs. Millington. She turned into a driveway and stopped beside a small, white clapboard house.

"There are real vines on the chimney!" Wanda's voice rose. She clapped her hands.

"Oh! Isn't this just *too* elegant!"

Boris Estervan chomped noisily on his breakfast toast and read the *Wall Street Journal* with the same avid interest he lavished on the racing form. He liked the phraseology in the *Journal*, the way they used CEO for chief executive officer and the way each interview*ee*, regardless of his business, made the nearly identical comments: "I don't know what this business is coming to . . . Our hands are tied . . . I doubt if our third quarter will reflect any gain over the second . . . foreign competition is killing us . . . we are in a cost-price squeeze and there just doesn't seem to be any way out . . ."

Such comments confirmed Estervan's view of American business in general despite the fact that his own enterprises, with the exception of the film which had been confiscated by the court, were doing handsomely.

There were times when Estervan longed to elevate the respectability factor of the Rosa Corporation and he had often thought how satisfying it would be to have the stock, now held in its entirety by his wife and himself, listed on one of the public exchanges. He could just imagine being interviewed by the *Journal* and obliging them with his own brand of bull.

Estervan credited the *Journal* with at least part of his graduation from small-time hoodlum to big business. It was simply an attitude of mind, he reasoned, although he was acutely aware that the CEOs he read about in both the *Journal* and *Fortune* magazine were of a different class than himself. Not that he trusted the sonsabitches—they did not fool Boris Estervan with their knotted ties, their spectacles and distinguished gray hair. He was convinced that the bigger the company they were supposed to command the more capable they were of eating their young. They could sit casually on polished board-room tables with an oil portrait of themselves hanging on the mahogany wall behind them and make fake-modest noises like, "My principal aim is to make sound suggestions to the superb team around me. They are the ones who really carry the ball."

Bull. The man who talked like that might have been born a gentleman but it was more certain that he was a liar who was about to take over his weakest competitor, thereby salting away another million for himself and the hell with his so-called team who would find themselves on their team ass if they failed to do exactly what their CEO told them to do.

Ever since he had seen the light in *Fortune* and the *Journal*, Estervan had tried to dress and talk like the man-eaters he saw in their pages. He did not really need glasses, but he wore them anyway. They suggested dignity, a quality obviously important in any project involving the accumulation of money. He had made a partially successful effort to clean up his language and speak like he supposed the real CEOs did, and he tried—with an equal lack of success—to improve his grammar. You did not learn to speak nice in the can. Too bad so many of his formative years had been spent in captivity.

Anyway, after so many years of independent enterprise, he was certain of one thing. Never would the Rosa Corporation hire one of those gentlemen assholes. They could not handle money unless it was en route to their own pockets and the Rosa Corporation whose business was almost entirely on a cash-basis had no room for sticky fingers. The porno theaters received payment in cash as did the adult entertainment centers. The go-go taverns sold only for cash right down to the last beer and pizza and the same held true for the laundromats and the slot machines allowed in the eastern part of the state. Only the film production unit, which Estervan now wished he had never heard of, had been forced to function on an invoice-basis, which meant that except for his own theaters the Rosa Corporation was at the mercy of every sleazy movie exhibitor in the United States. They would pay only as much as they pleased, ice the balance, and happy days. Estervan was still mystified that he had not considered the weakness of such a position before.

Estervan continued reading the *Journal* (there was an article on the New England shoe industry that he found absorbing), when his brother Leo entered through the kitchen door and sat down opposite him. He was a bulky man, bald-headed and given to perspiration and wheezing after the slightest exertion. He had spent his lifetime in the commanding shadow of his elder brother, who had managed to dominate him even during those several times when a prison wall stood between them.

Now Estervan did not trouble to look up from the *Journal*, or wish his brother a good morning. He asked, "Well? What did you find out?"

"Not too much. The guy is a Jew-lover for one thing."

"How do you know?"

"There's a plaque on his office wall from B'nai B'rith. Something he done for them. I didn't read it too careful."

"I fail to see how his being a Jew-lover can help us." There were times, Estervan considered, when Leo seemed almost hopelessly lacking in staying on whatever target he was assigned.

"He is also having the hots for a very young twist who works at Moran Shipyards."

"That's better. What about her?"

"Her name is Jean Pomeroy. She's got less than thirty years on her and a nice ass."

"You've seen her?"

"Right. I been really working on this, Boris."

"Don't tell me how hard you been working. Just give me something I can get a handle on."

"I can't find nothing more . . . so far. He's got a son at the university. They live together in one of those old wood dumps out on Maple Avenue. The place looks like it's falling down and you'd think a judge in his position would live better."

Estervan considered the statement while he ladled exactly one-half tablespoon of jam on what was left of his toast. Rosa's jam was too damn good, and sugar was bad for the liver. Nobody in the world could make jam like Rosa's. "I wonder what he's hiding," he said finally. "Any chance he's a fag?"

"I don't think so. Not from the way he behaves around that twist. I tailed them to a boat he owns down at the harbor. They hold hands when they walk."

"Well everybody's got something they have to hide. Don't tell me we're stuck with an honest judge because I hear enough of that crap from Martin Delgado, my hotshot lawyer. We need to get something on him so we can help him when he decides on my sentence. I need some leverage and I need it like right now. Almost any kind of a handle will do . . . he hates niggers, he sneaks drinks while he's up there on the bench, he tells women in his court he'll let them off easy if they give him a little action . . . anything like that will help him to think straight."

Leo reached for the coffee pot and Estervan pushed his hand aside.

"No. You don't have no time for coffee. You get your ass down to the city and come back here with some *useful* information. The days are going by and I'm beginning to worry he might make up his mind. We got to make sure he makes it up right."

As always at this hour of the morning, the State Building pulsed with activity. For here were housed both the county jail and the superior courts, as well as all those citizens honest, almost honest and dishonest who were directly involved with them. The halls were unimposing at the street entrances, but at the center of the building the banks of elevators had been clustered around an oval-shaped neo-Roman atrium of marble and mosaic, which for the very few who paused to appreciate it offered a certain clinical beauty. Both this lobby, the halls extending from it, and the identical floors above were pungent with a fusion of tobacco smoke, disinfectant and mop water.

The State Building had been constructed in the late twenties, just before the Depression and before architects and government planners were constrained by the Teutonic practical. Even the elevators, always jammed to capacity and frequently inoperative, reflected an earlier, more easygoing era when the state itself had been of relatively sparse population and the major communities within it barely qualified as overgrown towns rather than cities. A citizen who might have migrated to the far west even in the late thirties and found cause now to view the present hustle in the State Building would have trouble remembering when such an elaborate structure was considered a political boondoggle. And with some reason. Before the Second World War there was certainly not enough crime in the state to require even half the courtrooms, and such a large jail was considered a waste of taxpayers' money. This was not New York or Chicago or one of those monstrous encampments where the natives did so many dreadful things to each other. This was a peaceful area where life was as dull as the usually overcast skies. Here people drank a little, but not much. The citizens were outdoor-minded; it was hunting and fishing and boating for those with a few dollars to spare, as most people had, and most citizens tended gardens behind their own homes, and the neat lawns in front of them. There was no poverty—at least visible. The white population was a mixed bag of WASPs, Scandinavians, and Jews. There were many Orientals, mostly hardworking Japanese who became American citizens as fast as the law allowed, and there was a handful of black people who kept to themselves and created no more trouble than anyone else. Many people described the city as insufferably smug, and they were quite right. Those fancy people who took wine with their meals or drank mixed drinks must be foreigners.

Now after wars, booms, depressions and long-forgotten political manifestos, after the state was discovered by the rest of the United States and the revolution in American mores reached even to the hinterlands, the old State Building seemed always on the verge of exploding. The courts were months and sometimes years behind the calendar. The prison was an overcrowded purgatory, even though from some cell blocks the inspiring view of the sea and the mountains remained the same as it had always been. Now the entire building swarmed with bodies. There were lawyers both seedy and prim forced by the democracy of the elevators to press their bodies against their clients and the accusers of their clients. There were bail-bondsmen, subpoenaed witnesses and jury members with badges identifying them as such. There were citizens with bruises on their faces, black eyes, and newly bandaged parts which seemed to embarrass them. There were court recorders who even en route to or coming from the practice of their silent art managed to melt as totally into the background as they did in the courtrooms. There were television and newspaper reporters, deliberately scruffy to show their disregard for convention, but wearing their jeans and moccasins uniform in accordance with their professions' convention. There were law clerks of the judges, who were very young and serious, there were bailiffs, and squads of assistant district attorneys and public defenders, police in uniform, and deputies from the sheriff's department. There were beefy detectives in checked sports jackets and florid ties and middle-aged lawyers in gray flannel and old school ties . . . And there was the Honorable Julian Hickock who was greeted warmly by two black mop-and-bucket ladies. They asked after his health and he called them each by name, responding that if he felt any younger he would go back to law school.

Hickock waited along with an assembly of other people for an up-bound elevator and he exchanged "good mornings" with two of them whose names he could not remember. One, he knew, was a woman lawyer who had represented the husband in an ugly divorce case tried in his court. Now he recalled that she had been rather officious, but he did not remember her as being almost as tall as himself. That was the trouble with viewing humanity from an elevated bench. No doubt it did contribute to the majesty of the law, but perhaps it also removed the judge too far from the individuals he was supposed to be understanding, and, as a consequence, judging.

Hickock had no recollection of ever having seen the second person who greeted him. Since he wore a sheriff's department uniform, he assumed he must have been in his court at least once in the past. It was strange how individual faces merged into stereotypes, he thought, but then, how many faces had he looked down upon since he had first taken the bench? When did the mind start behaving like some overloaded computer and refuse to accept any more faces as belonging to individuals, and just store people away according to category? It seemed to make very little difference whether he was hearing a civil or a criminal case—the faces were still masks worn only for court sessions. He had often wondered what the real faces were like, at leisure, anywhere, without the masks of anxiety, greed, or fear.

There were the corporate lawyers, always poised, their case meticulously prepared by God knows how many paralegals, their data carefully researched. To a man they seemed to look up at him through bifocals.

There were various law enforcement officers who gave ritual testimony in suits so tight they seemed about to burst from the combined strain of muscle and fat. Or if they were female officers they seemed duty bound to deliver their testimony in pedantic monotones. While waiting to be called to the stand both types devoted themselves utterly to filling out their overtime pay claims.

Hickock was trying to estimate how many thousands of masks he had seen when the elevator doors opened and revealed a tight mass of humanity. How could so many people have business on the floors above and be all through with it by nine-thirty? As they flowed out of the elevator, his own group jostled each other slightly in anticipation, and almost immediately filled it again. Then all of them, holding their breaths as if they feared to be caught breathing, or fearful of catching whatever afflicted the strange nose poised less than a foot from their own, rose in absolute silence.

Hickock squeezed his way out of the elevator at the eighth floor and marched directly to his chambers. He paused in the anteroom and smiled at Lucinda Morrow. It occurred to him as it did almost every morning that he was now standing before a woman who could certainly qualify as the worst secretary in the world. Lucinda had been with him since the first week he had taken the bench, and in all those years what little ability she may have had when he inherited her from a former judge had gone steadily down hill. Lucinda rarely managed to type a letter without several typos, and frequently misspelled the addressee's name. She put calls through to Hickock from characters who wanted a judge to come at once to wherever they might be and settle a family feud, while she put prominent jurists and attorneys with important information he needed on hold.

Hickock had lost track of how many times he had threatened to fire Lucinda, and she had lost any fear she might have had that he might actually carry out his threat.

"How can you be so mean to me, Your Honor? Even you aren't perfect."

Lucinda was ever-ready to point out her boss's shortcomings, and once he became used to it he actually valued it. He knew he could never bring himself to actually discharge Lucinda, if only because her loyalty was unquestionable. And she kept him humble.

Since Dolores's death, Lucinda had appointed herself guardian of more Hickock family matters than she could handle. Hickock regarded her additional services as very much of a mixed blessing. She paid the household bills with a barely acceptable degree of accuracy although she sometimes entirely forgot to pay Nellie-Mae. The omission threw off Hickock's balance at the bank, caused Nellie-Mae to pout inexplicably until he pried the cause out of her, and failed to upset Lucinda in the slightest. Her "I'm sorry" was so practiced and sincere that Hickock now regarded it as a mere comma in her sentences of apologies.

Now Lucinda chirped, "Good morning, Your Honor!" She smiled and Hickock thought that her smile alone forgave the errors she would doubtless make this day. Lucinda was plump, yet her face had always intrigued him. There was a puckish quality about her eyes that softened his occasional desire to shake her. Damnit, how could you be angry or even really impatient with a chubby little spinster who bore her failures without lament and whose entire world orbited around your own?

"What kind of a day are we going to have?" Hickock said as he continued toward his inner office. Lucinda followed him, bringing a cup of tea which he knew would be too hot if it was not too cold. He would sip at it only because the act would please Lucinda. He disliked tea and wondered if he was ever going to find the heart to tell her so.

"Mr. Delgado called."

"Humph. What did he want?" Martin Delgado was the defending attorney in the Estervan case and, as Hickock was reminded, hardly a man he would meet for pleasure or anything else for that matter.

"He wanted to know where you were going to have lunch today and I told him as usual the Club."

"Lucinda . . .." Hickock paused to allow the exasperation to leave his voice. "Lucinda, did it occur to you for one moment that Martin Delgado belongs to the same club and if I failed to be on display at my regular table you would have told an untruth? How do you know I don't have a rendezvous with some gorgeous blond?"

Lucinda waved him off. "Really, Mr. Delgado is a very nice man. I hit him up for a contribution to Guide Dogs and he said a check would be in the mail today."

"That's just dandy. Now this office can be accused of passing favors for bribes." Hickock was convinced Lucinda had to be the most enthusiastic and successful campaigner in the history of Guide Dogs for the Blind. She "hit up" everyone regularly and on one campaign included the ancient crone who sometimes peddled newspapers in the lobby of the building.

"But she's blind herself," Hickock had protested. "Leave her in peace."

"She's only blind in one eye," Lucinda insisted. "So I only hit her for five instead of ten dollars."

"I suppose if Mr. Delgado had called to ask me to play golf you would make an appointment for me to meet him on the first tee even though you know damn well I don't play golf. That is, providing he reached into that overfat wallet of his and sent ten dollars for your pooches."

"Probably." Lucinda stood, smiling.

"Get out of here."

When she had left Hickock tipped back in his chair and smiled at the ceiling. There was another reason he knew, why he would find it impossible to fire Lucinda. Soon after meeting his friend Jean she had declared her a "very exciting young person."

Hickock's thoughts drifted back to the Estervan problem. Secretly he had cheered the jury's verdict, and had some trouble concealing his approval. It was very satisfying to realize that Boris Estervan, a local citizen of consistently dubious reputation, had finally tripped on his own petard. Now, Hickock had all the facts before him and he could reach a judgement without the distraction of lawyers, witnesses, juries, and all the ritual restrictions which prevailed in any court. Within a reasonable time he must decide how much punishment Boris Estervan would receive, and what form it would take. Because there were so many intervening factors that decision seemed to be more complex and difficult by the hour.

Everyone in this state who kept track of such people had known for years that Boris Estervan was hardly an admirable citizen—the trouble had always been to prove it. This was still a democracy, at least better than any other, Hickock mused, which meant that you could not throw a man or a woman in the slammer just because you disliked the way they thought, chewed their food, or conducted their daily activities. Even if a citizen was only trying to make a living pushing dope, stealing cars, or selling fake stock in a nonexistent company, you still had to *prove* he had been up to something illegal in a court of law. And citizens like Estervan covered their tracks accordingly. Even the IRS, who could usually find some shenanigan in anyone's tax report, could not find a flaw in

Estervan's records. Every penny they could trace had always been declared and the correct tax paid. Estervan's books were kept meticulously by a certified accounting firm of impeccable reputation. Likewise, he was represented in all legal matters by the long established and totally respectable firm of Horn, Delgado, Skinner and Dewitt. Horn was dead now and Martin Delgado was the senior partner. He was a man who believed in the power of suggestion and understatement, a combination which he knew how to use with marvelous effect upon his adversaries. Hickock could not think of another attorney whose courtroom manner was so deceptive. At times he appeared almost inept. During his opening address to a jury he would often stumble over his wordage, pretend that he could not find a note concerning a vital piece of evidence, or even hint that he, personally, took a dim view of his client's behavior.

The results were far more dramatic and effective than most of his more flamboyant opponents appreciated. Delgado knew every trick of the trade, from keeping his voice so soft (to suggest his reasonableness and tenderness), that the jury had to listen carefully or they would miss the whole show, to subtle demonstrations of humility before twelve heads whose thought processes according to his carefully disguised inference were far superior to his own. Whether Delgado was seeking outrageous compensation for a client who claimed a lumbering operation damaged his watering rights, or a widow who was trying to retrieve part of a fortune her husband had left to a nurse he met during the last week of his life, the man played upon a jury as a master tuning his favorite instrument.

Ordinarily Martin Delgado would never soil his well-manicured hands with a trial in criminal court. For one thing there was rarely enough money in it, and criminal lawyers were not considered true members of the legal hierarchy. There was a feeling based on nothing more than professional snobbery that perhaps some of their clients' improbity might have rubbed off on their attorneys. Yet with this case Delgado had no choice since he handled all of Estervan's complex business affairs.

"Adventures," Hickock thought, was an appropriate description of the sundry enterprises owned by Boris Estervan and his wife Rosa. It was she who held the actual titles to the six porno theaters and the eleven "adult education studios." Unfortunately for her spouse she did not own that certain feature film which Boris Estervan undoubtedly wished he had never made.

Despite the general public disapproval, there was nothing openly illegal in any of the Estervan establishments. They were operated as businesses straight through with all licenses paid promptly, employee compensation, insurance; whatever the law said must be, Estervan was prompt to provide. The porno theaters which gave wide-screen dimensions to hyperactive penises and vaginas in livid color were tolerated in the name of art. It was a proposition which Hickock reluctantly approved. Once a body of people set themselves up as censors there was no stopping them. Better to tolerate a few seamy old theaters in the run-down areas of the city than to have some pinch-lipped characters telling the rest of the citizens what they could and could not read or see.

The Estervan "adult education studios" were another matter. Everyone other than the most naive supposed the real business conducted behind their discreet fronts was prostitution. A man entered one of Estervan's studios powered by a lust which he was led to believe could be satisfied beyond his wildest dreams and for a reasonable amount. Once within he would be escorted by a young woman wearing a short see-through blouse to the "initiation room." There he would be introduced to his "tour guide," one of several employed by the establishment. Depending upon his degree of sophistication, the erstwhile traveler was already amused or goldfish-eyed by the time he heard the details of his forthcoming journey explained and he was asked to pay a passport fee of twenty dollars. He was told he could make a quickie tour of France for a mere twenty dollars additional, Germany was more expensive at thirty dollars. An "around the world" luxury cruise which he was assured would take the better part of an hour cost a flat fifty dollars, a true bargain, his guide insisted, in these inflationary times.

Depending on his affluence and curiosity the traveler made his choice and the tour began—usually in the "Oriental room." His guide, who had been required to memorize her brief lecture, rendered it to the accompaniment of appropriate reed instrument music. The walls of the Oriental room were embellished with a variety of photographs, illustrations, and statuary supposedly depicting the sexual activities and preferences of all Oriental peoples since earliest known history. After enlightening the traveler and allowing her voice to become increasingly full of promise the guide would make her pitch for one or more of the several aphrodisiacs displayed on an Oriental table. These ranged from straight estrogen pills at one dollar each to powdered rhinoceros horn at seventy-five dollars a vial, including sales tax. Normally the guide assisted her charge in making a decision by hinting that if he made a purchase he might very well become aware of the effects within the next several minutes. His reaction would supposedly make him irresistible to his guide, and as a consequence, a long pause on the trail would occur.

It was a typical Estervan operation, Hickock mused. Nothing was guaranteed and the buyer was allowed to hang himself. For the most part it was not even illegal; the tour guides, who were the most voluptuous Estervan's aides could find, were also intelligent and carefully trained. If they took a traveler to Germany, which featured Hamburg's notorious Reperbahm district, he was shown enough whips, swastikas, arm restrainers, manacles, and stocks to satisfy the most kinky tastes, and he was urged to fantasize all he pleased while he listened to a formal lecture on Teutonic sexuality since the time of the earliest Huns.

Much of the same routine was followed in the French, Spanish, Scandinavian, and African rooms, and the final result was *almost* always the same. The operations had moved so smoothly that the most unwilling traveler was usually surprised to discover he had been relieved of at least fifty dollars and had still not become any more familiar with his guide than a few suggestive caresses.

There was never any soliciting by Estervan's girl guides. It was unnecessary. The majority of their clientele had spent most of their cash by the time they had been "traveling" half an hour, and if he expressed outrage that the tour was finished and demanded more compliance on the part of his guide, two strong male "immigration" officers appeared and helped him out the back door. Most migrated meekly. Only those who were willing to pay even more got what they came for.

There were four adult education studios in the city and reportedly eleven others scattered throughout the state. All held the necessary business licenses, all local taxes were paid promptly, and all codes complied with. Most of the buildings housing the establishments were owned by the Rosa Corporation, which listed Estervan's wife as president. Boris himself was not even listed as an officer, but he did admit receiving occasional fees as a "consultant."

Since the conclusion of the trial Hickock had learned that Estervan's adult education studios were almost immune to interference from the vice squad. Although it was known that some customers were relieved of several hundred dollars while on tour, they were somehow made to feel they had received their money's worth, or were ashamed to report their bilking. Even more strange was the failure of the best undercover agents to persuade their guides to do anything more than was legally permissible. Hickock wondered if the girls were just extraordinarily careful or had someone in the various police departments always been ready to signal a warning?

When the existence of the studios had been brought to the attention of the jury by the prosecuting attorney, Delgado's rebuttal was quick and to the point. The activities within the studios, he insisted, were no more illegal or objectionable than could be found in any, say, Playboy Club, "the difference being," he explained, "that the studio bunnies offered the mental advantages of travel (however vicarious) and since no drinks were served the patrons were more inclined to be sober."

Estervan knew how to run a business even though he remained remote and classified himself as "semi-retired." His organization was well-staffed and usually well-advised—except for once, Hickock reminded himself. Just once the king had erred.

Estervan looked and behaved like the most solid of citizens. His smooth rather swarthy complexion reflected a number of interesting angularities and his eyes were so challenging those who met him were often compelled to look away. He claimed to be of Lebanese descent and Hickock found it odd that his air of majesty seemed so genuine. Others performed his deeds while his Rosa took the profits and deposited them only God knew where. Thus for years the man had managed to stay clean, a remarkable contrast to his much earlier record which Hickock now had before him.

While it was not an impressive rap sheet it did indicate that one Boris Estervan also known as Nessim Estervan, also known as Bruno Kartaba, had been somewhat less than a pillar of society.

1952: Elizabethtown, New Jersey. Assault with a deadly weapon. Hickock noted he served four years of a ten-year sentence on that one. Dannemora.
1956: Trenton, New Jersey. Conspiracy to defraud. Acquitted. Was he just trying to improve his financial situation after four years as a guest of the New Jersey taxpayers?
1956: Simple assault. Also in Trenton. This was puzzling since Estervan seemed to be too calculating to become involved in an ordinary altercation. He must have had a reason, but he was certainly not going to revive history now. Once again he had been acquitted. A good lawyer or a clumsy prosecutor?
1960: Back in Elizabethtown. Bribing a public official this time. Once more acquitted. But what had Estervan been up to during the years since his last bust? That was the trouble with rap sheets. They did nothing to illuminate the life of the culprit when he was offstage.
1966: Cleveland, Ohio. A federal matter this time. Evasion of income tax to unstated amounts for the years 1962, 1963 and 1964. Fined twenty thousand dollars. Nothing more? Sometimes the federal prosecutors were very clever and sometimes not so clever. Hickock supposed that Estervan had laughed all the way to the pay window. Still, it was interesting to speculate on how Estervan had made enough money in so few years to interest the IRS. And why had he migrated from New Jersey?
1975: Also in Cleveland. Operating an indecent establishment. Acquitted. Now there was a neat maneuver on the part of someone. Was that when Estervan began arranging his business affairs in such a way that he could only be identified as a "consultant"—therefore not responsible as an owner or operator? Until now?

Hickock realized that he must have considered the bare information before him at least a hundred times. As in all trials, it had not been made available to the judge until after the jury had brought in their verdict, yet now it was intended to provide Hickock with additional background before he pronounced sentence. If Estervan had never been arrested, or had no closer brush with the law than a traffic ticket, then he would probably receive a lighter sentence. On the other hand, his record during the past twenty years was not all that bad considering the nature of his various businesses and the company he might have kept. The prosecuting attorney had attempted to insinuate that Estervan could be closely related to the Mafia, but Hickock had been obliged to overrule him instantly. Hearsay and other unsubstantiated proofs were given no time in his court and of course Delgado had been on his feet calling objections before the jury heard too much.

Yet where did the man Estervan stand in society? Who was this human being who was apparently devoted to his wife Rosa and his daughter? The record said he contributed sizable amounts to charity (that had been checked and the details provided by Delgado's office). Here was a citizen who paid all his taxes or at least enough to keep the IRS and other agencies at bay. He was known to have helped underprivileged youths on several occasions. Here was a veteran of the landing on Omaha Beach during World War Two. What should be done with him now that one of his enterprises had misfired? He had probably been telling the truth in his deposition testimony when he declared in his high thin voice, "I really didn't know nothin' about it or I would have stopped it right away. I have a daughter myself. A guy would have to be real sick to go for that sort of thing. The people who did it were fired right away."

The trouble with being a judge, Hickock thought, is that you were asked to play God without being able to look down from on high and watch those you were judging over an extended period of time. While God's decisions were supposedly never influenced by money, the Lord did not have to contend with the vagaries of mortal law and artful lawyers.

What a dubious affair this whole business of judgment was. In actuality the law was common sense modified by the legislature. At best it was an improvisational drama presented by key players who seldom knew their lines. One man, one sometimes bumbling, a sometimes less than ordinary human being, presumed to dictate the future of another. Sometimes he was thought of as a lawyer who could not hack it in the competitive world and sometimes as a legal flunky of very questionable intelligence. It all depended on which team won—their opinion of the judge usually became the opposite of their original cause for being in court. There were magistrates (a term Hickock preferred to "judge"), who were far more dishonest than those who appeared before them. There were charlatans and fools and pompous asses who took themselves seriously rather than their office. And there were a great many men and women who tried to wear the black with something of the dignity and honor it deserved. Hickock hoped he might be one of them.

Yet how should any sound judgment be made about the irrational, the confused and complex animal who had taken on himself the title of "human"? There were some for whom punishment was meaningless; they were quite capable of persuading themselves they would never be caught, or if they were, that they were innocent of transgression. Some even found the prospect of risk an inducement, and the higher the gamble, the more seductive. Estervan had violated the law and should be punished . . . but how severely?

Here, Hickock thought, I sit in what a businessman would refer to as an office, yet because the law sleeps here the door becomes the entrance to my "chambers." I create nothing here nor do I direct others to make useful things. I do not buy or sell, repair bodies or provide any source for human amusement. Well, rarely. I do not transport things although I do direct that some humans be transported to oblivion. Pro tem.

Who authorizes me to perform this so-called honorable service? The public votes for a man like me every four years. Maybe they will put a check beside "Hickock" because they think it looks like an honest name. WASP. Okay in this area but how would it go in the Bronx or in Southern California, where a Jewish or Chicano name would be more trusted?

Still, very few of those who might bother to put an X beside the Hickock name will know me from a forest ranger, he thought. They will not know if I know the code of Hammurabi from the Morse, and they will not know if I am a soft or a hanging judge . . . and the worst part of it is I don't know either . . .

It was during times like this moment, Hickock supposed, that he might have been happier with the life of a sailor rather than being obliged to play the sage. A poor man, so often poorly represented in whatever court he stood before, knew instinctively that the odds were against him even if he was innocent. A rich man knew the chances of his going to prison were minimal in comparison. That was the way of the law and any judge who was halfway honest with himself knew it.

How then to justify so many difficult judgments—assuming the police were honest, the accused was honest, and the judge was honest? Lo! . . . not quite a miracle. For how about the law itself? Was it always honest? Nearly all laws were made by legislatures inspired by individuals or groups who wanted something started or stopped. The result was too often a hypocritical patchwork of awkward design.

I am confused because I am human, Hickock thought. I guess that's my excuse and my reality. And in spite of that handicap I am sworn to take two years, three, ten years or twenty of another human's life span and put it on ice. I do not know what that human is really like when he or she is *not* into mischief. Sometimes I manage to gather a smattering of whatever the hell it was that made them do whatever it was they did that is considered naughty by the tribe, but I still do not know what was and is in their heart and mind either before or after the event. Now what kind of a pompous fathead can suppose that every time he hands down a sentence he really believes he is absolutely right?

Hickock sighed and regretted his action instantly. What the hell business did he have sighing? The real agonizing was in the jail on the seventeenth floor. There, various humans wearing tan jumpsuits provided by the state were waiting for some judge provided by the state to look in his crystal ball and declare their immediate future. And sometimes not so immediate.

You there with the brown eyes, have the grace to open your purse without complaint and pay to your enemy the sum of ten, twenty, one hundred thousand dollars. You there with the blue eyes, submit sweetly to the man in uniform who will escort you to a dungeon where you will soon lose all contact with the rest of this world. For umpteen years. You there with the green eyes—since caning, the stocks, dunking, and whipping offends the American sense of ethics—take a walk and laugh your head off at the lack of a law to suit your crime or provide some compensation for your victim.

What was it like, Hickock wondered as he had countless times before, to know that at best you were going to spend the next five years of your life in a jungle surrounded by other wild animals? When you stood in issued uniform and reached out to touch the only wall with a view, you did not consider the cold steel bars as punishment. They became a symbol of revenge which was not what the law was supposed to be at all, but was certainly so in the eyes of most prisoners. Bars and locks made them all the more resentful and angry and convinced they had been given a bum rap. The prisons of the land were jammed with those who believed they had been wronged instead of being wrongdoers. Unless something was done to reform the system very soon, Hickock thought, an explosion was inevitable. It was all very neat and tidy to say that civilization had always depended on the habit of obeying laws, but in the United States at least, too many people were losing the habit or had never become addicted.

Estervan, though, was not one of the so-called new breed. He was no youth in rebellion against society or convinced the way to make a name for himself was to commit a felony and the more violent the better. Estervan was a survivor of youthful hard times and his past record indicated that he considered the law not so much as an enemy but as an inconvenience bristling with handy detour signs.

Why had Estervan been persuaded that his adult education studios and porno theaters were not enough to assure the future of his mini-empire? Why had a man who had previously never allowed caprice to influence his decisions suddenly given in to a latent taste for glamor? Could he also have fallen in love with a much younger woman and if so who was Julian Hickock to judge him? He claimed that he was tired of paying through the nose for the junk playing in his theaters. Other entrepreneurs, the kind of men Estervan understood, were making fortunes with such productions as *Wilder Than Wild* and *Come with the Wind*. Estervan had apparently found payment of rent for such art higher than he could tolerate and "Estervan Productions" was born. Never mind the moral view of his affairs. The law permitted his business to exist and therefore he had every right to promote it.

Estervan's desire to further exploit his business was quite normal even though it had led to his first mistake in a long time. His second was not maintaining closer supervision over the troops involved and one of them had grievously misjudged his boss. For seeking to please him by producing the very best and artful of porno films, the director had hired two sixteen-year-old girls to play the leading roles, thereby violating Title 9 RCW Section 2 of the state law covering child pornography.

All concerned were arrested and charged with committing a Class B felony.

When the jury had found them guilty Estervan himself was in trouble. It was just the sort of thing the district attorney's office had been praying for—almost anything to trip the elusive Estervan. Could it have been a twisted sense of vanity that had flawed his usual judgment? Why had he listed himself as executive producer of the film company? Even though he was not present when the girls were photographed the law said, "It is not a defense that the defendant did not know the victim's age."

His lawyer Delgado, hoping for a legal out, a hung jury, any last-minute rescue, had instructed the film director and the cameraman to plead "not guilty" to match Estervan's own defense. Another mistake, perhaps born of Delgado's secret hopelessness at winning the case. Although he had done his best to choose the most liberal-minded jurors available he had underestimated the average American's revulsion when the prosecution ran the film. The two mothers on the jury had been ready to have Estervan, the director, the cameraman, and even Delgado shot on the following morning. There had been moments when Hickock had almost felt sorry for Delgado, who must have foreseen his inevitable defeat. Presumably Estervan had refused any plea-bargaining and had made him fight to the finish.

The director and the cameraman were young, fast-money studs who were very much too smart for their own good. No matter who sat in final judgment on them they would probably be sent away for at least a few years (five were authorized). For all the good it would do. But Estervan?

What possible benefit would the public gain from sending a sixty-eight-year-old man away to live on the taxpayers rather than have him working to pay his share of taxes?

It cost at least fifty thousand dollars a year to keep a male prisoner in an American penitentiary, and confinement was not going to change Estervan's ways in the slightest. Would it make him feel remorse? Would he break down sobbing and say he was most awfully sorry? Was he likely to come out on parole after a year or so of good behavior and immediately start another film involving juveniles? Not a chance, Hickock was certain. Boris Estervan *was* sincerely remorseful, not because he gave a damn about the girls (who it turned out were anything but scout leaders in their community), but because he had been caught in a stupid mistake.

Since Estervan was certainly not a candidate for rehabilitation, what was a good solid reason for sending him to prison? Vengeance? If that was what the law intended then an old-style tar and feathering might be more effective—and a damn sight cheaper. Punishment? Since Estervan was guilty of an offense against the public eye then perhaps he should be blinded. That would teach him a lesson and satisfy the ancient public urge for a criminal's blood.

Or perhaps, Hickock reflected, I might recommend trial by ordeal as in ancient times. I could go down to the bay and pick up some clams. I could supply Delgado and the lawyer from the DA's office two limes. They could squeeze a few drops on their clams and the first one whose crustacean wiggled would win the sentence—five years suspended, or five years to be actually served. Water, fire and poison were all venerable decision-makers since the trials of antiquity and were still in use in remote areas of the world.

Or I might light two candles simultaneously, Hickock thought. See whose candle flickers out first. He is the loser. Shake the responsibility onto something that cannot interject and/or argue, and snooze along in your black robe while your salary keeps right on coming.

Now what the hell am I going to do with Boris Estervan?

Hickock picked up the phone and punched in a number. After a moment he heard her voice. "Miss Pomeroy? My name is Julian Hickock—"

"This is the drafting office. If you are looking for work I suggest you call employment."

"I have just received a certain message from on high."

"Would you please speak English, Mr.—? Sorry I didn't quite catch your name."

"By six o'clock tonight there will be a nice breeze from the southwest."

"You've been watching the *Today* show."

"No. I looked out the window. Could I liberate you at about five? We would still have two hours of daylight."

"How can I resist?"

"Please don't."

"Okay. See you."

He heard a click and Jean Pomeroy was gone. He replaced

the phone and caught himself before his mind flew out the window and landed on the deck of the *Freedom*. Stick to the work ethic, Elephant Ears. It is your middle-class WASP American heritage. It says here that every weekday you should sit either in this office or in court and determine the fate of citizens who are usually not WASP Americans of the third or fourth or fifth generations. It says right in the WASP middle-class rules and regulations that this is your burden for being born so incredibly lucky and you should not be thinking sinful thoughts like escaping to the natural world for several thousand breaths of fresh air. The privilege of the underprivileged is to sit in the sun without noticing or caring it is there.

And it also says here in WASP regulation Section A Paragraph 1 that she is too young for you.

Chapter Four

Jean Pomeroy slipped into her yellow coveralls and put on her hard hat. She took her camera off the drawing board and leaving the quiet of the drafting office descended into the raucous clatter of the shipyard. She walked through the fitful morning sun to the dry dock where a Coast Guard cutter was the center of noise and activity.

The cutter was an overage vessel of only two hundred feet now being fitted for extensive work in the Arctic. Heavier plates were being welded to her original hull for protection against ice, and an entirely new section was being added to the after part of her hull which hopefully would minimize ice damage to the propellers. The new section was innovative, and now that it was nearing reality Jean thought it appeared particularly graceful of line. She had done some of the original drawings on the project as well as some of the later working sectionals.

Now, looking up at a work she considered at least partly of her creation, her thoughts went back to the days at Ann Arbor and her four years at the University of Michigan. There at the School of Naval Architecture she had been one of two women students and she had hardly dared dream she would ever be allowed to design even a small part of a real ship. Yet there it was, its curving beauty the result of countless hours of working with the computers plus considerable old-fashioned human thinking.

She moved cautiously through the dry-dock clutter of electrical cables, hoses, and portable generators trying to find the best angle to photograph her "baby," as she had come to think of it. And she smiled inwardly as she made her way through the combined clutter of rivet hammers, the gruntings of heavy lift engines, and the hum of generators. She had no predetermined idea of what she could do with the photos when they were developed. It was doubtful if even Julian Hickock would be interested in such a souvenir of her labors, and certainly her mother would hardly appreciate a color print of a great hunk of steel. She would only be bewildered and therefore vaguely disapproving, as she had been of a photo Jean had once sent of Julian standing on the deck of the *Freedom*. That had been an obvious mistake because it had sparked a long advisory letter which covered in full the hazards of marrying an older man. The mistake had been compounded in a later telephone call, when seeking to calm her maternal fears, she had said she had no plans for marriage whatsoever and that she suspected Julian Hickock was of the same mind. Mother-daughter relationship became even further strained when a second advisory was issued: ". . . then how can you waste the best years of your life on a man who is apparently not serious? I don't care if he is a judge or a magistrate or whatever they call them. I don't know what your father will think if I even dare tell him . . . why, right now in your late twenties and early thirties is when your beauty really shines! . . ."

Alas, mother, it is well you cannot see your daughter's beauty shining, positively glistening beneath this hard-hat, and the glow of my gorgeous body not one whit diminished by these form-fitting balloon-butt coveralls. It is my duty, dear mother, to inform you that my baby up there, that magnificent hunk of steel, gives me a bigger charge for right now than all the squalling, pink-toed infants I have ever seen. Just as you've always said, too much the rebel in me, too much just like dear old dad.

Her father's life, she thought, was not full of regrets.

As she sought the best angles and light to photograph the after end of the vessel she tried to visualize what her mother would think if she could watch her daughter climbing thirty feet up a ladder to waste a whole roll of film on what would look to her like the side of a whale with a bad case of scrofula. She would not think, Jean decided. She would simply close her mind to the whole idea and wait until her daughter and the world returned to its senses.

When she had finished the roll and volleyed a few cracks with the huge black foreman on the job who said she must be nuts to waste film on something no one was going to look at, she settled the exchange by agreeing he was absolutely right, and also absolutely right that she should not be allowed away from her drawing board without an escort. And she agreed that the dimensions she had given on the plans were all wrong and had to be altered at great pains by the foreman who promised not to say anything to anybody so she would not lose her job.

"We need a face like yours around here to launch ships," he laughed.

It was while walking back to the drafting offices that she found herself thinking of Julian's daughter Sally. Their appreciation of each other was not unlike the mutual friendship she knew with her own father.

Sally was only nine years younger and might have been at least a little disturbed by the woman who had obviously become her father's dear friend. She might have thought it was the oldest story in the world . . . September song with even a financial threat, but during their two meetings Sally had reacted in exactly the opposite way. They had delighted in each other's company and had since exchanged several long distance calls.

It was a damn shame, Jean thought, that son Victor obviously felt so differently.

Since his court calendar was free on this morning Hickock spent his time clearing up a stack of mail that had accumulated during Estervan's trial. It had turned out to be an easy morning, and at precisely twelve o'clock he left his chambers and set out to cover the six blocks between the County Building and the Metropolitan Club, an establishment of so-called prominent civic fathers who occasionally reached out from their cocoon of inbreeding and awarded honorary memberships to the likes of judges and such political figures as they hoped might agree with their ultra-conservative views. The food was excellent, if a shade ponderous for Hickock's taste, but the price was even less than demanded by the average greasy spoon in the area. (The charter members, he thought, must have long ago made some preinflationary deal with the produce wholesalers, none of whom were likely to be invited to membership.) Best of all the Metropolitan Club enabled him to avoid the national curse of noontime standing in line and fighting for elbow room in city restaurants. Nor were his midday attempts at logical thought assailed by the clatter and chatter which he found so distracting that he had preferred brown-bagging his lunch before the Metropolitan altered his ways. Here, the privilege of near silence was enjoyed by the privileged, and with real, if bearable, twinges of social conscience, Hickock secretly conceded that the lack of decibels seemed worth almost any compromise.

Because his membership did not originate through the tribal right of a "good old boys" group Hickock knew only a very few of his fellow members, and those he did not know were rigid believers in the rights of privacy. It was a pretty tight WASP society, sprinkled with a select few Jews who had been born and raised in the city. Hickock usually took a magazine from the club's library if he planned to lunch alone amid such relative tranquility.

He was topping off his lunch with a cherry pie à la mode and reading the latest copy of *Wooden Boat* when he became aware that someone was standing beside him. He glanced up from what to him was a fascinating story on boat building in Morocco to see Martin Delgado.

"Hello, Julian. I envy you your pie à la mode. If I let myself go that route I'd weigh two hundred pounds."

"It's a question of self-discipline," Hickock said without smiling. "I rarely have it for breakfast."

He waited hoping Delgado would move on. No such luck.

"May I sit down a moment?" Delgado asked as he pulled back the other chair.

"I don't see how I can stop you since it's already too late."

"I'll only be a moment, then you can go back to your reading."

It was like Delgado to invite himself by action if he knew no invitation would come his way. He was one aggressive man, Hickock was reminded, with the hide of an armadillo. And he was very, very intelligent.

And therefore to be watched, he warned himself. Everything about the man was always in order. His suit appeared to have just come from the tailors. His Harvard tie was knotted with meticulous care and his iron-gray hair was carefully groomed. Hickock sensed that smoke screen of hesitant confusion which Delgado employed in a courtroom would not be trotted out just now. Whatever was lurking in Delgado's convoluted brain would be clearly outlined and there would be none of his stumbling oratory.

• • •

Hickock tried to smile as he remembered that Delgado's private practice brought him at least three times more money than his own salary as a public official; which proved, he thought, that while he was addressed as "Your Honor," plain Mister Delgado was three times smarter than he was.

They smiled at each other, thin smiles, the recognition of two professionals acceding to custom without offering or conceding anything of themselves.

"I do think our cuisine is the very best in town," Delgado said.

Hickock was once more impressed with the primness of his speech. He is so damned neat and orderly, he thought, that any minute now he is going to go up in a puff of smoke and reappear as Thaddius Hudson, one of his law professors who had once told him, "Hickock, if you ever get to be a magistrate of any rank, which in light of your grades I consider highly unlikely, I caution you to occasionally refresh yourself with remembering the trial of Socrates. Remind yourself that when his fate was determined he went his way peacefully, but not before he remarked to the jury, *Which of us, you or I, is going to the better fate, is unknown to all except God.*"

There were times, Hickock thought, when men like the one on the opposite side of the tablecloth caused him to think about a jigger of hemlock.

"How goes the sailing these days?"

"Thanks to you and your clients there has been damned little."

"Playing the piano much these days?"

"When I can."

Now how the hell did he know about the Cavemen? Hickock wondered. It was a rag-tag jazz combo composed of Tom Cookley, a black dentist who played the drums; Willy Ching, a prosperous Chinese restaurateur on the banjo; Paul England, a lumberman with an honest concern for the environment who thrummed the bass fiddle; and "Butch" Goldstein, a municipal court judge who played a very hot trumpet. The organization convened monthly in four different basements all with third-rate pianos which Hickock insisted was the sole reason for his third-rate playing. They were always more or less out of tune, but no one really cared. The true harmony was in the relations between the Cavemen themselves. Never had Hickock known such mutual admiration and affection.

Delgado said, "You're a lucky man to have so many talents, Julian. I'd be very unhappy to think they might ever be curtailed."

"Just what do you mean by that?"

Delgado took a gold pencil from his vest and slid his manicured fingers slowly up and down its length. His eyes were focused on the pencil rather than Hickock when he said, "I assume that by now you've read the presentencing report on my principal client, and I have been speculating on what you might think of it. There is no denying that my client made a few mistakes in the past, but you must have noted that was long ago and is certainly not pertinent to recent history. What I'm trying to say is that he has become a fine citizen and will continue to conduct himself as such. While the verdict did go against us in your court I've been wondering if a certain reasonableness on your part might steer us away from an appeal. What with one option and a few others available to us this thing could drag on for years. My client would like to have it settled."

"Would he?" Hickock made no attempt to conceal the sarcasm in his voice. "Well, so would I. But there are a lot of factors involved and I intend to take my time weighing them."

"Of course, of course. No one is trying to hurry you, Julian."

"And of course you know this entire conversation is unethical."

"Ah, but it is not. I deliberately chose a moment when you would be away from your chambers and I'm really here one might say only in the role of messenger."

Hickock raised his heavy black eyebrows and frowned. He detested the way Delgado used the archaic designation of "one," apparently as a ploy to impress listeners. What the hell was Delgado up to?

"Have you been retained by Western Union?"

Again he saw Delgado's thin smile.

"I've always admired your wit, Julian, but in this case it's somewhat inappropriate."

"This whole conversation is inappropriate, and I must tell you that you've not improved my digestion. The trial is over. Your client was found guilty. I'm presently considering an appropriate sentence for the crime he committed, which as you know can be up to five years. I haven't as yet reached any kind of decision and don't know when I will. Until that time, may I remind you that any communication between us must be extremely pertinent, and even a hint of your trying to influence my opinion would see you disbarred. Unless you're eager to tangle with the State Bar Association I suggest you leave me to what is left of my pie á la mode and depart . . . right now before my worst suspicions are confirmed."

Delgado switched the ends of his gold pencil and continued to caress it. He switched ends once again and examined the point as if he was looking down the barrel of a rifle.

"*Please*, Julian," he said softly, "give me credit for some intelligence. Of course I wouldn't be so foolish as to attempt to sway you. You've always been known as your own man and I've taken both pride and pleasure in our acquaintance. But one should look at the realities. There are lots of able lawyers who would love to have your job and you have an election coming next year. Those of us who have worked with you will naturally put our check by your name on the ballot, but how about the majority who do not know you? To convince them takes campaign money because the public just doesn't follow the conduct of a judge when he is in office as they do a politician's. For the most part they could care less what kind of decisions you hand down, unless you've been too soft with a rapist or a murderer. The majority of the voters haven't the slightest idea what a judge really does or what his election does or does not do to our judicial system. All it takes to shove you off the bench is for some reasonably clean lawyer, a man who bathes and shaves more or less regularly, to hang his photo all over the place and hire people to repeat his name as many times a day as his campaign chest can afford. Unless you can compete you might as well dust off your old shingle and start asking around a few firms for a partnership. Who knows? You might even go to work for Horn, Delgado, Skinner and DeWitt."

"I'm warning you, Martin. I don't like the goddamn trend of this conversation—"

"Don't be so owly. I've made no offers of any kind nor would I dream of doing so. I have simply pointed out certain realities in the hope you'll bear them in mind. Because it is conceivable that *someone else* might be backed very heavily by people who might have gathered the impression you were too hardnosed—"

"I wish I had a tape recording of this so I could hang you with it." Hickock took a forkful of ice cream and pie and regretted it. How could he be forceful about telling Delgado to get lost with a mouthful of food?

"No, you couldn't hang me. Because we are not talking about *your* finances, but about how affluent some still unknown individual might be who could surface later in the year. The point is—"

"Estervan must be paying you one hell of a lot of money for you to come up to me like this and sing that kind of song."

Delgado returned the gold pencil to his vest pocket and raised his eyes toward the heavy beamed ceiling. He had the air of a minister challenged irreverently by one of his flock. "I haven't said anything that is unethical or illegal. I'm only trying to reach some understanding with you as to the reluctance of my client to spend any time in confinement. And in that connection I'm instructed to deliver a message to you. It comes from Estervan's brother."

"I was not aware he had a brother." Of course, Hickock thought. Although Estervan was out on bail he was technically a prisoner. By shifting any communications onto a brother he escaped responsibility for any reaction to his message. It was very possible, he concluded, that this expedient had probably originated in the man who now sat opposite him.

Delgado was saying, "Mind you, Boris Estervan highly disapproves of his brother even though the family is close knit. If Boris must spend any considerable time away from his various enterprises, it's his brother who must take over, and surprisingly, that is a situation that is undesirable to both brothers. Now, Leo is of quite a different make-up than Boris, one might say he's rather hot-tempered and unpredictable. One might also suppose he would even resort to some sort of violence if a situation displeased him and he thought he could identify the cause."

Delgado became silent when one of the club's venerable waiters paused by the table and poured coffee for Hickock. The waiter glanced inquiringly at Delgado, who shook his head, then departed as silently as he had come.

When Delgado saw he was out of hearing range he said, "Julian, the fact is the man frightens me a little. I did my level best to make him take a more objective view of things, but he impressed me as the sort who allows passion to rule his thinking. After Boris was found guilty, Leo had what one might call a tantrum. I will not repeat the coarse manner in which he expressed his opinions on the injustices of the courts. When I eventually explained to him that it was not the jury but you who determined when and for how long his brother might be confined he insisted that I advise you, and I quote, to watch your step."

"I gather he is threatening me."

"One might say so, but then again I don't really know the man well and he may be all wind. It is simply that as one of your admirers it would greatly distress me if anything . . . happened—"

"I can take care of myself, thanks." In ten more seconds, Hickock thought, I am going to take this prissy bastard by the seat of his pants and personally escort him to the door.

"I hope you'll not underestimate two factors which I've tried to bring to your attention. The first is that Boris Estervan is a generous man and next year you'll be running for election. The second is Boris's brother, who suggested to me almost as an afterthought that he hoped you would not consider him so dumb that he would harm you personally."

"Is that all?"

"Yes. He did not elaborate."

"Okay, messenger boy, then I have one for you to deliver. You tell the Estervan brothers that I'll be reelected without their assistance and if it were offered I wouldn't take it. I'm a sworn judge in the superior court of this state, I take my duties fairly seriously and no one is going to tell me how to run my court or *help* me make decisions. If that's understood, you'll understand that if you were ever welcome at this table you are not now."

Delgado smiled tolerantly, as if to demonstrate his limitless patience. He pushed back his chair and got up slowly.

"I'm sorry about this, Julian. I'm most sincerely sorry to have troubled you. However I do hope you'll not allow your personal feelings to cloud your usual clear thinking. Enjoy your coffee."

Hickock watched him as he crossed the dining room, pausing occasionally to greet a fellow member. How badly, he thought, did he really want this job? Just being reelected every four years was a time-consuming exercise in frustration for anyone who was not a natural politician. Skill and devotion to the law were at the bottom of the qualification barrel. It was the best-known name that won every time, and advertising cost far more money than he ever hoped to have available. Only the federal judges could afford to relax. Appointed by the President for the duration of their careers, they were welcome to the job. Hickock just could not visualize corporate lawsuits and tax suits holding his attention while he waited for the occasional bank robber who gets caught. His court, by God, represented the real life, and the Estervans and the Delgados were just another challenge. It was always people versus The People. That was his bag.

The waiter appeared again and bent to Hickock's ear.

"Judge Goldstein would like a word with you, Your Honor."

Hickock glanced quickly around the room. "Where is he?"

"On the telephone in the hall, sir."

Hickock signed his lunch check. Well fine, there was no other voice he would rather hear at this moment than Butch Goldstein's swamp-frog basso.

Fundamental Butch, who presided over his municipal court with a marvelous mix of wisdom and compassion, was far more than a colleague; he was one of the Cavemen.

"Hey Julian," he rumbled, "your secretary tells me you're having hoi-poloi for lunch or are they having you?"

"My secretary is now fired for revealing my whereabouts to the world."

"Well I'm up in Jackass Valley."

"You must feel at home."

"You've got to help me. I've tried every other alternative."

"This sounds like it's going to cost me money."

"I've had a minor accident. I came up for the weekend to do a little climbing and talk to the rocks, you *comprende*?"

Hickock did comprehend all too well. Goldstein's wife Sarah was a nonstop conversationalist and to steal even a little tranquility he found it convenient to spend an occasional weekend by himself—as distant from his home as possible.

"My intention was to be in court this morning, but I had a flat tire . . ."

Conveniently? Hickock wondered.

"I was putting on the spare when the jack slipped . . . I'm not sure just how or why, but several hundred pounds of my car came down on my foot. The doctor says I have to stay here until the swelling goes down . . . at least three or four days. Meanwhile you are the only pro tem available who knows how to go by the book. So I'll appreciate it very much if you'll warm my bench until I can maneuver."

"But I'm not a municipal judge. I would have to be officially appointed by the mayor. And besides—"

"You are already appointed. I just talked to the mayor and he is delighted to have a man of your caliber take over for me."

"You sure the car didn't fall on your head? I don't know how to handle all those drunks, thieves, and prostitutes—"

"You'll think of something. Just go over to Court 4 right now. My staff is waiting for you and they know the drill on everything."

"But I'm all wrapped up in this Estervan thing—"

"It will keep. Just look solemn and wise and no one will ever know the difference."

"Thanks a lot," Hickock said sourly. "By the way, how bad is your foot?"

"Nothing that a few scotch and sodas won't cure."

Hickock was pleased that the click he heard in the telephone receiver was significant. No lengthy expressions of gratitude, or long explanations, and no compromising. Butch knew very well he would protest because he was spoiled by the much easier pace of the higher courts, but he also knew there would be no refusal. He knew that as long as Hickock was not actually sitting on his bench their friendship demanded unswerving service. And that, thought Hickock with a smile, was a far more pleasant subject for his present attention than Delgado and his manufactured threats.

It was noon before Wanda slipped her feet into a new pair of high wedgie shoes, checked her high cheekbones and full lips in a mirror to make sure they were still high and full, and told herself it was now or never. She just could not allow herself to linger any longer in the absolutely marvelous quiet of Mrs. Millington's house, where you could even hear your own breathing. Some different than the Clark Treatment Center. Every can kicked the decibel level over the moon but Clark had to be the noisiest place in this universe.

When Wanda descended the front steps and turned on to the sidewalk she saw that the sky had cleared and a warm sun splashed the tree leaves with a glittering light that made her think of ballet dancers. Heavenly days! The outside required being on the inside to appreciate it. Of course, she had never really seen a ballet, not the real thing with a live orchestra and girls and those muscular dudes jumping around, but once on late late TV, when she was just too tired to go after any more tricks, she had watched a performance. Only part of a show, that was, because after a while with all the jumping around and all that classical music which has no beat to it so a person just could not get with it, well, she just got tired and switched to another channel.

So why should she be remembering that ballet stuff this day? Because the trees were dancing in the wind? No way. What was really dancing was Wanda Usher, formerly of Winthrop, Tennessee, and points west.

Not really dancing either, more like just falling into the old sweet cream lady stroll like it was the most natural thing to do in the whole world. Funny how those things came back. If somebody was to put up five dollars for every mile Wanda Usher had done at the stroll she would be a billionaire. You better believe.

Mrs. Millington had said the bus stop was two blocks east, and the bus would go right to the center of the city. Ten minutes, only. So how handy could things be? There was no hurry now. Today, all there was to do was report to the probation officer and tell him . . . God forbid it should be a female . . . tell whoever that you were being a good girl and were already looking for work. Good afternoon and stay out of my hair.

That waste of time should take only about ten minutes and there would still be time to go to the bank. Little ol' Wanda may not be a billionaire, but at least she was a thousandaire. Damn straight. Right there in the little ol' First National Bank and drawing interest for the last two years was almost six thousand bucks which Sam had hung onto somehow and left to the best sweet cream main lady he ever had in his whole misspent life. That black bastard was now going to pay back what he took away even though he had been cold dead for two years. By now he would have forgot the time he was so high on coke he got his lawyer to make up a will, a real one, and left everything he had to his main lady. Which was unusual to say the least for a pimp, black or any other color.

Of course if you worked the west coast circuit you had to have a black pimp if you were going to survive—just like if you were working down in LA or the southwest then best to have a Chicano or an Oriental of some kind, and back east it would be a black or an Italian. And all things being equal Sam was a genuine boss pimp right there with the top pros grossing himself fifty, maybe seventy-five thousand a year out of only six girls. He was never no poop butt, no welfare pimp or Mack man. And no gorilla. He never beat a woman in his whole stable. A rat he was, but he had style and he knew how to shoot money terms with bartenders for girls who did better in those places, and he would not have anything to do with jiveasses, those flaky hos who moved around from one pimp to another.

Wanda's stroll became even slower and instinctively provocative as she envisioned Sam among the tree leaves, sitting up there on a branch, smiling and humming away a little tune like he always did when things were going along in a way that pleased him. He was a big man, well over six feet and weighing in around two hundred and ten. He was blue-black and sleek like the ravens in Tennessee, but he was born in the north and his accent was not black at all—just his deep and raunchy voice gave him away if you heard him on the telephone. "Right on!" he was always saying to you. "Right on!"

Sam ran his business pretty much by the book, the way Iceberg Slim had written it down for people in the fast life. He would have nothing to do with percentages, always saying they caused trouble. So he took *all* of the girls' money, but he took care of you. If you wanted to be an outlaw and work the streets yourself, go ahead, dum-dum, he would say, and see what happens. And of course it usually did. Indeed. No more than a few nights on the street doing a solo and sure enough the girl would find herself on the way to the can or worse doing a trick with some freak who wanted to take her apart limb by limb.

Not with Sam. With him you learned the business and everybody in his stable had to start as bottom woman. Well it did not take little ol' Wanda long. One day Sam said, "Okay, Wanda, you ready for this? I am hereby going to classify you as a thoroughbred. How you like that?"

Sam knew quality in a ho when he saw it and it was not much longer until he declared right out in front of everybody that you would be his main lady.

Jesus, the fast life was hard to believe now. Three or four o'clock every morning you turned your trick money over to Sam and if he felt like it he let you get in bed with him. And that was a privilege because there was not a girl in his stable was not crazy in love with Sam. He was a real sugar pimp, a sweet one, Lordy knew, when he wanted to be, and it must have been one of those nights when Deidre was conceived.

As she continued toward the bus stop Wanda saw a woman come out of a house near the corner. She saw her turn and lock the front door behind her. *Her* house, Wanda thought. Her very own *home* which she locked behind her whenever she decided to go away. To protect her things against people who did not have a house or even a place they could call home. That was the whole of it. Right there. This dolly had it made while plenty of others did not have it made. Eeney-meeney-miney-mo, grab what you can and never let go. Like look at her now tripping down the front steps from her porch and then down some more steps from *her* lawn to *her* sidewalk. Well at least her section of sidewalk. And can you believe she is wearing a hat? A little dinky thing perched on top of her hair which has to be dyed to keep out the gray.

When she reached the sidewalk the woman turned and started off briskly. Wanda quickened her pace to keep up with her. Now, she thought, there was what you call a lady. The heels of her shiny black pumps were going click-click-click along the cement, sharp little noises like a bird tapping something hard with its beak. Click-click. There she goes just as pretty as you please all wrapped up in her wonderful world and what had to be a three-hundred-dollar suit not including the accessories. Like her little matching purse which was not some leftover carpetbag but utterly neat and just big enough to hold credit cards and some cosmetic junk for when she felt like powdering her nose. Say she is about forty-some? Which would be an old bag in most parts of Tennessee, but in a neighborhood like this people kept their looks much better. It must be the water. You would read about such as her in some of the fancy magazines. She was wearing pantyhose and there was no sashaying around her butt. Good legs, small ass—Sam would have said "Right on."

Wanda was surprised to see the woman walk directly to the bus stop, pull back the cuff of her super-neat little black jacket and glance at her watch. Probably an anniversary gift. *Her*?

Taking a bus? Of course the *really* rich did things like that. They did not have to impress anybody with big cars and stuff. And not having to worry about parking her Mercedes was probably more convenient. People like her could ride a Tennessee mule to town and everybody would still know she was a genuine lady. So what? So could you if you wanted . . .

Wanda, why don't you quit kidding yourself? Remember how Aunt Louise used to say you could not make a silk purse out of a sow's ear?

Wanda knew a strange excitement when she came to stand beside the woman at the bus stop. Should she say something to her? Like, "You sure are beautiful, ma'am," which was fairly close to the facts. But if you did that she might think you were a dyke. Should she say, "Hey, is it not a nice day for taking a bus somewhere," or "shall we go shopping together?" or just something to keep this neat middle-aged woman handy so you could learn how to be like her . . . well, at least something like her—

Suddenly Wanda realized this total stranger was the first *real* person she had encountered since she got out of Clark; *real,* that is, because unlike Mrs. Millington who was much older, she did not know that Wanda Usher had just been sprung. She had no idea that the person standing next to her was an ex-con.

Well, something had to be said. They couldn't just stand there looking down the street for a bus that was not there yet.

Wanda enunciated very carefully when she asked the woman, "Could you tell me if this is where I catch the Number 3 bus?"

"Yes. It is."

"Thank you." Did the woman ask where she was going? She did not. Did she say anything at all like "the bus must be late" or "it will be along in a few minutes"? She did not. "Yes, it is." Three words and no more.

They stood in silence for only a few minutes before the bus came and halted with a grunt and a sigh. Wanda deliberately allowed the woman to precede her up the steps. She hoped the woman would take an unoccupied seat which would give her a perfect chance to sit beside her and then no way could she avoid at least some dialogue. No reason to give her a lesson on loneliness if there was nothing else to yak about but if she wanted one she would sure have a good professor.

Wanda was disappointed when she saw the woman take the

first available aisle seat next to a small bald-headed man who she thought looked like a plucked chicken. Jesus, did he look like better company than Wanda Usher? At least the woman gave her a teeny little smile as she passed down the aisle.

Wanda took one of the few available seats in the back of the bus and had to be content with a view of the woman's head in the distance. She forced herself to look away from her and think about other things. Like Sam and like how she was sure now that she would have no trouble staying away from the fast life. You better believe even if the bus passed right through the old district near First Avenue or Virginia and maybe she would even spy some old friends like Aggie, or Phyllis, or Trisha, or Stella, and it would not make a smidgin of difference. She could look right at them and say to get lost she was never going to take another trick as long as she lived. They could have all the servicemen, and diaper johns, and fast johns, and the talkers who were the really lonely hard-ons, and the freaks and conventioneers. Are you ready for this, old friends in the life? Little ol' Wanda is going to stay clean right out in this here wide wide world wherein it says you don't have to report for nothing to nobody except once a week to the probation officer which after a while you can do by telephone. And all you Aggies and Phyllises and Trishas and Stellas can become old fleabags if you want and which you sure will if you stay in the fast life or become types which is worse yet. Wanda has been away and she has had time enough to think these thoughts out. I have seen the light.

As the bus left the tree-lined residential area and became overwhelmed by concrete, Wanda thought about Deidre. She would be six now and where she was, no one was going to tell her mother. *Unfit mother,* that's what that Judge Hickock had said.

Okay, judge, you asked for it. You took Deidre away because of one little mistake. And you are going to pay for doing that to me. I will never see my Deidre again so she might as well be dead . . . and me too. She will grow up and have a name I won't know and I can't find out if she is happy or miserable or sick or well. I could maybe try looking up all the Deidres in the world about the right age as mine, but where do you go for that? Maybe you can find out, Judge Hickock, maybe when you are so goddamned miserable and so far down you can hardly find your next breath, maybe when I see you begging me to just put things back to normal again, then just maybe you'll understand how I been feeling this past three years and you'll say I was wrong to do what I did and so here is where Deidre is living and I hereby declare you can go see her at least once a month. Mr. *Dis*honorable Judge you will say I made one awful big mistake in sending you away and especially calling you an unfit mother. That's the way you are going to talk. Holler all you want, I won't care. I'll just watch you wear out your knees begging me to give you back your good life but it's going to be an eye for an eye. You killed me so figure out for yourself what kind of a problem you got on your hands. You can't shake it because Wanda Usher is one true survivor. *You better believe*.

As the bus stopped at the street corners near the center of the city Wanda was impressed with the changes since she had last worked the same pavements. An ugly glass office building had replaced the colorful little cluster of cigar, secondhand, and souvenir stores which only three years ago had always been a good starting point for the evening stroll. Give ten or fifteen minutes and a john was sure to come along and all you had to do was use just the slightest more hesitation in your stroll and he would get the message. If the john would come to a halt then any thoroughbred would have him nailed and half an hour later she could be right back on the same corner, fifty, maybe even a hundred dollars richer.

What was wrong with that? Why should that make anybody unfit? The johns were lonesome. Maybe their wives were frigid or invalids, or they were afraid to have babies, or who knew what? They wanted to do the natural thing which was healthy and it was all wrong to say they got diseased from prostitutes. People in the fast life were clean, they took very special care of themselves because they had to stay in business and it was a lot better for any john to get his jollies with a professional rather than some teen-age highschool girl who didn't know a douche from a dildo.

Once Sam got hold of some statistics which proved that eighty-five percent of the venereal disease in the United States was with teen-agers. So there, Judge Hickock, maybe you better think about your own daughter and ask yourself who is really *unfit*. And you better believe that word is an *obsession* with me.

At the next stop Wanda was prepared to look at the floor of

the bus until they had passed the corner. Because that was where they were living that awful New Year's Eve, Wanda and Sam sometimes, and little Deidre all the time. The flat was on the third floor and Deidre had her own little room which was awful small since it was part of a former hallway. That was a disadvantage, because there was never any lock on the door and Deidre had a habit of wandering in and out and sometimes waking up in the middle of the night asking for a glass of water. Which was okay usually because never never would her mother even think of doing tricks in that flat. Sam, of course, came there when he pleased, but that was different and he shared the bedroom just like they were married, which naturally Deidre thought was the situation. It was too bad Sam didn't pay too much attention to Deidre since he was her real dad, but he always asked how could he be sure of that, and the only answer you had was for God's sake can't you see she is half-white and half-black and you went on and on with that ridiculous argument until Sam said he was sick of the subject.

That bad New Year's Eve Sam brought that creep who said his name was Rollo to the flat, and they said let's celebrate this New Year so that nobody will forget. Hallelujah!

Rollo had his flaky girlfriend Juanita-something-or-other with him and they hardly got in the door before they brought out a whole lid of grass and started dusting PCP on their joints. Then they started fooling around with each other and pretty soon Juanita started going for Sam. Then Rollo said Wanda, you sure have a nice ass and I am going to have some of it. And then two more people came in who were friends of Sam, and they started shooting up and they got down in a hurry. And Stella came alone because her steady had already nodded out. She heard on the street that there was a real celebration going on at my place and pretty soon everybody was smacked back right out of their skins.

Except for a while, Wanda. Then just not to poop the party and to keep pace with Sam you took a few snorts of snow—just a line in one nostril really, but you weren't used to it since one thing in the life that never appealed to you was getting hooked on any kind of stuff.

From then on things got pretty fuzzy and there was some kind of fight between you and that Juanita for moving in on Sam. Then Deidre showed up all of a sudden, like she had dropped down out of the ceiling or something and there she was, right in the middle of things asking for a glass of water and everybody was so busy screwing around or nodded out she couldn't get any attention. And she started to cry and somehow that triggered something inside your dumb head because there was no lock on her door and you didn't want her to see any more than what she already had of what was going on.

Sam said, "Now you get rid of the kid because she's interfering with our New Year fun. I say again you get the kid outta here and stop her bawlin' right this goddamned minute or my friend Juanita and I is gettin' outta here to go have our own party."

That did it. Looking back these years it is some wonder how Wanda Usher who was from the real south to begin with and brought up to be halfway decent, at least to know the colored people had their own toilets and places on the bus, how in God's world did I get so hung up on a black pimp I cared whether he went off with Juanita or any other ho that might pass through his stable? How could I be so jealous of such a situation that I lost any sense I had left after only a few snorts of coke and one or two glasses of champagne? All right? So I am a highly emotional person and Deidre's yelling got to me, but did that mean I absolutely had to get her out of sight and sound?

Confused, that's what the situation was, you better believe it. So confused you could not stand it one more minute. There was that clothes closet out in the front hallway where the former tenant must have kept something valuable. It had a sliding bolt lock on the door and your poor, dumb, confused brain said loud and clear, That's a safe place to put Deidre and she won't be no more trouble to Sam or anybody else. Well . . .

Wanda took a deep breath and raised her anxious eyes to look out the bus window. Hey, right there is the corner where the flat used to be only now the whole building is gone. It is nothing but a parking lot. Somebody tore down the whole thing just like your life was torn down that night. There is not a trace of the building and there is not a trace of Deidre. Right there about fifty feet up in the empty air was where you last saw Deidre. With tears all over her face.

She didn't want to go in the closet, but you shoved her in anyway and slid the bolt until the door was locked. And about then or soon after you must have passed out. Because you don't remember nothing. Not what went on with Sam or Juanita or Stella or that Rollo or any other jerk that decided New Year's was so important.

It was daylight when that Rollo character woke up and said in a loud voice that he had to take a squirt. And he was still confused and of course he didn't know the layout of the place so instead of heading for the toilet which was back of the bedroom he went the other way thinking the front hall closet was where he wanted to go. He slid the bolt and found Deidre lying there and thank the Lordy he still had a few wits left. Deidre was damn near dead from suffocation because there was no air hardly in that closet and right away Rollo started giving her artificial respiration and yelling for everybody to get their eyes open and do something.

That all went on for quite a while before Stella said to call the EMT people and did it herself. She was still getting dressed and so was everybody else doing the same thing when the EMTs arrived like they came in some rocket. And the police were with them and so was the man who checked the marks on everybody's arms and read us our rights and said come along . . .

The bus left the corner where there was only an open parking lot now and while it continued deeper into the heart of the city Wanda thought the rest of that morning was something she did not care to think about ever again even though she had rehearsed the scene a thousand times in the last three years. It was tough enough to remember the rest of that January which was like a hundred years ago. First the arraignment with the public defender saying it was better to cop a plea of child abuse because the district attorney's office had in mind a charge of attempted murder. Of Deidre, can anybody believe? And then came the indictment which was when Sam disappeared from the face of the earth. Next came the pretrial hearing in front of Judge Hickock who asked if you wanted a jury trial or not. And that dumb public defender saying a jury might make things even worse so better say no . . . just depend on him and the judge.

'Bye Wanda. Unfit mother. 'Bye for three years. 'Bye Deidre. Hickock. I'm coming for you, judge.

• • •

Julian Hickock rolled up his black robe, tucked it under his arm, and passing through his outer chambers told Lucinda he would be unavailable until very late in the afternoon.

"I'm going to hold down Judge Goldstein's bench for a few days, but don't tell anyone. Have you got that perfectly clear?"

Lucinda nodded and smiled that bovine smile, but Hickock sensed that she was unhappy. He had been too blunt about her easy acceptance of Delgado. Hoping to cheer her he said, "I am going into the lower depths, down in the rough and tumble without knowing all the drill. If I have any dignity left when this chore is done it will be because no one has discovered how many mistakes I'll make. So please, censor your lips, will you?"

"Of course, Your Honor. Are you also unavailable to Miss Pomeroy if she should call?"

Hickock cocked his head and arched his black eyebrows. "Sometimes," he said slowly, "you are a puzzlement to me. Sometimes it seems to me you know more than you should."

"Isn't that a good secretary's prerogative?"

Hickock avoided a direct response. Tilting words with Lucinda was a devious pastime. Just when she seemed to be slipping out of phase was when she was at her best. He wondered why he should feel a tinge of guilt when he told her that any call from Miss Pomeroy was acceptable. "But if Mr. Delgado calls for another appointment or has any more messages to convey I am not available."

The telephone rang and Lucinda enunciated, "Judge Julian Hickock's chambers," in that special voice she used for incoming calls. She glanced up at Hickock and covered the phone with her hand.

"Are you in to your son?"

He took the phone and said, "Hi, Victor. How come you're not in class?"

Victor said he was between classes and was calling about Nellie-Mae. He had stopped by the hospital on the way to school and she was feeling depressed. "Could you stop by and see her on your way home? About six would be the best time."

"I sort of had in mind going for a sail. It looks like there might be some wind."

There was a long silence and for a moment Hickock thought Victor had hung up.

"Well, of course it's up to you."

Hickock could almost feel the hostility in his son's voice. I disappoint him at every turn, he thought. There seems to be nothing that I can do right. How in the hell did you work hard enough to send a kid to college and still have time enough for him when *he* has some free time?

And that is a real cop-out, he thought, because obviously he had time to take Jean Pomeroy sailing. As he hesitated he saw Lucinda was watching him carefully.

"Okay, son. I'll stop by and see her on my way home."

"I thought you were dining out."

"Right. Right. I guess I forgot."

"How could you?" The sarcasm in Victor's voice was as unmistakable as the fact that now Victor had certainly hung up.

Hickock handed the phone back to Lucinda. He closed his eyes and massaged them a moment with his fingers.

"Lucinda," he said finally, "you have known me a long time. Do you think I am cold-hearted or particularly selfish?"

"Not particularly. Sometimes we all have to be a little self-centered."

"You've been reading Dear Abby again. I don't need soapy wisdom. I need to be two or three people."

"You are."

"What do you mean by that?"

"For one thing you're honest with yourself. Then you hold down one of the most frightening jobs anyone can have. You're an average father with a score of one to one at this stage of the game. Your daughter thinks you sit on the right hand of God, and Victor thinks you need a guardian. That's enough for several people and should be a big enough slice of life for several people but you're not satisfied."

"Who said?"

"I do. How else do you account for Miss Pomeroy? She's a nice person but she's already a one-time loser."

"Are you by any chance referring to the fact that she has been married and divorced? Are you a new member of the Moral Majority or whatever that organization is that tries to return us to the nineteenth century? I am amazed at you, Lucinda. Be advised that divorcees, male or female, are not necessarily suffering from some hideous social disease." Hickock paused and his eyes narrowed as he bent over Lucinda's desk. "Now tell me. How the hell did you find out she has been married and divorced?"

"I made it my business."

"May I suggest that it is none of your business." He told himself that he was more frustrated than angry—or was the sensation of blood rising to his face just the result of Lucinda's pop-eyes seeing through to his deep embarrassment?

"Your well-being is my business, Your Honor."

"Stop smiling. You know I can't stand happy secretaries. You should feel overworked and sorry for yourself. Then you won't get into mischief—"

"I'm only trying to clear your myopia, Your Honor. At the risk of my underpaid and overworked job, I'm only trying to clarify for you that Miss Pomeroy is not Joan of Arc."

"Who said she was?" Hickock heard his voice rising unnaturally.

"Your starry eyes. The lady went to bat once and struck out. Just ask yourself why it might have happened and then put her back on a white horse if you feel like it."

Hickock pointed his finger at Lucinda. He was about to tell her that she had tried his patience once too often, then changed his mind. In the future, he thought, he would act his age. At least as long as Lucinda was looking.

"Call Miss Pomeroy," he said stiffly. "Tell her that due to unforeseen developments our sail is cancelled, *but* . . . I'll be at the appointed place for dinner."

Chapter Five

Although he had always been aware of life and customs in the municipal courts Hickock was not prepared for the staggering impact of the present-day work load. It had been a long time since he had worked these courts, first as a young public defender, and then as one of the city prosecutors. Now twenty years later it seemed all was much the same except for the increase in numbers.

All of what he now saw before him was what he had been reading about and occasionally hearing about from Butch and other municipal judges, but had only half-believed. It really is a zoo, he thought. Perhaps it was here in the lower courts that the gradual crumbling of urban societies was most apparent. The big kids who did the awful things did not appear in this court. Here was the sum of countless petty and often amateurish blundering by people who had trouble believing the law was not just a frivolous notion held by the powerful. Here were Americans who had been just a little bit out of line. The hardcase felons rarely appeared in the lower courts, nor did the murderers, and arsonists and various grand jury types like Estervan. These citizens were occasionally telling the truth when they said they were not aware they had done anything wrong.

They were also a mixed bag of clumsy liars who frequently underestimated the intelligence of everyone but themselves. Including the judge, Hickock reminded himself. Having pleaded guilty or not guilty during their arraignment, they were now prepared, at least in their own minds, to prove their innocence or twist their testimony until they said what they thought the judge wanted to hear. And usually they were wrong.

Behind the bench was a barren, ill-kept windowless room

smelling of overfilled ashtrays and the adjoining toilet which, like so many municipal buildings, was given a minimum of attention by the night cleaners. Here an occasional six-person jury was supposed to deliberate for at least long enough to convince the accused he had been given a fair trial, and here Hickock, as the temporary judge of Court 4, was supposed to slip into his black robe before entering the courtroom and mounting to the bench. Here he could relax during such recesses as he cared to designate.

On his way to Court 4 Hickock had passed through the main foyers of the Municipal Building and he had seen much that was unchanged if not quite so familiar as it once was. He was greeted warmly by a hefty sergeant of police who identified himself as a once-slim young patrolman Hickock had long ago cleared of a brutality charge. Escorting him to Courtroom 4, the sergeant indicated certain newcomers to the dreary stale-aired foyers. They passed a huge black woman who spread newspapers on the marble floor and slept the nights through. It was her right as a citizen in a public building, she claimed, and no one had the heart to throw her out although she was sometimes given to urinating wherever the urge compelled her. The foyers, she said, were her home.

There was Chester, a wino of great age who also slept in the foyers when he was not confined to the tank. Hickock, remembering Chester's earlier days, marvelled that he had any kidneys left.

"The doctors tell me," the sergeant said, "that Chester has a permanent blood alcohol percentage of point 28. They say that makes him a living miracle. Even the computers don't understand Chester, and the doctors keep paying him to be examined so they can find out how he does it. The money he gets is just enough for Chester to buy another jug of Muscatel."

Among the Monday morning regulars whose appearance in these courts was as predictable as the new week itself, Chester had by far the longest and most spectacular record. He had once been run down by a bus and suffered only minor bruises. He had fallen forty feet off the roof of the public market where he occasionally liked to give one of his incoherent orations and had broken only his wrist. He tumbled off one of the municipal wharves into the chill February waters of the bay. At the time he was clad only in a thin pair of pants and his dirty underwear and teams of police searched and dove half the night trying to find his body. The search had been officially abandoned when Chester finally bobbed to the surface, soaked and sober. He claimed he had gone for a walk on the water and had slept on the bottom and was therefore probably Jesus. If one of his rescuers would only show him true mercy and give him a shot of Muscatel to ward off a possible cold, he would be forgiven his sins.

It was citizens like Chester, Hickock mused, who drove all dogmatism from a man's mind. Who was to say Chester was naughty or even wrong? He insisted he was enjoying his life which was a better attitude than several of Hickock's acquaintances who had been in therapy, and he had survived innumerable solid citizens who had never touched a drop in their lives.

In the last foyer which echoed resoundingly with the heel-clickings of sundry municipal employees, they passed "the Wall Talker," now a well-past middle-aged man who blamed all the ills of the world on the walls in the Public Safety Building. When the walls misbehaved, which was almost every day, the man could be found addressing them earnestly.

Maybe, Hickock thought, the man was not as loony as he appeared. Like the Chileans who held a handy little god named Trauco responsible for whatever went wrong privately or nationally, the Wall Talker always had a place to unload his frustrations and he seemed to feel the better for it.

"This court is now in session, Judge Julian Hickock presiding. Will you please stand."

Hickock moved swiftly to the high-backed leather chair behind the bench and sat down. While he approved of the ceremony followed in all well-conducted courts, the spectacle of everyone rising in unison when Julian Hickock entered the room had always caused him embarrassment. Of course it is not me the man they are standing for, he reasoned. They are standing because some of them have been taken to the woodshed for a possible spanking and they are responding to an order. The population of this room stands because clothed in black they have instinctively beheld a father image and if I ever take it personally I am in trouble. The dignity of the law was a fine phrase as long as those who did the administrating kept their egos in cold storage. He had seen judges make an entrance which could only be matched by an opera star. They took their time, their normal walk became a pompous march reflecting what they hoped was the solemnity of the occasion and their exits, even when they called a recess to go to the toilet, were on the same grandiose scale. It was Hickock's practice to slip into the judicial chair as quickly as possible and thus signal everyone present they could be seated.

It was a small courtroom, one of several within the building and capable of accommodating some one hundred people including the accused, witnesses, lawyers, friends and families of those summoned, and the usual handful of spectators who spent the majority of their time drifting from court to court according to their curiosity about other people's troubles and the inclemency of the outside weather.

No matter how the dignity of the law was interpreted, Hickock knew that Court 4 was simply a holding pen of woes. During what was left of this day several individuals were going to be seriously inconvenienced, others would be angry, and a few might weep. There were bound to be those who felt wronged, cheated, outraged, and persecuted. Each to his own. There would be few victories if any, and many defeats. All the losers would automatically convince themselves they were suffering unjust punishment.

Hickock could not remember when if ever he had heard an accused say he deserved whatever penalty was handed down. The accused and found guilty never seemed to realize that all judges were limited in the severity and the leniency of their sentences. They could not twist the law too much without becoming guilty themselves. A judge was not a tribal leader as he had been in ancient times. The old boys could make up the law as they went along, allowing always for the counteracting values of love and war and the predilection of some human beings to exploit others. Those called upon to judge their fellows in less complicated times were lucky, Hickock thought. From the priestesses at the Oracle of Delphi to Confucius who above all sought a face-saving compromise in his decisions, their task as judges was to recognize the frailty of mankind and even protect it when they could. Yet they were also committed to the element of fear of their personal authority, enough to keep desperate supplicants at their distance.

Hickock slipped on his glasses, damning their need for close work and yet grateful that his distant vision was still excellent. The glasses were of "half-eye" design, a feature which allowed him to peer over them while they rested on his great nose. Jean had once said that at such times he looked like a peevish owl and he should be stuffed and preserved in a glass case. The vision pleased him, but he was not sure he would have enjoyed the image quite as much had it originated elsewhere.

Now he glanced at the large clock and the calendar on the far wall, and found the clock wrong by four hours which did not surprise him. Butch was an easy man with his time, an easy man with everything and hence much loved. Every knowing defense lawyer hoped to argue his case before Butch Goldstein. The chances are his client would get off with a reprimand, or if everything went wrong the sentence would be the lightest the law allowed. Hickock decided he was delighted to find the clock so awry—it was a symbol of Butch's basic distrust of the system and his total rejection of pomp. When he sat this bench he was in every respect just a good trumpet player trying to ease the troubles of other trumpet players. He identified easily with the troublemakers brought before him and for that Hickock envied him. Things went wrong for people, but why make a big fuss about it? A clock was four hours off the correct time—leave it be.

Hickock was amused to consider the contrast between two men doing the same job. The notion of having the clock set right probably had never occurred to Butch. He would be concerned only with the faces Hickock saw now looking up at him. And when his day was done he would forget them—utterly.

Hickock wished that his own sense of isolation was not always so predominant. There was too much time for balancing the scales, trying to identify the man Hickock with the accused, trying to exchange places with another being when actually their only common ground was the planet they stood on. He had come to think of the mental process as "the curse of the conscientious" and he was not at all sure it was a good indulgence.

It was a windowless room illuminated by tube lights reflecting against the high white ceiling. The effect was cold, Hickock thought, rather clinical and depressing in comparison with his own court which had several windows—and a dependable clock. The decor of Municipal Court 4 was relatively new, a blond veneer which for some inexplicable reason made Hickock wonder if he had not suddenly been transported to a suburban health clinic. There was none of the polished dark mahogany to be found in his own court and which somehow established its special and rather ponderous dignity.

Now the public benches were crowded with those who had been awaiting a judge, some of them most of the morning. Hickock leaned slightly forward and since the situation was somewhat unusual, he decided on an unusual approach.

"I regret the delay in opening of this court," he said evenly. "Judge Goldstein who would normally preside has been unavoidably detained and it took some time to locate me. My apologies to you attorneys for possible disruption of your schedule and to those called before this court whose patience may be strained. We will now proceed."

Just below the bench, sitting at desks on an elevated platform was the court clerk and a black woman who operated the tape recorder. The bailiff had his own desk just inside the fence separating the working area from the public seating. By leaning forward slightly Hickock could see the well-groomed head of the court clerk, a pleasant-looking lady who reached upward the full extent of her arm and handed him a sheaf of papers. "Your Honor, here is the case load for today," she said smiling.

Hickock flicked through the pages and was shocked at the volume. He wanted to ask if there had not been some mistake—certainly this ball of troubles could not be just for one judge in one day? Yet he was reluctant to show his naivete so soon. He heard the clerk saying, "We can start any time you are ready, Your Honor."

Hickock peered over his glasses at the long table where the public defender and one of the many attorneys from the prosecutor's office were seated. He recognized the defense attorney as John Exeter, a courthouse eccentric of almost legendary status. An honor graduate of Harvard Law School and a practical do-gooder, he had long ago forsaken any prospect of real wealth by choosing criminal defense as his field. As he often said of his specialty, "The blacks pay sometimes or at least the next time they need you, but the Indians just never pay at all." In court, John Exeter presented an extraordinary and incongruous figure and was sometimes mistaken for one of the accused rather than their defender. He was very tall and bent like a spruce in a heavy wind. His gray hair fell uncombed upon his perpetually hunched shoulders and swept down around his face until it joined his full beard. He shuffled when he walked as if his feet hurt intolerably. From a distance he presented an almost Christ-like appearance, a gentle man, perhaps an itinerant preacher. Hickock knew better. The perpetually grime-encrusted glasses through which John Exeter chose to view the seamy world around him concealed brilliant and piercing eyes and behind them lurked one of the finest legal minds in the land. "I have always been for the underdog," Exeter was fond of explaining in his theatrical fashion. The people in the judiciary and particularly the blacks and Chicanos and Indians who composed the majority of his clients knew he had long proven his claim. He was restless now as always, riffling through the cards and sheaf of papers which case by case listed the day's work.

In strong contrast to Exeter was the prosecutor for the day, a fresh-faced young woman who Hickock suspected could not possibly have been long out of law school. The court clerk had introduced her to him as Debbie . . . something, and he had already forgotten her last name. She was also flipping through the charge lists and Hickock noted she seemed utterly poised. It pleased him that at least the prospect of opposing Exeter did not seem to dismay her. Now she glanced up at him, smiled faintly and said, "If it please the court, the first on the calendar is Number 7629574 dash Y.U. for Uniform, Your Honor. Rachel Dinsmore?"

The bailiff opened the gate in the fence and beckoned to a diminutive woman who came haltingly forward. Hickock thought she looked exactly like Whistler's mother. The clerk asked her to raise her right hand and took her whispered oath that she would tell the truth and nothing but the truth. Hickock and every other professional knew it was an impossible promise even from the best intentioned of humans. The oath should read, "I will tell the truth as I see it."

This little old lady? *Forty-six* parking tickets? In a period of eight months? And for this sort of thing, Hickock thought, I have had to set aside Estervan?

"Madame," he said, wondering at his involuntary use of an address he could not recall ever having employed before. "Would you please explain to the court why it was necessary to swear out a warrant for your arrest? Is that the only way the city can get your attention? You had only to pay the small fine every time you found a tag on your car and that would have been the end of it."

"I am getting on," she said, "and I don't like to walk. And there are too damn many cars anyway."

Whistler's mother? Hickock looked more closely and saw a fierce glint behind her spectacles. And her jaw was set in a way that suggested no regrets whatsoever. "Mrs. Dinsmore, is it your opinion that cars other than your own should be banned from the city streets?"

Hickock knew it was a leading question and he was not surprised when John Exeter rose quickly to his feet and called out, "Your Honor, the lady . . . Mrs. Dinsmore has already pleaded guilty—"

Alert John Exeter. He sensed that if Mrs. Dinsmore were persuaded to say more she would talk herself into real trouble and reveal much more than was necessary. Good for you, John Exeter, Hickock thought. You sensed Whistler's mother had riled me. You are Protector of the Topdog as well as the Underdog. According to the charge sheet Mrs. Dinsmore's last ticket had been tucked under the windshield wiper of a brand-new Mercedes roadster. And her address was one of the most luxurious condominiums in the city.

"Are you on Social Security, Mrs. Dinsmore?"

"Yes. And it's miss."

"My apologies, *Miss* Dinsmore. And you are driving a Mercedes, is that correct?"

"What has that got to do with where I park it?"

"Nothing really, except it does. This court, and I hope every other court is for the protection and the prosecution of the well-off as well as the poor. The record demonstrates very clearly that you consider yourself above the law or at least so privileged that you can ignore the consequences of the law. I will give you the opportunity to reconsider that philosophy. I will fine you five hundred dollars which is the maximum allowed this court. I only regret that it is beyond my jurisdiction to suspend your license indefinitely."

Hickock was turning up the next page of the charge sheets as the prosecutor specified another long number and called out, "Antonio Saviatta?"

A policeman rose and escorted a thin, middle-aged man through the gate. He stood beside him more protectively than as if on guard and Hickock was reminded how all uniformed policemen squeaked, even when they made slight movements. It was their leather cartridge belts and holsters, their keys and cuffs and notebooks and all the paraphernalia of their office which created a sort of sinister melody until even their sparkling badges seemed to hum. Hickock was pleased to note the new style of officer which was gradually becoming the norm—at least in his city. There were no longer so many arrogant brutes whose potbellies were actually supported by their leather trappings. Now an entirely new type of well-educated, alert young men had chosen law enforcement and if there was any hope in the streets Hickock believed they might eventually provide it. They still squeaked, but the resemblance ended there. Yet give another ten years; would their comfortable civil service status and their constant exposure to the dark side of their city transform them into a reincarnation of their predecessors?

John Exeter was on his feet again. He ran his fingers through his wild gray hair and announced, "Your Honor, Mr. Saviatta is a two-twenty and I recommend the present charge be dismissed and the man sent to treatment center."

Hickock was puzzled. A "two-twenty"? What did that signify? To cover his ignorance he reread Antonio Saviatta's charge sheet. *Urinating in public.* A misdemeanor of little weight and certainly not an offense in the eyes of God, Hickock thought wryly. Yet in a supposedly modern city everyone could hardly be allowed to go about pissing where and when they pleased. Hence a law had been formulated to prohibit where such natural relief could be enjoyed. Hickock reminded himself that it was not always easy for strangers to find handy toilet facilities in any American city and a citizen in such obvious physical disarray as Antonio Saviatta would seem to be did not inspire a warm welcome into the discreet establishments.

Hickock saw the clerk watching him carefully; a signal that everyone was anxious to move on to the next case. After a moment their eyes met and he confessed his ignorance without having to say a word. She rose and whispered to him, "A two-twenty is a crazy, Your Honor."

Of course, of course, a code to save embarrassment. No one had the heart to come right out in court and proclaim a citizen was obviously demented. If proclaimed here the labeling had a too official ring and might do irreparable damage to an individual teetering on the borderline of lunacy.

Hickock studied the man a moment and saw that he was not really interested in his immediate fate. He was far off, his eyes seeing something no one else in the room could envision, and for a moment Hickock wondered if he was really a disturbed man or was he just clever enough to know a preoccupied behavior might help him be dismissed?

On the charge sheet Hickock saw a police notation, "Lily-waving prior to and after offense." That meant Saviatta had not only exposed himself, but had been shaking his penis in a provocative manner.

"Your Honor," John Exeter was saying, "I can't see where it would accomplish anything to keep Mr. Saviatta in jail. He needs help."

As we all do, Hickock thought.

"I agree. Mr. Saviatta, you will be transferred to the treatment center at Hillside where you can receive some obviously necessary care. Meanwhile all charges against you are dismissed. Do you understand?"

As the officer led Saviatta away, Hickock had difficulty erasing the look in Saviatta's eyes. They had said nothing and yet a great deal. They had seemed to say, Who am I? I am adrift in a sea of confusion, tall buildings yell down at me, the thunder of trucks and buses and airplanes pound at my ears and shake my brain until it refuses to stabilize. It takes confidence to live in a big city and who can find confidence in the streets? My head is tortured by the constant roaring everywhere, my eyes and nostrils are abused by fumes and my feet hurt on the boundless concrete. Help me. I am a lone man, a frightened, bewildered, unhappy little man trying to exist in an element of despair. Is it any wonder that my bladder leaks, that I mock the strength of this terrible establishment by shaking my penis in its face?

Of course it was unlikely, Hickock thought, that Saviatta had any such reactions. Yet his eyes said he did and they said so loud enough to leave this haunting impression. And to remind me that my business is compassion.

"I am drifting myself," Hickock muttered as he heard the prosecuting attorney calling out another long number and the name "Bettina Murray."

Hickock looked down upon an enormous black woman. Still

at her endless paper shuffling, the prosecutor was relating the charge in a straight monotone.

"Your Honor, Mrs. Murray was apprehended in the Safeway market at Twenty-first and Elm Street at two P.M. September 17. She had six prepackaged steaks, two pounds of butter, and a box of chocolate chip cookies concealed on her person."

While the court clerk took Bettina Murray's vow to tell only the truth, Hickock watched John Exeter. Apparently oblivious to the proceedings around him, he continued to rustle through his papers. Papers, an ocean of papers seemed to dominate the proceedings below the bench, volumes of papers crackled and hissed beneath the energetic fingers of five people by Hickock's count, all of them paid by the taxpayers to assure Bettina Murray and all her ilk would have a fair trial. Including myself, Hickock mused. He tried to put away a disturbing vision of a great modern building trying to vomit paper through windows that were never designed to be opened while hordes of judicial bureaucrats tried to stuff them into broken-down elevators. Simultaneously, multitudes of the accused were screaming for justice, but their papers were lost. At least, he concluded, it was better than thinking about his golf score or as some judges were sometimes preoccupied, with their next election.

Hello. Here was Bettina Murray insisting in a deep and melodious voice that she was not guilty of shoplifting. While his thoughts were drifting, she had hefted her bulk to the witness box and was glaring defiantly at the young female city attorney.

"Mrs. Murray, you were in the Safeway store at Twenty-first and Elm on September 17? That is correct?"

"Well now *exactly* how do you mean? I goes to the Safeway very frequently and I can't be just positive about the day."

"It was last Wednesday and according to the Safeway security officer's report and that of Officer Bunyan of the city police, you attempted to steal various items from the freezer and one shelf."

"Objection!" John Exeter yelled vehemently although Hickock noted he did not bother to look up from his papers. "The prosecutor has no right to use the word 'steal' since that fact is certainly not established."

"Sustained," Hickock muttered and he saw the city attorney blush. Serving the city as prosecutor was common among young law school graduates and even the best sometimes forgot their fundamentals when faced with real-life court. Now she obviously knew that she had erred. She was eager and she would learn—maybe.

"Mrs. Murray," she went on, now with more caution in her voice, "did you remove certain objects from the freezer and shelf which are normally for sale?"

Bettina Murray hesitated and glanced at Hickock. He gave her his best stone face and wished in this case that he would be allowed to see Bettina's past record of arrests. Something about her manner strongly suggested this was not her first time in court. But he was not allowed to know anything about Bettina Murray except what came out in testimony. Not until she was proven guilty could he make any judgment. That was the way things were supposed to be in this supposedly unbiased world and at least most judges made more than a token attempt to keep it that way.

"Well yeah, I did pick up a few items . . . sort of here and there you know . . . what I mean is you understand I mean I was fully intendin' to pay for them little items of course I was, but I didn't get no chance—"

"Mrs. Murray, would you tell the court how you managed to carry the items from the store?"

"Objection!" John Exeter cried out again. "Mrs. Murray never got out of the store and until she actually was, Your Honor, it is presumption of guilt that she did not intend to pay for the items."

"Sustained," Hickock said wearily. The police report before him described in detail how Bettina had managed, but now her intent had to be proven. While the big clock which was wrong by four hours ticked on. About a thousand dollars salary time, Hickock estimated, to prove the innocence or guilt of one Bettina Murray in a fifty-dollar matter.

Hickock watched while the young city attorney consulted her long note pad as if she would really find the truth there. He was sorry for her. She was fumbling her way through an easy case which he suspected was possibly what the black woman was hoping for. Bettina Murray herself had declined the offer of a jury trial because she was court wise and knew there was not a prayer of acquittal that way. Was the crafty hand of John Exeter hidden somewhere here? Had Bettina been advised some minor legal technicality just might get her off the hook with no more than a reprimand?

"Mrs. Murray," the prosecutor asked, "would you please describe for the court how you carried the items on your person?"

"They was in a bag, you know what I mean. Jes' an old bag."

"A shopping bag? With handles?"

"Yeah. That's about right . . . you know . . ." Bettina's voice became ever softer and a heavy frown contorted her features. If her eyes could kill, Hickock thought, the young lady from the city would be quite dead.

"Did you carry the bag in your hand?"

"No . . . well . . . not *exactly* . . ."

"Were you wearing a skirt on Wednesday?"

"I just can't remember . . . exactly . . ."

"Do you own a pair of pants?"

"No . . ." Bettina allowed a faint smile to crease her lower face, but her eyes retained their chill. "I might have a tad of trouble finding a pair to exactly fit."

A faint chuckle tiptoed through the courtroom. Hickock did not consider it worth even raising his gavel.

"Is it a fact, Mrs. Murray, that you were wearing a voluminous skirt and that your shopping bag was suspended between your legs by three cotton straps and that was where the Safeway Security Office saw you place the items and the female arresting officer found them?"

"I tell you I *was* going to pay for them. You don' listen to me."

"Do I understand you were going to enter the pay line and when you reached the cashier you were going to raise your skirt and take the items out of your bag and place them on the counter and pay whatever the charge and then reload them under your skirt? Isn't that a rather inconvenient way to shop, Mrs. Murray?"

"But I *was* . . . jus' 'cause I don't do things the way you folk do—"

Hickock saw the city attorney looking up at him quizzically. "I have no further questions, Your Honor."

Hickock waited for John Exeter's rebuttal. If he could find a way for Mrs. Murray to squirm out of this one he was indeed brilliant.

Exeter rose to his full height, scratched at his beard and then shuffled toward Mrs. Murray. "Your Honor, may I speak with the lady a moment?"

Hickock nodded and was not surprised when only seconds after the witness and Exeter had whispered together he called for a change of plea. "Mrs. Murray was confused, Your Honor, and now wishes to plead guilty. I recommend you take into consideration the fact that her intention was to take the food to her children and she did not intend to consume the items herself. The mercy of the court will certainly recognize the powerful drive of a mother obliged to feed her young."

Hickock wondered if Exeter was just feeling his way. Come on, Exeter! I'm new here and a little shaky on local procedure, but don't give me that mercy of the court business.

Hickock studied Bettina Murray's rap sheet which the clerk had just handed up to him. Once guilt had been either established or admitted he was entitled to as much information on the accused as was available. At least in part, his sentencing would depend on it and now Bettina Murray's lengthy record confirmed his impression that he was dealing with a professional. There were twelve arrests for shoplifting within as many years (God only knew how many times she had not been caught), four assaults, one with a deadly weapon, two resisting arrests and eleven traffic violations within the past four years. She had been convicted every time, except once because of a claimed need to support her children. The one exception cost her only ten days in jail.

"Are you on welfare, Mrs. Murray?" he asked.

"Well, sort of."

"What do you mean, 'sort of'?"

"Well more or less. You know, I qualify, if that's what you mean, Your Honor."

"Food stamps?"

"Yeah. An' it's no good I'm telling you, the way they been cuttin' out the poor people—"

Hickock cut her off. "At this time, Mrs. Murray, the court is not interested in your views on the actions of our government. What I need to know is how old are your children."

"Well . . . they is mostly in their twenties . . . you know, they grow *so* fast—"

"I gather there are six of them? One steak for each. You

must have been planning quite an occasion. Now please leave the witness stand, Mrs. Murray."

As she heaved her bulk from the chair John Exeter was quick to approach her side. He escorted her to a position directly in front of Hickock's bench.

Hickock put down his urge to deliver a lecture on the sanctity of private property, the welfare system as it was abused and the possibility of her twenty-year-olds scrounging for their own food. It was becoming very apparent that he would have to make things move faster or he would never get through the case load for this day. All right, from now on things would be settled huckety-buckety in true Butch Goldstein fashion.

"Mrs. Murray, I do not believe you ever had the slightest intention of paying for those items from the time you entered the store until you tried to leave. Therefore I am sentencing you to sixty days in jail with thirty suspended provided you have no arrests for any cause within the next year. Also for one year you will not enter any Safeway store. Anywhere. They don't want your business. Next case."

As Bettina Murray was led toward the waiting bailiff, Hickock waited for the court machinery to make one more revolution. He had time to reflect that by hitting Bettina Murray with a stiff sentence he had probably accomplished very little. It was almost without question that she would shoplift again—it was her way of life. She moved now as if arthritic, a belated bid for pity which he found hard to foster. She was unhappy because she had been caught, not because she had suddenly realized that she had broken the law. Yet the real loser now, he thought, was not Bettina Murray. It was her fellow citizens who were obliged to pay approximately fifty dollars a day for her care during the next thirty days, the cost of convicting her and transporting her, the cost of keeping her records, and the extra cost in food to other citizens because all stores had to maintain some kind of a security system. Crime did pay—through the nose of the honest.

There came before him now a Mr. Roger Leffler whose profession Hickock remembered had been practiced almost as long as prostitution. Leffler was a career pickpocket and freely admitted that he was a consummate artist in his field. He was a thin, gaunt little man given to expressive bird-flight movements of his hands combined with sporadic turnings and tiltings of his head. Hickock noted on his arrest report that he was also known as "the Magician." He had been apprehended in a shopping center while trying to relieve one Kito Kazumoto of his wallet. He had chosen the wrong pigeon for Mr. Kazumoto, who was present to identify him, was a two-time black-belt judo expert and had the hapless Leffler pinned to the ground and begging for mercy seconds after his talented fingers held his wallet.

Hickock was aware that the number of professional pickpockets in the United States was relatively small—if only because entering their tight fraternity was difficult and the apprenticeship hard. Although they were mostly loners they sometimes moved in groups from city to city, arriving like locusts and departing when police attention was aroused to the danger point. Most of the professionals knew each other and operated under a rigid caste system based upon their reputation for skill and resourcefulness. They made a good and steady living if not spectacular. Detectives on the pickpocket details of most cities knew them to be extraordinarily elusive and were rarely able to make an easy arrest. Yet Roger Leffler a.k.a. the Magician had erred and Hickock wondered why.

"Mr. Leffler, why did you choose Mr. Kazumoto as your victim? He is young, alert, and obviously in good physical shape. I would think you might have spotted easier prey."

Leffler shifted uneasily in the witness stand. He scratched at his large Adam's apple and stared thoughtfully at the ceiling.

"I dunno," he said without taking his eyes from the ceiling. "I guess it was some kind of a challenge."

"What did you think when Mr. Kazumoto brought you to ground?" Hickock found it very satisfying to employ a fox-hunting term in relation to Roger Leffler. He knew direct questions to the accused should originate with the prosecuting attorney, but in this case she was obviously not going to ask what he hoped to learn. Leffler's rap sheet was long only in time span—a mere three arrests and two convictions in what had been twenty years of operation. The man was obviously dedicated to his sly craft and Hickock suspected that a few years in prison would become a mere inconvenience.

Leffler had not responded; whatever it was that so captured his attention on the ceiling still held him—or so he pretended.

"I asked you a question, Mr. Leffler. Shall I repeat it or did you hear me the first time?"

Of course Leffler knew he could not be compelled to answer

any questions from anyone. He could remain dumb for the rest of the session and the worst that could happen to him would be a contempt charge.

Hickock saw that he was mistaken in assuming Leffler had chosen silence out of resentment at the proceedings. His voice sounded genuinely distressed when he said, "You know, judge, when that gentleman dumped me on my ass so easy, I just couldn't believe it . . . me . . . the Magician . . . me, a guy who everybody in my business knows. I got a reputation. And here I go out and pull an amateur bummer like that. Like some kind of impulse was driving me to it. It ain't natural and there is people in the business all over who are going to be laughing their heads off at you know who." Leffler's fingers fluttered through the air space in front of him as if he were seeking a tangible individual other than himself.

"Do I gather that you consider your encounter with Mr. Kazumoto and his wallet a disgrace to your record?"

"Correct . . . Your Honor. I still don't understand it. See, we got certain things in my business that us pros do and the dumdum amateurs don't do. Like when we lift a wallet see, all we want is the cash inside. I personally never fool with credit cards because it's too risky . . . there ain't enough time between the lift and trying to buy anything. So now we got the cash in hand we just don't throw the wallet in the gutter and walk away see? That ain't so nice for the guy who had the wallet see, not only his credit cards, maybe, but his lodge card, his driver's license, maybe Blue Cross and God knows what. He's got to spend the next two months getting everything back and it's one hell of a hassle the way things work nowadays. See? Everybody goofing off and on vacation and five-day weekends, it's a real pain in the ass for a guy that never done nothing to me. Follow?"

"I believe I do," Hickock said solemnly.

"So what we usually do if it's not too unhandy is drop the wallet in the nearest mail box and leave the rest to the Post Office Department. They got all the information they need right there and the man gets back his wallet in the next mail."

Hickock refrained from commenting that actual delivery might therefore take a very long time. Levity at the expense of the accused might be the style of some judges but it was not his.

There were a few more things he wanted to know before he

pronounced sentence. Leffler could be sent away for as much as half a year and he obviously knew it. His eyes were desperate and his head movements increased in frequency as if he was looking for a handy exit.

"How about ladies' purses, Mr. Leffler? What do you do about those?"

"I never did no purse-snatching, judge, in my whole life. That's for punks. And they usually get what they deserve . . . a sack full of junk and very little cash."

"You claim that you are not interested in purses?"

"Only if it's already open. Like some woman out shopping leaves hers set on the counter without paying too much attention to it . . . like then it is see, just beggin' for me to remove the cash and let the rest be. . . ."

"You can do that?"

"Sure. But if I do say so myself you got to have the fingers for it. It's not the easiest way to do a day's business, but when I make a lift people never know it . . . they think they must have left it at home or it dropped out somewheres."

Hickock found his candor so refreshing the idea that had been born when the prosecutor first put Leffler on the stand now seemed to be suddenly less bizarre. All right, Butch, you asked me to take over your court and you may wish you had thought of something else. Approve or disapprove you may be hearing about this for a long time. And the mayor may never forgive you for letting me be an old tribal leader sitting beneath a tree.

Hickock shuffled through the papers before him although they had nothing to do with the Leffler case. It was a deliberate pantomime intended to convince the accused as well as Goldstein's staff that he was having difficulty deciding what to do. On the contrary, Hickock thought with a slight smile, here is a wide-open invitation to practice what I preach, which is not exactly the law according to custom, but common sense. There is nothing violent about this man Leffler. He is not going to hurt anyone physically and to stash him away for one hundred and eighty days at the taxpayers' expense just because the law says I can is ridiculous. He is unable to make retribution to his victim because he failed to take anything from him so another solution is in order.

Hickock peered down at Leffler over his glasses. "Mr. Leffler, are you married?"

"Not presently."

"Divorced?"

"No. Not presently."

"Do you have any other employment other than your so-called profession?"

"Once in a while I cook . . . short order, see? I'm a good cook but see I won't join no union so it's tough to get work."

"Why won't you join the union?"

"I don't approve of the kind of people who are union bosses. Too many of them are crooks."

Hickock silenced the tittering in the courtroom with a snap of his gavel. "You are hardly in a position to comment on the integrity of others, Mr. Leffler, and this court is no place to air your unfounded remarks. For those in this room whose thinking might possibly be influenced by Mr. Leffler's comment I suggest you consider the source."

Hickock allowed a long pause to ensue while he reminded himself that people like Leffler were gypsies at heart and he was taking a very long chance in expecting him to change even temporarily. He noted from the arrest report that he had given his address as Apartment B-3 at a Sixteenth Street address.

"How long have you been living at your present address, Mr. Leffler?"

"Five, maybe six months."

"Is your rent paid up?"

"Yessir. I never was no dead-beat."

Hickock allowed a final pause then looking down at his papers rather than at Leffler he said very quietly, "Mr. Leffler, I am going to give you a choice. I sentence you to six months in the county jail with the days you have already served credited to that time. I am impressed with your tactile ability and believe it can be put to much better use. Therefore I will suspend sentence and place you on probation for a like time under the following conditions. You will remain in this city and you will report to a probation officer every thirty days. You will make every effort to obtain work as a cook whether it involves joining a union or not and if you fail to find such work or other legitimate employment within sixty days your original sentence will be automatically invoked. In addition you will immediately, on your release from the city jail, enroll in an Ameslan course offered at the Hearing and Speech Center on Eighteenth Avenue. If you don't know what Ameslan is, it's sign language and learning it will keep your hands out of mischief. The center has three consecutive courses.

"When you have completed all the courses, you will place yourself on call and volunteer to serve as translator in hospitals or wherever, between those who cannot hear or speak and those who can. You will serve three hundred hours of that work free of charge during the six months of your probation and any proven reluctance on your part to give your all to this program will automatically send you away. If that is all perfectly clear you may now make your choice."

Leffler's hands fluttered across the air space before him as if he was already communicating in Ameslan. "Judge," he said, "I'm an intelligent man. That ain't no choice. That's a sure thing."

The numbers and the names and the succession of woeful faces continued until a restlessness among the staff alerted Hickock that it was time for a brief recess. He was astounded at the swift passage of time—the pace had been so much different than the leisurely deliberations in superior court.

Fifteen minutes later he was back on the bench looking down once more on an apparently inexhaustible assembly of the anxious and unhappy. How did Butch Goldstein stand this every day and manage to keep his jolly nature? These people who came before him were not Estervans nor for the most part were they hard-core criminals. They were mostly just any judge's fellow Americans. Gathered in one place their numbers gave the impression the country was on the way to total decadence and Hickock found it necessary to remind himself that beyond this somehow soulless room there were the multitudes of Americans who had never been near a courtroom and never would be.

Then why these relatively few? He was more confident now; he thought he had a handle on the local procedures and he had even caught one of the supplicants employing what Butch called the old hat-pin trick. A man was in the witness stand accused of robbing parking meters. The city attorney had done a clean and quick job establishing that the man had somehow obtained a key to the meters and had been observed removing cash from twenty-six meters before he was arrested. John Exeter had been unable to offer much in the way of defense. Just before sentencing Hickock had glanced over the heads of those below him and by chance saw a woman stick something into the child beside her. The child immediately set up a howling and ran for the man in the witness box. The timing was too perfect as the sobbing little girl leaped for the waiting arms of her probable father.

Hickock watched the touching scene for only a moment before he said, "Thirty days, sir. Seven suspended for one year. And if you are caught in the parking meter business again it will be sixty days."

As the man stepped down the little girl ceased crying and seemed to have lost interest in her father. Hickock watched her return to the woman he supposed was her mother and his attention was almost immediately commanded by the next case. They followed one by one.

There was a feud in a middle-class WASP neighborhood which according to testimony was inspired by a barking poodle keeping one neighbor awake. Neighbor Anderson went to neighbor Bettencourt and complained. All was going reasonably well until neighbor Bettencourt's wife said her little Tinkerbelle could not possibly be heard next door and the insult had hurt Tinkerbelle's feelings. Neighbor Anderson threatened to shoot Tinkerbelle if he lost another night's sleep whereupon the poodle's mistress said if he did such a horrible thing she would burn down his house. Unfortunately, neighbor Anderson's wife overheard the threat and arrived on the run. She took a swing at Tinkerbelle's mistress and missed target. She did connect with the poodle who was in his mistress's arms and the battle was on. It had taken four policemen, three of whom received minor injuries, before the disturbance was over.

The prosecuting attorney made only a halfhearted attempt to lay blame on either of the parties. Both couples brought their own lawyers which allowed John Exeter to put up his feet and gaze at the ceiling. Both sides claimed retribution for medical bills incurred for treatment to various cuts and bruises and neighbor Anderson wanted payment for work hours he claimed he had lost. Both couples complained of police brutality.

All right, Solomon. What to do?

Hickock found temporary refuge in his paper shuffling again. Sending both couples to cool off in jail at the taxpayers' expense would obviously do no good although they seemed to deserve it. If they could afford lawyers then a fine might be in order, but was that enough to avoid a recurrence if Tinkerbelle found voice again?

He began slowly, "First as to police brutality. By your own testimony it seems the officers did not arrive until an atmosphere of brutality had been well-established by yourselves. And according to your neighbors who were innocent victims of your tempers the police did nothing more than pull you apart. The officers' injuries were minor, but did require treatment, and I will fine you the cost of that treatment to the city and the subsequent loss of duty time to the public safety. I will fine you an additional five hundred dollars each couple for disturbing the peace and for the same charge sentence all four of you to thirty days in jail—suspended provided you have no further contact with each other for the next sixty days. If at the end of that time the dog is still barking in a manner that would cause any normal person loss of sleep you may complain to this court and the dog will be put away. Finally, I admonish you to think about being good neighbors instead of contemplating vengeance because neither poodles nor judges are sympathetic to that emotion. Now go in peace and stay that way."

Hickock supposed that Butch Goldstein might not be too pleased with his sentencing. He would have been easier about feuding families—perhaps he would have just dismissed the case as unsolvable. But then what about neighbor Anderson's sleep and what if the next time Tinkerbelle became intolerable someone was seriously hurt in the resulting melee? Hickock passed a hand across his brow and raised his glasses so he could wipe at his eyes. For this, he thought, I graduated cum laude?

During the balance of the day Hickock dealt with four more cases of shoplifting, one being a man who had risked his personal freedom for a bag of Blue Bell Chips at thirty cents and a bottle of Tostitos Bean Dip at eighty-nine cents. There were two failures to pay business tax (both nude body painting studios), one case of operating a taxi without a city medallion, one attempted rape which Hickock, smiling wryly, passed on to his own superior court for hearing, one white man who had beat up the woman he was living with, and one black woman who had beat up the man she was living with. There were two cases of receiving stolen property, two lewd conducts, four young whites who had been vehicle prowling—three referred to juvenile court, one trespass which Hickock dismissed, and one interference with the city fire alarm system.

Hickock knew he had spent too much time on a case

involving a "Birth Control Demonstration Center" which, he considered secretly, was at least an imaginative way to describe a whorehouse. A point of law was raised almost immediately by John Exeter.

According to testimony which Hickock could only believe since the vice-squad officer actually compromised himself, he had entered the establishment on the pretext that he wanted more information on birth control. The girl who greeted him said he would have to wait since all the "therapists" were busy at the moment. She gave him a copy of the *National Geographic* magazine to pass the time and left the room.

After a few minutes the officer heard a commotion in the adjoining room and decided that rather than taking a chance on his possibly being recognized for what he was, he would seize the opportunity to make his arrest immediately.

He rapped sharply on the door to the adjoining room and announced as the law required, "This is the police! Open the door!"

Now the law said that the police must allow a *reasonable* time between the request and the actual opening of a door.

The officer heard a male and a female voice behind the door and further commotion until the female called out, "Just a minute!"

The officer did wait . . . a *reasonable* time? Fearing the suspects were taking so much time they would be dressed and appear innocent, he heaved his bulk against the door and it gave way. Unfortunately, it swung into the face of the girl, giving her a bruised cheek and a black eye. She was wearing only a slip, but she was obviously on her way to the door and was presumably about to open it.

John Exeter insisted she had not been given *reasonable* time after the officer knocked. Hickock studied the sweep second hand on his watch for thirty seconds and found he had no choice but to agree with him.

Case dismissed—and a reprimand for the officer who went away muttering that some judges just did not understand the kind of people he had to deal with.

An even greater time-consumer and somewhat of a puzzler for Hickock involved a picketing fracas on a mid-city construction project. He thought it was a matter that should have been passed on to a higher court, but decided to at least give it a hearing at the insistence of a trio of union lawyers who he suspected preferred to take their chances with him. There was also a lawyer who introduced himself as representing the ACLU and said that he was attending only in the capacity of an observer. Considering his own long record of liberalism, Hickock found his presence more annoying than inspiring. His court did not need professional do-gooders to protect the weak. That was John Exeter's job.

The pickets had been ill-advised or their emotions had been running so high they must have ceased thinking. They had physically prevented other workers on the job from entering the area, which violated their right to work as well as their right to freedom of movement. Then they blocked traffic which was a second mistake because the police arrived to straighten things out. The pickets were ordered to disperse, but refused. Their rights to assemble were being violated. And the whole thing started because the pickets insisted that the construction firm was not giving equal opportunity to minority workers.

Hickock became unsure of himself and he longed for a young assistant to research books on this matter. What did the *law* say? Were the police powers to force dispersal *sovereign*—always? But in the lower courts every judge was his own one-man band. Butch Goldstein, all is forgiven. Please come home.

The pickets had fought the police, which was of course resisting arrest, but had the police given them *reasonable* time to disperse? Additionally, there were two citizens who had no connection whatsoever with the strike. They were just passing by and decided to join the fight. They were Halleby and Watson, both unemployed lumberjacks.

The situation at the time had been cloudy and became more so now as both sides presented their views. The Equal Opportunity Commission had also sent a lawyer who only succeeded in further muddying the case.

Hello there, Julian Hickock, what is the legal answer, and more importantly, what is right and fair? You there, young man from Portage Lake, Wisconsin, you there in the black robe and the solemn demeanor, what are you going to do about enforcing laws that are basically in conflict with the Constitution? Speak, oracle, and they had better be words of wisdom. Here was a matter in which all involved were right and everyone was wrong.

Hickock tried to put himself on the picket line, but found it difficult since he had never been on one. So watch it, he thought. A judge's decisions quite naturally depended upon his sense of values and those depended upon his social, economic, and to some extent his political background. Sometimes even a judge's religious faith could bend clear thinking. Here, in a different form was the age-old challenge to most judges. How could a man who had never stolen judge a thief; how could a man who had never lived in a ghetto judge people who did? Most judges were influenced by the accumulation of their life experience when they handed down even the most minor decisions; only if they knew the power of their background and kept guard against it could they hope to remain at least tolerably impartial.

Hickock suddenly recalled that the ancient Irish had a possible solution to the problem. Legend had it that a gold collar was placed around the neck of a judge and if his decision was just it would expand. If it was otherwise, the collar would seize up and choke him. Well, Julian?

"As for the legitimate pickets I will fine each of you one hundred dollars with fifty suspended . . . that amount to be paid by your union who encouraged your behavior. I will dismiss the resisting arrests charge since that would start a record for some of you. In addition I urge each of you to read the Constitution. While you have a perfect right to picket as well as freedom of speech, nowhere in that document will you find license to obstruct a peace officer in his duty."

Hickock glanced up at the clock and frowned. If he subtracted four hours it was well after five, which confirmed his belief that it had been a very long afternoon. At least the Watson-Halleby case was the last on the calendar. In his own court he could continue a case until the following day because the volume was much less. But here, anything carried over set the judge back a like amount the next day.

Halleby and Watson were standing below him, their faces turned expectantly upward.

"As for you, Mr. Halleby, and you, Mr. Watson, I will fine you one hundred dollars each which I believe is a reasonable charge for the fun you thought you would have. Or you may take five days in jail. I might also suggest that in the future you keep your fists out of other people's business."

As Hickock started to rise he heard the clerk call out eagerly, "Everyone please stand!"

Hickock was off the bench and through the door before the muffled sound of people rising had subsided. He slipped out of his black robe and rolled it under his arm. He took off his glasses, stuffed them in his shirt pocket, and made his way rapidly through the back hallway until he came to a fire exit. He descended four flights of stairs so fast that he found himself thinking of long-ago exits from school, in Portage Lake. Had the work he had done this day to justify his existence on this planet been so unpleasant that he had to beat such a hasty retreat? No, damnit. It might not always have been pleasant, but it was necessary and he thought he had done a reasonably good job.

His haste, he knew, originated in quite another area. It was two blocks to the County Courthouse Building and by the time he stopped at his chambers it would be close to six o'clock. Five minutes there to wash and freshen up. Then another twenty minutes bailing his car out of the parking lot (he was going to buy a bicycle by God, and save enough in just parking fees to give the *Freedom* a new sail). Driving to the hospital would take another twenty minutes, then thirty minutes with Nellie-Mae . . . and then? Then another twenty minutes to Jean Pomeroy's place, which would make him no more than half an hour late for dinner. Slow down, you old goat. You are not a teen-ager bound for the senior prom. What do you think she will do if you're late? Evaporate?

Chapter Six

Hickock was still smiling at his haste when he entered his chambers and marched past Lucinda. "You still here?" he said without pausing. "Thought you'd be long gone."

He noticed only that another woman was sitting in the reception chair opposite Lucinda and assumed she was one of her friends. He continued into his office and was hanging up his robe when he heard Lucinda behind him.

He turned to see Lucinda looking down at the floor, an escape Hickock knew she employed when she was dubious about his approval. "Your Honor, I have a confession to make," she began.

"Oh boy, at this hour of the day? Are you aware I'm not a priest?"

"I've been worried about your home life with Nellie-Mae gone. You and Victor rattling around in that big house and making do as you can. It isn't natural somehow and you're beginning to look peaked."

"Lucinda. I have been on this earth more than half a century and I think I'm capable of—"

"It would be much better and easier if you had a temporary housekeeper . . . someone to dust, clean, do the laundry and maybe even a little cooking. Now wouldn't that be nicer to come home to than a mess?"

"The house is not a mess." A lie, of course. "Go away now, Mother Hubbard. We will survive."

Lucinda continued as if she had not heard him.

"That young lady in the outer office is the first applicant for the job and she's anxious to go to work right away. Tonight even."

"I'm not going to be at home for dinner tonight and may I be so bold as to inquire how an applicant for a job that does not exist just happens to show up in your office?"

"Well," Lucinda said, warming to what was obviously a favorite project. "I've been so worried about you and Victor. I called two employment agencies first and they just laughed at me. Asked where had I been the last twenty years—no one, but no one wanted to do housework these days. So finally I took an ad in the newspaper. She read it and ran right down here and that's what I call a rare and proper attitude. You don't find much respect for the work ethic these days. Will you please talk to her? Pretty please? Just give her two or three minutes. She's a very nice girl with a sort of cute southern way of talking."

"Make it a half minute and I'll get rid of her. Anything to stop you nagging me. Tell her to sit over there. I'll be right back."

He pointed to a chair opposite his desk, entered the washroom, and closed the door behind him. He took off his jacket, rolled up his shirt sleeves, and washed his face and hands. He took a bottle of aftershave from the closet over the sink, poured a little pool of it in the palm of his hand and rubbed it around his face. All his movements were automatic and mechanical because he had developed a new and thought-provoking interest in what he observed in the mirror.

Not too bad, really, he decided, although he could have wished for a little less of the overseasoned, overcooked look about his face. Dewlaps were beginning to form to the east and west of his jaw line. Look better on a turkey. The blood veins on the knob of his nose held promise of future blossoming. Be more careful about whiskey. Old wives' tale. This evening the heavy pouches beneath his eyes seemed to be worse than ever—matched luggage. And good God, the eyes! They were weary and flecked with red—from all day reading of the mortal sins of others. He decided the whole silly face was worth hardly a half-smile. Back in Portage Lake the friends of his youth often had themselves a time kidding him about his black eyebrows, long legs, and bag ears. "The Stork," "Elephant Ears," "Owl Eyes," he had answered to them all then as good-naturedly as he could manage. And now, Julian, have the guts to judge the judge. Can you conceive of that ugly puss being treasured by a much younger woman or had you just better limp away over the horizon whistling "September Song"?

Nuts. Go for broke, Hickock. People like Jean Pomeroy were not to be found just every day.

He was still slipping into his jacket when he reentered his office and saw that he was not alone. Talk about a one-track mind! In the space of only a few minutes he had entirely forgotten his agreement to see this woman.

He circled her warily and stopped behind his desk. "Hello," he said. "I understand you're looking for work."

She was not really a woman, he thought, still more of a girl. Twenty-some. Clean-cut and well-scrubbed. Hair swept back and tied in a bun. Neat and bright-eyed. Looked like the sort of girl his daughter Sally went to school with.

"Yessir," Wanda said evenly. "I'm real handy around the house and I like to work. I'm new here in town and I need money bad." She took a deep breath, and Hickock hoped she was not about to cry. "I'm afraid. In fact I'm right desperate, sir. I've been praying to God I'll get a job today because my landlady may throw me out if I don't."

Hickock found himself wanting to tell Lucinda to stop meddling with his personal life. Damnit, there was no substitute for Nellie-Mae. He glanced at his watch. Just as he had feared, he was not going to get through this in five minutes.

"Your Honor, I'm real scared, y'know. Petrified. I mean the whole world seems to be closing in on me. I mean all I can think about is I'm a stranger in this city and I don't know nobody and what will I do if I don't get work?"

Maybe, Hickock thought, I am creeping up on senility. There was something vaguely familiar about this young woman, but still nothing to give a true fix. He wondered momentarily why he felt so much on the defensive with her. Maybe it was her eyes, that were almost too intent on him—cat's eyes, a hot brown if there was such a color.

Hickock tried to settle back in his chair but after being confined to the bench a full day he was hungry for any kind of action. He became distinctly uncomfortable as he realized that it was not just the passage of time that disturbed him. Did everyone his age have this occasional notion that the face of a complete stranger was familiar to them, or had he just seen too many faces per day and they had all dissolved into one along with the names he could not remember?

He saw her cross her legs demurely and lean forward. Her

eyes were so pleading he was compelled to look away. "*Please*, judge, I like to work, but I can't get any in this city because I have no local references. And back east where I come from my husband wouldn't let me work. A real macho type, but when he started working out on me I had to leave him, know what I mean? It's hard to start your life in a new city. I mean, I wonder if I can handle it alone. The only friends I have in this world are back there and I don't have nobody here to talk to. I want to make something of myself. Of course I don't want to do nothin' but housework for the rest of my life, but I do need a starter, understand? I want to be part of a good scene where people like you just get up in the morning and know they have to be someplace and off they go to wherever it is. I mean, I want to earn my way and have people like you say hi or good morning at like seven or eight o'clock instead of just getting a grunt from my husband who was so macho he didn't believe he ought to work except on a punching bag—"

Hickock interrupted. "I don't want to be unsympathetic but it seems to me your problem might be better solved at an employment agency. I have no experience in hiring—"

"I went to those people as soon as I hit the city. They all said no references, no job. They said I didn't have no skills and so their commission was not worth the trouble. So I'm a kind of nonperson I guess you might say. If you'll just give me a job even for a few days and I please you then I can sure get work in some hospital where they need people to clean the toilets and wash dishes and stuff like that. I mean I'm willing to do *anything*, I don't care what it is. I'll scrub floors, baby-sit, take care of old people, there ain't anything little ol' Wanda won't do just to feel like one of the real people."

"I can't understand why you're having so much trouble. It's been my impression that a person who is willing can always find some kind of work." *That* is a pretty damn pompous statement, Hickock thought. He tried to remember when he had ever been unemployed, and realized that except for his schooldays he never had been.

"Don't you see, Your Honor? My landlady won't wait until next week. This is Monday, and she wants her rent by Friday. Mrs. Millington is her name and you wouldn't believe what she charges for her dumpy little rooms. Of course I could go on public assistance, but I'd rather sleep in the streets before I'd do that. I want to be a part of things . . . somewhere. What I mean is, *I got to feel like I belong in this city*, and if I don't have some kind of a job then it's pretty hopeless . . ."

Her voice trailed off. Silence fell between them. There passed a moment when Hickock thought she was going to resume her plea, but apparently she was too close to tears.

"What did you say your name was?" he asked. "Sorry. I'm not very good with names."

"Wanda Raleigh. I don't care about any fancy hourly pay, judge. Just give me enough to eat and pay Mrs. Millington. I'm real thrifty and I'll get by. If I could just go back to Mrs. Millington's tonight and say to her, guess what, Mrs. Millington, I got a job and I have to go to bed early tonight so I'll be bright-eyed and bushy-tailed tomorrow morning . . . I know you're gonna say I need patience and everything will work out and that's like my daddy used to say when he was bringing me up so nice and all, which is okay if you're not in the same fix I am right at this particular time. I need a job, judge. I need one *real bad*. Please help me?"

Hickock massaged his brow and stared at the top of his desk. He hated making quick decisions (hello, Mr. Leffler, who had just learned the hard way), but Nellie-Mae would be waiting and every minute he delayed now subtracted from the few hours in this day when he could relax . . . come on now, he thought, what's really distracting you is the amount of time you're losing with Jean Pomeroy.

He studied the palms of his hands as if he might find the answer between them. The learned judge was turning to reading palms. His own. He stared out the window as if seeking an answer from the sky. Damnit all, he really didn't want to have to cope with this, and yet she seemed so sincere. "Well," he said, "I'll tell you what. The woman who keeps house for my son and myself is temporarily in the hospital. Our place is a mess and needs cleaning. I'll pay whatever the going wage is for two or three days, which should be enough at least to get the crust off things. Meanwhile, you can look for a permanent job." As he stood up he wondered why he could not rid himself of the notion that he had seen this girl somewhere before.

He was unprepared for her reaction. She rose quickly, took hold of his hand and kissed it. "You will never know how much what you just said means to me. Your Honor, you are some kind of man!"

To cover his embarrassment Hickock reached quickly for a note pad and scribbled a number. He was flustered—how could a man think straight when a woman grabbed his hand and kissed it? As if I was the Pope, or the Procurator of Macedonia, for God's sake. He knew he was blushing, and if it would not look so ridiculous he would prefer to climb under the desk until she was gone.

"Here is my address," he said quickly. "If you come tomorrow morning about eight I can show you where the vacuum cleaner . . . if I can find it . . . and how to operate the washer-dryer . . . if I can remember how myself. Now if you'll excuse me . . ."

When she bought the miniature house Jean Pomeroy had many misgivings; it had been what was known as a "working man's bungalow." It had been hastily and cheaply built in the early 1920s and none of the innumerable tenants and owners had put a penny in it since. Once she had seen it the house became the only material thing she had ever yearned to own and it had taken all of her savings plus two thousand dollars borrowed from her father to make the place her own. Since that memorable day there had been many times when she wished she had surrendered to her secret voice and burned her obsession to the ground. Only her stubborn nature (a true Pomeroy mule, her father had said), survived the reconstruction problems which she estimated as being in the thousands. She found it necessary to remind herself at least once a day that a house was a home no matter how humble.

Before the house there had been Steve, a tall red-bearded, banker's son who was always seeking his identity and, as she realized too late, had no intention of finding it. Yet he was an amusing companion and eventually developed into an easygoing if rather dull man. Now Jean could not imagine why she had married him except that he was handy at the time and her mother had approved. *All* mothers approved of Steve. They said he was "sweet," little knowing she slowly realized, how sweet he was.

From the beginning the marriage had been a farce. It began on the wedding night when Steve said so much champagne had given him a headache and would Jean mind awfully if they postponed consummation of their union until the following night. The strange headache persisted through the second and third nights of their honeymoon and on the fourth she endured a short, fumbling, notably unenthusiastic tussle with her groom that in no way resembled her past occasional experiences. There was no passion involved and certainly no relaxed aftermath.

A month passed. She blamed herself for their arid relationship until Steve confessed that while he liked female companionship, physical contact with the opposite sex made him queasy. "I hope you understand," he said as if he was discussing a menu, "that I prefer the company of men. In bed as well as elsewhere."

He thought they could manage, nevertheless. After all, their families knew each other and they came from common backgrounds. Marriage, he explained, could be convenient for both of them if they were careful not to make it inconvenient.

Jean had left him with a pleasant farewell note, the wedding ring, and half the first month's rent on their furnished apartment. Then she went to see the Pomeroy family lawyer.

That brief episode was almost forgotten now. She had made a mistake and she was determined it would not embitter her. One way, she knew, was to find something quite different to occupy her overactive mind and the little house had been the answer.

Two years passed before "Tumbledown Manor" began to resemble her original dream. Little by little, working nights and weekends she had transformed the sagging shack into a proud little shelter freshly painted green with white trim. She had done much of the work herself, knocking down a partition between two tiny bedrooms to make one relatively comfortable room. By devouring "how to" books she managed to repaper the dingy walls, install new plumbing including a glass stall shower the full size of the old bathtub. She made her own bookshelves and laid the rock for the fireplace which replaced the original stinking oil stove. She painted the stained fir floors a light cream to brighten the living room and in time found the right throw rugs to enliven the color. She hired outside help for the electrical system only because the insurance company insisted a licensed professional do the work.

Now at last she hoped the house was an honest reflection of herself. There was a neat exterior and inside the comfortable clutter of her book collection which included everything from Tom Wolfe to Melville and Mailer to Buckleu, the three marine paintings she had picked up at an auction, and the two prints of Homer masterpieces in her bedroom. There was her ornate brass bed which always reminded her of the year she had spent as an exchange student in France. She did not care if the decor seemed odd for a woman. Jean Pomeroy was born an individualist and would stay that way.

The few guests who eventually came to Tumbledown Manor congratulated Jean on her perception in visualizing charm where there had been only ruin. In response she smiled modestly and refrained from telling them that the sole governing reason for her purchase was a passion for living above a tree-lined street in a quiet neighborhood.

It seemed almost preordained that Julian Hickock would enter her life almost immediately after her absorption in the house had been satisfied. Or was he the cause of her waning interest? She found it very difficult to care about much else when she was so certain that for the first time in her life she was deeply in love. Since that first rainy afternoon when he had invited her aboard *Freedom* she had carried on many very private conversations with herself concerning the matter of Julian Hickock. Without actually uttering a word her mind repeated the same trite questions over and over again. "What is this thing with Julian Hickock who is old enough to be your father? What is so special about him that a lot of other men don't have . . . men more of your own tender years or thereabouts? Why can't you at least fall for a man of your own generation?"

For a while, during the period when they had gone to dinner at Julian's favorite Chinese restaurant, there were several times her thoughts seemed to have been stuck in the same "why bother" groove. By then he had explained about his present life and had hinted that it was not altogether satisfying. Gradually, almost imperceptibly, her mental conversations had changed. . . . If he doesn't like his present status why doesn't he do something about it? Which would mean marrying someone, right? And who might that be since there do not seem to be any candidates on the horizon? At least any he was willing to talk about. But then Steve had not been overly informative about his preferences until after it was too late. Julian seemed so solid and utterly free of hang-ups. If he had a fault the worst might be his sometimes annoying tendency to deprecate himself, which was really a kind of excessive modesty. Of course one day I may discover that he is really Bluebeard's long-lost brother, but until then I will happily die in his arms.

When Jean's father came to visit her for a week she discovered that in spite of her initial joy in his company, a week could be a long time. He was still a most energetic man and the years he had given to his small, modestly profitable steel foundry had apparently preserved his youthful appearance. He was short and broad shouldered, and though powerful of hand she knew him to be the most gentle of men.

She had given him her bed, protesting she would be perfectly comfortable sleeping on the couch in the living room—which was a fat lie. It might have been lack of sleep that accounted for her rash decision on the fourth night of his stay.

"I love you madly," she said with a directness Ben had always said she must have inherited from him and certainly not from her mother, "but I think we're both getting a little bored looking at each other. We're running out of subject material and there isn't time to develop new ones. We've discussed all our relatives and everything that has happened in Michigan for the last twenty years. I don't think you're really fascinated with what I do all day at the shipyard . . ."

She decided against confessing that she was no longer listening to his adventures in the Second World War, yet something had to be done about the frequent silences between them. "If we talk about mother we might say things we would wish we had not said. If I had a TV set we could watch it for a while, but I'll bet not very long and discussing politics isn't our bag. That leaves us with the subjects of you and me, which is very rich in your case because you have been around a while, but discussing a twenty-nine-year-old, protected, WASP, career-minded, over-educated female must be about as exciting as pulling taffy. Just because I went to Naval Architects' School and managed to graduate and get a job practically the next week does not, I realize, make me very interesting."

Ben chuckled, a habit which came to him frequently and easily. "Okay. I can take a hint. I'll go home tomorrow."

"Now, now . . . that's not what I want at all. I was just thinking we might enjoy looking at a new face . . . like say, for dinner tomorrow night."

"Like whose face?"

"I have a friend you might find interesting."

"Male or female? Your mother will have a fit if you ring in another woman just for me."

"Now, daddy, what difference does it make?"

He looked at her carefully. "I've been wondering about your private life. Now I'm reassured. What's his name?"

"Julian."

"That's a nice name. Sort of old-fashioned for a young fellow. Does he earn an honest living?"

"He's a superior court judge."

"I never heard of a judge, especially superior type, under fifty . . ." It was then that her father's eyes had suddenly narrowed, and a mischievous smile played around his lips. "Don't tell me my little one and only daughter is involved with a much older man?"

"Let's say he's mature."

Jean Pomeroy considered the dinner party she gave for three on the following evening one of the most nervous occasions of her life.

The first half-hour had been a trifle stiff in spite of the double whiskey and soda she had prepared for her father before Julian actually arrived. Scotch always made Ben glow a bit and become even more easygoing than normal, but it had not quite eased all his shock when he shook hands with their guest. Long silences followed until Julian had a drink in his hand and toasted a welcome to the city for her father. Then she had watched anxiously while the two men circled each other. They were certainly not hostile but still assessing, like two bulls in a corral, she thought, until her father smiled and said, "Well, sir, aren't you on the young side to be a superior court judge?"

And Julian had responded, "The state just happened to have some spare black robes, mostly oversize. One of them just happened to fit me so there went the future of another promising lawyer."

"I thought judges were elected."

"This is my first term on the bench. The governor appointed me to fill a vacancy, but next year I'll have to run for election and as the politicians say, I'm running scared."

Jean saw that they were not quite off and running but they were at least at the post. She eased toward the kitchen. A lamb roast tonight, Julian's favorite and not just coincidentally, her father's.

Even while she opened the oven door long enough to sniff at the roast she listened to her father and Julian launch into a discussion on the merits of and demerits of electing judges. Why was she so anxious for them to approve of each other? Did she have a father complex?

At least on the surface the dinner itself was as she had planned it—soft music on the stereo Ben had brought as an arrival present, corny candlelight with popovers, and her father pouring wine; perhaps a bit too generously since he became more talkative than she had ever known him.

"What are we going to do about all these murderers and rapists?" he asked Julian, *Asked,* not demanded, she was happy to note. "There's too damn much babying of criminals in this country."

"I wish I knew. Every case is different, every person is different—"

"In the case of murder it seems to me the result is the same. How the hell can any judge even consider less than the death penalty when some young punk kills his mother and father? Or some other nut kills a whole string of people just for kicks? Don't you believe a freak like Charles Manson should be shot at sunrise or any other time of the day it's convenient? And what about assassins who are always taking potshots at our presidents? What are we supposed to do . . . sit back and smile?"

"I wish I could give you a straight answer, but my thoughts keep changing. Hammurabi, for example, was quite the believer in an eye for an eye. His code says that if a contractor builds a house and the house falls down on the owner and kills him, the contractor must die. If the house collapsed and killed the owner's son, the builder's son must be put to death. That was the way things were done almost four thousand years ago. I like to think we've made at least some progress since then."

"Sounds to me like you might be what we call a bleeding heart judge back home. I hope you don't consider yourself one of those characters."

"I don't know . . . maybe I am. I just try to call the shots as I see them and hope I'm right. I suppose there is still some of the old lynch mob in all of us. If we are hurt or think we have been threatened we want vengeance. If a judge refuses to go along with the gang he is known as a liberal and sooner or later will be looking for a job."

"Well, damnit all, judge, what are we going to do? We can't continue to just let all the wild animals out of the cage and hope for the best. We've got a war going on and won't admit it. In a war you kill the enemy. Don't you believe in capital punishment?"

"No." Jean was pleased to hear Julian's flat negative. He was so rarely adamant about anything (part of his judicial make-up, she presumed), and it was refreshing to discover he could be so certain. "I doubt someone who's about to commit a crime of passion stops to think about the future . . . theirs or anyone else's. I doubt very much if the average murderer pauses long enough to think he might hang for the deed. A contract hit man is another matter. But they are careful, deliberate professionals who unfortunately are almost never caught—"

"Our easygoing way with criminals is changing our whole society. We've got locks on locks and too many people carrying guns to protect themselves! It's insanity! No one in this country feels entirely safe."

Jean was alarmed at the rising tone in her father's voice. And Julian too, seemed flushed and overintense. "Gentlemen," she said nervously, "If we are going to pound the table perhaps I should remove the silverware?"

Hickock barely hesitated. "What with one thing and another, from hostile Indians to civil battles, I doubt everyone has ever felt safe. We have a big roaring country, populated by extremely vigorous and passionate hybrids of every nationality. We're not a Scandinavian country with more or less one racial line in our heritage, or a Germany with its instinctive penchant for discipline, or a France or Italy with its tight-knit families, all of which contribute to a sense of security. We're a hodgepodge of people and we are constantly changing our sense of values and even of right and wrong. As long as there are haves and have-nots there is going to be social friction, and as long as we have the energy to love and hate we are going to multiply and kill. And I will now get off the soap box."

"If things are really so bad in the good old USA," Jean said, "maybe it's time I served the hemlock."

Why had she ever suggested this evening? Ye gods, they were playing men are men and will not be stopped.

Ben said, "I read a story in *Time* about the increase in rapes. The numbers were astronomical."

Hickock said Ben should realize that statistics could be deceptive even when they had not been manipulated by special interests. "There's no question that we have more crime than we had ten years ago or twenty or thirty years ago. The numbers are up. But those same numbers never indicate the enormous increase in our population. The proportion of crime to the number of people has not increased very much. We have to remember that a police department in need of new equipment or convinced they need more staff is going to emphasize the crime numbers every chance they have. And then there are the politicians who sense how unhappy people are about murderers and rapists in general and are anxious to tell the media how gung-ho they are to hang or shoot the nearest handy suspect."

"But how do you feel when a murderer comes before you? If you just give him a slap on the wrist he'll go out and murder someone else—"

"Not if I can help it. But there's the catch. I want to be absolutely sure the person is guilty before I even think about a penalty."

"I just wish you guys on the bench would give as much consideration to the victim and the family and stop worrying so much about the criminal. Is the guy guilty or not. If he is hang the bastard. That's the way it ought to be and isn't."

Jean picked up her dessert fork and rapped smartly on her wineglass. "Knock it off now. I'm not going to have the two men I most admire arguing over my sponge cake. You'll blame me for your indigestion."

Hickock leaned back in his chair and laughed. "Your dad's right. But it's the jury who makes the decision on guilty or not. It would be so simple if I could just open a vein and if I don't bleed to death in a matter of minutes, the person is probably innocent."

Later when Julian had left, the questions she had been sure would arise came right along on schedule. She had suggested Ben sit down and read a book, but he insisted on helping her with the dishes. "Next time you come to visit, dad, you will find a dishwasher here even if I have to steal one."

"Don't. Your judge friend wouldn't approve. Nice guy, by the way. Interesting. Some judges I've met have an inflated opinion of themselves. I liked his modesty. . . ."

"That's one of his problems, I think. He says that when he's judging others he must first judge himself and when that happens, he becomes very unhappy. He says he sinks below the Plimsoll mark and he says it too often."

"What's a Plimsoll mark?"

"A circle with some horizontal lines. Every ship is required to have one on the hull. If the ship sails with water above her Plimsoll mark she's too heavily loaded and probably unsafe at sea."

There followed the long pause for which she had been waiting. Dear old dad, she thought, you are so obvious you might as well have a flashing neon sign across your forehead.

"Mind if I ask you a sort of personal question?"

"You're my father, aren't you?"

"Are you very much in love with him?"

"You bet."

"It's quite obvious."

"Then why do you ask?"

"I was just wondering if he's married."

"What if he was?" She might just as well discover if her beloved father had caught the soap opera disease from her mother. Certainly, she thought, he could not qualify for her exalted life membership league, but possibly he had been taken on as a patron or sustaining member.

"If he is, then that's bad news. You two seem to get along so well."

"Listen, dear father, and try to keep an open mind. Ever since I was a little girl I've heard you talk about other men and sometimes use that phrase 'he's his own man.' Well, I'm my own woman. If I fall for a man it's entirely my own doing. No one ties me to a stake and says I *have* to do anything much less fall in love. If I get hurt along the way it's my fault for putting myself in such a position—not anyone else's."

"You're telling me to keep my nose out of your business. Since you are the fruit of my loins I find that impossible."

She crossed the kitchen and put her arms around him. She kissed him gently on both cheeks and said, "God bless you. Since it will probably relieve your mind be advised that Julian is a widower."

"Ah." She was not sure whether the sound he emitted was just a sigh of relief, a note of congratulation, or simply a query for more information.

"Which is another of Julian's problems, I *think*. Somehow

he blames himself for his wife's death. I don't know why, he's reluctant to talk about her—"

"Around you I would say that's quite natural."

"Whatever, he carries a guilt complex. I think that's maybe what makes him so different. It isn't that he lacks self-confidence, it's just that he measures his faults against what he thinks ought to be the rest of the world's standards and he's convinced himself he doesn't measure up."

"Since when did you become an amateur head-shrinker?"

"Since Julian. I am trying to stop him underestimating himself. He carries the world on his shoulders and I'm trying to knock it off."

"Good luck. Just don't knock yourself out trying."

"There's another problem we share but can't solve. Julian has a son who does not approve of me, which is putting it mildly."

"He's afraid you might move into mother's territory?"

"You're very perceptive, dad."

"There are other qualities in me you'll discover as you grow older. Someday you're going to realize that I'm also intelligent, charming, and handsome. With another two feet in height I would really ride tall in the saddle."

"Hey man, there you go! Have some more scotch."

"How old is the son?"

"Nineteen. And Julian thinks the world of him. I think it's part of his guilt complex. He's terrified of failing him."

"Any other children?"

"A daughter, Sally. She's in school back east and is delightful. We talk once in a while on the phone. She does like me."

"Then I would guess the son was very attached to the mother."

"As I said, you are a very perceptive man."

"Maybe," Ben said quietly, "the son will grow up one of these days. And maybe his father is just a strong man who has the guts to recognize his own weaknesses."

And that was all he said, she remembered now. Her father had stayed one more day but had not brought up Julian's name again. Even when she took him to the airport and held him long and tightly before he turned away he simply said, "Take care of yourself, girl. I just want you to be happy."

She watched until his short, powerful figure disappeared

down the long hall and thought that as long as he was alive she had no real cause in the world for unhappiness.

Now almost two months after her father had departed, Julian was still her man, although tonight he was already late for dinner . . . not exactly a capital offense. And the problem of Victor showed no signs of going away. Make do, she thought, and count your blessings. A few years with Julian Hickock, she told herself once again after a thousand times of saying the same thing, was better than a lifetime with any man she had met so far. There were the years of P.J. (pre-Julian), and she hoped there would never be an after-Julian.

The telephone rang. She ran to it. She was sure it must be Julian saying he would be even later or worse, could not come at all.

"Hello," she said anxiously.

She did not recognize the male voice. It was high and whining, and it scared her.

Chapter Seven

Now weren't that nice, Wanda thought. That Lucinda was a real blabber-mouth, had told Wanda all about the Hickock family and how the judge was busting his ass to get to the hospital so he could be sweet to some nigger who hurt herself not minding her own business. And he was the same man who took children away from their legitimate mothers?

She decided it was too early to go to a movie, so it was back to Mrs. Millington's and maybe watch TV for a couple hours or read the dictionary, which was very educational indeed if you could stand that sort of thing. It was different now. Out in the free air there were so many choices of things to do.

While she waited for a bus Wanda found Hickock's address persisted in clicking through her thoughts. Like some computer, she decided. Ten-eleven Maple Avenue—not that she had not memorized that address long before she got out of Clark. It had been bubbling up in her thoughts ever since she had made it her business to find out where a certain judge lived—it used to help pass the time just imagining going there and doing all sorts of things to get even.

She asked the bus driver to tell her when he made a stop near 1011 Maple. So why not have a look at tomorrow's assignment? It was almost six-thirty by her new watch and there was nothing else to do except go down in the wrong part of the city and run into old friends, back on the merry-go-round . . . More important things were on the schedule and maybe nearby the judge's house somewhere a person could find a hamburger or a Colonel Saunders. A person could die of hunger in this area of the city, nothing but houses that must cost like you would not believe.

The driver was displeased when she confessed she had no idea how much the fare was. When you've been away for three years it takes a while to get the hang of a lot of little things. He said grumpily that he would let her off at Clover Street and she could walk north one block to Maple Avenue.

Almost at once Wanda found herself drifting right back into her old ho stroll. Of course there would not be any johns looking for a party in this kind of neighborhood. Everything was so neat it looked like a postcard, real houses with a couple of cars and the kids' bikes scattered around and everybody had their shades up as if they weren't afraid of people seeing what was going on inside. In one place there's this man and there he is sitting reading the newspaper with his coat and tie on, for God's sake! Still, at this hour. Like he didn't understand it was the end of the day. Where I come from the guys get in their shirt sleeves once they finish work. They go home to their hang-titted women and cuss them out some while they have a few beers and tell the kids to get the hell out of their sight so they can have some peace. In Tennessee.

And now then, here is this old woman and two kids watching the boob tube like it was any time of day. Why wasn't she out in back cooking if she was going to be a wife? One of the kids looked a little like Deidre did three years back. Well, some, anyway. Deidre was more dark, naturally, and didn't have such a button nose. Oh God, tell me where Deidre is and I'll become a nun. Promise.

It is a yellow evening, she thought, and as she hummed softly to relieve her melancholy she decided they were the best kind with the sun smearing everything with gold, including people, like the man walking toward her with no hat. He was walking along at a good clip, but he was white-haired except on one side and a fringe along the top where the last of the sun hit. Get this character. The man passes right on by without so much as a hesitation and on the way he says lovely evening isn't it as straight as you please plus a little smile and he keeps right on going. Like, what kind of people live this way? There is just no noise at all, like everybody but a few people are dead and this is like some ghost city. Nobody is yelling at anybody to go screw themselves and nobody is screaming because their man is beating them up. There are no buses roaring and so far no sirens. Where's the fuzz? There is not one high-flying long-legged dude strutting down the street.

This area is like a tomb. It gives you the creeps. Even as cool as Sam always was he could not take this laid back. Sam knew his streets and everybody almost on them but he didn't know no street like this. You could hear the trees growing. There is not even any food smells here let alone the odor of some good Colombian grass. Do these people get anything to eat? And what do they do nights for a charge? I mean, do they screw around or are they just too respectable even to do that?

This scene, Wanda decided, was pure unbelievable. Just like in the magazines. Only this was for real—unless she was dreaming which was entirely possible considering what a weird day this had been anyway.

It was 1011 all right. Second house from the corner—needed paint and kind of rundown-looking in general. Kind of disappointing for a judge to have because judges made a bundle and this house was just old frame wood with a porch that looked like it might have been imported from Tennessee. Two stories so the bedrooms must be upstairs. And how about the pickup truck in the judge's driveway? Real ancient iron.

Wanda took a few steps up the driveway and was surprised to see a young fellow working on the engine. He straightened to smile at her.

He had to be, he thought, he *had* to be because there was the same nose and the same heavy eyebrows still developing. He was young and long-legged just like his father, but he was smiling and that was something she had never seen the father do.

"Hi," he said cheerfully. He wiped his hands on a rag and continued to smile. Beautiful blond hair, beautiful teeth, boy, if all the diaper johns she had initiated had been this handsome . . .

"Hi," she said, surprised to hear she could put the same old invitation just by lingering on that one word as if she had not even tried for three years. Once a thoroughbred, always a thoroughbred. "This is 1011? I guess this is Judge Hickock's house?"

"I guess it is. Looking for someone?"

"Well . . ." She wished she had looked in her purse mirror before this meeting. Maybe her eyes needed a touch up. Or her lips. "I'm Wanda Raleigh."

"Pleased to meet you."

"Are you Judge Hickock's son?"

"Right. The name's Victor."

She saw that his eyes were questioning and she knew that

sooner or later she was going to have to explain, but why hurry? There were suddenly certain things going on in her mind that had not been there before; never ever occurred to her in fact and now here was what might be called a golden opportunity presented on a golden evening right standing there in front of her and it would be a shame to blow such an opportunity before it had a chance to develop. Like there was maybe going to have to be some switching done here, and maybe the final result could be even better than she had planned. Okay, get with it then.

"Is this your pickup?"

"All mine. It's still a little shabby but I'm working on it."

"I declare, it is the best paint job I ever did see. I just always have loved deep green cars. They have real class, know what I mean? I mean red and yellow pickups are too flashy and black, well that's for dune buggies and stuff like that, and blue, well you know, might be all right for a girl." She hesitated, surprised at herself. Where did she get so educated on the subject since she had never given pickups the time of day before? "Did you paint it yourself?"

"Sure, and I sort of goofed here and there."

"And do you keep it running too?"

"Naturally."

"Could I hear the engine run?"

He smiled and she thought, hey, this kid is something else. He should be in the movies or have I been away too long?

"As a matter of fact I've been tinkering with the distributor and then the mixture trying to get a lower idling speed so I was about to fire up anyway. These old Chevys have a cooling problem, that is they run too cool at first and are hard to keep down where you get that nice smooth, round sound until they're very hot. It's the nature of the beast, I guess."

"I see. That's very *very* interesting."

"I guess you just didn't come by here to hear an old engine idling, though. If you're looking for my father he's not here right now."

She had to tell him sooner or later and it might as well be now. "I've already seen your father . . . I . . . I'm supposed to come to work here tomorrow morning, and well, I just thought since it's such a nice evening and I haven't anything else to do anyway I might as well find out where the place is and then, y'know, I wouldn't be late in the morning . . . know what I mean?"

She saw that he was puzzled and she wondered why his eyes had suddenly turned cold.

"My father hired you? For what?"

"To clean up the house. He said it's a mess."

"That's for sure." He laughed and Wanda told herself this kid needed an agent.

He said, "I hope you don't mind me saying you don't look like any cleaning lady I've ever seen."

"Of course I'll only be temporary."

"Yeah. Nellie-Mae will be coming back soon."

"I like old cars. Y'know, they have something the new cars don't seem to have. Especially pickups that show some lovin' care, know what I mean? I guess you would call it dignity, know what I mean? And who cares about tripping around in one of the new little compacts. They don't do a thing for me. I like to ride in pickups. You just sit up there in the cab looking down on all the world, you can see what's going on. You're not down on the concrete worrying about getting stepped on like you were sitting on a rollerskate. Right?" She thought, here I am making such a pitch to this kid I'm liable to start believing it myself. Sam who never drove nothing but Cadillacs must be having himself a laughing fit.

"Right." Victor closed down the hood and climbed into the driver's seat. He patted the stack of books in the middle of the seat and said they would just have to wait a few minutes. "First things first," he added.

Victor started the engine and listened intently to the throaty rumble of the exhaust. Wanda pushed back her hair and cupped one hand around her left ear. She looked up at him and gave him what Sam had once called her hundred-dollar ho smile, the very same that finally got her to be Sam's main lady, gave it to him right between the eyes. And she said, "It sure does purr like a little sleepy kitten. Beautiful."

She warned herself not to overdo things. The kid was no dummy so she should just give it to him a little at a time. Still, diaper johns were always skittish and sometimes you had to practically hog-tie them before they got the message.

She waited for him to be satisfied with his efforts, then asked, "Do you know where Fourteenth and Elm is?"

"Sure. It's not very far, maybe a mile and a half."

"Do you know what bus I take to get there? That's where I'm living."

He hesitated, then even quicker than she had hoped he said, "I have to do a lot of studying tonight, but if you're ready to go right now I'll drive you home."

"Say, that *is* real nice of you."

She tried to keep her movements casual as she walked around to the opposite side of the truck and climbed into the seat beside him. She saw that he was still smiling and she was struck by a new thought. Hey! Here all of a sudden, all prepackaged like in some Safeway store was maybe the answer? The big, *big* answer? Hey, I mean the entire picture is just as clear as the glass in the windshield not to mention the owner of this razzle-dazzle pickup's gorgeous blue eyes.

All *right* . . .

Almost a full week had passed since Hickock had visited the hospital, and he was somewhat taken aback by Nellie-Mae's appearance. "You've lost weight. Who are you trying to be, Lena Horne?" He wished he had thought of something else to say. Why did everyone who visited a hospital patient feel obligated to augment their arrival with some hopefully cheerful remark? The patient hardly needed the efforts of amateur wits to relieve their misery.

"I'm down to the basic lard," Nellie-Mae said. "Pretty soon I'll just be two hundred pounds of skin and bones from lying here and worrying."

"The doctor says you can come home in about a week."

She frowned and shook her head unhappily. "Victor says the moths and the spiders have taken over the house."

"It's not quite that bad, but you're sure missed." He decided not to tell her about her temporary replacement. Ten-eleven was Nellie-Mae's home and most women were touchy about who laid a hand on their territory. "Don't worry about us. I even remembered to wind the clock."

"I worry about you and Victor being alone there without a referee. I'm afraid something unpleasant could happen if you two lock horns without me there to pull you apart."

"It gets a little rocky now and then, but we'll make it."

"Victor tells me you've been spending a lot of time with the woman," Nellie-Mae said flatly and unsmiling.

"He's exaggerating again."

"Are you thinking about marrying her?"

Suddenly Hickock wished he had not come to the hospital. It seemed incredible that after all the years he had known her, he had forgotten how Nellie-Mae always ran a direct line between her heart and mouth. She had no notion of subtleties of any sort, nor was she capable of twisting words to circle an embarrassing topic. She would make a terrible lawyer, God bless her.

"I admit to having given the matter some consideration," he said as blandly as he could manage. "But she's very young."

"How young?"

"Twenty-nine. Going on thirty."

"Has she been married before? I hope she doesn't have an ex-husband in the bushes. They can give trouble."

"She's been married and divorced. I hardly think that categorized her as a permanent reject. Sometimes divorce is necessary for the survival of both parties."

"You sure are becoming one mighty liberal judge. Next thing I know you may be dancing in a disco . . . living high, wide and handsome. I understand she's not much older than Sally."

"I am acutely aware of that."

"What's she do all day long? How does she maintain herself, or do you?"

"Absolutely not. She's not about to take anything from anyone. Very independent. She's a marine architect."

"She must be smart. Then how come she has such a yen for you? Does she need a father or something? You sure she isn't after your money?"

"You really know how to make a guy's day. No, she's not after my money because she knows I don't have any. And if you're suggesting I'm too old for her you're probably right."

"I knew that sooner or later some gal was going to be fooled by that insidious charm of yours, but I'd just feel better if I was sure it's the right one this time. I don't want to see you going through the worry you had the last time. Does she drink much?"

"No. Hardly at all."

"That's hopeful. How's crime?"

It was also typical of Nellie-Mae, Hickock knew, to change subjects instantly. Her mind cut clean through the flesh, viewed the bones, and opened a new subject. Now staring at the ceiling she said, "I worry about how you're going to pay for this hospital. They don't pay you any more than they do a head garbage man. How do they expect to get a good man to be a judge when they don't pay more. The house needs fixing in all departments and one of these days that heap you drive around in is going to say no more, Your Honor. I am hereby going to lay down and die right here in the middle of the street."

"I assure you I'll not let that happen. If I see slow death approaching I'll take out my thirty-eight and shoot it right between the headlights."

"What have you done about that bad man . . . what's his name? The one who makes the dirty movies."

"Estervan. The jury found him guilty. I'm still trying to figure out what to do with him."

"How about chopping off his head?"

"The law does not call for beheading in his case."

"Well, make up a new law."

"You and Draco would have got along just dandy."

"Who is this Draco? I've heard his name before . . . somewhere . . . my memory's not getting any better loafing around in this bed."

"He was one of the ancient Greeks. He was asked to write down the laws of Greece for the first time and people said they were written in blood. Just above everything a person did from stealing fruit to murder called for the same penalty. Death."

"I hope you throw the book at Mr. Estervan."

"I'm trying to decide what kind of book to throw. Just sending him away to prison for a few years would be the easy solution, but it won't really accomplish anything. Believe it or not, we need Mr. Estervan."

"For what? You say a man like that is wanted by anyone but the FBI?"

"He works and pays taxes. Can every good American say the same? He's been in a rotten business, but I like to think he will now get out of at least part of it. And while he may be technically guilty I'm really not convinced he actually knew the girls were juveniles. He's too smart to run such a risk knowingly. And incidentally, I've learned that the girls were anything but angels. They both have a very colorful juvenile record."

"I don't care. There's no excuse for that sort of thing. Of course I'm just a poor black woman who don't know about the law, *but* if I was the judge that man would be hanged tomorrow morning." She smiled brightly, amused at her own put-on of the accent.

"Why wait until then? Anyway, via one legal maneuver or another a man like Estervan can postpone the actual serving of his sentence, sometimes for years. He might appeal the verdict and the appellate court might find something technically wrong with the case I've missed and reverse the decision. Meanwhile time goes on. It takes money, but the distance between the conduct and the results of a rich man's trial and that of a poor American is incalcuable, I admit it . . . Still, if you want to head a lynch mob," he said, "your system would soon put both you and me out of a job."

"Never mind. I'd like to lynch a few honkies like him just for old time's sake. What are you having for dinner tonight?"

"I'm going out to dinner."

"With the woman?"

He nodded. If the day ever came when he would be forced to present Jean to Nellie-Mae he knew it was going to be a nervous occasion.

She asked what Victor was going to do for his evening meal. "He's a young animal and you have to feed him regularly or he'll bite. Something is eating at him and you have to be very careful. Sally, she's pure sugar and cream and you never have to worry about her. But Victor? He's going to fight you for a while and maybe all his life if you just mess with him a little bit. He believes in himself just like you do . . . he believes in what he believes all the way and the only way he's going to change his mind is to let time pass."

"Meanwhile I'm not getting any younger."

"Meanwhile . . . if the woman is really the right one for you she can wait."

They sat in the last of the twilight, the pickup's exhaust still grumbling while Wanda listened to Victor. He had pulled up in front of Mrs. Millington's house and now she wished they had stopped farther down the street just in case Mrs. Millington might be owly about her coming home with what might look like a boyfriend when she had just got out of the treatment center this morning.

"You really got a lot of heavy stuff to unload," she commented as Victor told her how tough it was to be a sophomore in a big university where the competition was unbelievable.

At first he had been quite shy and she worried that he might tell his father not to hire her at all, but during the drive from 1011 she was pleased to see him open up with the good ol' male true confessions and she knew it was because she had done just the same thing any intelligent woman did once she passed fourteen or fifteen which was to make a man talk about himself.

Victor seemed surprised that she had not gone to college. Well, did every female he knew go to some university? She warned herself to ease around that one because right here sitting beside her was the goal line. Rah-rah-rah for the old college try. Right away here on the first day out here was the solution presented like in your lap. What you have been thinking for three long years was like a soup and right here was maybe the spice for that soup. If you just knocked off Judge Hickock like any one of the several ways you had thought out and planned so many times he might not even feel any pain . . . or maybe only for a few minutes. Then he would be dead which of course he deserved to be.

It was almost too much. If it worked you could shove it to the judge real good. You make him cry before he died. You could make him cry his heart out. And who is going to be laughing inside no matter what happens afterward? Just laid back and smiling her head off will be Wanda Usher.

"Understand," she explained, "we were a very high-class family, but there was just no way for me to go to college. Understand we surely did not have one of the largest plantations in Tennessee, not one of those huge places, but we did have enough to live very well on until my father bought this horse that was real mean."

Should she give the horse a name? No, that was too much.

"Anyway, the horse kicked my father and made him a cripple, and then my mother got sick too and I was the only one around could bring home any money. Mind you I did not think like so many girls in Tennessee that work of any kind was beneath me, but some of the jobs I had to take to keep everybody in the family fed were pretty God-awful. I worked at everything I could until I was coming home one day and a friend told me . . ."

Wanda paused. She was going to tell him her parents were

killed when the plantation caught fire and burned to the ground, but that sounded too corny. She decided to let her father live a little while longer. ". . . My mother, she was killed in an auto accident—"

"So was mine."

It was unreal how this was working out. A lollapalooza! Right away now they were sharing something. Here she was making up all kinds of stuff and not having any idea this good-looking kid would have been there himself with his mother dead because of an auto accident. Who is setting up the pins here? It was fantastic the way this whole thing was working out.

Wanda's voice became ever more confidential in tone as she told him, "That tragedy with my mother was sort of the beginning of the end, know what I mean? Here we are, just me and my father and he had to go to a rest home so somebody could look after him because I just could not work hard enough to pay for that sort of place unless the government helped." She liked the immediacy of her presentation. She could just see her father limping around in that home. "I get letters from my father all the time, real long wonderful letters telling me how much he loves me and how much he appreciates all I done for him. It is to laugh but in one letter he told me that some day I would probably be a cover girl on one of the magazines and stuff like that, know what I mean? He writes the most beautiful letters it just sometimes makes me cry to read them."

Victor should read some of her father's letters. If it could be done. If anybody knew who in the hell her father was or if he could write more than an X for his name . . . And she sure as hell was not going to tell him that the family name Raleigh which sounded so sort of aristocratic came from the pack of cigarettes in her purse.

The snagger now was how to get Victor to understand where she had been for the last three years if he got nosy. That macho husband back east might present problems. "So there I was—either get myself up north and get enough money to go to college or stay down near dad and keep scraping up the pennies. Have you ever been in the south? I mean like Tennessee?"

"No. I always wanted to go, but ever since mom died I haven't felt much like doing anything except going to the U and just getting by from day to day. It's funny, kind of weird sometimes because she keeps sort of coming back in my thoughts . . . sometimes when I'm trying to concentrate in one of my classes when we're supposed to be listening to some boring lecture—"

"I know what you mean, Victor. Losing a parent is absolutely the most awful thing that can happen to a person . . . a young person that is. By the way, how old are you?"

"Nineteen."

"What a coincidence. That's almost the same age I am. Well, I'll *be*."

Plus four years, Wanda thought, but there was no sense in telling him her real age. It might be unhandy later on.

"I like the way you look," Victor said abruptly, "and your voice. I like to hear you talk . . . How come you live here if it's not your family house?"

"Well, that's a long story and since you've unloaded so much on me maybe you won't mind if I lay something heavy on you. Because it seems to me you are a very sympathetic person, I mean there is something inside you that almost shines and says whatever it is you are going to say."

Jesus, she thought, watching his eyes, maybe I've already gone too far. Maybe I should let him talk, but he still has the engine running like gas was one cent a gallon and I can't let him get away just yet. I can keep his interest as long as I'm yakking about him, but sooner or later I got to tell him about me.

"When I first came out of Dixie," she said, allowing a tone of lament to touch her voice, "I worked in various places until one of my employers said I would have to let him make love to me or lose my job. Well that sort of thing just never happened to me before. I did not really, cross my heart, ever think he was really going to do anything like he did and I was entirely ignorant what to do and what not to do. So then several months later there I am pregnant, and finally I have a beautiful daughter . . . but I have long ago been fired by my employer who said I was a dumb bitch to have any baby at all. So then I sort of moved around a lot, y'know, it's not easy to find work when you have to take good care of a baby which I certainly did want to do. I wouldn't want to come right out and say that I was the best mother in the world, but I guess maybe I was in the top ten. I really was.

"But I was awful lonely and I married a guy who was all

macho, but what I *didn't* know is that he loves his muscles more than work, so *I* have to support *him*. Finally I had enough of that and ran away with my daughter to make a new life for me.

"Well, comes three years ago and I am hired to be the clean-up lady in this person's apartment who is planning to give a big party on New Year's Eve. I am supposed to come to the place right after midnight when everybody is supposed to go home. They were going to have coffee and cake and maybe some champagne to celebrate. So I asked if I could bring my daughter with me when I reported for work because of course I couldn't afford a baby-sitter who would be getting more money than I was for doing the cleaning up . . ."

Wanda sighed and rubbed at her eyes as if they pained her. She was sure she could cry if she really needed it, but that was not yet necessary because Victor seemed to be hanging on every word, and why not? "All right? I go there and much to my surprise the party was still going on even though it was after midnight. I don't know what to do because I was living a long way from this place and I barely had bus fare as it was . . . certainly I could not go home and wait and then come back again. It would already be the next morning, understand? So I tell my daughter she can sleep on the bedroom floor where nobody was even though it is still a little noisy from the guests singing once in a while . . . old Swedish and Norwegian songs because most of them are squareheads. Well, I get my daughter all bedded down and am sitting there waiting when this man comes into the room and offers me a glass of champagne and he says I can't possibly sit in there all alone and start off the New Year the way I am doing . . . just sitting there . . .

". . . So never in my life before did I ever have champagne, and I thought well it is the New Year and things will go better for my daughter and . . . and so I will just do what the man says . . .

". . . Well that was almost the last thing I remember. I don't know what was in that champagne or maybe it was just the champagne itself, but I don't remember one single thing from the time I had even half a glass. It was unreal. The next thing I knew it was morning and the police were there and my poor little daughter was sick and some men in white coats were working on her . . ."

Wanda paused and looked straight ahead. She raised her head, knowing her profile was her best angle, like Sam said no black woman could ever have a profile like that. And she was pleased because from here on she was going to think of the New Year's night as just like she was telling it now.

". . . Well, I get the blame for everything and because I have no money I have to take a public defender who is an idiot first class. And this public defender who is supposed to be a real lawyer tells me it will be much easier if I plead guilty to all the terrible things that were being said about me, including accusations that I was a prostitute and all such terrible lies about how I had mistreated Deidre, that's my daughter's name, and the first thing I know there I am being taken off to women's treatment center . . ."

Wanda hesitated. If what Lucinda had said was right the kid and his father did not exactly see eye to eye on everything, but maybe she had told him too much. "The thing is," she went on, "I just *had* to tell somebody about all this . . . somebody from here . . . it helps me feel I belong in this strange city. But please, don't tell your father. Maybe he wouldn't hire me if he knew all about this and that and there I'd be right out on the street which is where my landlady throws people who don't pay on the nose. Through it too. Please promise you won't say a word?"

"Okay. I don't see any special reason why he has to know. . . . Not that it matters, but were you really a prostitute? It's none of my business but—"

"You're being decent to me, least I can do is be straight with you. Yes, I was, sort of, anyway. Frankly, I was plain hungry, but it was only for a little while."

Victor was silent a moment and she was not sure he had been listening to her or to the continuing rumble of his damned motor. He was just sitting there like some great big gorgeous hunk of young stud looking at his hands on the steering wheel. Jesus, were his knuckles more interesting than what she had just said? He got the ten-dollar front-row seat at this great drama and there is no reaction whatsoever from the kid.

"Okay," Victor said finally. "I have to go now. Homework and I'm supposed to be in class by nine . . ."

Don't press it, Wanda. Take your time. An inspiration that comes on like a thunderbolt needs a soft place to land.

She opened the door and eased herself down to the curbing.

"Do you ever have dreams, Victor? Like about getting away from everybody in this world . . . maybe with somebody who needs you?"

She hoped he could see her eyes in the twilight because they were promising him so much. If he could only read.

"I guess I have thought about it . . ."

"Dreaming . . . I think it's about the best thing a person can do in this world. Don't you think a person can accomplish just about anything if they dream?"

"I guess . . ."

"You sure are real nice to drive me home."

"No problem." He hesitated. "Oh . . . about my father. He's sort of hard-headed . . . but underneath I think he means well. Still, if you don't want him to know, be careful what you tell him. The less the better. I sort of found that out a long time ago."

He was smiling that smile of his when he said it. She closed the door. "I'm sure your father means well. But in my humble opinion he has a long way to go to match up with his son. Night-night."

They waved, and as he rumbled away she gave him *her* hundred-dollar smile—the one Sam always said was like money in the bank.

Chapter Eight

With the wine and the curry which Hickock pronounced as very superior he told her about his day in Goldstein's court.

"You obviously found it exhilarating," Jean said.

"That's not quite the right word. But I have to admit it keeps a guy on his toes. In my own court there's almost always a jury involved, which makes it a different ballgame. The lawyers are out to win no matter what they have to do. It begins right with the evidentiary hearings, goes through the pretrial hearing, the *voir dire* when they select the jury members, and their opening statements. Sometimes I sit up there on my mountain and wonder what the hell is going on—"

"If you don't know who does?"

"Good question. The trouble is I'm strapped up there on my bench, removed from the action. I have to listen or at least keep my eyes open while some lawyer stalls for time with a long interrogation that is about as relevant to the basics of the case as this salad. If the lawyer is too clever I hate to watch what he's doing to the jury and if he's not very smart I can watch the jury's eyes and see them lose sympathy for his poor client whether he's defending or prosecuting. There are times when I think I got lost between my chambers and the bench and have wound up in Disneyland. In Butch's court I have a lot more to do than just referee."

"If I were in trouble I would prefer to be judged by Julian Hickock."

"Don't be too sure. There's nothing worse than a maverick judge and sometimes I am. I keep remembering how Oliver Cromwell told the Scots before some battle I can't remember the name of, '. . . I beseech ye, in the bowels of Christ, think ye that ye may be mistaken.'"

"Have ye ever been?"

"Too many times. The trouble is a judge is supposed to be neutral and that can neuter him. We can't just holler down to some windbag who is trying to pry his client out of a conviction that his argument is a bunch of malarky. He finds some psychiatrist who for a fee is willing to say the accused is insane and so he didn't know what he was doing, whatever it was, and juries tend to believe experts. The obvious fact that the accused knew exactly what he was doing and is probably as sane as anyone in the courtroom somehow gets lost in the arguments and there's not much I can do to get things back on track . . . My compliments to the chef on this salad. It's as pure and simple as its creator."

"You are full of malarky for saying so and I love it. Can I come see you in action someday?"

"You won't see much action and you're bound to be disappointed unless you know what is going on behind all the formalities. When I get the chance these days I'm playing things pretty sneaky. One of the victims of our system is the victim. If someone brings suit over a financial matter the aggrieved at least stands a chance of some sort of compensation. But it's a rare day in any court when a crime victim gets more than a sympathetic nod and usually not even that. A few states are trying to do something about it, but apathy runs the show until it's *you* who is hit over the head. You have to twist around the law and practically go underground to help the victim get a square deal. It's just plain wrong to send people off to prison, pay them and keep them and if they have one, never touch their personal bank accounts. In some cases the very money they stole can be drawing interest for them while they're in the can."

"I don't understand why you can't just say hey there you with the bludgeon. You hit so-and-so over the head so you owe him a hundred dollars. Pay it off by a certain time."

"If you were in Singapore or a lot of other countries that would happen, but our law in most states including this one looks the other way. We do everything possible to protect the rights of the criminal and nothing to help his victim. Once in a while I can get away with awarding some compensation on the sly, but some day some smartass is going to appeal and try to get me sacked."

"Would that break your heart?"

"No. I'd get more sailing in and maybe even my piano playing would improve." And that was pure malarky, he thought. Now that he had grown into the judicial world he knew it would be very hard to turn back.

She reached across the table and took his hand. "I love you," she said simply ". . . but I'm a little concerned about something . . ."

He tried to smile. "You've decided we have a generation gap problem."

"They don't make men like you any longer—"

"The model must have been defective. I have to admit that going to a disco doesn't appeal to me." He watched her eyes. Note, he thought, she did not respond to my crack about our age difference. That is not good.

"I didn't want to spoil our dinner and the wonderful sense of being comfortable together but I have to tell you that just before you came I received a phone call. It worried me. I think it was a man, but I'm not positive because the voice was high and whining. For a moment I thought it might be a joke or an obscene phone call because it sounded like he was trying to disguise his voice. First he asked if I was Jean Pomeroy and when I said yes he told me to give you a message."

Hickock lost his sense of relaxation as he tried to visualize who would know about their relationship and have any reason to believe Jean was the best way to reach him.

"Whoever it was said, you tell your friend that if he's a smart judge he'll understand that if you are too hard on certain people you can only expect them to be hard on you. He said he was getting old and had no time to waste. Then whoever it was asked twice if I had the message and advised me to write it down. I asked who could I say was calling? That's when Mr. Whoever-It-Was hung up."

Hickock groaned. There were times when his work had been baffling and disillusioning, but never before had it intruded on his private life . . . in this case, very private. Estervan, of course. Who else? The high whining voice was a giveaway, just as he must have intended it to be. Only a few days back he had discovered among all the other papers relating to the case one which described Estervan's record during the Second World War. He had been twice decorated for gallantry, two battlefield promotions and a Purple Heart for multiple wounds. Certainly no one could fault Estervan for not serving his country during that period and it was only right to weigh those achievements against his previous and later rap sheet. Now he remembered that one of Estervan's wounds had been in his neck, which had damaged his vocal chords and resulted in that peculiar voice. Estervan had made a mistake in sending Delgado around on the pretense of delivering a message; now in his anxiety he had made a second and even more serious mistake in revealing that he had gone to the trouble to find out about Jean. It was becoming ever more difficult to keep an objective view about Boris Estervan. Justice be damned.

"Do you know who it is?" she asked.

"I do. Let me do the worrying about him, I've already developed the habit."

Hickock dismissed the sudden notion that Estervan might threaten or even harm Jean. He was not that stupid—or could it be that his fear of returning to prison had destroyed his judgment?

He rose and moved around behind her chair. He placed his hands gently on her shoulders and then very slowly allowed them to slide down over her breasts and finally to her waist. He kissed her hair then her ears and neck as tenderly as his fingers caressed her body.

Her breathing quickened and he whispered, "About any dessert. I'd just as soon skip it."

"Right."

"Well . . . ?"

"Right."

Hickock left his car in the driveway behind Victor's pickup and mounted the front steps of 1011. The house was totally dark, and he supposed Victor must have gone to bed. It was only eleven o'clock so why was he tiptoeing across the porch of his own house in this ridiculous fashion? Why should he experience this unaccountable sense of guilt and what the hell happened to his sense of humor? Maybe, he thought, I should go to a shrink and find out why a man of nearly sixty returns home like a schoolboy. Why should he be concerned about waking up his son instead of the other way around?

He fitted his key into the lock—apparently Victor had not expected him to come home at all—and entered the front hall. As he switched on the light he realized that the soft warmth of Jean's body was still with him. At her door he had held her in his arms for a parting embrace and she had said she wished he did not have to go home, that after such a night it would be much more fulfilling to wake up at his side. And he'd answered, "I don't have to go home . . . but I do."

"Victor?"

"Yes. Get back inside before you're arrested for exposure. Or worse, catch cold."

Now in his empty, silent house, he thought, good night, my lady. If for nothing else, thank you for making me aware of how very lonely I have been.

He wound the grandfather clock by pulling up the weights, checked it against his wristwatch and found with considerable satisfaction that they agreed. It was reassuring to discover that at least some mechanically active instruments could be relied upon. Perhaps he should try to balance such reasonableness against the frailties of his professional life. Something must be done very soon about Estervan, but just sending him off to five or ten years in a prison was not going to accomplish anything.

As he climbed the stairs toward his bedroom his anger at Estervan for intruding upon his personal life diminished. There were dishonest judges who would never have allowed such a situation to develop in the first place. They would have accepted some kind of reward from Estervan for their wisdom and leniency and that would be the end of it. Well, he wasn't one of them. But on the other hand whatever Boris Estervan had done to personally annoy him must not be allowed to influence the sentencing for his crime. The only dependable factor that kept people from settling their grievances by tearing each other to pieces in the ancient style was still the law. And the court, presently in the person of Julian Hickock, was the blade of the law. He'd better try not to allow anything to tarnish it. Noble sentiments. So get on with it, judge.

Hickock paused briefly outside the door to Victor's bedroom. And he saw again those times not so long ago when they had been such good companions. They had sailed together in *Freedom* from the time Victor was five or six until his mother was killed.

Had Victor really changed since Jean had entered his life or was it just his imagination? Maybe it was just old-fashioned jealousy, the need for affection that Victor might feel subconsciously he had lost. Maybe just a fragment of him had departed temporarily. It did not seem logical that a man could lose a whole son if they had once been close. How about you . . . judger of men? Maybe you are the one who has changed. The father sets the tone of a relationship so something must be wrong with the way you're doing things.

Hickock moved on to his own room and as he hung up his clothes and threw his shirt into the mountain of laundry that something must be done about tomorrow morning by *someone* (a little organization here, please), he tried to concentrate on ways to reestablish the once so rewarding relation with Victor. Damnit, nothing else counted as much right now, not Estervan, not Nellie-Mae, not the damned laundry . . . not even Jean could be allowed to interfere with what had to be rejuvenated between father and son. All right, judge. Now judge yourself once more. How did you turn Victor away and what did you do? Be an honest judge and admit that the trouble began soon after Dolores was killed. Was it possible that Victor somehow blamed you for an accident even though it happened more than five miles from this house? It might have been better if the two of you had taken a trip together right after the accident, somewhere . . . chartered a little boat for a sail through the West Indies . . . somewhere there might have been an opportunity to sit down and level with each other.

Hickock slipped naked into bed, turned out his reading light, and stared at the rectangular blob of light on the ceiling created by the street light. No, he had not shown any overpowering grief when Dolores was gone. It was not his way. He was sorry that her life had been cut off in middle age, but he had not been devastated and perhaps Victor had found that conduct unforgivable. Perhaps at that time he should have been told that the love that had once flourished between his parents had been drowned long ago in Dolores's devotion to the bottle. Perhaps he should have come right out and told him that his mother had not only become a constant worry, but also a complete pain in the ass when she was alone with her husband. Perhaps he should have been told that her performance in front of her son and daughter was strictly that—a virtuoso performance, sometimes of Academy Award proportions. She had two voices—one for her public and her children, and one for her husband. And two personalities, the public angel and the melancholy drunken wife. Nellie-Mae understood because in spite of every caution she had occasionally been witness to Dolores's less than charming ways. And apparently daughter Sally had not been entirely deceived. It had not been long after Dolores's funeral when he had returned home from an evening of playing Dixieland jazz and found a note on his pillow. It was written in Sally's unmistakably generous hand and it said, "A great man is one who has not lost his child's heart."

There had been no way to tell Sally how much the note had meant to him just at that time.

Okay then, was it fair to destroy Victor's revered image of his mother on the off chance it might bring him back to his father? Nuts. There had to be some other way.

Hickock had hoped to fall asleep quickly, but he could not seem to turn off his thoughts. That girl, what was her name . . . Sandra something? Her pathetic little face flashed across his mind. No, it was Wanda. She was coming in the morning, one hoped, to make things at least look better. No wonder he thought he'd seen her before . . . somewhere . . . sometimes he was convinced he'd seen every type in the human race, thousands of faces staring up at him perched on his bench. And certainly there were thousands of young American women just like her—usually not overbright and rarely with more than an elementary education. They were drifters, they came like a weed to a large garden of children, he thought drowsily . . . so many that they seldom heard the word "love" until it was spoken by a stranger. By then it was too late to have any real meaning. They had been shoved and kicked by their world until by the time they were twenty they were burned out—just from fighting. They no longer looked for happiness because they were convinced it did not exist.

His mind refused to settle down. He asked himself if most men had pinwheels of thought fighting off sleep like this. Maybe he read too much. There was some kind of crime study made at UCLA (one of fifty thousand studies), he recalled wryly, and unless his memory tricked him it was on violence . . . something about an experiment among first-grade children to see if a later predilection for violence could be detected in the young. Supposing they did find Johnny Appleseed might have the ingredients to make him a one-day mugger, rapist, or killer? What could be done about it? You can't confine anyone for a crime they haven't yet committed, or perhaps had yet to plan. So? Do you inoculate them with some magic substance in the same way you eliminate any other disease? Wasn't that control of the species? How far should the so-called honest citizens go in crime prevention? All right, we *do* lock up the mentally incompetent whether they have done anything or not. We brush them under the carpet and try to ignore their existence. And that includes many just plain alcoholics. They did it to mentally defective teen-agers in the Middle Ages . . . gave them to the guillotine. Is that any way to run a railroad?

Come now, sweet slumber, the wind is fair and you're not taking me. Anywhere.

He rolled over and made a determined effort to think of something soothing. Instead he saw the face of that girl again. It was a strangely appealing face, and maybe that was why he kept thinking about her . . . She very vaguely reminded him of a young woman he had once sent away for child abuse. But that young woman had been much thinner and a blond as far as he could remember. And much older. No, she couldn't be the same. Too many cases . . . too many faces. What had been *her* name? Had he made a mistake in locking up a woman like that for whatever time it was? God Almighty, if he had been wrong then he was the one who should be put away. Were his views on that sort of case changing or was he just mellowing? Yet look what she had done with her child. Where should a man stand these days when the *Gideon* decision just damn well about proved locking people up was a mistake in the majority of cases? They let a thousand inmates free in Florida because they'd not had an attorney when they were convicted. All at once. The very development Jean's father had thought outrageous. And what happened? It took a few years, but the return-to-prison percentage for those just let go was half the rate of those who served out their full terms. Which just about proved there were a lot of people in prison who should really not be there. Hickock, you are becoming a marshmallow judge. Why don't you take up psalm singing and join the Salvation Army?

Chapter Nine

The kitchen at 1011 matched the era of the house. Here Nellie-Mae had presided over an area as large as the adjacent dining room. Years back a dishwasher had been added, but the stove was still the old four-burner gas upright with an overhead oven that had been installed during the twenties. The kitchen sink was copper and the counters were beechwood, now sticky from neglect.

The Hickock family dishes and silverware were stored in the narrow pantry which separated the kitchen from the dining room, and it was here that Hickock and his son encountered each other and exchanged their morning greetings. While he sought in a drawer for a knife and fork Victor said, "This has got to be the most inefficient way ever invented to get breakfast."

"What's the trouble, son?"

"We come in here for our plates and utensils and take everything into the kitchen where the food is. Then we haul it all right through here to the dining room and everything stays there for about thirty minutes while we eat. Then we haul the whole thing back through here to the kitchen where supposedly we clean up. Sooner or later we haul the whole works right back here, put it away, and the next meal do the whole thing over again. I don't care if it was the way people did things a long time ago. It's crazy and I realize now why mom never liked it."

"Has it occurred to you that some people in this world are so happy to have anything to eat they are not particularly concerned about where they dine?"

"Come on. Don't give me that old starving African, Nicaraguan, Indian Third World bit. According to our economics professor it's not a world problem any more."

"I would guess your professor dines well on his steak-tenure. Hunger is not a problem until you haven't eaten lately. Meanwhile, would you rather eat in the kitchen?"

"In this house? Unthinkable." Victor's voice rose as if he were mocking an oration. "This is the Honorable Judge Hickock's house where tradition prevails forever. Let no new ideas enter here because the old way is the best way and be damned to the twentieth century!"

Hickock decided not to react. Instead he was again impressed with his son's vigor, and his handsomeness. Except for his ears and perhaps his nose, which unfortunately resembled his father's, he looked like his mother. There was the same intensity of coloring, and the same flashing blue eyes which had made Dolores such a stunning woman. As they moved to the kitchen and began preparing their separate breakfasts Hickock said, "This place may be a bit on the old-fashioned side, but it's the only home we have. Things will look better when Nellie-Mae takes charge again."

"What if Nellie-Mae can't get around like she used to? That hip injury isn't funny. Did you go to the hospital?"

Hickock said that he had spent half an hour with Nellie-Mae and that they had enjoyed a nice talk.

"Did you ask the doctor about her?"

"No. I didn't see one around."

"Well, I did. And he says it will be a while before she'll be moving around normally."

"We'll work something out. I've hired a girl to come in and do some cleaning today. Temporarily, of course . . ."

"I know."

Hickock slipped two eggs into the pot of boiling water and almost immediately saw one of them crack and develop a short white tail. Damnit, how could you boil a pair of eggs exactly four minutes without having the water boiling when you started? And somewhere someone had once said if you put the eggs in water that was too hot they would crack which one of them sure as hell just did. Nellie-Mae knew the secret, but a dumb judge just could not get it right.

He checked his watch and what Victor had said suddenly echoed back to him through his preoccupation with the eggs. "How did you know about the girl?"

"She came by here last night while you were out whooping it up."

Hickock's hand paused as he cut through a muffin for toasting. The sarcasm in Victor's voice was thick. He was about to explain that he had not exactly been whooping it up, whatever activity that might include, then changed his mind. In a way Victor was right.

He asked Victor what he had thought of the new housekeeper.

"She seemed like an okay girl. I gave her a ride home." Victor picked up the coffee pot and two cups and started for the dining room. "To hear her tell it she'd had quite a life."

"What's her name? I can't remember it for the life of me."

"Wanda. Sometimes I'm surprised when you remember mine."

Control yourself, Hickock instructed his temper, but couldn't resist, "May I say that since the day of your birth you have given me cause, both good and otherwise, not to forget you."

"Spoken like a true judge."

And of course, Hickock told himself, he was right. Still . . .

Later in the dining room, Victor broke the silence between them. "Do you think all prostitutes are bad?"

Hickock swallowed an overlarge bite of toast with difficulty. One of the dubious pleasures of close coexistence with a teenager was the flat questions so often launched from behind some hidden barricade.

"Why do you ask?"

"Because I want to know how you feel about them."

"Morally or legally?"

"Both."

"That's some question at this hour of the morning. Well . . . we do have laws against prostitution and it's my job to abide by them, even enforce them."

"Regardless of the reasons for it? Like paying the grocery bills?"

He's baiting me, Hickock thought. He's deliberately trying to knock me off my perch at seven-thirty in the morning while I am trying to enjoy one overcooked egg and one with water in it. Patience. Nellie-Mae is not here to pull you apart.

"Are you saying that if someone sells it for cash to make a living that's wrong, but if they give it away or legitimize it somehow . . . say a calculating, ambitious woman marries a guy so he'll support her in the style she wants . . . that's okay?"

"I don't make the law and I don't personally approve of the law against prostitution. It should not be a crime because it is victimless . . . most usually. And the male is seldom if ever arrested, and the pimps almost never. The girls get a bad deal from the time they begin until they're too old or broken to work any longer. I'm very glad that they rarely show up in my own court . . . when they do I try not to consider it too seriously . . . now that's enough of the subject. For now, at this hour, anyway."

Hickock hoped but doubted that he had settled the matter. Almost without pausing he asked the usual morning question about how school had gone for Victor for the preceding day and he received the usual monosyllabic grunt. After another long silence he saw Victor get up and start carrying his plate and cup to the kitchen. He asked him how he was doing financially these days.

"Now that you've brought it up, I was wondering if I could float a small loan."

"How much are you thinking about?"

"A hundred dollars should handle it."

"That's quite some bundle. *It* being—?"

"My pickup. I need four shock-absorbers while I still have some teeth. I can buy them secondhand, install them myself so it will be a good investment. I'll get more than my money back if I ever decide to sell the pickup."

"You will, some day. But I wonder if a potential buyer will care that you replaced shock-absorbers. As for such an excellent investment, unless you have some definite plans for paying me back it will be *my* money, not yours that will be returned."

"I bow to your wisdom, Your Honor."

Sometimes, Hickock decided, his son struck him as an unsalvageable fathead. But then youth at this stage teetered along an ever more uncertain road. There had been a time, he remembered, when he had held his own father in something just barely above contempt. "When do you need the money?"

"ASAP, if it's convenient."

"To anyone but a banker, lending money is always inconvenient." Now why, he thought, did he always seem to include some pomposity in any conversation with his son? He managed to avoid such temptations when speaking from the bench and he was certainly not given to aphorisms, parables and old chestnuts in daily conversation. Yet almost invariably Victor had to suffer some verbal flak, and by this time he had considerable excuse for sighing when he sensed its approach. "I think I do have a hundred-dollar bill stuck away in a drawer upstairs for such emergencies. We'll float your loan when I come down. We'll peg your rate of interest according to the national prime rate."

Victor thanked him, and Hickock knew or hoped he knew that his smile was not based on financial reward. Victor also said that it was unlikely he would be home for dinner since he was a candidate for the track team and the tryouts would certainly extend into the evening. It would be easier to eat at the university dining hall. He agreed to pick up potatoes and lettuce at the market on the way home. All were in short supply at 1011. "And if you can, pick up some oatmeal cookies," Hickock added. "Nellie-Mae has some kind of prejudice against them and won't make or buy them so while she's away I'm going to cheat on her. I could live on oatmeal cookies."

The doorbell rang. Victor put down his plate and cup and went to the front hallway. After a moment he returned with Wanda. As they exchanged "good mornings" Hickock was reassured. Now he was certain he had never seen her before. She was wearing a simple blouse and skirt that might have seemed just right on a kindergarten teacher. Her hair was swept back in a bun and she wore no make-up. She was wearing simple black slippers with low heels, which was probably one reason why, Hickock decided, she looked so much smaller than she had the day before. She presented an altogether well-scrubbed look and her large brown eyes were now filled with sincerity. She stood with her hands clasped behind her and her chin tilted upward as she said, "I'm ready to go to work. Ready and able. Just show me where a few things are and leave the rest to me."

Victor picked up his plate and coffee cup and started for the kitchen. Wanda moved quickly between him and the swinging pantry door. She reached for his plate and cup. "Here, let me take these. You go study and get smart. I'll do everything. Please."

As Victor relinquished the dish and cup Hickock saw him

smile. His eyes said he was pleased to be relieved of a chore, but that was not all.

He said to Victor, "You show her how to operate the dishwasher and I'll go through the vacuum drill with her afterward."

Hickock climbed the stairs to his room where he put on a tie, a rather bright red one which he thought might best match the relative circus atmosphere of Butch Goldstein's court, and a sports jacket. There was no use looking like a judge when off-duty unless running for election, and that was not quite yet. Then he supposed he would be obliged to make various appearances and perhaps inflict a few Rotarians and Kiwanian assemblies with speeches. Somehow, without spending far more than he could afford, he must attract attention and a solemn look would be important. Damnit, the whole business of electing judges was wrong unless it involved some poor justice of the peace in a small town where everyone involved knew each other, including most of the voters. Big city judges, who carried most of the judicial responsibility, should not have their careers on the line every time politicians and bureaucrats were in or out of jobs. Very few judges could support an honest campaign chest, which was wasted money anyway, and as for the time lost in campaigning, that was a direct loss to the community. A judge should be moving his calendar ahead with all the dispatch possible and not postpone the reading of a brief or even interrupt a trial itself because of some commitment to an election. Democracy, Hickock grumbled, was not perfect. More perfect than anything else, though . . .

He stood before the full-length mirror a moment assessing his image. A bit stooped. Sign of age. When was a man too old for a woman? Perhaps, as Sally had said, when he let his heart grow old. Pants need pressing. Jacket rumpled. Where the hell did Nellie-Mae take things to be cleaned and pressed? Sentimental fool, no doubt, silly old man possibly. Still Jean needed a mature man or at least that was what she claimed. And you could do with a shoeshine, my mature friend.

He stepped away from the mirror and went to his bureau. He pulled out the hollow top drawer and reached far back. His fingers encountered something metallic and cold, and it took him a moment to realize it was the service pistol he had been issued during the Korean War. It had been in the drawer for at least twenty years and he had fired it a grand total of approximately twelve times on the military range at Fort Sill. To qualify. To qualify that he could not hit a North Korean with the silly weapon if he had stood obligingly right in front of him. And to eventually qualify as a criminal, for the gun was government issue and the law specified that all items be returned to the quartermaster on separation from service. A cooperative supply sergeant had winked and suggested he might like to keep his sidearm as a souvenir and he had done just that. A qualified thief, and where was the FBI which was supposed to track down all stolen government property?

As he moved the gun aside he thought that he might do well to recall the gun next time he was obliged to judge a thief. Or was harangued by an advocate of a gun control law. Of course the damned things should be banned, but where did you start? They were certainly the root of unending tragedy in America, and no sportsman in his right mind would claim they were useful to hunters, but how did you stop the bad guys from buying them?

Just beside the gun he found the old leather breast-pocket wallet he was looking for. There were five one-hundred-dollar bills inside and he removed one. Like the gun there was no sound reason for keeping so much money, but then he had never thought of it as real money, since it was "found" money. The Cavemen had won first prize in a jazz festival four years ago and here, still untouched, was his share. He had always intended to deposit the money in the bank, but his usual procrastination had prevailed. Likewise he had long considered turning the gun over to the police. Really? And confess you were a long-time thief who has suddenly seen the light? Perhaps you might try cooking up a story explaining how you came by this weapon which of course you never saw before in your entire life. Even with your fingerprints on it. There must be some mistake, Your Honor.

He replaced the gun and wallet in the drawer and as he did so his eye caught the leather-framed photograph of Dolores which still held so familiar a position on his bureau that he realized it had become part of the furniture itself and he had not actually paused to look at it for years.

It was a very good portrait and seemed to have caught Dolores at the very peak of her life. It had been taken when she was about thirty-five and had not yet discovered vodka could be sipped regularly without its odor betraying the swallower.

Now he regarded it as the portrait of a once-upon-a-time lady in another, almost forgotten world.

What happened to people from one decade or even half a decade to the next? So many times, they seemed to change organically as well as mentally. He reflected momentarily on his few friends remaining from the days of Dolores. Some had grown and expanded while others had turned inward and some had begun a forlorn retreat until they were dead. Couples they had associated with had fallen away from each other, God knew why. Such things were not discussed, or at least not in detail. It was difficult to understand why people who had children and had spent thirty-odd years together suddenly found new life springs elsewhere. And there were others who bore up right to the very end of one or the other, celebrating silver and golden anniversaries and becoming either devastated or vastly relieved when their partner had at last left them in peace. The Hickocks, he remembered, had behaved like so many of their peers, beginning in bliss and then standing back to watch almost helplessly as corrosion crept through their relationship.

In time things followed what he now recognized as the normal pattern of his class. There was church together on Sundays, not so much because they were concerned for appearances; it was just that they were both reaching for something solid to hang onto. Dolores's relatives came and went with increasing frequency. They were worried because a marriage they could view only vicariously and in which they believed they held a proprietary interest was threatening to fall apart.

And of course that was undoubtedly what had originally troubled Victor and it still prevailed. He had looked for an excuse for his mother's behavior when she was alive, and he continued to do so after she was killed. When his world collapsed he had to find an instant villain. The bad guy was his father, who would now, more than two years later, like to know how his role could be tolerably reversed.

Hickock studied the portrait of Dolores a moment longer and decided it would be very fitting if she would reach out from wherever she was and return his son to him before it was too late.

He smiled sourly. Cracking up, old friend. Plea-bargaining with the photo of a ghost who had never been particularly generous or feeling even when she was in the best of health. God only knew how to get Victor back into the fold. A mortal father could only keep trying.

He closed the drawer and almost immediately opened it again. He took out the remaining four hundred-dollar bills and placed them in his wallet. The new cleaning girl was going to be alone in the house nearly all day and if she became overly curious there was no sense in placing temptation in her path. After all . . .

After all, he thought unhappily, prudence in this situation was based on suspicion and unless a person was exceedingly careful, bitterness came along soon afterward.

Then there was wariness. There was old man Estervan still on the horizon, squatting like a bug full of poison and quite capable of doing some very nasty things if he wanted to. No matter what sentence was handed down Delgado would probably file an immediate appeal. If the appeal succeeded in getting his client off without some kind of penalty he would still be very angry at Julian Hickock.

There was no way to outguess what Estervan might have in mind, but it was now apparent he might play very rough. He obviously did not understand how any man in his right senses could reject an offer of money, particularly when it might prevent the breaking of his rice bowl. In his eyes he would not be bribing a judge but contributing to his term of office because he had the wisdom to cooperate. Maybe the best thing to do then was to accept a hefty contribution to the Hickock campaign chest and give him a stiff sentence anyway.

Hickock rejected the idea instantly. If you go that route, he thought, remember what happened to Faust. Maybe he should call Delgado and advise him in no uncertain terms that his client was stumbling into ever deeper trouble with his various messages. And also let him know that if his client ever again phoned Jean Pomeroy or in any way interfered with her life, he would see his bail cancelled immediately and Boris Estervan would most certainly receive the maximum sentence under the law.

As he descended the stairs and headed for the kitchen Hickock was wondering how the Delgado-Estervan team had found out about Jean Pomeroy. It was getting late, coming up fast on nine and he was due, black robe and all, in Butch

Goldstein's court at nine-thirty. For the nitty-gritty of the world.

He had descended the stairs charged with gusto for the day's work ahead of him. The law, he thought, could be a drag and the lingo of lawyers soporific, but there were times when his job could be the most exciting and absorbing in the world.

He marched rapidly across the dining room and through the pantry. "Woe is me," he muttered as he became newly conscious of the domestic chaos about him. "A bachelor's housework is never done." Now where the hell did Nellie-Mae keep the vacuum cleaner? He pushed open the door and saw Victor bent over the dishwasher. He was filling the little receptacle with soap powder and smiling up at Wanda. She was standing beside him, apparently intrigued with the interior of the dishwasher.

What suddenly interested, and concerned, Hickock was her hand on the back of Victor's neck, and the way she so quickly withdrew it as she heard him enter.

Chapter Ten

It was nearly noon before Wanda decided she was making progress. She scrubbed down the kitchen counters until they lost their dull film, cleaned the stove of assorted food droppings and dreamed of finer things while she shoved a mop around the kitchen floor. She told herself that she was not bucking for a permanent job and that she had swabbed all the damned floors she ever would for the rest of her days. All she wanted was to make things look like she had worked while the Hickocks were gone. It might take some time to renew her contacts with the people she needed, and to make all the arrangements she could foresee. From the way Victor Hickock talked it would be at least two weeks before the nigger would be back on the job so there was no sweat there.

The sweat was all in that first meeting with his father, but everything went as advertised. Of course you really did not look one bit like when you were living with Sam and in the life. Nearly ten pounds more and a whole different hair-do and no lipstick or eye make-up or nothin'. You get out of the habit in a place like Clark. Hello, Mrs. Raleigh, with the macho husband back east. Hello, Mrs. Raleigh, who is like a new person. You better believe.

The first problem was to find the man who called himself Manuel and still keep away from the area the probation officer had insisted was an absolute no-no. That, she thought, was where the action was, but it would be just awful to get busted just because of geography. The area was a temptation, all right. It was the same sort of scene there that could be found at Thomas Circle in Washington, D.C., or Eighth and Fifty-sixth in New York, or on Twelfth Street near the Mulholland in Kansas City or Rush Street in Chicago. These were just some of the areas where girls worked the street and they were very comfortable places to be if you knew your way around. Bless the memory of those true friends. It didn't make no difference if they were sweet cream ladies, flat-backers, outlaws, or even jiveasses, they were okay people trying to survive.

People didn't mind knowing that sex was for sale as long as the salespeople stayed out of sight. You could have whorehouses all over the city and most of the city fathers would drop by sooner or later sometimes just to prove to their pals how macho they were. But oh my God don't even think, don't admit for one second that such a place existed or that maybe your name was in the madam's little black book. As long as the vice squad got their little piece now and then and some little presents to go with it, and the city fathers got their jollies without their families knowing about it, then everything was just fine. But just you let a handful of girls hit the street so people could see them and boy, did everybody start to holler! The eyesight of our sweet wives are being insulted. Our daughters will get some ideas and lose their super-precious virginity. What about the morals of our sons who will all get the clap and the boo-bo and become sterile because these evil women have hauled them off to Sodom and Gomorrah. She paused a moment to consider who Sodom and Gomorrah might be. Funny, she had heard about them for years and they were part of the Bible so maybe they were in the life. Anyway the very same city fathers who had been screwing their ears flat would have the very same girls arrested if they went outside to do business like any other business.

The same gents who were busy all day making money and stabbing each other in the back while they were doing it did not want any eyesores strolling around the streets of their fair city. Even if you paid taxes and were willing to buy some kind of a business license like anybody else that sells stuff . . . they just won't admit that your product has a market. And they are the best customers, believe it.

There is no john like an establishment john because you know exactly how he is going to behave. You get him in a room and he spends the first five minutes looking for recording devices, and peepholes and mirrors and making sure the door is locked. Then while he's counting out his money he treats you to a lecture on how he never does this but this is his birthday or the Fourth of July or the doctor has just told him he has not got cancer or some other damn reason for him to reward himself.

Then for sure he promises you a bonus if you are "extra nice" to him. Only he is careful not to specify how much the bonus is going to be and what you are supposed to do to earn it. Sometimes you feel like asking him if he will put you on the company pension plan if you are extra, *extra* nice to him. And would he include health insurance and credit union privileges which his secretary who does not put out to bosses gets whether she asks for it or not.

Who is getting the shaft here? In more ways than one. Now the guy fumbles around and tries to prove he is the wild bull of the pampas which is all in his imagination. But he figures he has never seen this female before and never will again so let her rip and he is still grunting when he falls away.

And then panic sets in. He asks you for the tenth time if you are diseased, are you positive, are you absolutely sure, and so forth and on and on. And he rushes over to the bowl and spends the next five minutes washing himself and complaining that the water is too hot or too cold and haven't you got an unused bar of soap. Then he gets dressed like lickety-split and has the usual total lapse of memory about any bonus while he is counting the money in his wallet to make sure it's all there.

In closing he says it was nice meeting you and see you around sometime and gives you the " 'bye baby" and you give him the "toodle-ooo" or some such silly and he is gone.

Block to block maybe twenty minutes and you have yourself twenty, thirty, fifty dollars which is about the same pay per hour as a welterweight lawyer. At least they don't take out Social Security or federal tax. Some girl said we should take a depletion allowance like we were an oil well.

Okay. One down and an unknown time to go before some cop decides he don't care for you being so visible. You are embarrassing your fellow citizens who would like to throw stones at you for making a living. Maybe that union, COYOTE, could help, but getting the right kind of recognition and maybe someday making legal what sure had to be if people would only be honest about human nature, was going to be a long haul. Here in this city, which was sure no San Francisco, the area around First and Virginia or Fourteenth and Beasley could be full of people from the life. Unless the weather was stinking. Then they all went in their holes. Of course there was nothing like San Francisco where there were so many areas—Eddy and Taylor for black girls and junkies, Market and Taylor for teen-age boys, and the regular Mason, Powell, Post and Hyde walks which was always loaded with johns. A thoroughbred could average a hundred, maybe even two hundred a night in San Francisco—depending on the weather and conventions. God bless the IRS, who allowed write-offs for conventioneers. A lot of them charged tricks to their credit cards or their hotel bills. "Entertainment." And the hotels took their cut without even a fast thank you. Everybody from the bellman to the house dick took a slice while the chamber of commerce looked the other way. Hypocritical fatheads.

The thing was that here in this kind of half-ass city it was very difficult to contact Manuel unless you could spend some time in the area. Because Manuel liked to stay invisible as much as possible, and took his customers only by reference, that is, he would not even discuss a deal unless he knew the reputation of him or her who he was talking with. The best thing about Manuel was that he was a good friend of Sam's in the old days. And he knew little ol' Wanda was Sam's main lady. Now the thing was with Sam dead which Manuel was bound to hear about sooner or later, would he remember?

Wanda knew it would be useless to start calling people in the life until at least noon. She had brought her little book with her, the same black book every working girl carried and kept the names and phone numbers of johns who might be helpful someday or people in the life who just might fill in some lonely night when you just didn't feel like turning a trick. The book was fairly well up-to-date because they were lenient about phone calls at Clark providing you made them collect. Stella's number was still good and so were quite a few of the others. Manuel's number was not in anybody's book, you better believe, but a message could be relayed to him by the right parties and he would call back. When he felt like it. Which presented a problem because he certainly could not be calling back when the Hickocks were at home and the only phone at Mrs. Millington's was in the kitchen. The thing to do then was to start calling about noon and ask whoever was awake to start the wheels moving . . .

Wanda vacuumed the dining room, then the front hallway, and finally the living room—sort of in between the chairs without moving them around too much since this is *not* my regular line of work?

She paused frequently to examine various objects which

interested her in the living room. The judge sure did a lot of reading. Books were scattered all over the place, dull-looking stuff like *Lectures on Literature* by that guy Nabokov, wasn't he the same guy who wrote *Lolita* which you read the very first year at Clark? And here was *Centennial* which hardly nobody in prison could get through. And the *Harper Dictionary of Contemporary Usage*, and stuff like the *University of Pennsylvania Law Review* and magazines like *Judges Journal, Judicature*, and, for God's sake, *Criminal Procedure Evidence Appellate Procedure*. And something called *The Literate Naval Architect*. Real zingy stuff.

She became entranced with a large atlas, exploring it until the chiming of the big clock in the front hall reminded her that she had been idling for almost an hour and there was still a lot of work to do before she got on the horn. Everything in this room could do with some dusting, but she had better vacuum upstairs first. The front hall only had throw rugs over the bare floors so they could be given just a lick and a promise and nobody would know the difference.

As she carried the vacuum up the stairs she paused to study several framed photographs which were hung opposite the balustrade. There was a photo of Victor in a football outfit and she noted his number was forty-nine. He looked only a little younger in the photograph so she supposed it had been taken when he was in highschool. His gorgeous hair was shorter then and his ears looked even bigger in the next photo which showed him in cap and gown. Graduating, for sure.

It must be nice to graduate from someplace. What a difference from your own life, and look here is obviously his sister in two photos. She was wearing a cheerleader's outfit in one picture and cap and gown in the other. And both of them *still* in school. What a difference from little ol' Wanda with that busing to a school where most of the students were black and fighting and smartassing to the teachers until if you didn't join the crowd they knocked you down and kicked the bejesus out of you right while you were waiting for the bus. It took about a month until you told Aunt Louise there was no way you were going to go back to such a zoo . . . no how. Aunt Louise found another school which was not so bad and you managed to stay in there until the ninth grade when one of the teachers started to make passes at you. He said he would give you a failure unless you let him ding around with you and you yanked his beard when he pulled down your halter strap and grabbed at your tit. For just thirteen, he said, you sure had some nice melons. When you complained to the principal she said you were a liar because the teacher said he never touched you and from then on *all* the teachers started to hassle you and that was the end of the ninth grade for little ol' Wanda. Who needed it anyway? There was more education to be had at Clark in three years than in any school in the world and there was almost no race stuff, even the niggers were regular people, and there was no hassling by anybody as long as you stayed with the rules and minded your own business.

But when you looked at kids like these Hickocks who were almost right in your own age bracket and here they were just loading up their brain cells without thinking for one second about money or being hassled or worrying about how maybe they might get busted for some damn little thing that didn't amount to a tiny little mound of Mexican beans . . .

It took Wanda a long time to ascend the stairs because there were so many things to look at. There was a photo of a white-haired woman who looked like she might have been Judge Hickock's mother. How would she have felt if her son was taken away from her? How would that fancy-looking lady feel if she was called an unfit mother—?

And are you ready for *this?* Was the judge a Jew? One of those characters who changed their names? Here was a plaque from B'nai B'rith saying Judge Julian Hickock was honored for distinguished service in behalf of *human* rights. Ho, ho. Is Wanda Usher not a human? Didn't Deidre have a right to stay with her real mother? Somebody should tell the Jews that Julian Hickock was the closest thing to a murderer anybody could be and still not actually do it. You better believe all the Jews were not as smart as they were supposed to be or they would never have given an award to Judge Hickock. If they were going to plant trees in the martyr's forest in Israel like it said here, they should plant one in the name of little ol' Wanda Usher who was like she told Victor maybe the best mother in the whole world. And give Wanda another tree for being brave after her whole life was ruined because of one judge who thought working girls were unfit . . .

Anybody can look around this house and all that goes with it and see that Judge Hickock is not exactly suffering one bit. So his wife does go get herself killed—that was a couple of years ago and ever since what is he doing? Mourning his heart out? He has got to be shacking up with some amateur that's for sure. He had that look in his eye, like a contented rooster, y'know. It is perfectly all right for him who is supposed to be such a respectable judge to be laying some sweet young thing who does not absolutely have to make a living with her body because she can do something else. It is perfectly all right because she don't take no actual cash on the barrelhead, and she does her tricks in her own home instead of in some flea-bitten hotel. All the ladies and gentlemen in the whole city would not be very much surprised to find out that Judge Julian Hickock who had lost his dear wife, poor man, was getting a little on the side, y'know. They would understand it and smile their little smiles while they nodded their heads up and down like some mechanical dolls and they would not think there was nothing wrong at all about a judge getting a little no matter what it said in the Bible about fornicating and such. It worked for the people like him because he was part of the whole lousy, unfair establishment which made up the rules saying it is perfectly okay for us to screw around all we want to, providing we do it out of sight and do not say nothing whatsoever about the other guy's wife or her husband. Those are the rules. You can even do a little screwing around at the country club while dancing and everybody is going to look the other way, but just let a few honest working girls get into the act and off to the can they go for a month or so. Or longer. Longer . . .

We are an offense to the public eye, *they* say. *They* say it is bad for business if you work the downtown streets when for Christ's sake the shops have been closed for at least four hours before you could find one single lady working the street. It is crazy, it is ding-a-ling. The cops are always hassling the girls and saying to get your ass moving in high gear when you are already at a dog trot. They make cracks from the safety of their patrol cars, trying to get a rise out of you or nail you for loitering if you so much as stop ten seconds to say why don't you spend more time arresting robbers and murderers and protecting the public like the heroes you're supposed to be instead of hassling women who never hurt nobody? Indeed.

At the top of the stairs Wanda came on a mahogany table with a large silver bowl set in the middle of it. She picked up the bowl and read the engraving on the side.

Winner. First Place. Channel Handicap Race.
Freedom
Skipper: Julian Hickock
Aug. 1, 1975

It was real silver. It had to be because it was so heavy, and had one of those marks on the bottom. It had to be worth maybe one hundred, maybe two hundred to some fence, but not from little ol'Wanda. Wanda was never a thief and never would be. People's property was theirs, like it was sacred or something and all the thieves she had ever known, which was a fair number, were all jerks and that included some of the girls at Clark. You could have no respect for them no matter how nice they appeared on the surface.

She replaced the bowl and entered the first door at the top of the stairs. It was obviously Victor's room because there were college pennants on the wall and Superman posters and a desk covered with a whole bunch of books and a beat-up guitar leaning against the radiator. She saw that the single bed was neatly made, and she was amazed at the collection of clothes in the closet—the kid must have more than a dozen shirts.

Wanda found the wall outlet, plugged in the vacuum and ran it back and forth over the throw rug for a few minutes. When she decided the rug had enough she turned off the vacuum and went through Victor's desk drawers without touching anything. It had occurred to her that Victor might have some kind of a record that maybe it would be helpful to know about it. Even a speeding ticket or maybe a marijuana bust would sort of set the tone. But there was not one thing. Clean as a whistle this kid. Of course he would not have kept traffic tickets—probably if he had any his father fixed them for him, but just the same you would think he must have done something wrong and would maybe leave some kind of leftover around. There was a dirty book in the bottom drawer. Jesus, how could people get a charge out of looking at that stuff? There was nothing else worth looking at in the drawer, just some odds and ends like athletic medals, some camping utensils, a jar of pennies and umpteen pencils. In the top drawer there was a calculator with an instruction book, a small camera which no fence would give you the time of day for, and would you believe little books of poetry? And not a single piece of stereo equipment in his room. This Victor was something else. He was not even a Jesus freak because there was no religious stuff around, not even any of those Oriental Hairy Christa things that so many kids got their jollies out of these days.

She was vaguely disappointed when she left Victor's room, but her spirits rose when she entered the door at the end of the balcony and found herself in the master bedroom. Master, indeed. Are you ready for this absolutely huge polished oak bed like they have in the movies? Like in old-time houses where the rich people lived or if they were in Europe where princes and queens and even kings lived. Right before your very own eyes is this bed with carvings all over the backboard and big knobs on the footboard and a bench to sit on at the end. A sports palace. Would you believe in a bed like this you could do it cross-wise or any combination and still have room to play hopscotch. And the judge slept here *alone?*

It suddenly occurred to Wanda that the sudden appearance of goose pimples on her arms might be related to the ghostly feelings she now experienced. Maybe, she thought, I am being born again. Maybe that old life, the fast life, disappeared when I died and here I am starting all over again like in reincarnation? I am a great lady and this is my bedchamber and the servants are all downstairs waiting for me to order something.

She dropped the handle of the vacuum and began to pirouette around the room. And twirling slowly with her eyes half-closed she saw the long and filmy nightgown she was wearing. She could feel it clinging to her. It swirled about her fine legs with the gentle night breeze, she heard the night cries of birds beyond the windows, and the fragrance of expensive perfume was everywhere about her. She paused in her progress around the room as she made a decision. Should she order up a bottle of champagne to celebrate the first anniversary of her marriage to the count or should she just have the servants bring up some warm milk flavored ever so slightly with vanilla to make her sleep better? She moved slowly toward the bed. She was composed. Cool. Was there anything neater than this? She spread her arms wide because she was a rich sleep-walker, an heiress worth billions of dollars but afflicted with this terrible disease which caused her to walk in her sleep . . . through the gardens . . . through the great rooms of the castle . . . especially on moonlit nights.

She had a terrific idea. It would be neat to take just five or ten minutes and really do it.

The bed was unmade and the covers thrown back. She approached it and kicked off her shoes. Then slowly, moving just exactly like a real sleep-walker would do, she lowered herself into the bed and pulled up the covers. She closed her eyes tight and thought this was without doubt the neatest thing she had ever done. Here was little ol' Wanda lying in this enormous bed without anybody hassling her . . . without a care in the world. Could you believe?

The sheets were so soft and smooth even though the judge had been sleeping here only a few hours ago. Forget the judge. Get him out of your new world. So-o-o soft . . .

Instinctively, her body began to undulate. Her hips moved very slightly at first and then with gradually increasing intensity. She groaned softly. This was so sensational it should be put down in some diary. She touched herself and thought she might be on the verge of having an orgasm. Would you believe? A solo performance by the late, great Sam's main lady! Right here with all the trimmings. At Clark sometimes, locked in her cell when the loneliness was just too much she did like everybody else did except the old hags. But this was different. Here in this castle everything was different . . .

Chapter Eleven

As Victor Hickock drove his pickup toward the university campus he listened as usual to the cheap radio which came with the vehicle when he bought it. He disliked hard rock music, but despaired of finding anything else on the dial. One of these days he was going to buy a tape cassette, but not until he had more spare cash—of which there was certainly none at the moment. It was unbelievable how expensive it was to support one piece of ancient iron. You could tell the guys who had cars and those who had steady girlfriends. They were both broke. And even without a girlfriend here was a cash-flow problem. So who needed a girl even if she was an equal rights champ and was willing to carry her part of the load?

So no tape cassette yet. First a hundred bucks worth of new shocks then maybe think about such goodies.

The news on the radio was usually so boring it was hard to listen to the same old stuff. There were the troubles in Ireland which went on and on and no one seemed to understand. And there were the troubles in Israel which so many people pretended to understand. And the sports which could be fairly interesting at times.

The news was on the radio now and he was about to switch it off when he heard something that caught his attention. He had failed to hear the beginning, which he regretted instantly.

". . . attorney said during arguments before the court Tuesday that prisoners should at least have a hearing before being sent out of state. Parker was convicted of murder in 1975 for mailing a pipe bomb that killed County Superior Court Judge Harvey Saxon. Parker was transferred to more than half a dozen prisons in three states in a year, his attorney said . . ."

Victor took a deep breath and switched off the radio. He wanted to think. *Killed* a judge?

If someone killed his father it would be awful. He would be the only male Hickock around which was not exactly a tremendous idea when you came right down to it. Sure, the old man was a pain most of the time. He just could not get his act together and most of his ideas were like pre-Civil War, but he guessed he did mean well and he was not always knocking himself out with martinis or bourbon like so many of the other guys' dads were always doing. True, he had that woman who was way too young for him, but as long as he didn't marry her it would probably turn out all right. She would find a younger guy sooner or later. He hoped . . .

Actually, he decided as he drove on to the campus itself, he probably should be proud of the old man. People looked up to him and he was always getting some kind of honor from some group or other. And basically he was a pretty nice guy and there was no denying he was a damn good sailor. Made a boat move in a whisper of wind. And everyone who knew the *Freedom* swore he had some sort of silent engine hidden in the bilge. Yeah, there had been some fun times together with him, smiling like he was sharing a real secret and showing you how to trim the sails and especially the main so it would seem there was hidden power of some kind helping things along. And showing you how to anchor in behind the kelp when it was blowing hard and there was no place else to go. Good times, the two of you sitting down in the cabin with only the kerosene light, scrounging up an old can of Dinty Moore stew because it was the only thing to eat on board . . .

What with college and all there was not so much of that sort of thing now. In fact there was not any. Why? Because of that Jean Pomeroy, that's why. She was always invited and the way she moved in and sort of took charge of things in the galley you would think she was a member of the family. Well, humor the old boy. He's the only father you have and if he wasn't around to hassle you about this and that you would miss him.

That business about killing a judge. That made a guy think.

Lucinda said, "Good morning, Your Honor," as Hickock entered and passed through the outer office of his chambers. He was so preoccupied that he almost neglected to return her greeting; this damn Estervan case was driving him up the wall. Or was it through the floor? Lucinda brought him to a halt just before he entered his chambers. "Your Honor, this gentleman is Terry Undergood from the DA's office—"

Hickock looked up from the floor which seemed to command an increasing amount of his attention these days and saw a young blond man with a wisp of a moustache rise from the chair opposite Lucinda's desk. The young man held out his hand and in taking it Hickock knew only vague displeasure. The hand was limp, soft, and moist. He caught himself thinking the man's hands were almost the trademark of young lawyers these days. Nonsense, Hickock, the moment you categorize others by age then you allow a process of isolation to begin.

Hickock smiled as warmly as he could manage and asked what he could do for the young man.

"I need a warrant, Your Honor. We'd like to go through Boris Estervan's house and of course need to be legal about it."

"Why do you feel the need to go through his house?"

Undergood glanced at Lucinda and asked if they might continue their conversation in Hickock's chambers.

Hickock waved a hand toward his open door. He followed Undergood through the door and he was surprised when he saw him close it behind him. Whose office was this anyway? Was he wrong in feeling this rather shifty young man had usurped a privilege? Damnit, if this conversation was to be so confidential, if there was some kind of security risk in his own secretary hearing it, then he should be formally warned. It should then be *his* choice whether to leave the door opened or closed.

Undergood's voice actually took on a condescending tone when he said, "Your Honor, we think it's possible that Boris Estervan may be part of the Mafia, or at least closely connected to it."

"You *think?* Do you mind telling me why your office has such a notion?"

"At the moment we don't have too much to go on. However, we have reviewed Estervan's tax reports and it seems to us there may be more than just porno theaters, a movie, and perhaps a few whorehouses involved. If you'll sign a warrant we can poke around until we find something—"

"Aren't you a little late? The man has already been tried and found guilty by a jury. It's up to me now to handle the sentencing."

"We think that maybe we can hang him for something more.

If you would have your girl type up a warrant I could take it over to the office with me right now and we could get going by this afternoon."

"And that would be very convenient, would it not?"

"Yes, Your Honor. If you want to put it that way. I hope it's not an inconvenience for you at this hour."

Hickock reached for his half-eyeglasses and wiped them cautiously with the end of his red tie. It was a gesture he employed when he was telling his temper to simmer down. He glanced at Undergood over his glasses several times while trying to decide whether it was his righteous air that so annoyed him or his suit which fit as if it had been tailor-made around him.

"The DA is most anxious to have this warrant activated," Undergood said as if he sensed Hickock needed urging.

"*Is* he now? Do I understand correctly, Mr. . . . sorry, I'm very bad at names, but do I understand that your office has no new hard evidence to support your theory? You have nothing that I can stand here and read . . . some facts rather than your suspicions? You don't know exactly what you're looking for or where it is in his house. So you're just exploring? Well now, I'll do some assuming and that is that you are an attorney and should have been familiar with *Boyd v. U.S.*, not to mention the Fourth Amendment."

"If I may point out, Your Honor, Estervan himself is a fact. He's a proven criminal—"

"That's one of the reasons we have a Fourth Amendment. Boris Estervan is also an American citizen and as such is entitled to the sanctity of his home. We are not a police state and I for one am not going to be party to making one—"

"But this is Boris Estervan we're talking about, Your Honor!"

"I don't give a damn who we're talking about—white, crooked, black, green, red, gay or straight. Unless you come here with some exact evidence that proves Estervan is violating laws other than the one he has already been convicted for, I am not about to help you barge into his house and go poking around, as you put it. How the hell would you like it if a squad of ying-yangs you never saw before in your life arrived at your front door and said get lost we are going through all your effects and that includes your wife's kimono?"

Hickock's voice had risen much more in volume than he

intended and he found it even more ill-matched to Undergood's quasi-simper.

"*Well,* Your Honor . . . I hardly know how to respond. Although I must say that we in the DA's office might find it not overly amusing to be identified by one of our local judges as ying-yangs. We might think it even more odd that a judge of your stature would be defending an individual of Estervan's caliber."

"I'm not defending Boris Estervan. I'm defending the Constitution. You heard me the first time, Mr. Goodbody or whatever your name is . . . when you have hard evidence such as I've described you come back here and if I'm satisfied it complies with the Bill of Rights I'll issue a warrant. And finally I hope you people are smart enough not to try any wire-tapping or bugging. Until then, good day."

Undergood shrugged his shoulders and reached up to smooth his blond hair. "Very well, Your Honor. I do hope the DA will not be too disappointed."

If that guy had a skirt, Hickock thought as his caller went through the door, he would have flounced it. And then he thought, now why the hell did I do that? Why should I stand up for the rights of a no good bum who plays by his own rules and never gave a hoot in hell about anyone else? With the possible exception of his family. And if he actually was one of that notable family loosely known as the Mafia, that was even worse.

But where did you start? If the police were allowed to go around poking through homes just because they *thought* they might find something incriminating then we might as well fold up the show. He remembered *Mapp v. Ohio* in 1961. Same situation almost. The Mapp woman sold pornography to anyone . . . kids, whoever. The police were frustrated for lack of evidence so they broke into her place of business—her house. They found plenty of obscene material, but the Mapp woman took her case all the way to the Supreme Court. Her conviction was dismissed. Evidence gained in an unlawful manner.

Now of course there was bound to be some flak from the DA's office because Goodbody had departed with his nose very much out of joint. It would not be in the least surprising if he planted a few nasty riddles keyed to why Judge Julian Hickock was so soft on a suspected Mafia tribesman. Anything like that could be very damaging when election time came.

Hickock pulled at his long nose and thought that as long as he understood his enemies and kept on guard, survival was at least possible. He understood the DA because he had often seen a reflection of the man's driving ambition in his overeager assistants, and he thought that he understood Estervan because he was also a survivor.

He took his black robe off the hanger, rolled it beneath his arm and started for the outer office. As he passed Lucinda's desk she held up her hand. "I have a call for you."

"I'm late. I've got to be in Butch's court."

"It's Mr. Delgado." She held out the phone.

Hickock hesitated, reached for the phone then changed his mind. "Tell him I'm not here."

"I did. He says he knows you're here because he just met Mr. Undergood down in the lobby."

Hickock retrieved the phone. "All right, Martin, what can I do for you? I warn you I've already had enough aggravation this morning."

"So I understand. And I certainly can't blame you. I don't know why the DA hires so many kooks. I just wanted to interject my congratulations on your attitude. I'm sure my client will be extremely pleased to learn you're willing to take a just view of things. Perhaps I am being premature, but it would not surprise me at all if your campaign's fiscal problems were, so to speak, a thing of the past."

Fast, Hickock thought. Very fast. His expectations had been fulfilled before he was really ready. Within the space of ten or fifteen minutes a whole case could get out of hand unless you stayed right on top of it.

Hickock deliberately kept his voice casual. Maybe it was worthwhile trying to bait these scummy people, go along with them until they hung themselves with a direct bribe to a judge and have a stack of witnesses on hand for testimony. "That's very interesting, Martin. You'll understand that I don't care to discuss such matters over the telephone. But there is one little thing I'd like you to do for me."

"Certainly, Your Honor. Name it."

Was there a cutting sarcasm in the way he said "Your Honor"? "Would you mind advising your client that my friends do not welcome calls from total strangers and are not interested in his philosophical remarks on the concern of judges for their fellow man. And furthermore, if he should attempt to make another such call my disposition will take a very sharp turn for the worse. Do I make myself perfectly clear?"

There was a moment's silence in the phone then Delgado said, "I will so advise my client."

Suddenly Hickock knew a sense of pity for Martin Delgado. He was a rich man and his extraordinary fees were a reflection of his legal skills. But he had sold himself out and the sour part of his surrender was that he knew it.

Shortly after noon Delgado was able to contact Boris Estervan on the telephone. He was still at home waiting for Rosa to finish making his lunch; green peppers and rice, he explained, contributed greatly to a man's longevity and potency. Estervan then discussed the nuances of Rosa's ever-tricky health in far more detail than Delgado cared to hear about. As he listened to a recital of Rosa's impending mastectomy, the discovery of a displaced retina in her left eye, and the ill fit of her new upper dental plate, he concluded that Estervan must be very solidly in love with his rickety Rosa. As the high thin voice continued with even more details of Rosa's deterioration Delgado tipped far back in his heavy leather chair and waggled his expensive shoes in the air. He contemplated their need for a shine and his own wife's insatiable demands in and out of bed. He was reminded that the only reason he could afford the magnificent view from the most luxurious suite of offices in the most prestigious building in the city, not to mention his hedonistic wife, depended on his ability to interest himself in other people's troubles. Or at least appear to be interested. Even in people like Boris Estervan.

Far below, like ants scurrying about their work, were the peons of the city. Royalty, he thought, was up here, high in the sky with a view over the entire metropolis, a view limited only by the green of the suburbs stretching along the horizon. Horn, Delgado, Skinner and Dewitt were doing very well indeed, thank you, and let the surviving senior partner be the first to warn himself that clients like Estervan who paid his fees promptly and without complaint had to be attended. Even if the immediate request or need had no bearing on his main problem. It was the way an imaginative law firm could take on a new client, assist him with some minor difficulty or as simple a matter as incorporating the individual, or perhaps formalizing the adoption of a child. The game began with that initial kick-off whatever it might be, and proceeded relentlessly until the takeover of all affairs was complete. There were always tax matters to be discussed at one hundred and fifty dollars an hour (talk slowly with long pauses to take notes), there were various advisories to be issued both on the telephone and in person regarding the sale or acquisition of property, the collection of insurance from reluctant insuring companies, family difficulties apparently unsolvable between husband and wife, intrusion of undesirable neighbors upon the client's property, a child with a car accident (even a minor fender bender could consume many hours of a lawyer's time if the driver was still a teen-ager), tax-deductible gifts to be carefully prepared against legal challenges by the IRS, and sometimes the most lucrative of all, the preparation of wills for the client and his family. Any lawyer worth his shingle saw to it that if he could not be appointed executor then the blood relative who was chosen for the job was made to feel so innocent of an executor's duties he must forth-with continue employing the firm to do the actual work. And that, in this day of complex inheritance taxes to say nothing of the obligatory sales of properties now useless to the deceased, could demand untold hours of legal work and paper shuffling. At one hundred dollars an hour. Minimum. And then of course if some criminal matter was involved . . . well, shall we say there is a surcharge? And *not* depending on win, lose, or draw.

Therefore, Delgado thought, it was relatively easy to be tolerant of Estervan's high whining voice and the various complaints and fears which were the mark of his almost total insecurity.

". . . whatsamatter with that sonbitchin' judge?" Estervan wanted to know. "Did you tell him we are willing to make things easy for him if he does for me? Whatsamatter with him he don't like his job or something? He's got a rich uncle? Whatsamatter he don't give with some decision? Christ Almighty, it's drivin' me crazy with this waiting bit. I can't get nothing done. I got to know where I stand before I make some important decisions . . . I mean how the hell can I plan something for next year when I don't know if I'll be in the can or sitting on my ass in Mexico or Florida or like that? What does he say? Christ Almighty, he must have *some* idea what he's goin' to do by this time."

Delgado adopted his most conciliatory tone, the suave, steadfast manner that had captured the total faith of hundreds of clients. Not for him to appear concerned if things were going badly. If a situation turned out to be a loser there was plenty of time to shake one's head and appear disheartened at the unfairness of the judicial system.

"Julian is a strange man," Delgado said carefully. "He keeps himself very unapproachable."

"You call him Julian? What are you, brothers or something? You call him Julian, you must be able to tell him to call off his dogs."

"He's deliberating. I would guess that he is beginning to see the light. An incident occurred this morning which might confirm his changes of attitude." Delgado was always careful to use the words "guess" and "might" or sometimes "just might" in any dialogue with a client. It accented the positive without risking the later necessity of eating one's words. It was a science known as waffling.

He told Estervan about his chance meeting with Undergood, a young lawyer from the district attorney's office and added, "I would guess we might take our judge's refusal of a search warrant to indicate he *may* be swinging around to our side. Of course one can't be certain—"

"Look, how about you name a figure, you know like they did in that book they made a movie out of . . . about the godfather? It was a crock, but the idea of making an offer he can't refuse is not all that bad. How about you start with a hundred grand? It would be worth it. I'm too old to spend any more time in the can. My arthritis would kill me."

"I would guess Julian Hickock would not settle for any sum so offered. Furthermore I would be disbarred and probably sent away myself for even attempting to bribe a judge. Now, if Julian won't take money for his campaign chest, even given anonymously, his feelings might be influenced if he knew we were giving, say a hundred thousand, to some worthy cause . . . say the Boy Scouts, or the symphony, or something of the sort. You'd also get a tax deduction. If he was made properly aware of the donation and its effect on whatever charity if they did *not* receive it and he still refused then he would be denying funds to some worthy cause. In that kind of a set-up he just might discover a new conscience."

"Suppose I give away that kind of money and he still sends me away? Where am I then except out a hundred grand and in the can to boot? I don't much care for the odds."

"That's the chance you have to take. What you've got to understand is that Julian Hickock is no ordinary judge. I had my whole staff working on him and they couldn't find a spot on his record. We uncovered the girlfriend finally, but there's not much we can do with that. After all, he is a widower and there is nothing unusual about a man in that position having an affair."

"You sure she's not a hooker? Maybe there's something we can lay on her."

"Absolutely not. She's very respectable and she is gainfully employed. And while we are on the subject, Boris, I'm obliged to give you a piece of advice."

"That's what I'm paying you for. I tell you right now I don't like the smell of things with this crackpot judge. He must be one of those holy God-Bless-America Moral Majority guys and I don't trust them."

"Just because we furnished you with the girl's name and phone number did not mean you should contact her."

"How'd you know I called her?"

"We know and I'd suggest that your call was a mistake. For your own good may I beg you to consult with me before you make any more moves like that? It's very difficult for me to work on your behalf and then find out through a third party that you've done something on your own. The very least that can happen is I wind up with egg on my face."

"All I did was just pass on a little good advice to her dumb boyfriend. Since I can't talk direct to him I thought she'd pass it on. If he had a wife I would have done the same thing . . ."

Delgado sighed as he looked over the vast pincushion of buildings below his windows. Estervan's high whine was beginning to get on his nerves. How could he explain Hickock's code of ethics to a man like Estervan? "The point is, Boris, the girl is not a part of Hickock's official life. I suspect he does not take happily to anyone, let alone you, intruding on his more private interests. So please, in the interests of our present problem, do *not* do that again."

Delgado hesitated. A question had haunted him from the

very beginning of his long association with Boris Estervan and he had not yet found the nerve to ask it. This morning's episode had brought it bouncing once more to the surface. It was a question he must risk asking even if it offended his client.

He decided to be as casual as possible about it since it was equivalent to asking a total stranger if he had a venereal disease. "And by the way, Boris, we've always shared openly in our relations with each other because we trust each other implicitly. You simply cannot keep any secrets from your attorney if he thinks it would have any effect on what he tries to do for you . . ."

Delgado told himself that he could hardly make a more diplomatic approach.

"Okay, what's bugging you, pal?"

"I must ask you, in all confidence, of course . . . do you have or have you ever *had,* any connection with the so-called Mafia?"

Delgado heard what sounded like a high cackle in the phone. Supposedly, he hoped, Estervan was trying to chuckle.

"Of course not. I got no use for them bastards. Who needs 'em?"

"Thank you, Boris." Delgado closed his eyes for a moment. "I am relieved."

There followed a long silence, then Delgado heard a whining so high in pitch it sounded almost falsetto.

"Okay, you listen to me now, pal. I know how guys like that operate. They got ideals. When you meet a crazy man you got to go a little nuts yourself if you want to negotiate. There was a character back in the east part of the state owned the local newspaper and he was giving one of my places a bad time with one of them clean-up campaigns. Okay? So we called on him and told him to stop it because it was very bad for our business. Know what he said? Get lost, I have my principles. So we offered him five grand for a thousand subscriptions to his little rag which had a total circulation of two thousand. Told him he could throw the subscriptions in the trash barrel as far as we were concerned. Know what he did? He said no, he thought our little business was bad for the moral image of his little hick town. So what do we do? We buy his little rag for ten times what it's worth, ten thousand. We sell it back to him for five thousand. His ideals are satisfied and so are his principles and he don't feel like writing any more uncomplimentary editorials about our little business. Everybody is happy and I'm sure we can do the same thing with this Judge Hickock. We just have to make it easy for him to be realistic, you follow me?"

"Yes, Boris. I do follow you. If it were some other judge there is one chance in a thousand it might work, but with Hickock I don't think we'd stand a prayer if we offered him a billion. We would only make things worse."

"Then what am I supposed to do? Pray?"

"I'll do that for you."

"You have a better connection than I have. You keep me informed and if he doesn't see my way pretty soon we'll just have to go hard ball. For a lousy five grand I can have him put away—"

"Don't talk like that. Don't even *think* like that." Delgado was more frightened than surprised. How far should he go along with people like this? "You don't seem to understand, Boris. You have been found guilty by a jury of committing a felony—"

"I don't give a fuck what the jury decided! I didn't know them girls were underage. I wasn't even there when they were hired or photographed—"

"We've been through all that a hundred times. You just can't turn back the clock on a jury."

Estervan's voice rose until it became a screech. "I got a lot goin' on now . . . lots of enterprises and I can't run 'em the way they should be from the can. I don't care how many arms and legs I have to break I *ain't goin'*, understand? Now you work it out or I will. It's my ass and by God I'm going to take care of it!"

Delgado heard a click. Would he, he asked himself, still represent Boris Estervan if he were on trial for murdering a judge . . . ?

Chapter Twelve

Martin Delgado had no more hung up his telephone and switched off the device which recorded all conversations with his more contentious clients than another communication was established between two citizens of the city.

After waiting through several unanswered signals (the empty sound was so lonelylike, Wanda thought, you can always tell when a number is not going to answer), she finally captured a woman named Nancy, who kept a phone by her bed.

It was well past noon when Wanda said, "Hi, Nancy. Are you ready for this? It's Wanda Usher in the flesh. Just calling to see how things are in Glocca Morra."

Wanda had made up her opening line and rehearsed it several times before she was finally able to use it. She had only to change the salutation for each call.

"Well, well . . . when did you get loose? I am still half-asleep. Where are you, what's doing?"

"I'm considering several job offers. I'm here. Playing it straight, know what I mean?"

"You're telling me you're leaving the life?"

Wanda was pleased to note that Nancy sounded incredulous. She sure had her attention.

Nancy was saying, "You better give that some more thought, Wanda. Things are pretty good these days. I never saw so many johns and all loaded. Of course lots of Japs, they have the money you know, and lots of foreigners like English and Germans . . . you name them, honey. Are you coming to see us? It's good to hear your voice."

Sometimes, Wanda remembered, Nancy could be a little vague and get awful mixed up in her thinking. She was a speed crank. It didn't make no difference what kind of amphetamine—whites, crosses, Quaaludes, you name it—Nancy was always ready for a trip. But she did stay away from the hard stuff. And she is certainly a friend, Wanda thought. Her and Nancy's friends in the life must stretch from coast to coast the way they moved around, but you all hung together somehow until one day somebody just disappeared. Nancy, who used to work the same block and sometimes right together as a team, was real special. She must be almost thirty now and she would flip if she could see her old pal sitting here on this enormous bed just taking it easy like there was no tomorrow.

"Listen, hon, I got a different last name now, Raleigh if anybody happens to ask you, but I still can't come to see you for a while yet because I'll be back in the can if I get caught even walking down Virginia Street. Or anywhere around there, know what I mean?"

"You're on some kind of probation." Nancy said flatly—a statement rather than a question. "As soon as it's over will you come by to say hello?"

"You know you can depend on little ol' Wanda."

They discussed their looks and figures for several minutes. Nancy complained of a weight problem. Wanda claimed her skin had become terribly dry at Clark. Wanda asked about Gertrude Collins, Trisha, Hillary, Stella, and Cecily, all of them working girls. Then she inquired about the welfare of Harvey, Big Mack, Pee-Wee Rogers and Pete the Indian who pimped for them or were just boyfriends. She was told most of them had disappeared from the local scene and then they got to speaking about the death of that nice guy Sam. They did not mention Deidre.

"It isn't at all the same here, honey," Nancy lamented. "Maybe there's more money around and the cops still blow hot and cold as you never know where you are, but it just isn't the same. You would not believe the new girls on the street. Some aren't old enough to have real tits and they don't know a condom from a rucksack, which some of them carry right along with them when they're working the street. It's unreal. We got females wandering around in Mother Hubbard shawls, lumberjack boots, no make-up at all and God only knows when they last had a bath. They got no idea of money. Some of them would take on a snake for five dollars. Talk about kinkies and freaks. You would not believe."

They covered every detail of the local scene until Wanda felt they had reestablished their relationship soundly enough for her to ask the special question. "Nancy. Do you know how to get a message to Manuel?"

There was a long silence before Nancy acknowledged that she had heard the question. Finally she said, "Why do you want to talk to him?"

"Maybe I don't. Maybe I do. It's just something I have on my mind."

"Okay. I'll see if I can find out if he's alive or dead. Sometimes those guys don't last very long."

Wanda agreed and they fell to talking about a new diet combined with exercises guaranteed to take weight off the hips and put it on the breasts.

Long after she had said " 'bye" and "see you around" Wanda stood uncertainly by the telephone. There was just so much to think about and the time to get a handle on it was now. Like don't lose the ballgame around here which could happen if every little detail is not accounted for. Like okay, you make up the judge's bed so he won't know there's been any person in it. Then you vacuum around the bedroom here and there so it looks real neat. Then you go through the drawers in the chiffonier and what do you find besides shirts and socks and stuff like that? A rod. It's loaded and so heavy you can hardly hold it out at full arm's length like they do in the movies. You rehearse. You point it at the pillow where the judge's head would be and say "Bang!" Then "bang-bang-bang!" again while you pump some more bullets into the rest of him. And there he is lying there just as plain as if he really was and he is wringing his hands and saying, "Please, Wanda! Oh please don't kill me, Wanda! I know in my heart that you are not and never have been an unfit mother and I hereby swear what I done was wrong. And I will do everything possible to get Deidre back to you" . . . and on and on.

You let him stew and get his eyes full of tears for as long as you please then you let him have it. The first one right between the eyes. Wanda the markswoman. Wanda the unfit mother in the opinion of certain people who are now extremely dead and don't know it.

She left the front hallway and went to the living room where she stood with her back to the fireplace. She found it easy to pretend there was a fire burning behind her—big yule logs like in some castle.

Okay, so let's really face it, Wanda. Wasting the judge is not going to be enough because it'll be over so quick. So he's scared for a few minutes at most? Then he don't know nothing. Dead people don't know they're dead. You're standing there in his bedroom getting your jollies just watching him die and right away the ballgame is over. Except for you. You're standing there beside the bed with his gun in your hand which is out of ammunition because it's all in the judge. And then what happens? You don't forget to wipe your fingerprints off the rod and put it down beside him so it looks like he done it to himself? No way. Any dumb cop will know the rod had been fired from some distance and soon enough he is going to know you have been working for the judge right in this house and right away he is looking at you. So okay, you done it in self-defense because the judge was trying to rape you. Maybe you could describe all the terrible things he demanded you submit to, awful kinky acts—but you refused and there was a fight and you don't remember how it happened, but there he was all of a sudden, dead. He thought he could take advantage of you just because once upon a time you were a working girl. And some psychiatrist could say she was in such a state of shock at the idea of her body being violated when it had suffered so much all her life that she was nuts at the time this thing happened. She was so nuts she didn't have no idea what she or he did and therefore she should be given treatment and especially fresh air. And all the time you can be bawling like a loony over what you done because you could never bring yourself to hurt a fly.

Still there was something wrong about just knowing the judge was plain dead. He has got to suffer like you did. He has got to see *his* life explode and then go around on his hands and knees trying to pick up the pieces. Look. Anybody can just die. But if you bust their hopes forever then you got something real heavy going as who should know better?

The thing to do was not get impatient. Play it very cool. The right time would come sooner or later and then little ol' Wanda Usher formerly of Winthrop, Tennessee would hit the front pages everywhere. You better believe.

That evening Julian Hickock was slumped in his favorite heavy leather chair at 1011 reading contentedly of life at sea in Nelson's time. Stomping the quarter deck of his man-of-war Commodore Hickock had just ordered the decks cleared for action and heard the drummers beat to quarters when he also heard the telephone ringing in the front hall. Commodore Hickock sighed and sheathed his saber as he rose reluctantly and walked to the phone. It was Butch Goldstein, who Hickock decided was in much too jolly of voice for comfort. There was that good-old-reliable-friend manner that foretold trouble.

"First the bad news. I'm so immobile I won't be able to make band practice Saturday night. Doctor says the Cavemen will have to get along without the world's hottest clarinet."

"We'll never recover from such a setback."

"The good news is that you'll have another week warming my bench."

"You can't do that to me. There's got to be some kind of a law against it."

"What's the beef? Aren't you enjoying yourself?"

"I hate to make decisions. And in your court I have to make fifty or more a day. It's bad for my digestion. I've about decided that I don't know how to deal with the kind of people who come into your place—"

"They're all sweethearts. Where is your love for humanity? You will never meet nicer people than you will in my court. They are all innocent of any wrongdoing. You just ask them."

"I have."

"I don't know how you guys are going to get through 'Sleepy Lagoon' without me. Try to stay in tune for a change."

"Just worry about getting yourself back in a black robe. It may surprise you to learn I have other things to do."

Actually, Hickock realized on the following afternoon, he was beginning to like working the municipal court. He sensed that he was getting into the rhythm of the environment and he liked the pace which was so much faster and more colorful than in his own territory. Now he found himself absorbed in listening to a Mrs. Digby, an elderly lady who was pointing her cane at two black youths. She identified them as the pair who had mugged her on the previous Saturday night. Her face was badly bruised and one eye was still swollen almost shut. She said there were bruises all over her body. According to her story she had been to the library reading about stamp collecting, which was her hobby. She stayed until closing time and then walked to the bus stop, which was only half a block away. Suddenly she was hit hard from behind and was propelled into the bushes which fringed the library grounds. Fully aware of what was happening she had clung to her purse which she now admitted had been a mistake. She was hit repeatedly about the face and kicked when she was finally brought to ground. She was called a number of filthy names as one assailant held her while the other ripped open her purse and took out the twenty-two dollars she knew was there. They kicked her several more times before they departed, angry that she was not carrying more money.

John Exeter was on hand to defend the youths and Hickock watched carefully as he uncoupled his lanky frame and hitched his pants up to cover what had been an inch view of his bare belly. He was wearing his usual red smock coat and it appeared that his hair and beard had not been groomed for days. Yet anyone who underestimated him, Hickock had already learned, was making a bad mistake.

Exeter shuffled to the witness stand, batted at an invisible fly in the air, then shook his head forlornly. He pointed at the two black youths who stood defiantly near the defense desk. Hickock thought that if they were actually guilty then they certainly showed no remorse.

Exeter addressed the lady in his most tolerant and kindly voice. "Mrs. Digby," he said, "are you sure that those two young men were the ones who mugged you?"

"Of course I'm sure." Mrs. Digby banged her cane lightly against the floor to emphasize her conviction.

"Can you tell me what your attackers were wearing when the incident took place? Can you tell me exactly if they were wearing their shirt tails in or out, or were they wearing tennis shoes or boots, or Levi's or slacks?"

"Well, one of them had a white T-shirt."

"But you don't know which one?"

"Objection," the attorney from the prosecutor's office called. Today she was the same very young woman Hickock still knew only as "Debbie," and he was reminded once more of his leaky memory for names. Damnit, he would learn and retain her last name if he accomplished nothing else this day. Her astuteness deserved his respect. "The defense is putting words into the victim's mouth," she said.

"Sustained."

Exeter bowed his head and said, "Do you know which one of these men was wearing a white T-shirt?"

"No. What difference does it make? Those are dangerous young men and they should be punished."

And I agree, Hickock thought secretly. He had always reserved a special place in his judicial thinking for muggers even though they never came to his higher court. He knew that if they attacked elderly people he would not have been at all against hanging them up by the thumbs both before and after their maximum prison sentences. He knew it was a barbaric way of thinking, and he was somewhat ashamed of his unequivocal stand on muggings but in his heart he believed they were the worst sort of barbarians and should be treated in a language they understood. And yet there were some individuals who held no fear of punishment and for some of those it could even be an inducement.

John Exeter scratched at his beard as if totally confused. "Mrs. Digby," he said softly, "can you tell the court which one of the young men had an Afro haircut?"

Mrs. Digby hesitated. "No . . ."

"But one of then did?"

"Yes."

"Did your attackers take their time or were they in a hurry?"

Hickock noted that neither of the young men now had an Afro haircut. Nor were they wearing T-shirts. Both were well-groomed and wearing identical blue shirts.

"Did your attackers take their time or were they hurried about it?"

"They were in a hurry. They said so."

"Then it is correct for me to assume the whole regrettable episode took less than five minutes? Perhaps even less than three minutes?"

"I don't know. I don't carry a watch, or those people would have taken it."

"You are entitled to that assumption, Mrs. Digby, but not to the assumption that every pair of black young Americans who happen to be on the street were your attackers."

Exeter paused and looked up at Hickock. "Your Honor, if I may address the court directly and thus save us all some time, Mrs. Digby had an unfortunate encounter in the dark with two male individuals. The total time of the attack was undoubtedly less than five minutes. She cannot say what they were wearing and she cannot identify one from the other even with such an outstanding feature as an Afro haircut. It would seem very remarkable indeed then that in the dark, surrounded by bushes which must have made the area nearly black, that without being able to see anything else the lady did manage to see two black faces with such clarity that after four days she is able to so positively identify them as these two young Americans. If I may suggest, Your Honor, this case should be dismissed."

Hickock studied the faces of the youths hoping to discover at least a hint of regret in their eyes. Nothing. Damnit all, these two characters were obviously guilty and were confident they had got away with it. Was this sort of affair the reason justice was always portrayed as blindfolded and guessing at the scales. The police had picked them up thirty minutes after the attack on Mrs. Digby and in the same neighborhood. They were trying to hot-wire a car when apprehended and the total sum of money in their combined possession at the time was twenty-two dollars. The police had not as yet learned of the recent mugging in the area because the terrified and injured Mrs. Digby was over an hour in finding help. Had the patrolmen known they might have checked the suspects' fists more closely and their clothing for signs of blood, but as it was they were hauled in only for attempted theft. The evidence on the mugging, as John Exeter so easily demonstrated, had been purely circumstantial.

Hickock removed his half-eyes and looked long at the young men. They were not powerful, but rather frail of physique. He remembered the cocky little bounce to their walk, the go-to-hell swagger intended to inform the world how tough they were. Their eyes troubled him . . . he saw only contempt for himself, for their victim, for everyone surrounding them and even for John Exeter, who worked in their behalf. I am their enemy, he thought. They hate all I stand for, and a part of the reason is because it does not require much thinking to hate. Exeter had identified them as young Americans and he was right—they were the poor and twisted of the black ghetto and their numbers in this land of supposed equal opportunity were becoming astronomical. Their eyes said they had been cheated of a life that had barely begun. Their eyes said we are pure hatred, we are going to rob and beat and kill because as far as we can see that is the only way we are going to get our share of what there is out there, whatever it is—beyond the ghetto. Their eyes said of course we are going to do it again and next time we may throw in a rape if things look right. There is not one damned thing you can do to us unless you can *prove* beyond a reasonable doubt that we did it. And we know that as the laws now stand that is damned difficult. We are this country's number one problem.

Hickock became disheartened with himself and with the system when he took a deep breath and was obliged to say, "Dismissed."

Although he did his utmost, Hickock had trouble dismissing the case of Mrs. Digby from his thoughts. He caught himself only half-listening to a man who had failed to pay his business tax, followed by two other liars who had been arrested for driving without a license because they had "lost" them. There was no record of either man ever having one. Hickock kept seeing Mrs. Digby being helped down from the witness stand by John Exeter of all people, and then being turned over to her daughter, who escorted her painful progress toward the exit.

The problem with the black youths was upsetting enough, but the almost total lack of concern in the system for all *victims* of violent crime made him deeply angry. All of the protective devices of the law were designed to protect the criminal and the victims were left licking their own wounds. The criminal was provided a free lawyer to plead his case; the victim usually had to pay someone. As if they had not paid enough, he thought. Victims of violent crime rarely learned what the law did with those who had made their lives so miserable unless they were able to attend the actual trial and sentencing. Even worse, they were never informed about the actions of the various parole boards and so were unaware they might be free. If the victim had appeared in court and testified against them as Mrs. Digby had just done, they never knew when the newly released convict might return for his revenge.

Hickock knew that his own state had funded a small aid-to-victims program . . . something like a million and a half dollars, a tiny fraction of the budget. At the same time the legislature, through some Alice in Wonderland wisdom, had appropriated one hundred and twenty thousand dollars for tobacco products for prisoners. Poor Mrs. Digby. Running a very poor second to a can of snuff.

Hickock called for the next case which was that of a man named Farraday who Hickock began to suspect was in dire need of mental help if he was not planning a revolution. And it struck Hickock that it was a very healthy thing that you were allowed to plot all the revolutions you desired in this country as long as you did not assemble enough weapons to launch a successful revolt. It seemed that Mr. Farraday, a soft-spoken apologetic man, was ready and able to carry out at least a minor coup.

Acting on a neighbor's complaint that Farraday was endangering his life, the police had obtained a search warrant and found cached in the Farraday basement six machine guns, twenty submachine guns, twenty-one cases of dynamite, two bazookas, five automatic rifles, two antitank guns, forty bayonets and one hundred five pistols of various calibers and design. There was ammunition for every weapon and enough to fight a major battle.

In his quiet way Mr. Farraday appeared to be perplexed at his arrest and the charge of reckless endangerment. He wanted to know what had happened to the sacred right of Americans to bear arms as guaranteed by the Constitution just like the National Rifle Association kept saying.

"You are embellishing the Second Amendment," Hickock said. "The Constitution does not endorse anyone's right to bear arms even for lawful purposes. The Second Amendment which you have twisted to your convenience only guarantees that *Congress* will not take a direct hand in any confiscation of arms. It specifies that control will be left to the police. Surprised, Mr. Farraday? Perhaps you have been misled. Now where do you buy your arsenal?"

"You pick it up here and there. You just have to shop around a little. Surplus stores, hock shops, junkyards . . . you never know when you might come across a jewel."

"Like a little old antitank gun?"

"Right. Just now I'm looking for a small howitzer."

"What do you plan to do with it?"

Farraday seemed surprised at the question. "I need it for my collection."

Hickock leaned far forward because Farraday spoke so softly he was having trouble hearing him. "Let me ask you something, Mr. Farraday. If an intercontinental ballistic missile came on the market would you be interested in acquiring one?"

"Why heavens, yes! But then I'm not sure I could afford to build a silo."

"How about an atomic bomb?"

"Well now, that's something *else*. I didn't know there were any available. I can't imagine anything I would rather add to my collection."

When Hickock thought he had recovered at least some degree of solemnity he looked down at Mr. Farraday. Here was a real puzzler and Farraday's utter sincerity was no help. He was sitting quietly now, his hands folded in his lap, his head moving with birdlike alertness as his eyes examined each individual in the courtroom. He did not appear to be in the least frightened or even worried.

His puzzlement is my puzzlement, Hickock thought. He had shown paid-in-full receipts for every item in his basement. There was no record of his ever having used any of the weapons.

Hickock softly whistled "Buttermilk Sky" to himself, one of his better piano renditions. He suddenly saw himself as if from a distance, as if he was merely one interested spectator. Here was a man, structurally elevated above his fellow men, supposedly dignified in appearance, hopefully not swollen with his own importance as he picked a bit of lint from his black robe; here was this normally stable individual caught whistling a sentimental ditty that had nothing whatsoever to do with the immediate environment let alone the matter at hand.

He became aware that he was actually enjoying himself. Only war itself, Hickock thought, could be a crazier enterprise than what had so engaged citizen Farraday. We put ordinary lunatics in the nut farm while other men are encouraged to destroy irreplaceable forests and pollute every last moving body of water in the country.

Hickock tried to calculate how many man-hours Mr. Farraday might have devoted to his collection, and he wished that he had the gall to ask him how much money he had invested in a hobby which he did not intend to employ in its full potential.

The key, he decided, was that there just was no true logic in this affair. And the key was that the law was at times only half-logical itself and rarely made provision for the formless nature of human instability. At least the law lived and was thus flexible to a degree. The ultimate confusion lay in its long history of cross-breeding which invited odd interpretations. Yet in the case of Mr. Farraday the law was reasonably clear. The man could not be tried for a crime he had not committed, nor for a transgression he might have been contemplating. Unlike a similar situation in many countries, Mr. Farraday was not *guilty* of anything. The law also said that it was against the law for anyone to confiscate his private property or even hold it as hostage unless he owed money on it. Note the Puritan bow to commercialism there, judge. And if on some excuse, a species of court order could be devised which would undoubtedly call on a handy city ordinance for support, then perhaps Mr. Farraday could be forced to move his tempting collection to some remote site in the countryside. Check, but far from checkmate. If Farraday had as much intelligence as he seemed to have he would find a lawyer and insist that all the potentially dangerous collections of dynamite such as were standard at any construction site in the city be likewise removed.

So what is your verdict, oh jury of one? You can't send a nice man like Mr. Farraday off to the slammer because the charge of "reckless endangerment" is so far only his neighbor's opinion of something that might happen. Yet if you let him go back to his lethal playthings he may one day blow up the neighborhood whether he wants to or not. And you, as the prime protector of his playthings, are not going to feel very good about yourself.

"Mr. Farraday," Hickock said, "can you give me some idea, even a general idea, what might happen if your house caught fire and the flames reached your basement?"

"It would be disastrous."

"Why? Specifically, what do you think would happen?"

"I would probably lose my whole collection."

"Ah . . ." Hickock breathed softly. It had been a long time, he thought, since he had seen a hedgehog. Never mind that Mr. Farraday might lose his own life or that he might blow his neighbors to a considerable altitude. His collection would be no more.

"Do I take it then, Mr. Farraday, that you do not feel any responsibility toward your neighbors' welfare?"

"Oh sure. I guess they are okay people, but I can do what I like with my own property. This is a free country."

Hickock thought of his little boat and how his father had pondered for months over her name. As a man holding quite a different and now old-fashioned concept of the word "freedom," he had finally decided to bestow it on his most precious creation. This was the 1980s and here was Mr. Farraday, smug as could be, using his so-called freedom as a bandwagon and be damned to how much noise it made en route. I take care of me and you look after yourself.

"You are correct, Mr. Farraday, this is a free country and you are free to go. I wish there was some legal way for this court to restrain your enthusiasm for toys that can kill, but the law does not provide any."

Hickock nodded at the prosecuting attorney and handed the complaint down to the clerk. He said, "Dismissed," and hoped some of his frustration was evident. I am here, he thought unhappily, to judge the individual within the system, not the system. "Next case?"

It was John Exeter again, now with a pair of prostitutes. On his advice they had pleaded guilty to the charge of soliciting. Hickock tried to assess them as they moved to a position almost directly below him. They stood flanking Exeter and Hickock asked Debbie the prosecutor if she would like to put them on the witness stand. She smiled enigmatically and said since the girls had already pleaded guilty she thought it might waste the court's time.

John Exeter said, "These ladies have pleaded guilty but, Your Honor, I suggest the charge be amended to soliciting without a license. It is true they *were* soliciting, but not for the purposes of prostitution."

Hickock saw a faint smile touch the faces of the girls. They were both barely twenty, he supposed, but their eyes were old and instinct told him this was far from the first time they had been before a court. Both were blonds. They were certainly not beautiful to look on, and the girl named Jody bore the unfortunate suggestion of a harelip. Still, they had made an obvious effort to look their best in spite of the ill-fitting jumpsuits issued to all occupants of the city jail.

Were they smiling or smirking? Impossible to tell. He warned himself not to consider them as professionals until they had been heard and he had examined their past records. All right, Mr. Exeter, he thought, I'll play along with you and see where this leads. Up to a point. "What do you mean," he asked John Exeter, "by saying not guilty to the charge as defined?"

"May it please the court, these ladies had no intention of selling anything of a physical nature."

Hickock looked directly at the girls. He was annoyed with Exeter's domination of the moment and he wanted to shoulder him aside. "What were you up to then that obviously made the police believe otherwise?"

The shorter of the two girls said something, but her reply

was so near a whisper Hickock failed to hear it. He asked her to repeat herself.

"We were selling insurance," she said demurely.

Exeter pulled on his beard and glanced benignly on his charges. "That is the truth, Your Honor. These ladies are both qualified saleswomen. Here are the certificates they received on graduation from school."

Exeter handed two diplomas to the clerk who passed them up to Hickock. They were fancy enough, he thought, with all the proper scroll work. "The Elite School of Insurance hereby declares Jody Baker to be a graduate bona fide salesperson. Having completed the required course of study . . ."

There were two illegible signatures along the bottom of the diploma and a red seal. The second document carried the name of Ginger Hattrup.

"Are these your real names?" Hickock inquired.

Both girls nodded.

"Where is this school located? There seems to be no address on these documents."

"In San Francisco," Ginger said.

"And there's one in Boston," Jody said with true alma mater spirit.

"How long is the course of training?"

Hickock was not surprised when Exeter broke in to the exchange "Your Honor, if I may say so, that question is not pertinent to the case. These ladies were arrested on a false charge and their activities prior to that time cannot . . . excuse me sir, should not be the concern of the court at present."

Hickock saw the gleam in Exeter's eyes even through his nearly opaque glasses. And he thought, we both know damn well these girls are hookers and what we wish so secretly is that they had never been brought in here. We are both on the same side, but we must maintain the hypocrisy of assuming these two enterprising businesswomen are a menace to society and should therefore be severely chastised for their sinful behavior.

He consulted the police arrest report again. "Let me get this straight. You were both selling insurance on the corner of First and Virginia at ten o'clock at night? Isn't that rather an odd hour to be doing business?"

Ginger said, "That's the best time, Your Honor. You see, a lot of our clients are so busy during the day hours they have no time to listen. So we just make our pitch in the evening."

"What kind of insurance do you sell?"

"Any kind. Except life. Mostly casualty . . . on your car, or your valuables, like that, you know. Like if you break a leg or your TV set catches fire . . . you know what I mean?"

"I assume you take the first premium in cash?"

"That's customary, Your Honor."

Debbie, the prosecutor, stood up and broke her bemused silence. "Your Honor, I have here two complaints from the Better Business Bureau. They allege these girls have taken sums ranging from thirty to fifty dollars and given worthless receipts on nonexistent insurance companies in return. I agree they are here on the wrong charge. It should be fraud."

"Did those who bought policies receive any reward other than a receipt?"

"Yes. In both cases acts of prostitution were performed."

"Wait a minute. Were two separate transactions involved here? After the policies were sold did the customer negotiate and agree to pay an additional sum of money for any service provided by these girls?"

"Apparently not, Your Honor," the prosecutor admitted.

"Absolutely not," John Exeter insisted.

Hickock noticed that both Ginger and Jody were shaking their heads in the negative. Here is one for you, Butch Goldstein. You unravel this one. "Do I understand then that *after* the so-called policies were sold certain relations developed between purchaser and salesperson?"

Exeter said, "That is true, Your Honor. And I would suggest those relations are none of our business. Whatever happened after the sale of the policies was given freely to the customer."

"Were there any witnesses to these later relations? I can find nothing specific in the police report. Are there any witnesses in the courtroom who would care to testify in this matter?"

Hickock surveyed the public area of the courtroom hopefully but he saw no response. There was only a silence supported by the purring of the air-conditioning system. He asked the clerk for any records on Ginger and Jody. He would like to find some kind of verdict that would seem something less than a total mockery.

He found the rap sheets on both girls confirmed his first impressions. He counted twelve arrests for Jody and seven for Ginger, all for engaging in or encouraging acts of prostitution. They had left a trail of convictions from Boston to San

Francisco, San Diego, Denver and Seattle. They were true pros and he thought it was a shame their resourcefulness could not be directed into some other endeavors. Yet their present arrest and detention in the city jail was wrong. The police had erred in making the wrong charge and the girls knew it. There was, as yet, no law against free sex "between willing adults" as the phrasing went, and there was no law against soliciting for insurance on the street or anywhere else. The only illegal aspect of the transaction was fraud and the girls knew those who had bought their "policies" were extremely unlikely to appear against them. Checkmate.

Hickock pulled on his nose and looked down at the girls. "I am going to dismiss the charge of prostitution against you for lack of evidence," he said as solemnly as he could manage. "I will fine you twenty-five dollars each for soliciting without a business license. As soon as you are released from jail I suggest you leave town. I assure you the next time you are caught selling phony insurance and giving your customers a bonus on their premium payment the police will know that the charge will be fraud and I will see to it that you will go away for a much longer time than you would for prostitution."

Ginger and Jody smiled. John Exeter's eyes were smiling behind his clouded glasses, and even Debbie the prosecutor was compelled to smile. Hickock, so as not to betray himself, declared a recess.

Chapter Thirteen

Two days later Wanda stood a little back from the living room window at 1011. From this vantage she could easily watch the street below without being conspicuous herself and she found the situation pleasing. She had once been to the aquarium in San Diego and she had been entranced with the notion that the fish were looking at her rather than the other way around. Here it was the same. She was looking out on another world, all so peaceful and secure.

She especially watched the end of the street because she was waiting for Victor. It was already four o'clock and he had said he would be out of his last class by three-thirty and then intended to come directly home.

And sure enough there he was, green pickup and all. Hello Mr. Gorgeous. Welcome back to 1011 where little ol' Wanda is waiting faithfully like one of the local housewives—with her chores all done and pretty dress all rigged for the evening.

She waited, counting the seconds because her timing had to be just right. As the green pickup slowed, then turned into the driveway, she let herself out the front door and started down the steps from the porch. As Victor turned off the engine she walked past the pickup and halted. "Well, hello," she said, maintaining her hundred-dollar smile. And she was careful to look surprised.

"Hi."

"Hey, this *is* nice. I just happened to finish my work as you drove up. Did you learn a lot today?"

"I learned how dumb I am. Anthropology."

"I'm not even sure what it is." And that's for damn sure, she thought. "Is it some kind of a bug maybe?"

They both laughed and she started to walk away. Not too fast, she reminded herself.

"Don't go yet."

"Why not? I'm all through for the day. I think maybe I'll do a little studying myself tonight. Mrs. Millington, she's my landlady, she has this book on calligraphy see? And I just have always loved writing like that . . . so pretty and elegant, y'know what I mean? I think maybe that would be a very good thing for me to do professionally, writing out invitations to weddings and funerals and banquets and such and I could work right at home. Just work and get paid so much per word and nobody bugging me."

"It sounds great . . ." Victor hesitated. She saw that he was staring at her blouse, which she had left unbuttoned at the top—the first three buttons, just down to the cleavage, just enough to give him a hint at what Sam always claimed were the most beautiful boobs in the world.

"I suppose you're going home," Victor said.

"Yes. I'll have to wait a while for the right bus, but it's a nice afternoon. It's really one of my favorite hours of the day, things all sort of laid back, y'know what I mean. People are sort of through for the day and they all get mellow and, well, don't you think that this is sort of a romantic time of day . . . a time for dreaming like we talked about when you drove me home the first time—"

"Would you like me to drive you home?"

"Oh, Vic, please don't think I was *hinting*. No thanks. No, it's too much trouble for you, I can take the bus with no problem. Really."

"Come on. Jump in."

Jesus, that smile on this kid . . . She did her best to appear reluctant as she moved toward the open door. "You are real super-nice. But I don't want to bother you. Really, I can take the bus, I like it . . ." And so forth.

On the way to Mrs. Millington's house Wanda asked Victor if he sometimes got hungry around this time of day, and she was pleased to learn that they shared such a natural and healthy reaction.

"It's good to share things, y'know. I think sharing is the best thing two people can do together . . ."

She was encouraged when Victor so promptly agreed to make a detour and share the experience of having ice cream together. It just proved a person did not lose *all* their appeal because they were in cold storage for three years.

Wanda found it difficult to hold back her enthusiasm when Victor chose a place called Freddie's, which he explained was a hang-out for people from the university. He greeted several of the customers, who responded heartily. Wanda noticed one of the students whistled his approval of Victor's companion and she was even more pleased when another called out, "Hey Vic! How come you're so *lucky?*"

Wanda also noticed that Victor made no attempt at introductions, a breach of etiquette which would not be tolerated in the life. But never mind, this was a whole different world where the people were not so suspicious of strangers. Many of these people lived in real houses. Here they were in this super-clean place with the jukebox going and people jabbering and laughing and gobbling up cokes and ice cream and pies and yoghurt and health foods like you would not believe. And Victor took on a good listen while you explained some more about how come you were forced into a life that you never wanted and never wanted to go near again. "I just don't know what I'd do if I ever got arrested again . . . for just any reason. I might even kill myself. It's an old family tradition in Tennessee. If one of the Raleighs was disgraced in any way that's just what they did. Believe me, Vic, this little lady is going to make like a saint forever, y'know what I mean . . . like Saint Wanda, and maybe you will light candles in my honor."

They both laughed, and when their laughter subsided Wanda asked him if she could lick his spoon because his ice cream had been a different flavor. She did so carefully, making sure Victor was watching her tongue caress the spoon. Her tongue continued with occasional explorations of her lips and even the air around her mouth while she asked him if he had a steady girlfriend. And she appeared to be shocked when he said that he did not have any steady at present because he was too busy just trying to stay in the university.

"Victor I don't feel like we're strangers any longer so if you promise not to get scared or nothing like that there's something I'd like to say to you. I mean I'm not trying to butter you up or anything like that, but I just can't help telling you that you're one of the most intelligent and interesting men I've ever met. I'm like to burst with pride to think that Wanda Raleigh who has had her problems in life is sitting right here sharing time and thoughts with Victor Hickock. I mean that. Of course I know this will never happen again because of the kind of people we are, I mean I'm a nobody and you're you and it isn't likely that people who are brought up so differently are likely to come together very often, know what I mean?"

She reached out and seemed to accidentally touch his hand.

"That's why if you never happen to ask me out for ice cream or anything else again I'll certainly understand. Not that I would be lonely, I guess I could wrangle a date with some of those candycane boys like are a dime a dozen everywhere, but some guy like you who's not afraid of being seen with somebody like me, well, I tell you, that's pretty special. Being alone in the world has a lot of drawbacks, Victor. You look around you and you see everybody else is doubled up, okay? I mean this world is not made for singles even though it *sounds* good and you think you can do as you please. Only it doesn't work that way. You get stepped on if you're alone and have nobody to stand up for you . . . I have to tell you right here and now that all I ask of this old world is one good friend to just be . . . just somebody to *be,* somebody I can unload on if I absolutely have to . . ."

She reached for a paper napkin and managed to touch his hand again. "I don't know why I'm laying all this heavy stuff on you, Vic. I'm sorry and I promise, I'll never do it again." She laughed and patted at her lips with the napkin. "I bet I bored you and you're too much of a gentleman to say so. Well, anyway, I thank you for listening while I blabber on. At least I can tell you that down south where I come from being called a true gentleman is considered the highest compliment anybody can ever give or hear."

She waited, watching his eyes, and she told herself that unless she was mistaken, Victor was actually blushing. For God's sake, blushing at nineteen? You don't suppose this great big gorgeous hunk could still be a virgin, do you?

Victor said, "I guess my family has its traditions too. I guess we only partly make ourselves, the rest we inherit. In some ways that's sort of what anthropology is all about—"

Wanda gave him her complete and devoted attention for more than an hour while he held forth on the hereditary behavior of the Papuans, the Aleuts, and the Celts. She was not at all sure she had ever met any of the sort of people he was talking about and while she was trying to listen she had trouble concentrating. For new thoughts kept biting at her attention.

Little by little, she decided, she was beginning to come up with some more real ideas. Maybe . . . like suppose maybe this Victor was for real . . . like suppose he could be *very* useful if he was given the chance to grow up? Could he help it if his father thought the sun rose and set with him? Could she? No, but she could damn well take advantage of it.

Hey, Mr. Gorgeous, somehow I *got* to figure out how we can spend more time together.

Hickock had good sailing in *Freedom* over the weekend. At breakfast on Saturday he had invited Victor to go along, but the invitation had been declined. "Any special reason, Vic? It looks like there is going to be a fine breeze."

"No special reason."

"You're leveling with me?"

"Yes I'm leveling with you. I just don't feel like sailing. And I've got a lot of homework to do."

Hickock had studied his son's eyes for a moment, hoping to discover why for the first time he could recall Victor was not interested in sailing. It had always been a passion they had shared despite other intrusions and problems. Victor was an equally avid reader of nautical tales; everything from Slocum's voyages to Conrad, Melville and Montserrat were treasured in his library. Like his father, Victor considered *Freedom* a living member of the family and a substantial part of her smart appearance was due to the time and devoted labor he had put into her.

"Is it because Jean is going?" Hickock asked.

"No. It's not because your friend is going."

"Well something is eating you. Do you mind sharing it with a relative who tries to have your welfare at heart?"

"I have my problems just like anyone else. And you have yours. Why double them up?"

"Because I'm your father, damnit!"

"And you feel duty bound to look after me, right?"

"Oh come off it." Hickock had to take several long and deep breaths to restore his patience. He knew he had strained his tolerance and he was sure that was a mistake with Victor in his current mood. A very edgy young man this morning, he thought; stubborn like his mother and just as unpredictable.

He tried and failed to recall any specific reactions toward his own father when he was Victor's age. There had been the normal frustrations, he supposed, and perhaps some resentments because the young are so easily wounded, but was this the same?

Hickock was grateful for the weather on both days. Although a glowering overcast left the water a dull chromium from horizon to horizon a spanking wind blew steady as a trade and seemed to sweep away all his concerns. Sitting at the helm of *Freedom* he rediscovered the sensual pleasures of wave and wind playing with his ship and he tried to think of an appropriate way to express his gratitude.

Freedom's bow collided with a sea sending a shower of cold salt spray aft. It struck Hickock full in the face and he yelled out his joy as loud as he could. He continued to shout exuberantly at the wind and the boisterous seas until Jean came from below and stood laughing in the hatchway. She asked whatever had happened to his dignity.

Later when the wind diminished and relative quiet descended on the *Freedom* he listened to the guttural whispering of the water against her hull and he thought that he must be at least on the outskirts of heaven.

He found enormous satisfaction in watching Jean's bereted head pop up in the hatchway, linger for a time while she smiled at the sky and the gloomy horizon, and then descend again.

"Are you going to spend all day down there? You're missing a glorious sail."

"I'm keeping an eye on a wonderful smelling wood stove and the growing pains of my drunkard's stew. I've laced it with so much burgundy it's a fire hazard."

"How about a dollop for the Ancient Mariner?"

She disappeared momentarily then returned with a mug of burgundy. She handed it to him. "For the man I love," she said simply.

"To the woman of my heart." He raised the cup in a salute.

He met her eyes directly then looked into his cup. "Silly speech for a man my age, isn't it?"

"Of course not. You just made my hour. How would you like to try for the whole year?"

"How do I manage that?"

"Just share yourself with me. The bad as well as the good. I'm Jean, remember? I may not have your wisdom, but I'm not a child and not to be pampered. I'm a full-grown woman who knows when something is troubling you."

She glanced up and along the luff of the sail and said, "You're luffing. Not paying attention to your business. Why not tell me what you're worrying about?"

"I'm not worried about anything. How could I be with all this?" He made a sweeping gesture at the horizon.

"I have a hunch that you're not telling the full truth and nothing but."

"Okay. Maybe not." His laugh sounded hollow even to himself.

"Are you worried about that dreadful man with the high voice?"

"Not recently. Mostly it's Victor. I can't seem to do anything right. I can't get our relationship back where it ought to be . . . or where *I* think it ought to be. I'm running out of patience and if I don't watch it I can destroy the whole works and that will be a hell of a mess."

A long silence fell between them.

Finally Jean announced she was going to spoil the day and make a speech. "Maybe I've been sipping too much of the stew's burgundy and you should tell me it is none of my business and that I should jump overboard . . . or maybe you'll throw me overboard, but it seems to me you are too much inclined to carry the weight of the world around on your shoulders. People make their own situations, or at least that's what I think. You can rationalize and persuade all you want and most people are going to carry right on whatever track they set for themselves. Victor's old enough to think for himself and just at this time he probably likes to think he can get along without you . . . and certainly without me. You have got to stop placing the blame for everything on yourself . . .

"You say you're in love with me and I believe you, and I'm honored and thrilled and wake up mornings shouting at the air around me that this found joy is mine for as long as I deserve it. I just don't understand how a person like me can be so lucky. I mean it. You have tremendous inner strength. It isn't always visible, but it's there and everyone who meets you knows it. It's your control of yourself even when you are unsure. Ordinary people like me need you in a thousand ways . . . I can't explain why I love you. Maybe it is just the way you move, the way you talk, your mouth, your wonderful big ears and that sail of a nose. They have all become very precious to me. I've never met any man like you and I never expect to in this life and I don't care what anyone says or thinks about the difference in our ages. So you are old enough to be my father. The point is you are not my father, and if you think I would trade you for some half-baked reject of my own age who wants to talk about his golf game or his identity or how the world doesn't understand him all the time, you don't know the woman who is now under sail with you. Under *full* sail and unless we go on the rocks for lack of care and attention I foresee a long long voyage together . . .

"But there *is* one thing that bugs me, and that's your lack of appreciation for yourself. You are one very special individual and don't ever think you are not. I know you play God all day long but please step down from your golden throne more often. Keep remembering that even God made some mistakes and you will too. Be a peasant for a while. It won't hurt you. Now, do you want to tie the anchor around my neck and give me the heave-ho or shall I just slip quietly over the side?"

A grin crept across Hickock's face. He said carefully, "Getting rid of you would be easy. I could tell the police there had been an accident. But you're out of reach. Come here."

She left the hatch and moved toward his extended arm. He pulled her down beside him and steered with his foot. He kissed her long and hard and held her tightly until at last she broke away. "Your nose is cold," she said.

She nestled down against him while he held *Freedom* on course, and he thought that never in his life had he been so content.

"You are absolutely right," he said at last. "I probably need that speech of yours at least once a month. And I hereby vow to cease worrying about Victor."

She pressed against him, brought his free hand to her lips and kissed his fingers. "Maybe he has a new girlfriend."

"If so I hope he has my luck."

"For a captain who had a right to make me walk the plank you say the nicest things . . ."

They made hot mulled wine together when they reached port during that last of Sunday evening and then devoured the stew. Less than an hour later Hickock drove her home and they parted quickly. Jean said she had to be on the job very early in the morning since the Coast Guard ship was being launched and she wanted to watch her very own chunk of steel slip into the water. As he waited while she unlocked her door she said, "I forgot to ask. How is your new housekeeper working out?"

"I don't really know. She's in and out. I really haven't seen much of her. But she's sticking with the job longer than I thought she would and at least the place looks cleaner."

Chapter Fourteen

There was nothing in this whole wide world that a person could not do if they really wanted to, Wanda decided. And if you had friends in this world, real loyal friends like were in the life, then getting things done became just that much easier. And even obstacles like nosey Mrs. Millington could be overcome. Boy, that woman would buy fried ice cream.

When Wanda thought of that phrase in relation to Mrs. Millington she chuckled to herself. It was a standard term used at Clark for any inmate who believed everything they were told. Still, you could never tell for sure about these do-gooder types. They had a lot of kooks in their organizations and if you did anything wrong in their eyes why sometimes they just stopped knowing you.

So *real* friends without any built-in hostilities are important when you are going in to a gig like this. It seemed just impossible that almost two weeks had gone by since liberation day at Clark. Must get Nancy to understand that there was two numbers she can call when everything is ready. She can call at Mrs. Millington's during normal office hours and say she is your probation officer calling about a job. And while she is at it Nancy can tell Mrs. Millington what a super person you are. She can even bring in the old plantation if she wants since Nancy sure heard the story a few times when some john would ask about your accent.

If I'm not at Mrs. Millington's try the judge's number, but not before ten in the morning and not after two in the afternoon when Victor just might pick up the phone at the wrong time and overhear a conversation that is none of his business. This is *not yet* his business.

Nancy has to get ahold of Manuel, and that's not easy in itself because he's so slippery. You better believe Manuel can disappear into thin air right in front of your eyes. Manuel is trouble within a million miles.

At least Nancy was real, right out of the good old days of the life. Like a hundred-and-ten-year-old kid, she is, says she looks awful and is getting fat and will meet you in her favorite bakery when everything is ready.

Nancy would not know a real worry if she saw one. All she has to do is turn a few tricks a night, hope she doesn't get a dose and go home to sleep like a baby while ol' Wanda is worrying about how she is going to get everything together.

There's always the unexpected to be handled, like that bird-brain probation officer Mrs. Holland calling Mrs. Millington's house. She says she has some kind of a job for Wanda Usher and she better get down there. Who needs her interference at this critical point in time? So to get her off your back and make sure she don't somehow screw up your plans for the future you drop by her office and give her the old bug-eyed attention these people thrive on. You tell her your name is now Raleigh so she don't screw *that* up and she understands you want to take your old married name back in memory of your late husband who was killed in a motorcycle accident while you were away. It was just like at Clark. You tell them what they want to hear . . . how you have seen the light and will never no more get in any kind of trouble. "Yes, Mrs. Holland, I *am* thinking about my future . . . yes, Mrs. Holland I *know* I am not going to be beautiful forever . . . Mrs. Holland I certainly am going to *involve* myself in the community in every way I can."

It was all so easy this time because you could say how you were working your fingers to the bone at the judge's house. The job Mrs. Holland had available was a fry cook at some dump way out in the west end of the city and the pay was a bare squeak above minimum. And they wanted somebody right this minute. It took some squirming to get out of that one. Can you imagine sitting there and talking to this creep who don't know nothing but social work all her dumb life, telling her all about how you can't let the judge down because he is depending on you like you were one of the family?

Well there has been some progress in that department. There it was last Wednesday afternoon and Victor comes home from school late—almost five and you are just leaving. So he says his father is not coming home to dinner and how would you like to cook up a meal with him?

You tell him why yes it just so happens that you do not have another engagement this particular evening. You give him a laugh saying you will have to call your agent because there is so much demand for your company. You do not want Mrs. Millington to worry about how you might be kidnapped or worse if you don't arrive right on schedule.

And what does Victor want for his dinner? Are you ready for this? Sausage and sauerkraut. Now anybody who is from Tennessee and can't cook up sausage and sauerkraut until it is like God-food is automatically turned over to the Ku Klux Klan. So away we go with pots and pans flying and when you finally sit down right there in the dining room with the silverware and candles and all, Mr. Gorgeous eats his head off.

Finally when he is sitting back and patting his belly, says he like he is suddenly the president of the world, "I guess you've seen an awful lot of things in your life, haven't you? I mean here I am nineteen and when you come right down to it about all I've done is go to school."

"That's a good place to be." And *that* remark sure as hell came from the heart.

"I suppose," says he, "you must have met an awful lot of interesting characters in your life?"

Interesting? Now there was a handy word that could not begin to describe some of the ding-a-lings you've known.

". . . and I suppose," he went right on without waiting for an answer, "that some times in your . . . well, your profession . . . you might sort of . . . I don't know how to say this . . . you might really go for some of the customers?"

All of a sudden he was real nervous, twitching in his chair, fiddling with the silverware, like he just *had* to know all about you. Was that good or bad?

"What I mean is," he rattled on, "and I hope you don't mind my getting personal . . . is that considering you were only doing it for money, did you ever feel like, y'know . . . going steady with anybody and maybe just sort of living together without any money involved?"

What a question. It is to wonder what he would have thought if you told him about Sam who happened to be black. A real big temptation to tell him about Sam just to shake him up some, but how broad-minded is this white boy? He might get turned off completely and that would never do. Don't mess with success.

All is extremely mellow when he is leaning back in his chair pretending to look at the chandelier over the table which you now see needs dusting. He is leaning back like some big contented blond bear and he says, ". . . I suppose you know a lot more about sex than most people. Pardon me. I didn't mean that to sound the way I guess it does and I don't want to offend you. But the things is, see, it seems to me sex rules a big part of our lives. I mean ever since the beginning of history . . . Cleopatra, Queen Elizabeth the First, Napoleon. All those people and more changed the course of history just because they had the hots for someone. Look . . . I wouldn't tell this to anyone else, but the truth is I don't know much about it."

"Don't tell me you've never been in love, Victor Hickock."

"I guess I could say I have. But only once really. Her family moved back to the east and it sort of dissolved . . . the feeling between us, that is. And then I was pretty much into athletics at school. I know one thing, love takes a lot of your time. I can't tell you how far behind I got on everything when Cindy lived here—close by, just down in the next block."

"Cindy is a nice name."

"Cindy was a nice girl. But she didn't know about certain things and we never quite did it because she was so damned scared all the time."

"Maybe that was just as well." Hey, what was this turning into? An advice column to young studs and virgins? The kid was obviously feeling horny, but if you came right out and told him so he might think it was an invitation. And you're not ready for that. Not yet, son of the judge . . . But how to carry on a conversation like that without sounding like a fruit brain or a tin canary? Just because a girl sells it does that mean she's a swami? But one thing was for sure, some of the best loving in the whole history of the world had been done by whores so don't knock it.

Which is more or less what you told Victor while you did the dishes together—except about Sam, which subject might cool the increasing temperature in Victor's pants. Like to bust, he was when he said, "Wanda I've got to tell you that all the girls at the university seem sort of nothing compared to a person like you. They don't have anything to say except what youth hostel they stayed in when they went to Austria last summer and who's getting pledged to which sorority and what movie, for God's sake, they went to see instead of studying. They don't know about life like you do . . . and life interests me."

Well, bully for you, boy. Are you ready for this? It interests me too. And let me clue you that when you blow three years of your life you never can get it back.

He goes on, "I want you to know that I know you're going to have a tough time getting a new start, rehabilitated, all that, and if you ever need any help . . . well, I want you to know you can count on me."

Jesus, here is Sir Galahad. You should have asked him where was his white horse.

The clincher was yet to come. You are both exiting the kitchen when you just accidentally bump into each other. Accidentally? In the pantry naturally where accidents like that are bound to happen because it's so narrow in there. But he did it. All the time he's pretending to be so innocent and all when really he's just been maneuvering around to one thing. So why not let him play out his little game?

You hear him say, "Well, here goes" or something like that, and he grabs you. You better believe it's like being grabbed by a polar bear which is one of the most powerful creatures in the world according to the *National Geographic*. He is hanging on and pressing his instant hard-on against you and how are you supposed to breathe when suffocation is due in the next ten seconds.

"Hey, watch it, man. I break easy."

But King Kong does not hear for a long minute or so. He is like unconscious, totally ignorant of the way your boobs are being crushed against his rib cage. He's like a volcano, this kid, and what a lover he will be if somebody can just tame him. Which is not on the duty agenda for Wanda Usher just *yet* . . .

Suddenly, he backs away and while you're getting your wind back he says, "I'm very sorry, truly sorry. I don't know what happened to me. I guess that just because of your . . . well, your past . . . some lousy instinct got hold of me, I forgot you work here and I shouldn't take advantage of that."

Hallelujah. Hello to the Boy Scout with the most merit badges. So the kid is horny? After two hours all alone in this house you sure lost your touch if he wasn't.

Says he, "I might as well admit that there's something . . . look, the truth is I find you extremely attractive."

"Likewise, I'm sure, Victor. I have a very hard time behaving myself around here."

He took a long deep breath. You could see he was almost biting off his lower lip before he got up the gumption to say, "We could go up to my room."

"And have the judge come home and find me still here? No way. Vic, I got to be very careful for the next year. I'm still on probation, and the least little thing I do that somebody thinks is wrong and they'll send me away again. You wouldn't want to see that happen, would you?"

"I told you. I'm completely on your side. If you get in trouble, let me know and I'll come running."

And he *would*. He was flashing those eyes and if you asked him to knock down the pantry he would charge right into the wall, to get into li'l ol' Wanda.

"Look, Victor. We got to be a little realistic about this. Maybe we can arrange to meet somewhere else, know what I mean? Somewhere miles from here. It would be different then, I wouldn't feel like your father was hanging over us . . . like I could relax, understand? I mean if it worked out maybe we could spend the whole night together . . ."

When he wanted to know, right that very second. You were both whispering by now as if there was anybody to hear you. There was no cat in the Hickock house, but if one walked across the floor you would both jump ten feet in the air. ". . . Understand?" you carried on with more truth than you could believe, "I need a little time to think things over. This starting a new life is very complicated and means a lot of adjustments. I have a lot of things to work out in my mind. Okay?"

"Okay. I just have to say I really . . . well . . . enjoy your company. Some people are like that, y'know. They come together and match right away . . . it's like nuclear fusion."

"I'd like to hear more about that stuff."

Mr. Gorgeous was smiling his smile and he kept it beaming all the way while he drove you home to Mrs. Millington's. There was a long embrace before you got out and you gave the kid a French one that he was not likely to forget very soon.

No question, things were moving right along. Are you listening, judge?

• • •

Boris Estervan was watching television with his brother Leo. I am allergic to him, he thought. He makes my brain break out in a rash, but what the hell, he's the only brother I got. People of the same blood, the only way to get rid of relatives was to die.

Estervan did not like television either, but he endured it now because he was watching a biblical story about Jews and Jews fascinated him. They did things without fuss which he liked and they put their money where their mouth was. And mostly they stayed out of jail, which was quite an accomplishment he always admired.

The painful realization that he might be prison-bound himself swept over Estervan like a wave, as it had done many times a day ever since that unpleasant final session in Judge Hickock's courtroom.

Estervan sipped gently at the glass of Postum which Rosa had prepared for him. It was his customary prebedtime drink. He had never had anything to do with hard liquor although he did occasionally enjoy a small glass of wine with dinner. He had no use for heavy drinkers. "They make mistakes," he declared in his reedy voice, "and I got no time in my business for mistake-makers." One of his staff had made a mistake and as a result he, Boris Estervan, was threatened with a long prison sentence. Now he could not be sure whether he was angrier at that goddamned film director who cast the girls, or the jury who condemned everybody who had anything to do with the production.

Estervan's brother Leo was a borderline case as a mistake-maker. He had to be watched at all times and not allowed to think for himself. Which was why he was reasonably dependable as a gofer, but certainly not to be trusted in any sort of executive capacity.

When events in the Holy Land were replaced with a strident commercial Estervan wiped at the thin moustache the Postum had left on his upper lip and said to his brother, "I've been thinking. There are God knows how many judges in this country and it's sure a fact that all of them are not honest. But we happen to get one who is supposed to be. So what do we do? Either we have been given some false info on this Judge Hickock or we are approaching him in the wrong way. *If* he really is allergic to taking other people's money which is still hard for me to believe, then maybe we ought to work on his pucker factor a little bit . . . just easy at first . . . just enough until he gets the message. Are you with me?"

"Well, not exactly," Leo said.

Of course the dumb sonofabitch was not paying attention. His eyes were anchored on the television set's commercial on constipation. It figured. Like Leo's mind. If there was anybody else around who could be trusted other than a blood relative then he sure as hell would talk to him rather than Leo. But these days you took what you could get.

"What I'm thinking," Estervan went on more slowly, "is that if this judge is actually so honest he doesn't have good sense then we need a gimmick of some kind to open his mind. For example, there's his girlfriend . . . she might be the answer, and if we can't work through her then he has a son who might come in handy . . . or maybe a combination of the two."

Estervan studied the strange mixture of cunning and stupidity he always saw in his brother's face. Maybe there was some way he could turn state's evidence and tell the DA's office that it was Leo who had hired the girls. Should he be responsible for his brother's actions? Make him chairman of the Rosa Corporation maybe . . . retroactive . . . dated back several months when you were both in Florida. They could send Leo away for a few seasons and nobody would miss him . . . least of all his brother. And as a reward for his cooperation he, Boris Estervan, would be let off the hook. It might be worthwhile having Delgado check into that project.

Estervan reconsidered. Put that idea away in the back pocket until the last minute. The judge would be thinking of saving his face. He had to be put on the right thinking track *before* he reached a decision. And time was getting short. Son or girlfriend? Or both? Which was the most important to a judge who refused to think like a reasonable man?

"I may have a little job I want you to do," he said to Leo. "So don't go running off out of town somewhere, understand?"

"Sure. I wasn't planning on going anywhere."

Watching Leo's face in the glow from the television set he wondered if *he* was not being unreasonable. Did it make sense to trust Leo with any assignment out of the ordinary? "What I am thinking is that we don't know enough. We're like General

MacArthur who was trying to fight in Korea without full information. In other words, I need a scout, just like a football coach—and you're elected."

"What do you want me to do?"

"Follow Hickock's kid around until you get something on him. Hell, all kids are in some kind of trouble these days."

"Suppose he's clean?"

God spare me from negative-thinking relatives, Estervan thought. Great men did not have to employ relatives on their staff which is one reason they got great. "If he's really clean then we'll have to fix it so he isn't. It's as simple as that."

"What about his woman?"

"I dunno." Estervan concentrated a moment on the various opportunities offered by Hickock's obvious devotion to the Pomeroy woman. Just how she could be useful was difficult to foresee, but if things got much tighter that might very well be the way to go. A pity Hickock was without a wife. It would have been so simple.

Estervan decided he could wait no longer before he put some kind of a program into action. He told himself that as a good businessman he should never forget that timing was everything. The son . . . perhaps. The Pomeroy woman . . . another perhaps? As soon as he had a little more information—

"Starting as of now," he said to Leo, "I want you up with the birds. And I want you on the job tailing the kid and the girl. Monday I want you back here every day with a bundle of news on both of them. Any questions?"

"No questions."

Estervan slipped uneasily back into the Holy Land. But in the slow revolution of his thoughts the trials of the Jews as portrayed on the television screen were no competition for the new line of survival he envisioned.

Chapter Fifteen

It was the first time he had ever tried anything like this and he could feel the excitement building in his stomach. And a few other places, Victor thought. Somewhere deep in his groin, he felt a roiling sensation, a hungry and pleasurable aching that became so powerful he wanted to jump out of the pickup and run all the way to his destination. The old adrenaline, he thought, the old adrenaline flowing just as it did before a football game. There were also little tingling spikes along the back of his neck which now and then crept on up to his scalp. Even the weather was cooperating, a rainy night for this was just right. If some of his friends knew about it they'd turn green, no question.

Victor had the windshield wipers turned up to maximum speed. He was driving very carefully. The last thing he wanted was even a fender-bender, let alone a real accident that would take up time and throw everything off schedule.

He smiled. It was hard to concentrate on freeway traffic when there was something so much better to think about. And that better something was Wanda. Hey, there was some *woman*. Of course a guy would never get serious with someone like Wanda, but if you knew about her and understood you just had to respect the hell out of her. She wasn't one bit spoiled like so damn many of the girls on campus and she had plenty to say . . . in that special tone of voice . . . all soft and sexy like her body. Just being within a few feet of her . . . well, tonight was the night.

Victor turned up the volume on the radio. The Tin Cans were playing "Jessie's Girl" which was not such hard rock a guy could stand it. Especially on a night like tonight. He rolled back and forth with the music, keeping the beat. Who would ever think that Vic Hickock was going to be at a place called the Green Shutter Inn holed up in his own tepee on a night like this. With squaw.

When he saw the sign Galvin Circle he turned off the freeway. He turned right at the end of the exit then doubled back for two blocks until he saw the neon sign Green S——tter Inn. He noticed that the *h* and *u* were apparently not working but who cared. This was the address of paradise.

He parked the pickup and sat listening to the rain bouncing off the cab roof and the hood. He was ten minutes ahead of time, but no matter. All he had to do was make a run for the bright lights, where a red neon sign said Office, register, take the room key and call Wanda at eight-fifteen.

His mouth was dry and now the aching sensation returned down below. It came upon him in hurried little drumbeats of surging intensity. He thought that he could jump from where he sat directly to the bright lights and move through the air so fast he would never get a drop of rain on him. Yea-a-a, Superman!

He turned off the ignition and took his small overnight bag from the seat beside him. It contained his toilet articles, a bathrobe, slippers and a paperback volume of one of the Hornblower series. Just in case. Just in case he lost his cool waiting for Wanda. She said it would not be longer than half an hour at the most.

He opened the door, started to descend from the pickup and halted as he felt something press hard against his rump. His wallet. The hundred dollars for the shocks plus some fifty more was in there and maybe it was not such a smart idea to be carrying that much cash on a night like this might be?

He eased himself back to the seat and closed the door. He pulled his wallet from his hip pocket and removed the hundred-dollar bill. He was about to put it in the glove compartment when he changed his mind. It wasn't that Wanda couldn't be trusted. It was just this place . . .

He removed the two twenty- and one ten-dollar bills he had allocated for this night—could buy a truck-type chromium side mirror for the pickup with that kind of change—but first things first and what was going to happen tonight was a real *first* . . .

He stuffed the three bills in the pocket of his jacket and leaving the hundred-dollar bill in the wallet he placed it in the glove compartment. Now. All bases covered. Ready and able. The time was exactly two minutes until eight.

He locked the door of the pickup and bounded across several puddles of water before he reached the shelter of the motel's portico. There he slipped the keys to the pickup in his overnight bag, flicked the raindrops out of his hair, took a deep breath and, walking very straight, entered the door marked Reception. A fat lady with one drooping eyelid greeted him. "Hi."

"Hi." Suddenly Victor found himself tongue-tied. The fat lady had not moved, and the way she looked him up and down from her perch behind the counter made him very uncomfortable. He tried to calm himself. Relax, Vic, there's no way she can know what's on tonight's schedule. Oh yeah . . . ?

"What can I do for you, young man?"

"Well . . . I'm supposed to have a reservation."

"Do you now. What's the name?"

"Raleigh. Like the cigarette." Cool as an old pro.

He brought his overnight bag around in front of him where she could see it and know that he was going to be a real guest. He watched her fat thumbs flipping through a card index. Her thumbs paused. "For two?"

"Er . . . yes. Right."

"Okay. Sign here. That'll be thirty-three dollars with tax. Sure rainy out ain't it?"

Victor agreed that it was rainy out and signed Victor Raleigh just as he had planned a hundred times since Wanda had thought up all the details of how to do this thing. It was much easier than he had thought it would be. The fat lady did not even look displeased when she handed him the key to Room 20.

She said, "I suppose it was the wife made the reservation. She sure got a nice accent. You both from the south?"

"No, I'm not." Hey, don't rush things lady. The *wife?* Hey, that would drive the guys bananas.

The fat lady raised her arm to point and Victor was so fascinated watching her flesh quiver with the movement he almost forgot what she said. "You go down the hall past the bar and the newsstand to the very end, then turn left."

"Thanks, thanks a lot."

As he turned away he heard her say, "Enjoy yourself."

He passed the bar where a jukebox was banging out "Back on Black." He caught the odor of stale beer and tobacco smoke. This was really going to happen. All the problems were out of the way. And his watch said it was eight-oh-four. Right on schedule.

He paused just long enough to look in the bar. He saw several couples pawing each other in the semi-darkness and a lone customer at the bar itself. She was a plump woman and from what he could see in the dim light, apparently red-haired. She stared at him and he saw her smile invitingly.

This certainly was some place. *The* place . . .

Leo Estervan was relieved to find the parking lot at the Green Shutter Inn was far from crowded. It enabled him to park his car a considerable distance from the pickup he had been following and observe the interesting behavior of the pickup's driver from an inconspicuous position.

He saw the driver sit in the pickup for several minutes before he got out, then run across the lot and pause before he actually entered the Green Shutter Inn. He saw that he was carrying a small bag and he wondered why. Why would this kid leave a nice home and come to a dump like this?

Leo Estervan decided that he must be running some kind of delivery service.

He sighed when he thought about the view through the rain. He knew the Green Shutter Inn was a favorite gathering place for junkies and sometimes for hookers who got a reduced room rate if they brought their johns around regular. There was also a little card action, nothing fancy, two-hundred-dollar pots. Still it sure as hell was not a place anyone would expect to find the Hickock kid. Well, you never knew . . .

Victor let himself into the room and closed the door. He threw the overnight bag on the large double bed and followed it immediately, making a long leap and landing on his knees. He bounced up and down several times.

He bounced high, flipped around in mid-air, and landed on his back. He laughed at himself, then reached out lazily for the telephone. Mrs. Millington's number was easy to remember—one, one, six, one, after the prefix which was the same as his own. Easy when it had been clicking off in his mind ever since Wanda said she was willing to tell Mrs. Millington a lie—just for this. She was supposed to be going to spend the night with a friend. Well, she *was*. He heard the ringing sound once and there she was. That voice. A guy could go out of his gourd just listening to that voice. Husky, like sharing a secret.

"Hi. Everything okay, Mr. Raleigh?"

"You know it. Hurry up."

"I'll be along. It always takes longer to get a cab on rainy nights. Just keep your britches up."

"Okay. Hurry."

After he hung up the phone he spread his arms wide and lay spreadeagled for a moment. He stared at a large brown spot on the ceiling and saw that in the center of the blemish there was a tumerous projection which resembled a female breast; not as full and well-rounded as Wanda's naturally, but there it was.

He decided the roof must be leaking and he hoped the water would not find its way to the bed, not for at least several hours. And he tried, desperately, to think of other things.

Wanda hung up the phone and lit a cigarette. She inhaled deeply then pursed her lips and blew a long feather of smoke at the ceiling. Mrs. Millington was uptight about people smoking.

Wanda left the phone and went to the breakfast nook where she poured another glass of Mrs. Millington's sherry. Why the old rascal had been hiding it all the time, way back in the broom closet where she thought no one would ever know she had it. And two-thirds full. Sweet sherry, awful icky. She took a sip of the sherry and smacked her lips. Now what about this? Here is Wanda Usher Raleigh who really never had anything much to do with alcohol getting a little heat on all by herself. Of course, it was a kind of celebration, or liberation was a better word. Because everything was set. Perfect organization. Everything you owned was already at Nancy's, who said just come and stay as long as you like. Now there was a friend. Everything was down there at her place except the overnight bag, which was right there on the kitchen sink . . . waiting. So was Victor. Do him good. Talk about building up a heat . . . the kid was already on fire. Okay, okay, I'll call a taxi. In a minute . . . as soon as I finish this cigarette which Mrs. Millington would have a fit about if she was home.

She should complain. There were sixty bucks pinned to Mrs. M's pillow which was more than Mrs. M could have spent on your room and board. *You are not obligated to nobody.*

She took another sip of the sherry and watched the rivulets of rain snaking down the window. Mrs. M was off to one of her political meetings where she was some kind of delegate or some such and she had put a little tin badge on her dress which said who she was before she left. As if it made any difference.

As if those persons didn't know that all elections were rigged anyways and that the voting business was just going through the motions to keep the peasants quiet while the big boys took over. Like, hey . . . *you* there . . . you want to be a judge Mr. Julian Hickock? You want to call people unfit mothers and send them away from their kid forever? Hey, it's easy. Just you keep your nose clean and don't disgrace us good people and never forget for one second who put you there.

She took another sip of the sherry, and held it in her mouth for a moment before she swallowed. There was a pad by the phone and she had previously noted on it the number of the cab company. It was part of the preplanning. Everything was down to the last detail. According to her horoscope and the rhythm chart would you believe it was also just the right time of the month?

In the overnight bag was everything she needed—and all paid for. Nancy had finally caught up with Manuel and arranged for a delivery of twenty balloons—enough stuff to choke a horse.

"Excuse me, madame. I must call my chauffeur," she said aloud.

She dialed the taxi number and was told to expect one in twenty minutes. Okay, Victor would wait and meanwhile there was one final detail to be taken care of. Let there be no hard feelings, madame.

Wanda strolled back to the breakfast nook and considered finishing off what was left of the sherry. Mrs. M probably forgot she still had the bottle.

She changed her mind. No and no-no. This night was too important. Absolutely nothing could go wrong and she wanted to enjoy every minute of it. And with a full brain kit, not all sloshed up. After all, it had been a long, long time since she had a man and this one was going to be something special.

She sat down in the breakfast nook and placed the lined tablet Mrs. Millington used for ordering groceries before her. She took the ballpoint out of her purse, the same one she had used at Clark. She had written some great poetry with this pen; everybody who read it in the *But the Spirit Is Free* agreed to that. Now writing was more difficult because there was no one around to correct her spelling, but if she kept the lines nice and straight with good spaces between the words there was no need to worry about how good the letter would be.

Dear Missus Millinton—
Hello and good-by. I have left 60 dollars on your pillo because I am going away. I dont belong here. I guess I dont belong much of anywhere. Since I was a little girl I have been *around* you mite say. I never saw no plantation. Is that the way you spell it?

Wanda sucked on the top end of the pen for a while and then clicked it against her teeth while she thought of all the things she would like to say to Mrs. Millington if only she knew how to spell better. But in the life where she did not have to wear a name tag so people would know who she was, and there were very few people who could write with good spelling. Some of them could hardly write their name. Jesus, you certainly did not have to win a prize in penmanship to lie back and spread your legs.

Well missus Millinton I am going away from your nice house tonite and I want to thank you for all you did. The sponsering and such.
When I am gone think of me. Okay?
You are a nice woman and I thank you for all you done to make life easy for me. Some people should not be given any help because it spoils there war with the world.
I write you this poem so you will remember me.

Wanda made several attempts before she was satisfied with the way she wanted to end her letter. At last she wrote:

On a rainy nite the streets are wet
And all the smart girls are inside
Don't forget,
They know each other by name and smile,
And never does once call another one vile.
So if there is a real home for the likes of me,
Then the street itself is the place to be.

Goodby. You should lock your front door more often.

She signed the paper with a flourish.

Wanda Usher Raleigh

Victor arched his back and reached with his powerful arms to the top of the headboard. He pulled himself up and down several times, slowly, the hard way.

He rolled slowly off the bed and went to the windows. He pulled on the strings of the venetian blind until he could see out. The view was of the parking lot and there was his good old pickup just sitting there.

He closed the blinds, took his toilet kit out of the overnight bag and entered the bathroom. It looked like a good shower even if the curtain was crummy. Maybe they could take one together? He opened his toilet kit and placed it on one side of the washbasin. She would take the other side, he thought, and the two kits would look sort of nice standing there together. He took out a small bottle of aftershave, squirted a few drops in the palm of his hand and patted his face. He inhaled and hoped he had not used too much.

He glanced at his watch. Only five minutes had passed since they had talked. It was going to be a nervous time until she came to the door. So cool it. Criminee! He had forgotten to give her the room number. Never mind. He would meet her at the door.

For a time he studied his image in the bathroom mirror. Not too shabby, but how about a beard? Well-groomed like, say . . . Sir Walter Raleigh? There you have it. He reached into his toilet kit again and took out a long comb. He ran it through his hair carefully. He could do with a haircut but right there would go at least five gallons of gas for the pickup.

He left the bathroom and began experimenting with various lighting effects in relation to the bed. The reading lamp was too bright, it would spoil everything—like being in a hospital. He turned it off and groping in the sudden darkness found the switch by the door. He flipped it on and frowned at the two lights in the ceiling. Terrible. Turned the skin almost blue.

There was a cheap chandelier over the round table by the window. He turned out the ceiling light and turned on the chandelier. Okay for a card game maybe, but probably if you were lying on the bed it would shine right in the eyes. He went to the bed and lay down testing his theory, and he found it correct. Absolutely would not do.

How about leaving the bathroom light on and then cracking the door just enough so the bed would be just softly illuminated—to say nothing of the people in it?

No, a better idea. He rolled quickly out of the bed and turned off the chandelier light. He went to the venetian blind and pulled gently on the strings. As the blind opened he looked over his shoulder at the bed. The reflected light from the parking lot and the red neon over the entrance to the Green Shutter fell across the bed in a pattern of slits that made it sort of mysterious. He could almost see Wanda lying there in those strips of light, her hair all tousled—flicking her tongue around her lips the way she did . . .

He began to pace the room in the semi-darkness. He thought about reading the Hornblower book, knew he couldn't. How could he concentrate on an ancient naval battle at a time like this. He checked his watch again. Twenty minutes since his call to Wanda. He had better get himself out in front. She should show up any minute now.

For about five minutes now Leo Estervan had been watching the Hickock kid standing beneath the motel portico and it was for damn sure he had not just stepped out for a breath of the night air. He would look at his pickup occasionally, but most of the time he was looking down the street. Now who would he be waiting to meet in a place like the Green Shutter? There were times when Boris was like a psychic, he could smell things . . . like maybe this Hickock kid *did* have some sort of a problem that could be helped along a little . . .

Leo watched a taxi pull to a stop under the portico and he saw a young woman emerge from it. There was something about that woman, something vaguely familiar. He saw her hand her little kit-bag to the Hickock kid, who was smiling all over. Like they was some honeymoon couple, for God's sake. In the Green Shutter?

He saw them turn for the doorway, the cab pulled away, and there was her face. He had her made. It was the same face he had seen a few times at stag parties when a few years back the boys used to call in a couple of hookers to liven up the evening. Sure as hell she was the one . . . had a big black pimp who got sent away and killed for something or other so the story went . . .

Leo scratched at his brow. Her name? For the life of him he could not remember her name, but he did recall many other things. Now she looked older, but not much because she was just a kid when he first saw her. Cantankerous little bitch. Always getting kidded about her accent and all the boys thought she was pretty special. *Sam* . . . that was his name, but what was hers? And she was sent away too, right? And here she was with young Hickock? Well, well . . .

He checked his watch and squirmed about in the car seat until he was reasonably comfortable. He hoped he would not have too long to wait.

After they entered the room Victor locked the door behind them. "Well, here we are."

He reached for her, but she sidestepped and crossed to the far side of the room. There she removed her plastic raincoat, shook it once and hung it in the closet. She crossed to the cracked mirror in the bathroom door and smoothed her egg-white dress to conform more surely to her hip line. White like in virgin, she thought—a little cracked like the mirror. It was her best dress bought from a catalogue during her last days at Clark—the white dress she had saved for the day she would make like a butterfly and turn into a different person.

"You look wonderful," Victor said. "You should've let me pay the cab fare."

"No. It's my treat. This is a very special night, Victor." It would be many months before he knew how really special a night this was going to be.

"Well . . ." he said, approaching her in the half-light from the window.

She decided not to smile; not the hundred-dollar smile or any other kind. She was going to do this perfect, the true thoroughbred way. Jesus, but he was one good-looking kid. Everything about him was in just the right proportion. Now the important thing was to make absolutely sure—

She met him in the middle of the room and slipped into his arms. She tipped her head back and opened her mouth, inviting his lips. "Let yourself go, honey," she whispered.

He pressed her to him and their bodies undulated slowly together. After a time she pulled slightly away and began to unbutton his shirt. She made little humming noises deep in her throat. Jesus, there was not an ounce of fat on the kid. A super-stud and didn't know it. There must be a hundred girls who would give it to him for free. Including this one. He and his poppa would pay later.

She unfastened his belt and then took her hands away. She twirled around, pulled the egg-white dress over her head, and tossed it on the table. She kicked off her shoes and still with her back to him she removed her brassiere, garter belt, and stockings. She cast them away from her one after another until they made a little pile on the table and in seconds she stood naked before him. Every gesture in the transformation had been made with practiced economy, just as she had done so many times she had long ago lost count.

Now she stood demurely, and somehow in spite of her calm and expert manner, managed to create an air of mischief and excitement. "Are you going to just stand there all night?" she asked. Then she ran to the bed, pulled back the covers, and slipped beneath them.

He came to the side of the bed, tearing at his clothes.

"Please, Vic. Please . . . hurry—"

She reached for him and pulled him down upon her and almost immediately became lost in her frenzy. Never in her life had she been so anxious for a man to explode within her. Not just once. More like the Fourth of July . . . like all the fireworks going off over and over again. He was so sweet, the poor hungry kid, and so strong. His breathing was like he just finished running fifty miles. Was it because he was so new at it?

At last his whole body became much less rigid and he was saying over and over in little spurts of words, "Oh boy . . . oh boy, oh *boy* . . ."

"I want you to never forget this night," she said.

"No way . . . I never will."

You better believe, she thought. "Rest now," she said. "We wouldn't want Mr. Raleigh all worn out too soon. Lay back for a little R and R, know what I mean? I'm going to give you some special treatment."

Pushing gently she eased away from him. When he was stretched out face down she got to her knees and straddled him. She began a slow massage of his legs.

She took her time. Listening for the gentle moans of pleasure which arose from him as she explored each new area of his body. Occasionally she would whisper, "Sleep now, my prince, sleep . . . sleep." Moving her hands slowly and with the instinctive rhythm that had served her customers so often in the past, she reveled in the thought that now it was complete. What she felt sure Victor had left inside her was now irreversible unless she tampered with things, which was certainly not part of her plans.

There was plenty of time now. The iridescent glow from the electric clock on the night table said it was still five minutes until ten—they had been joined with each other hardly more than an hour and a half. How little time it took, she thought, to make a new life.

As she moved along his body she found her own body responding to the slow oscillation of her hand movements. And soon she knew a powerful sense of moving in a dream which for a time she blamed on the eerie effect of the faint bars of light streaking through the venetian blinds. What would it be like to be a real Mrs. Raleigh with this boy-man the mister? They would have kids . . . maybe call them Jeremy and Karen, and the boy would look like Victor. And you better believe their mother was going to be waiting for them when they came home from school. All right kids, here we go—let's get with the homework and don't give me no fancy stuff about doing your own thing. You're going to learn the three Rs or your mother will know the reason why . . . even if she had to learn right along with you. You're going to learn to read a book, and figure how to get rich, and write long letters to the editor telling what's wrong with the world. And nobody, but nobody on the whole goddamned planet Earth is ever going to have a chance to say that Mrs. Victor Raleigh is an unfit mother. No . . . they are going to elect her head of the PTA and there will be Cub Scouts meeting every Thursday at the Raleigh house and messy cakes and knot tying and everybody taking oaths of allegiance to the flag and like that.

Was it impossible? Did she dare think that maybe her and the real Victor . . . ?

No. Never. Not in this life, Wanda Usher Raleigh. Don't even think about it.

Her hands continued their caressing as she bent down to kiss the back of his neck. "Vic," she asked, softly, "do you like children?"

He mumbled and she realized he was nearly asleep. "I guess . . .hey . . .it's okay with you, isn't it . . . ? I mean—"

"Sure."

She continued her massaging, and there was a moment when she thought she ought to cry, at least a little, but tears would not come. The reason, she decided, was that suddenly she was singing inside . . . it was hard to believe that half of what she had set out to do was now done. Hallelujah. This was no time for bawling. This fine Hickock body beneath her was as good as on its way to a year or so in the bucket or at the very least a long and stiff probation. And would the old man be uptight! You will have to let him stay alive long enough to watch his precious kid in deep trouble. Let him be humiliated . . .

She paused again, letting her hands rest while she listened to Victor's langorous breathing. He was asleep, but it could only have been for a few minutes.

She glanced at the clock. Ten minutes since they had talked. Not enough.

Now she was watching the clock and when she had continued her massaging for another five minutes and bent down once more to assure herself of Victor's heavy breathing, she moved away from him and eased her feet to the floor. She dressed almost as quickly as she had undressed. She moved cautiously to her overnight bag and removed the twenty balloons of cocaine. That robber Manuel had hit her for nineteen hundred dollars! But he didn't ask questions and he was the only sure game in town. There had to be that much of the stuff to make things look right.

She tiptoed through the darkness until she entered the bathroom. There she took a moment to orient herself. Finally she placed the balloons behind the mirror over the washbasin. She succeeded in closing the mirror without making a sound.

She returned to the room and bent silently to pick up her shoes. She slipped them into her overnight bag and knew a moment of fright when her raincoat made a rustling sound as she took it out of the closet. But Victor did not stir.

She moved silently to the door and took a long time removing the chain latch. Again she was satisfied that she had made no sound. She glanced over her shoulder at the rumpled bed in the bars of light, then pulled the door open very slowly. She slipped out into the hall and closed the door behind her. Not a sound.

She slipped into her shoes and took a deep breath. She straightened her spine. Right on, Wanda Usher Raleigh! Right now at half after ten this night was liberation time. Wanda

Usher knew herself, she did. And when she set out to do something she didn't fool around.

As she started rapidly down the hallway she began to hum a tune. She could recall only the first few words of the lyrics yet she found them deeply satisfying. "Goin' home . . . goin' home . . . da-dee-dee-da . . ."

She passed the bar and thought she could do with a little less volume of music when she saw how close the pay phone was to the action. Never mind, maybe it was better that way. She reached into her purse and found the two numbers she had so carefully recorded on a slip of paper. With the paper were the two quarters she had also been careful to provide. So what if the phone company had raised their rates since she had been in Clark? Wanda thought ahead. Everything was all planned out . . .

The first number was the taxi company. She would be picked up in twenty minutes. Guaranteed.

The second number was more interesting and she hoped the sound of music in the background would not keep anybody from hearing what she had to say. She spoke briefly to a Lieutenant McReady in the police department. Narcotics division—*the man*.

"Here's a bust for you." She gave him the bare facts, refused to give him her name and hung up. What she could use now was fresh air.

She picked up her overnight bag and walked out to the portico. When she lit a cigarette she noticed that her hand was shaking ever so slightly. Well, it was exciting, this was real life. There would be no tricks though. Just settle down at Nancy's and wait until the most beautiful baby in the world was ready to enter the world.

She watched the rain for a time and she thought that life was full of contradictions. Here she was at eleven o'clock of an evening, would you believe, up and around of her own free will and no need to even think about johns or wading through puddles in her wedgies. The taxi would be along in a few minutes and she would leave all this behind—never to be seen again. If the man came first so who cared? She had a perfect right to stand where she was standing and she didn't have to say boo to no one.

She thought for a moment about her *condition* . . . how about that, being already in a condition? So twenty years from now nobody would care how she got in that condition. Like with all the Ushers nobody would give a damn who the ancestors were. Suddenly Wanda thought she might add tears to the rain. *Mrs*. Raleigh? Or who should she be tonight when she was nobody? Mrs. Usher? She had never seen even a photo of her real mother and nobody ever bothered to tell her whether she was a Miss or a Mrs. Usher. Senator Smith, I am pleased to have you meet my mother who is invisible like a ghost. She was here a minute ago, but she disappeared. She dissolved in the rain. It's a little habit she has. All you got to admit is that I came out of somebody. Or did I? My name is Usher or so they say, and the woman who named me Wanda was gone so fast I wonder if she was ever really there. Poof! Like that senator, so let's just assume I was a test tube baby and I'll take you across the ballroom to meet my father who is not ever around either. He has been in Texas looking after his oil wells. He never come within a million miles of his little ol' Wanda and I don't know if his name was Usher or something else. Like Hickock maybe? How about that, Senator Smith? How about having a judge for a father? That's a real kick considering that I think he's a porcupine and he thinks I am an unfit mother . . .

She saw the lights of a taxi in the distance and flipped her cigarette into the rain. Simultaneously she felt a heavy hand on her shoulder. She spun around to look into the face of a man she thought she had seen before . . . somewhere . . .

"Nice night for ducks," Leo Estervan said with a half-smile. His hand slipped down and took a strong hold on her arm.

"What do you want? Take your damned hand away—" She felt the pressure of his fingers increase and something—something from the old ho days triggered an alarm. Her belly told her and her eyes told her and every instinct in her body confirmed her building fear that here was bad trouble.

"I just want to have a little talk with you," Leo said.

"You leave me *alone*." She thought of screaming, but no one would ever hear her over the sound of the music and if they did maybe they would call the police. Which would wreck everything. "That's my taxi coming," she protested as he shoved her into the rain.

"No problem, I'll drive you where you want to go."

"Let go of me," she said, knowing a struggle would be useless. He was a powerful man and as they crossed the parking lot he never once exposed himself so she could knee him. If she had spiked heels she might have smashed one down on the arch of his foot, a trick all the girls in the life knew, but in wedgies . . .

He led her straight to a sedan, opened the rear door, shoved her inside and followed her. He closed the door, snapped down the lock and lightened the pressure of his hand under her arm.

"Now we can have our little talk—"

"What are you? Some kind of a cop?"

"You know better. So relax. It took me a little time to make you, but I finally did. You were Sam's woman, but I can't remember your name. You got sent away. How many years ago was it?"

"I'm not puttin' out, so don't get any ideas."

"Oh no? What are you doin' here with young Hickock? Or does he get it for free?"

She watched the taxi arrive now, the driver disappear momentarily inside the motel lobby and after less than a minute reappear, go back into his taxi, and as he turned off the "engaged" light and drove away it seemed as if all her great hopes went with him.

The idea that she might escape if she did a trick with this creep beside her flashed across her mind. If that was all he was after—She dismissed the thought. *No* one was going to foul up what was inside of her now, no matter what. He could kill her first.

"What do you want?"

"Just a little information. Like I said. What you doin' in a dump like this with the Hickock boy?"

"I don't know anybody with such a name."

"Don't you?" He slapped her so hard her eyes watered. "Now listen. I don't have all night and I want straight answers."

"Go to hell."

Before she had a chance to pull back he slapped her again and twisted her arm until she cried out. "You want this working body to be covered with bruises? You don't have no Sam now. That much I can remember. Now what name are you goin' under these days?" He twisted her arm again.

"Wanda." She would not cry. Not even if he did kill her. Or beg either.

He let go of her and slapped his knee. "Sure! Now it all

comes together. You had some kind of a mess with your kid . . . and Hickock was the judge. I read about it . . . Okay. Now back to square one. What are you up to here with his kid?"

"It's no damn business of yours—"

She saw his attention was suddenly diverted and she heard him say slowly as if he had made a happy discovery, "Hello . . . ?"

Following his stare she saw a car pull to a quick stop beneath the portico. It was unmarked but it was also unmistakable with its flickering green light on the top. Two men got out and entered the motel at a fast walk. The *man* . . .

"Well, well. This is a busy place," Leo said. "Maybe I been missin' somethin'."

He was fascinated with the lighted area of the portico. One door of the car was left open and occasionally they could hear the strident tones of the police radio. Her thoughts kept leap-frogging over each other. Everything had worked out so perfect . . . and now . . .

Try sweetness and light. "Please . . . can I go now?"

With his eyes still on the portico he said, "Hell no, I want to stay for the rest of the show."

Wanda studied his profile. She *had* seen him before—somewhere. Somewhere way back, before she went off to Clark. He knew Sam or at least had heard about him so he must have been one of that city crowd who used to give stag parties and invite girls in to perform. Usually they were a bunch of clowns but they paid well and whenever a girl had a chance to work a party she took it. "I wish I could give you the clap," she said.

He laughed and said he wouldn't touch a hooker like her with a ten-foot pole. Somebody had swiped his eleven-footer. And then he raised his eyebrows, cocked his head and said, "Well now what do you make of that?"

He nodded toward the portico where the two men appeared with Victor between them.

When she saw he was handcuffed she caught her breath and in spite of herself thought, "Damn you, Judge Hickock, why did you have to have such a nice guy for a son . . ."

She saw the men shove Victor into the back seat of the car and lock the door from the outside. The sight made her cringe and for a moment she thought she actually might cry. It was the way Victor was holding his head, looking at the ground, beat, all bewildered. "If I don't get out of here I think I'll throw up," she said.

"You damn well better not." He slapped her again. Her ears rang and she closed her eyes. When she opened them again the green light on top of the police car was no longer flashing, and she shook herself and took a deep breath. For she knew she was being watched intently.

"What is this?" Leo asked. "What gives with you and the kid and the cops? This seems to be my night for meeting up with old friends. I got a lot of buddies down at the department, and I know those guys. But I don't understand what they're doing coming here and making your john their guest of honor. The whole deal smells to me. And you goin' to tell me about it or do I have to beat it out of you?"

Although she didn't know this man she had seen his kind before and she had no doubt that he would beat her close to death if he felt like it. She knew it happened to other girls in the life. And there was something else to think about . . . if he got really rough he could make her abort or something, louse up her insides . . . And if *that* happened, dear sweet Jesus, there went the whole ballgame . . .

"Are you two into some hard stuff . . . ? It don't make no sense, you don't look like a junkie and neither does he."

She tried to think of an answer that would turn him away, came up empty . . . Oh God, how can I unscramble my brain?

He cupped his hand over her left breast and squeezed it, gradually increasing the pressure. "You gonna start talkin' or am I going to follow the cops and say, Hey, you guys forgot somethin'. There's no charge for delivery. Now how come cops come just in time to pick up the kid and not you?"

She could no longer endure the pain. "Please, *please* stop, I'll tell you . . ."

And she told him then that Victor Hickock had just paid her for a trick and there was nothing more to it. She did not know anything about cops arriving . . .

"That was just a *fluke* that you just happened to leave at the right time? How much did the kid pay you?"

"A hundred."

"Big spender, that kid." He yanked the purse from her hand and fingered through it. He found three tens and a five-dollar bill along with some change. "He got a charge account with you?" He snapped the purse shut and tossed it in the front seat.

"Yeah."

"You're lyin'. And I haven't got all night."

He slapped her so hard her head bounced against the back of the seat. When she started to scream he seized the skirt of her plastic raincoat to protect his knuckles and jammed his fist between her lips. He held her until she began to choke. She groaned, shook her head violently. Finally he took his fist away.

"Okay," she gasped.

"Now start at the start. How come you know young Hickock in the first place?"

By the time she had regained her breath she thought she had the solution. She told him that her girlfriend Nancy worked house and hotel calls and tonight she was too busy when Victor wanted a girl. A lot of the kids at the university were into calling escort services and such just for a new kind of kick, she guessed. She, may God strike her dead this minute in the back of this car, did not know what brought the cops around just when he happened to arrive.

And for a while she was convinced the bastard believed her . . . he said what she had said was all very interesting and he would drive her home wherever that was. She thought of having him drive her to Mrs. Millington's but quickly decided that was a lousy idea . . . And anyway, it was more believable if he took her to Nancy's, whose apartment was in the right district.

Leo Estervan drove very conservatively through the rain, relaxed and almost genial now, his seat pushed far back and half-reclined, a man physically too large for his car. He asked Wanda about Clark and how long she was away and when she would be off probation and she told him she was already free to do as she pleased which was why she had gone back to the life some time ago.

"And how do you feel about Judge Hickock?" he asked as they stopped before Nancy's apartment building.

"I hate him. He took my kid away."

She reached for the door lock. Please God, let Nancy be home because all I want in the world right now is a strong shoulder.

As she started to open the door Leo grabbed her by the neck

and jerked her back to the seat. "You lyin' little bitch. You want to be a cripple for life or are you goin' to tell me how come you know young Hickock."

There was just enough light from the street lamp to reveal Leo's eyes and she knew he meant what he said. She glanced hopelessly down the deserted street. The rest of the human race had vanished. There was only the everlasting muffled vibration of the city.

"Okay." She sighed. Jesus, she had to say something because he was doubling his fist again. "Okay, *okay*. Are you ready for this? I used to work for Judge Hickock."

"Doin' what?"

"Cleaning his house. It was a long time ago."

"How long? You still got a key to his house?"

". . . yeah."

Leo pondered her answer for a moment, then reached across her and unlatched the door. "Better for you if we stay friends," he said. "Now let's go up together and make sure your friend Nancy's for real. Then I want the telephone number here and don't change it. My name is Leo. When and if I call I want your attention. Any questions?"

She saw, to her horror, that he was actually smiling.

Chapter Sixteen

Hickock awoke to the sound of rain pounding on the roof outside his bedroom window. The roof extended over the front porch of 1011 and when he had bought the house (in that other life of so long ago), he had not realized how comforting the roof could be, enabling him as it did to tell the intensity of almost any rain that fell without getting out of bed. A nice self-indulgence. Every morning when he did get up he would stand at the window for a few moments looking down at the street and he would know from the surface of the roof if it had rained during the night, or if there was a heavy dew he would know that a fine day was probable and in the winter the shingles obligingly turned white with frost as if to tell him it was going to be a chilly day.

On this morning he saw that it was raining so hard the whole roof hissed, and when the heavy droplets splattered they formed miniature crowns of water. Now he watched the creation and instant collapse of the crowns, and yawned mightily. The thought came that if it continued to rain as it had since Saturday night he was going to start building an ark.

His mind was not thoroughly roused and he wished he had not had that final brandy with Jean before they went ashore from the *Freedom*. He reminded himself with a smile that there had been a time when he could take a few brandies after dinner and never know the difference the next morning, but those days were obviously gone. Just one, which could hardly be considered heavy consumption, added to the single jigger of rum in water he had taken before they had dinner was now telling him that he was no longer in his prime. Oh yes, and there had been half a glass of red wine with dinner. So little to be felt so long afterward.

He yawned again and smiled at his inclination on this gray

morning to reflect on his age. Sixty? That could hardly be considered middle-aged since he did not know anyone who had lived one hundred and twenty years. What was he then? Forget it. Don't say the word.

He was about to turn away from the window when he noticed suddenly that Victor's pickup was not parked in its usual place in the driveway. Hickock went to the side window which looked down directly upon the driveway hoping to see it parked against the house or back by the garage. He was disappointed to see only raindrops plopping into the puddles along the driveway.

Hickock slipped into his bathrobe and the straw Japanese slippers he had worn ever since his service in Korea. He opened his door, marched across the balcony and knocked on Victor's door. "Hey, Vic. Are you awake?"

There was no sound beyond the door. He opened the door very slowly and carefully, already convinced that he would not see his son. The bed had been made and had obviously not been occupied during the night. "Well I'll be damned." He checked the room and Victor's bathroom for notes but found nothing. His toothbrushes were missing and so was his razor, which was reassuring. He had obviously planned to be away.

As he walked thoughtfully back to his own bathroom he tried to remember if Victor had said anything during their last conversation that might give him a clue. He was not exactly sure why he was so uneasy. Victor had been gone Saturday night and now Sunday night as well. Had he said anything at all to him that might provoke him into moving out?

Victor had not seemed to be particularly resentful when he declined the invitation to go sailing over the weekend. Saturday morning at breakfast they had discussed the bad news about Nellie-Mae. The doctor now recommended she remain in the hospital for another two weeks at least. They agreed they would both pitch in and wait on her when she did come home since it would certainly be a little time before she was capable of using the stairs. Until then Wanda could at least keep the place livable. Maybe he should tell her to start coming on the weekends as well.

As he shaved and showered Hickock managed to dispel the gloom which seemed to have started this day. Victor was old enough and certainly big enough to take care of himself. He did not need a nursemaid. Even so, Hickock thought, if he had not heard anything from him before he left for the courthouse he was going to call the university and ask if he had reported for classes.

As he shaved he said to the mirror that he was becoming worse than an old maid. At nineteen youth was gone and early manhood had a way of being wondrously unpredictable.

He was making his breakfast when he heard the telephone ringing in the front hall. He sprinted through the pantry and across the dining room, but by the time he got to the telephone it had stopped ringing. When he picked it up there was only a dial tone. Then I'll use it, he thought, as he dialed Jean Pomeroy's number.

"You're up early," he said.

"I always am. I just tried to call you." There was something about her voice that made Hickock uneasy. She sounded guarded.

"That's nice. I can't imagine anyone in the world I'd rather hear from at this hour. I must have been in the kitchen or the shower. Speaking of which, better take a bumbershoot to work today." He was trying to be as light as he could, but he was not finding it easy. Victor's absence at breakfast had renewed his worrying. Why the hell couldn't people always fit into nice little slots and behave themselves?

Jean said, "What I called about is something . . . well, I don't want to worry you, but I think I should tell you. There are really two things and I don't even know if they're related. I started early to work this morning and when I was backing out of the parking place in front of my house a car came along and hit mine—"

"Were you hurt?"

"No, no. I'm perfectly all right. Not a scratch, but my poor little Volkswagen has a crumpled fender on the left front side and I'm hopping mad because whoever it was speeded up after he did the dirty deed and kept right on going."

"Did you get his license number?"

"No. It was raining so hard I couldn't even be sure what kind of a car it was except it was a big American type. The thing is, and now don't get all in a lather . . . but it did occur to me that well . . . the way it happened so quickly . . . it did look like it might have been deliberate."

"What makes you think so?"

"There weren't any other cars around and he had the whole

street to himself. Why should he swerve over and just nip my fender and then get right back toward the middle of the street?"

"I don't know but we'll sure as hell try to find out."

"Of course he could have been drunk, but then something else happened. When I came back into the house and made an appointment to have the fender fixed . . . you know you have to treat those tinsmiths like royalty these days or they grant you an interview next year some time . . . and I had to call my insurance company . . . well I did all that, and I'm having a hard time bringing myself to tell you this part. Anyway, when I started out the door again the phone rang and there was that funny-voiced man again . . . the one with the parrot throat? He said he had another message he wanted to give you. He said that just to prove he was a nice guy he was going to do you one big favor and it did not involve money. He said he hoped after you got the message you would take a more reasonable look at his problem. That man scares me, Julian. I think he's crazy."

"What was the message? I'll handle him later." For openers I'll revoke his bail, Hickock decided.

"He said you should call Martin Delgado right away. He is not in his office yet so you're supposed to call him at home. Here is his number."

Hickock found that he had to exercise very deliberate control over his hand to scribble down the number.

"I'm going to be awfully late to work," Jean was saying. "But for heaven's sake call me when you can. I'm dying to find out what the message was."

"Do you want me to come by and pick you up? I could be there in twenty minutes."

"No. Get your business done and call me later. I'll be just fine. My love to you."

"Mine to you."

Hickock stood by the phone debating whether he should dignify any message from Estervan by complying with his suggestion. If Delgado had anything to say that was new to his client's case it was he who should initiate the call.

He paced back and forth in front of the telephone as if it were a living thing. And in a way, he thought, it was. It could serve as a go-between for a cunning lawyer whose legal morals were of dubious integrity and the law itself as represented by one Julian Hickock. Here was a classic case of the poor, the rich, and the law. Delgado was unquestionably one of the most skillful lawyers who had ever passed the state bar. With enough maneuvering and a successful impression on the appeals court he could still get his client off the hook no matter how carefully it had been sharpened. And his bill would be what he thought the traffic could bear—in this case Hickock guessed at least one hundred thousand dollars. It was impossible to visualize a poor man or even a citizen of ordinary financial resources receiving the same love and tender care as Boris Estervan enjoyed.

Frowning at the telephone he left it and went to the kitchen, where he made himself a pot of coffee and burnt the toast. Then he went back to the dining room and sat in his usual place at the head of the table. He wanted to put some salt on the toast because he thought it might make the charcoal tastier, but he could not find the shaker. How could items which were longtime fixtures in a home, things like salt shakers and those special fruit spoons that Dolores had bought at a long ago auction disappear so easily? Sometimes he thought, life at 1011 became very close to intolerable because of the big and invisible hole in the floor that everything he needed fell through. Sometimes it was appealing to think about selling the whole works down to the last bedsheet and moving into a nice hotel. And there to die of acute self-indulgence.

He heard the hallway clock bonging nine times and pushed back his chair. He was due in his chambers at ten on this Monday morning to meet with the chairwoman of the local Victims of Violent Crimes, a rather loose organization made up of what he considered might be the most tragic citizens of all, the people whose children had either been kidnapped, raped or murdered, or all three and had banded together for sympathy and in the hope of making a few changes in the judicial system. For the moment at least, their demands were certainly not unreasonable. They wanted the culprits who had scorched their lives to suffer at least some punishment regardless of legal gymnastics. They wanted to know when and where the culprits would be tried and most of all they wanted to be advised when they were about to be released. When a violence-prone psychopath was released on probation it was very uncomfortable to realize that he might not come out of prison loving all the world. He just might be hungering for revenge upon those who had testified against him. They wanted a representative on the parole board, someone who would stand up to the bleeding hearts and waffling bureaucrats who declared who stayed in and who got out. They wanted a judge as one of their trustees and Hickock was inclined to accept their invitation.

Hickock dismissed the subject from his mind and thought about Delgado. This message business from a convicted felon was ridiculous. Obviously Estervan knew that he could not communicate directly with his judge so he had chosen the only method available. Or was there more than just propaganda in his own behalf involved? Could Estervan have really been responsible for the car that had collided with Jean's?

Perhaps, he thought, he had stalled long enough. Long enough, he hoped, to inform Delgado that he was not overly anxious to hear what he had to say. And next he had better do something about finding Victor. Two nights away without any notice conjured up all kinds of nasty visions.

"Well, Martin, what can I do for you?"

"Maybe it's the other way around, Julian. I'm so glad you called me, because you have a problem."

Hickock did not like the sound of his voice at all. He was too smug, too sure of himself.

"Your problem is that I'm going to see your friend Estervan's bail revoked this very morning. You can contact him in the slammer as soon as I get the paperwork cranking."

"Now, now, Julian. I wouldn't do that if I were you."

Hickock's tone was biting. "Well, be advised I am fed up with these so-called messages that come to me via everything but carrier pigeon. And I am wondering if your client's not so fine hand has been involved in another event which just took place this morning." He decided against telling him about Jean and the hit-and-run driver. Why should Martin Delgado of all people know Jean even existed? "So in order to get my beauty sleep I am going to put him in cold storage until I find just the right spot for his future."

"Julian . . . Boris Estervan knows where your son is."

Hickock caught his breath and felt his heart begin to pound. *Estervan* knew?

"Julian, I have two sons myself and while they are not quite as old as your boy I do sympathize with your predicament. I suppose all of us parents have our special problems these days . . . it is hard to blame any one thing directly . . . it's our culture . . . I guess you would say it is the times—"

"What the hell are you talking about? Where is Victor?"

"In the county jail. I'm truly sorry to be the one to tell you, Julian. Neither one of us would have known if it hadn't have been for Boris Estervan."

"What's he got to do with it? And what's Victor supposed to have done?"

"He's in on a narcotics rap. Dealing. He was jailed Saturday night and for some reason he was booked under the name of Raleigh. Boris called me the minute he heard about it."

"He must be mistaken. Why would he hear anything about my son?"

"My esteemed client does not share his sources of information with me. But sometimes I think he has more informants than the CIA."

"I just don't believe you."

"Okay Julian. But is your son at home?"

Hickock felt his stomach turn over. He hated the tone in Delgado's voice. He wanted to slam down the phone.

"My client has many connections, Julian. Both in and out of jails. He does the people who are in them favors. Sometimes they return favors. He's really a big-hearted guy. He even gave me the name of the narcotics lieutenant who arrested your son. His name is George McReady and you can reach him at the department on Extension 233."

"Why didn't Victor call me? If it's true that he's in jail he's entitled to call."

"That I don't know. I'll be in my office all day if I can help you."

"I guess I thank you." Hickock hung up the phone very carefully.

He stood motionless for a moment, trying not to believe what he had heard, then trying to organize his thoughts. There must be something very wrong. It was simply impossible to visualize Victor of all people as a dealer in narcotics. Of any kind. He had not thought to ask what kind. Some marijuana possibly . . . at the worst peddling it to other students—Victor? It was inconceivable.

Hickock recalled the several times he had counseled other families, so-called nice families who had suddenly discovered their kids were in trouble. In times passed, even fifty years ago or less in America, this sort of thing just did not happen. If something did go wrong within a nice family it was an extremely rare event and the offender was shipped away to sea for a few years or sent out west or to Alaska or somewhere out of sight. Presumably then he would mature, see the folly of his actions and establish himself as a stalwart member of the community. Now kids from all walks of life were committing crimes they could not have imagined when he was their age—

"You dogmatic idiot," he said aloud. Condemning before he knew all the facts. Mentally charging his own son with a crime when all he had was the word of a felon and his opportunist lawyer. They're trying to obligate me, and they're damn near succeeding.

He looked for the telephone book. Like everything else in the house it was not in its usual place on the telephone stand and it was certainly not in the hallway. Nothing was as it should be.

He dialed information and asked for the number of the police department. The operator offered several numbers. Was it an emergency? Little did she know. Administration? No. Garage? No. Traffic? *No,* damnit. Hickock asked her if she had anything under narcotics and found he could barely pronounce the word. How about inspectors? Yes, yes.

He copied the number, took a deep breath to curb his impatience and dialed. He asked for Extension 233. The man who answered said he would have to put him on hold. Finally a man said, "McReady."

Hickock introduced himself, trying to keep the quaver out of his voice. How different things were when your own were involved! He asked McReady if he had made an arrest on Saturday night.

"Yessir. I did."

"Can I have some details?"

"No, sir. I can't do that over the telephone."

"Why not? I'm Judge Hickock."

"You tell me that, but how do I know?"

"Is the individual in custody?"

"Yes. You can read about it in the paper."

"How long are you going to be there?"

"All day. We never quit work around here."

Hickock said thanks and put down the telephone. The morning paper, of course. He had been so rattled ever since leaving his bed that he had forgotten to bring in the paper.

He ran to the front door, found the paper and tore at the rain wrapping. Still standing on the porch he searched anxiously on the page which normally offered the weekend's events in municipal court. He found one small item noting that a white male named Raleigh had been apprehended while engaged in the sale of narcotics. The arresting officers estimated there had been more than a thousand dollars worth of cocaine in his possession.

Raleigh? That was the name the housekeeper had given him. He thought to call Inspector McReady back and ask for a description of the suspect and changed his mind. McReady was not likely to give further details on the telephone.

Boris Estervan was still at the breakfast table staring out the window and brooding upon what the rains might be doing to his rose garden when his brother arrived and complained that the rain was so heavy he could not see to drive very well and had thereby been in a minor accident. He explained that he had taken one of the Rosa Corporation cars and knew that under the circumstances his brother would not mind if it got scratched up a bit. Especially after the fine service he had provided on Saturday night.

"What do you mean, under the circumstances?" Estervan had just finished eating one of Rosa's waffles, which was not sitting very well, and the sight of Leo at this hour of the morning added to anxiety about his roses did not improve his digestion. Now the idiot had been in an accident which if he said was minor probably meant the company car was totaled.

"I took the Mercury because it's fast in the getaway," Leo was saying. "There was no one else around anyways so I'm sure no one saw it."

"Saw what?"

"The accident, Boris. Why are you so grumpy this morning? I get up at dawn to do what you want done and I get no thanks. Between so early this morning and so late Saturday night I'm getting awful short on my sleep."

"Do I understand you've been in a hit-and-run accident? If so that's not very smart considering the fact that you are even remotely connected with me. In the future you will remember that we do not get along and almost never see each other. And start using your brain if you have one. Now . . . why didn't you stop?"

"Because I knew you wouldn't want me to. You said just give her something to think about and that's exactly what I done. I nipped her fender good because it was only one of them little Volkswagens. It didn't do no great damage, but I'm sure it scared her."

"If you are talking about Judge Hickock's girlfriend I think I'll have a heart attack. I'm a sick man, Leo. Don't aggravate me any more than you ordinarily do."

"Look! I'm bringing you good news. Just like I did on Saturday when I found the kid and the hooker was in business together. What more do you want in two short days? This morning I'm waiting down the block almost a full hour before Hickock's woman goes to work. I begin to think she is never going to leave. I have her car spotted in its parking place from way last night—"

"Was she hurt?" There was a choking sound in Estervan's throat.

"Nah . . . you told me to lay it on her easy."

Estervan's voice rose to a screech as he pounded his fist on the table. "I did *not* tell you to try and kill her! How can you be so goddamn dumb? Have you ever heard of conspiracy to commit murder? Do you realize what that would do to my case if they found out you were driving that car? How in the name of God did I wind up with you as a brother?"

Estervan was panting with his efforts to make his voice behave, but his vehemence was beyond the capacity of his throat and he choked until bits of waffle flecked his lips.

"Listen to me," he said when he finally regained his composure. "Listen to me very carefully and don't even *try* to think of doing anything on your own hook now or in the future. Just leave all the thinking to me. First rule. Be careful you don't hurt that broad. We don't want any blood on our hands. There are other ways to make life miserable for her until she gets the idea and passes it along to her judge friend—"

The telephone rang and Estervan picked it up quickly. He cupped his hand over his free ear as if to exclude all extraneous noise and his face brightened as he listened. "Are you positive?" he asked the telephone.

He nodded affirmatively, listened a moment longer, then replaced the telephone. He pursed his lips and ran his tongue around his teeth. He looked at his brother questioningly. "I suppose there is no chance in the world that even you could have tailed the wrong kid Saturday night, is there? Tell me it can't be so."

"No chance. I was with him from the time he left his home. I saw cops come and take him away, and even the hooker admits it was him. What more do you want?"

Estervan appeared not to have heard his brother. He continued to stare fixedly at the telephone as if it might soothe the uncertainty in his eyes. "What I don't understand," he said finally, "is why the kid won't talk to nobody—not one word. About anything. He also won't give his real name."

"Who told you?"

Still staring at the telephone Estervan said, "A little bird. Now why isn't he crying for his daddy?"

A husky red-bearded man came from behind a line of desks and introduced himself. "George McReady, sir. What can I do for you?"

Hickock handed him his card, which McReady read at a glance.

"Oh, yes . . . uh, Your Honor. You called about that coke bust Saturday. It was just one of those routine things. Nothing special. I apologize, but you'll understand we just can't give out much information on the phone."

McReady paused as he assessed his visitor. "It isn't very often that we meet judges who are interested in our work. We need all the help we can get from the courts these days. The trouble is, if you'll excuse me, judge, we can't seem to get you guys to understand what we're up against."

"Saturday night. Did you take a young man in custody who gave his name as Raleigh?"

"Correct."

"What does he look like?"

"Big. Like all kids are now. But he's a funny one. Never picked up anybody like him. I read him the *Miranda* and he clammed up. Won't say a word to anyone about anything. I even had to get his name from the motel register."

"Motel?"

"Yeah, the Green Shutter Inn. Junkies love the place. They can get stoned and nobody bothers them."

"Did you actually see him selling?"

"Look, judge, I been in this business a long time. And it isn't getting any easier. Why? Okay . . . I'll take a chance and tell you . . . because judges tie our hands right behind our backs. I think it was way back in 1966 or so that some federal judge ruled we can't do any real interrogation if the suspect objects. So how are we supposed to find out who did anything? I used to work in homicide and in the old days we solved about ninety percent of the murders. Today I doubt if the boys are hitting thirty percent. Excuse me, but you people asked for it. We just work here."

"I asked you a question, lieutenant. I would appreciate an answer. Did you actually see the individual selling cocaine or anything else?"

"Judge, listen to me, will you? I don't like to go into any lecture on life in these United States at this hour of a Monday morning, but maybe if I can get the idea across to you, maybe you'll pass it along to other judges and eventually some good will come of it. First of all this character who calls himself Raleigh is not talking to anybody. He dummies up tight. We don't believe that's his real name but he won't give any other. He won't say where he lives or works or is from. He is smart and he knows if he keeps clammed up we just might not have a case that will stand up in one of your courts. We can't identify him. His prints are back from the computer in Washington and he comes up clean . . . no record at all, which is a little hard for me to believe."

"Why should it be?"

"He had twenty balloons of coke with him in his room and nothing else except an overnight bag. He sure wasn't in that particular motel just for a rest cure or to sit up and watch the late late movie. That place has a reputation that's not quite the same as a Holiday Inn. When we arrive and knock on the door he opens up instantly. He's obviously expecting customers and he's very very surprised and disappointed to see us. We find the stuff in the bathroom and of course he claims he never saw it before in his life. Which is standard procedure. From that time on he is what you might call nonverbal, which is also standard in most such cases.

"Now, judge, since you came all the way over here to our building to ask about this character let me tell you that when I identified myself to the motel clerk she finally agreed to give me his name, but when I asked if he had been there before or if there had been anything unusual about his behavior she told me to get lost. That's the way with people these days, judge. They don't cooperate with us because they don't have to. I'll tell you personally and I don't really care what you think of me, but the system stinks. The public doesn't back us up and the judges don't back us up so where does that leave us? Now that I've got that off my chest I'll apologize again. There was nothing personal in what I just said. And since this Raleigh kid has cost me two nights sleep trying to get a word out of him edgewise, I think I'll go home and take a morning nap."

"May I remind you, lieutenant, that it happens to be Congress and the legislatures, not the judges, who make the laws."

"I don't care who's responsible. It isn't working and you know it as well as I do."

Hickock was only half-listening because the question that had been burning a hole in his thoughts could no longer be postponed. He cleared his throat and stared at the floor for a moment. "Could you give me a little better idea what the kid, as you call him, looks like?"

McReady hesitated and Hickock wondered if he already knew the answer he dreaded.

"We-ell . . ."

Hickock decided that McReady had a particularly annoying way of rolling the word "well" around his slablike teeth.

"We-ell . . ." McReady repeated, "like I say, he's big. Of course it wouldn't present any problem for you to go up to the jail right now and see him although I can't imagine why you'd bother. I'd say . . . well, hell . . . to tell you the honest truth, judge, come to think of it, he looks a little like a young version of you."

Hickock took a deep breath and managed to look straight into McReady's eyes. He found, not surprisingly, that he was rapidly developing a dislike for the man. He said, "That's not altogether surprising."

McReady arched one tawny eyebrow and laid a finger against his nose. He took his time before he lowered his eyebrow again and his voice took on a new and decidedly bitter tone.

"Your Honor, let me tell you something that may be news to you. Now that you have condescended to *de*scend from your high and mighty throne and have a look down here at us working stiffs, let me tell you that you came to a place where the troops don't like judges very much. If you are the least bit interested I'm gonna give it to you straight . . ."

McReady moved his well-worn shoulder holster half an inch

around his rib cage as if the minute adjustment made it more comfortable. "Down here in these parts we don't often get to see a real genuine in-the-flesh judge, so we have developed the idea that too many of them don't know what goes on here and don't care. We work our asses off down here, sometimes eighteen hours a day . . . and plenty of nights too. Every time we leave this building on a business call we don't know for sure if we'll ever come back. Sure, the spaced-out junkies don't give us much trouble, but pushers are a different breed. And they don't like it when we break their rice bowl. Sometimes when we go out on a job things don't work out just so fine and dandy as they do in the movies. Sometimes one of our guys just gets beat up . . . not too bad, mind you, a few cuts here and there, a thick lip, and a black eye or so, just enough to sort of spoil a guy's day. And then every year or so somebody around here never comes back to his desk because they got him downstairs in the morgue, on a slab, laid out all prettylike except for the multiple knife wounds like my long-time partner Jimmie Dinsamira had. It's discouraging to see that sort of thing happen, especially when Jimmie had been twenty-five years on the force and had a nice wife and four kids who had some cause to wonder what kind of an ignoramus let the sonofabitch loose that killed him. Especially when that sonofabitch had a record eighteen miles long . . ."

McReady readjusted his shoulder holster again and the gesture seemed to give him added confidence.

"Now, judge, I can see you are not giving me your full attention, but maybe you should. I don't know or care much what your interest in young Raleigh is, but to me he's just another pusher who's court-wise enough to keep his mouth shut. If he ponies up his bail by this noon it won't surprise me at all since none of those characters are hurting for money.

"Now just one thing before you leave this dirty, worn-out old office full of dumb cops, judge. Just one second before you go back to your nice clean chambers and kick some of the moths out of your law books. The Raleigh kid is not the only pain in the ass we have encountered lately. Between one thing and another I haven't had a decent night's sleep for a week so if I sound a little testy it's because I'm plumb tired.

"And, judge, let me tell you something . . . we hate pushers here because we know them. We also know that there is no such animal as an average pusher. They are not all slick-looking black dudes or Puerto Ricans or what have you, and they have a thousand disguises. And not all of them throw money around. They can look innocent as choirboys and live like monks so no matter what you tell me about maybe we are jumping to conclusions around here, it does not sell me that he is a case of mistaken identity. And finally, judge, just in case you have been nursing some thought that somehow the whole thing just did not happen and I could be persuaded to forget it . . . just *you* forget it. Maybe young Raleigh is a friend of yours or a relation's relation. I don't care. Maybe you are a friend of the mayor and the chief and can manage to have me fired if I don't seem to think your Raleigh is the scout leader he looks like. The fact that he's young and does *not* have a beard cuts no ice. I'll regret being fired because my heart has been in this goddamned job, but my wife will consider it a blessing because she likes to have me spend an occasional night at home. My kids, who think I live here instead of there, will feel likewise, as will my dog, who is not quite sure if this rare visitor to his territory is to be trusted. Now, any further questions, judge?"

Hickock realized that his feelings about McReady were mellowing. For a moment he thought to defend his own profession—McReady should sit on a bench for a while if he wanted to see the ultimate in tarnished human images, but he decided against it. Someday he hoped to benefit by McReady's street knowledge and perhaps show him why so many apparently inconsistent decisions were made by judges.

"Well, lieutenant," he said solemnly, "there are two countries I know about that have very little trouble with drug pushers. They are Singapore and Iran. They stand them up against a wall and shoot them. Sometimes with full TV coverage. Anyway, have a nice day."

Hickock found the wait for an elevator to his chambers interminable. When he finally reached his floor the sharp rapping of his heels on the corridor's marble floor reflected his impatience.

He was certain now that the so-called Mr. Raleigh was his son Victor and his first instinct had been to go directly to the county jail. He had actually started in that direction after he left McReady, but he suddenly realized that parental concern was getting in the way of clear thinking. Trying to talk with anyone in jail was a miserable business. There were very few people who could keep their spirits up in such a wretched atmosphere. No, the thing to do was get cracking on the formalities because the sooner Victor was *out* of jail the earlier they could try to sort things out.

Meanwhile he reminded himself that a man who retains himself for a lawyer has hired a fool for a lawyer.

He moved at a half-jog toward his chambers and his pace did not slacken as he passed Lucinda in the outer office. "See if you can get me Nathan Wolfmann. Right away."

He continued into his chambers, sat down quickly in his big leather chair and rubbed at his great nose while he waited. It was very odd, he thought, how people who had been the most casual acquaintances sometimes had a way of becoming vitally important, and the transformation took only seconds. Three years back, Nathan Wolfmann, as the then-current president of the local B'nai B'rith, had invited Hickock to be the guest speaker at their annual banquet celebrating Rosh Hashana. His subject had been on a favorite theme, major judicial decisions in history, and apparently the talk had been quite successful. Nathan had been grateful for his appearance since he said guest speakers who could tolerate kosher food were rare, and those who could be entertaining on such a heavy theme more so. Nathan Wolfmann was a lawyer specializing in criminal cases and his professional reputation was at least on par with Delgado's.

Lucinda said on the telephone that her feelings were hurt because he had been in such a hurry he had not even said good morning. She also said that Nathan Wolfmann was on the other line.

"Nathan?"

"Julian. Warm greetings from the firm of Wolfmann, Haphazard, Reckless, Protocol and Driving."

Hickock knew that Wolfmann was a loner, a rare lawyer who took pride in the individuality of his office. Young lawyers stayed only for a short period under his devoted tutelage. Instead of taking them in as partners he urged them to go out on their own to small towns where they were so much needed and eschew the rich fees of the big cities.

Now Wolfmann's sonorous voice reminded Hickock that he was one of the most charming and fascinating men he had ever met. "I hope you're not calling me just because you have a problem," he said.

"I'm afraid I do. I've been informed that my son Victor is in the county jail charged with selling narcotics. He's there under the name of Raleigh and apparently refuses to talk to anyone. He won't even give his right name."

"Oh? Would he be trying to protect you?"

"I don't know. I can't believe the story, but there it is."

Wolfmann said that he was very sorry and asked when Victor had been arrested. "Of course I will get right with it, Julian. I'll try to get him released to your custody, but you'll probably have to put up some bail. Of course if he skips town I'm afraid you'll be in a very sticky situation."

"I don't give a damn about my situation. He's my son. He's in trouble and I want to help him with everything I've got."

"Write a note for his release and sign it. I'll send someone over for it. And difficult though it may be, try to relax. Avoid spicy foods for the next few days. If he was arrested Saturday night he's probably in arraignment court right now. Paperwork and this and that takes a spell, but he should be available by midafternoon. I'll call you."

"I'll be there ten minutes after I hear from you . . ." Hickock hesitated. "And tell him I love him."

Chapter Seventeen

Using the house as security Hickock had borrowed the bail money from his bank without, he was relieved to learn, having to explain what it was for. So old 1011 was once more in hock. And the scene in Nathan Wolfmann's office had hardly been less embarrassing. Victor, after a strangely formal thanks for his release, remained stubbornly reluctant to discuss the matter. He said, "I have a lot of thinking to do. And a jail is no place to do it. Please give me some time."

Hickock and Wolfmann had exchanged glances, which said plainly they agreed that nothing would be accomplished by contesting Victor's mood. During his arraignment that morning he had refused to say a word except "not guilty" to the charge—*possession of and sale of narcotics*. He had refused to talk to the public defender, the bailiff, the jail officers, or anyone else.

There had been a brief exploratory conversation after they had left Wolfmann's office. It was already very late in the afternoon and Hickock was driving Victor home to 1011.

"By the way. Where's your pickup?"

"At the Green Shutter Inn . . . I hope."

"We better stop by and let you bring it home. Do you have the key?"

"Yes."

"I assume you understand that I'm now legally as well as morally responsible for you. If you should leave town I would have a lot of new problems."

"I'm very sorry you have any."

Hickock had waited until he was sure the pickup started and then drove away. He saw Victor following him for a time in his rearview mirror. Later, when he checked again, he saw that the pickup was no longer behind him. Maybe, he thought hopefully, he had to stop for gas.

Hickock had been at 1011 nearly a full hour before Victor arrived. Vowing not to ask what had taken him so long en route he said, "Apparently our friend Wanda decided not to come to work today. Things are sort of in a mess around here."

Victor had shrugged his shoulders and started up the stairs.

"Just a minute, son. The name you chose . . . was it just a coincidence that it happens to be the same as our housekeeper? If there's something between you two maybe now's the time to get it off your chest—"

"Now is not the time. I've got a lot of thinking to do. I'd like you to be patient with me . . . dad."

"Sure." As he watched him climb the steps toward his room Hickock realized it had been a very long time since Victor had called him "dad."

That evening they sat at opposite ends of the dining room table and Hickock thought the distance between them could only be measured in light years. He had opened a can of vegetable stew and Victor had made a plain lettuce salad which along with a rather stale loaf of rye bread composed their evening meal. It had been prepared in conversational silence which was relieved only by the kitchen radio's omnipresent monologue of manufactured news.

Hickock sat back in his chair and tried to seem relaxed. "This stew is pretty awful," he began. "You have to be extremely hungry to appreciate it." And I have certainly lost my appetite, he thought. If Victor would just come out of his protective shell and say that he was so hungry he could eat anything or say he was not hungry, or say that the food in the jail was worse, or *something,* then maybe the tick-tocking of the big clock in the front hall would not sound so loud. But Victor showed no sign that he had heard anything.

"Sooner or later we are going to have to communicate, Vic. We have to face all the facts in this thing and get on with our lives. You have to get back to school and I have to get back to my court and, among other things, a man named Estervan."

Hickock wished he had not mentioned Estervan. His name seemed to be the wrong note to touch on at this moment. It clanged harshly like metal to metal. Victor knew at least something about his case and if he was as innocent as he said he might justifiably resent being thrown in the same mental bag with him. On the other hand if it had not been for Estervan, Victor would still be in jail. But damnit all, where was the truth? What was Victor Hickock of 1011 Maple Avenue doing in a sleazy motel with twenty grams of cocaine?

"Look here, son, you know, or should know that I'm for you one hundred percent no matter what you've done. And I *always* will be. But I can't help you if you won't talk and the longer you hold your tongue the tougher it is . . . all the rationalizing I do falls to pieces when it seems you're trying to hide something from me. So answer me just one question. What were you hoping to accomplish by giving the police a false name? Were you trying to protect me or yourself or both . . . ?"

Silence took over the dining room once more, but Hickock was determined to break it. He waited as long as he could bear it then put his fork carefully on his plate and smacked his fist down on the table. "Answer me, damnit!"

Victor kept his eyes directed at the tabletop when he said, "You."

"All right. We make progress. I appreciate your consideration for my good name, and yes it is probable that any press stories on this incident would not help my chances for election. But I assure you I don't give a hoot in hell what *anyone* says if it means we are not together on this thing. You can tell me what it's all about, no holds barred, but I can no longer be kept in the dark. You are accused of a felony, which is a very serious charge. If it can be proved that you have broken the law you could be sent away for a long time and it is very unlikely that the judge who will hear your case will be lenient because you are my son."

Intolerable silence again.

"There is just so much I can do, Vic. We are very lucky to have Nate Wolfmann on our team, but even he can't work without knowing the full truth. What I want you to understand right now is that this thing just won't go away because we don't like it. If you fail to show up in court at the appointed hour ten days from now, a pair of cops will come and take you there. I'm not trying to scare you. I just want you to recognize that is the way things are going to be. I believe you're innocent because you have said so, but you are my son and I'm naturally prejudiced in your favor. A jury won't be unless you give them the chance . . . offer them something on which to hang their belief on that a nice guy like Vic Hickock would not be mixed up in such an affair. Am I getting through to you?"

"Yes," Victor said finally, "and you have since the beginning. The trouble is you say you believe one thing and you think the other. You say you are one hundred percent behind me, but you talk to me as if I was guilty. I am very sorry this happened, but at least I know where I stand. In your fine preformed, prefabricated, judicial mind I have to be guilty."

"I did *not* say that, nor have I suggested it."

"Then why are you telling me I can be sent away? Is that what happens to people who are innocent . . . I haven't had any sleep for two nights, what with one thing and another. I don't ever want to go near a jail again. I knew there was no use telling the police anything. Their minds are made up. The same when I went to court this morning. And now you. I can see it in your eyes. *Sure* you're willing to help me. Duty calls. And you are a duty-bound person."

Hear him out, Hickock warned himself. I've just got to sit here and take it so he can let off steam to someone. If he'll just let it all out maybe I'll find out how he got mixed up in this in the first place.

"This has been an education for me," Victor was saying. "Now I know what it's like to even look like you are on the wrong side of the law. You don't have to break a law to be hauled off to jail. You just have to look like you did. Now I know what it's like to be a definite maybe."

By God, Hickock thought, he is right. Some uninvited genie in his brain had reversed his natural prejudice in favor of his son and he had subconsciously found him guilty on purely circumstantial evidence. It occurred to him suddenly that he would not have assessed a total stranger so impulsively.

"Well, something was wrong, Victor, with whatever you were doing. Otherwise I can only assume the police would not have been involved. All right, you are totally innocent. But will you please help me by giving me just one little thing to stand on? Will you please tell me what you were doing in that motel and why narcotics were found in your possession? I am trying with everything that is in me to understand why those things happened to be. If you can prove you weren't involved let me call Nate and get him started on having the case dismissed."

"Can you do that? Just like that?"

"I can if we can come up with some new hard evidence that will back up your plea of not guilty. It's much easier to stop the legal machinery now than it will be later."

Victor rose very slowly from his chair, stretched his arms toward the ceiling and yawned. "If I wasn't so beat I would go down to the hospital and see Nellie-Mae. She wouldn't need any diagrams or lengthy explanations to convince her that what I say is true. Because Nellie-Mae thinks with her heart instead of her brain. Whatever I said she would take as the truth without any ands or buts about it . . ."

Victor lowered his arms and placed both fists on the table. With his shoulders hunched forward he leaned across the table and his voice held a fierce quality Hickock had never heard before. "If you ever *had* much sense of tolerance it died somewhere along the way," he said. "You have been sitting up there on your throne for so long you don't know what goes on with the real people in this world. You have been judging others and telling people they were wrong and dishing out punishment for them without anyone ever judging *you*. Well, I do now. And I say I don't want your help. If our so-called judicial system is as good as you seem to think it is I don't need it . . . or anyone else's. I'm not guilty and if the system is any good then I'll be found not guilty. I know I'm young and you think I'm not dry behind the ears. And maybe you're right. But I shouldn't need a clever expensive lawyer to get me off for something I haven't done. When they ask me in court to tell the truth and nothing but . . . I will. And if I don't walk out the door then I'll know what a lousy system employs you."

Victor picked up his plate and water glass and passed quickly through the pantry door to the kitchen. After a moment Hickock heard him climbing the back stairs and knew he had gone to his room.

Hickock put his head in his hands and closed his eyes. He sat motionless at the table for a long time. And he knew that although there were no tears he was weeping for his only son. My generation, he thought, was a long time losing our ideals even with the help of wars. Now the young became realists almost before they had a chance to dream.

Despite his exhaustion Victor found he could not sleep. His thoughts fluttered like butterflies between visions of Wanda and the sharp-edged memories of his two nights in the county jail.

Where *was* Wanda? After his father had dropped him at the Green Shutter parking lot he had driven the pickup to Mrs. Millington's house. Nice woman. She had met him at the door and told him that Wanda had left. She did not know for where.

Of course, he decided, it was still possible that Wanda had nothing to do with the stuff the police found in the bathroom. It could have been left by a previous occupant and the maid had not bothered to look in the bathroom cabinet when she changed the linens. But if so why had Wanda left while he was sleeping? They were *supposed* to have had breakfast together.

Once again he tried to recall those terrific hours they had spent in each other's arms. And once again he could not find a single act of Wanda's behavior that would indicate she wanted to make trouble. After the police arrived he tried to believe . . . needed to believe . . . that she had somehow heard their coming and had, understandably, made a hasty escape. Since she was on probation she would naturally want to avoid any contact with the police. Would have to. But now? She had left Mrs. Millington's with no forwarding address. She had paid what she thought she owed—sixty dollars, which Mrs. Millington said was unnecessary. "She was such a nice girl . . . I'm afraid I shall be worrying about her," the lady had said, and he had promised that if he heard anything he would let her know.

It was inconceivable that a girl in Wanda's circumstances could afford to by that much cocaine. *There* was the number one sticker. And that was one reason why from the very beginning he had kept his mouth shut. Why unfairly involve Wanda with police trouble, any more than his father . . . but now since she had left her sponsor with no explanation or address things were looking to be considerably different . . .

Would Wanda, if it *was* Wanda, do such a thing?

Victor found it difficult to believe that he was lying in his comfortable bed in this large silent house occupied by only one other human being. For the first time he was acutely aware that only a few miles away in the same city other people were trying to sleep although their chances of finding any real rest were almost nil. All night long they would endure the banging and clashing and snicking sound of metal sliding into metal as cell doors and entrance doors were opened and closed. Toilets were always roaring and hissing because there were not nearly enough bowls for the inhabitants of the larger cells and not all of the smaller cells had relief facilities.

No one except those in the drunk tank seemed to sleep in the county jail. The inmates babbled all night long spilling their woes through the bars to each other, to themselves, to the world at large. They told mainly of the bum raps that had resulted in their present confinement. Only rarely did anyone admit he had actually done what the authorities said he had done. Such a confession would have shocked the prisoner community.

The reception area for arriving prisoners was painted a sickly urine yellow and the booking officer looked out from behind a glass-enclosed area painted the same color. McReady and his partner, a man he had introduced as a Jack Simpson . . . or was it Stinson . . . left as soon as the routine of booking was completed.

McReady said to the booking officer, "This smartass has been told his rights and read the *Miranda*. He understands English but he's not speaking it. When he gets used to the scenery around here somebody ought to have a chat with him and find out what his real name is. Right now just book him under Raleigh, white male about twenty, place of residence unknown, and put him on hold until tomorrow. It's worth taking a few hours of my Sunday to see if we can get him to communicate." Then McReady had looked at him for a moment as if he had discovered a variety of creature he did not recognize and he said to the urine-yellow room, "Anybody who has so little to say must have a lot to say. So you think about it, pal, and tomorrow being the Sabbath maybe you'll feel more like singing."

He had been issued a pair of yellow short-sleeved coveralls and worn tennis shoes, then a very young uniformed officer escorted him to a small room painted yellow. He was instructed to stand in front of a white wall and be photographed. The officer informed him that the number board hung around his neck indicated he was the nine thousand and fifty-first prisoner to be photographed this year. Afterward the officer asked him if he had ever been fingerprinted. Obviously he believed he was talking to a drug dealer and obviously everyone else was convinced of the same thing no matter what Victor Hickock chose to say. So the hell with all of them. They could find out their mistake the hard way.

The patch on the officer's sleeve moved up and down as he shrugged and began his business. He grabbed Victor's right wrist and took a print of his full hand and then the fingers one by one. He went through the same motions with the left hand, cleared an errant smudge off one print and handed Victor a piece of tissue to clean his hands. He was asked if he wanted to make a telephone call and he had declined with a shake of his head.

He was escorted back to the booking desk where a third officer pressed a button on a dung-colored gate and took him through a wall of bars. Once beyond the gate the officer halted, closed the gate and removed those damned handcuffs. It was incredible how automatically guilty they made a man look and feel. They passed a uniformed officer who was tipped back in his chair by an inner gate. He looked up from the newspaper he was reading only long enough to press another button. They passed through the second gate, and as Victor now remembered he had heard a telephone ringing insistently somewhere far behind him. It was the last sound he heard of a world that he had previously taken for granted.

As he was led down an alleyway between two rows of barred cells he had looked straight ahead. Anger, he hoped, would save him from the fear that threatened to overwhelm him. His peripheral vision told him that there were people everywhere, moving, looking, yelling and grunting.

"We'll put you in the executive suite," the jailer said, reaching to his belt for a small ring of ordinary keys. "It's the only place we have left. Saturday night, y'know. We'll have people stashed out in the hallway before morning."

At the end of the cell block the jailer stopped and unlocked a door which was not barred. It was a very ordinary heavy metal door with a single diamond-shaped port in the top half. "This here," the jailer said, like a tour guide, "is where we used to keep the mops and buckets and disinfectant and stuff like that, but we had to move them downstairs and use this space. I dunno what we're goin' to do if the county doesn't come up with more money to build more space."

The jailer pulled the door open and Victor stepped through it. He heard the door slam behind him, heard the snick sound of the heavy lock's movement. He saw three black faces staring at him as he stood beneath the single bare bulb hanging from the ceiling. He saw two double bunks; the upper and lower on his left were both occupied and in the lower on his right sat a huge barefooted black man. He said without smiling, "Welcome to the broom closet, honky." He nodded at the galvanized steel trough which had apparently been used to wash mops and brushes. "You want a wash you go there. You want a drink you go same place. You want to piss you call for the jailer an' he take you away. What's your name, man?"

Victor made no reply.

"All right. Nobody here cares anyway. Your bunk up here above me. You snore an' I kill you."

The big black man lit a cigarette and blew smoke at Victor. "What you here for, whitey? Tell us your troubles."

Victor kept his silence.

"Okay. You got a ticket for overtime parking. Just don' move around too much up there tonight. You keep me awake tonight and I be in a bad mood so I kill you in the morning." He laughed dryly and the others laughed with him.

From that moment on all three black men had ignored him although they kept up an almost continuous patois between themselves through the night and part of Sunday. Then two of them were taken away. The big black man was replaced by a scruffy white man who kept chattering to himself when he was not coughing and noisily clearing his throat.

Yearning for sleep Victor rolled over on his other side. In his mind he saw flickering images of the Green Shutter Inn. They jumped and scattered in sequence, like an old movie. It had been McReady's partner who tore the place apart. It seemed less than a minute before he was holding those twenty rubber balloons under his nose and saying he supposed their existence was a total surprise to him.

Surprise? Well it sure as hell was. Saying they must have been left behind by the person who had the room before only made McReady laugh. He asked if that was so, then what were you doing here? And from that moment on his big clam-up . . .

Victor rose from his bed and put on a bathrobe. Sleep seemed out of the question for a while. He sat down at his desk and started to write a letter to his sister. He was certainly not going to charge a long distance phone call to his father. Not the way things stood between them right now . . .

Dear Sally,

A lot of things have happened around here and it's a good thing you are back east. I have been in jail for the first time in my life. It was quite an experience. You can imagine how dad took it.

The worst part is that I am not guilty of what they say. Selling drugs. You know I don't even smoke pot. Dad seems to think I'm guilty . . . or at least isn't concerned I'm innocent . . . although he did bail me out. I guess I was pretty mad at him tonight, he's so iron-headed.

So far the papers have not found out that Judge Hickock's son was arrested, but probably they will in a few days and I'm sorry about that. Stone-headed though dad may be, he does not deserve that sort of thing.

I now have a whole new attitude toward people who find themselves on the wrong side of the law. The way it is now is unreal and unless we do something about it soon the jails and prisons all over are going to explode.

1011 misses you and so do I. Every time I pass your room I think of the fine old talks we had together there and mom coming in and telling us to quit our jabbering and get to sleep. Remember?

Well, sleep is what I have to try now. My eyes won't stay open and my mind won't stay closed, but my face is about to fall on this paper . . .

Your jailhouse brother,
Victor

Chapter Eighteen

It should have been a glorious morning. Hickock thought as he eased his car into the street. There was an electric crispness in the air, the sunlight was mellowing, and the first ambers of autumn flecked the trees. But it was an uneasy morning, to put it mildly. Victor had still been in the shower when he called goodbye, so the inevitable tension of conversation between them was delayed. But not the deep anxiety Hickock felt about his son's situation.

Hickock drove directly to the hospital because he wanted to see Nellie-Mae and tell her what happened. She was sitting up in bed waiting for her breakfast tray when he arrived, and he had barely said good morning and inquired after her night's rest when she noticed his anxiety.

"You're troubled, Julian."

"What makes you think so?"

"I know that face of yours in the morning. It's like a mirror to me. I can tell whether you like your eggs straight or over just by the way your eyebrows wiggle. You can't keep secrets from Nellie-Mae, you know that. Is the young woman giving you trouble?"

Hickock managed a smile and said, "Not yet." And then he told her as much as he knew about Victor and their problem.

"I knew you two were going to get in trouble. Dope! My Victor? I just can't believe it."

"He says he's innocent, which I want to believe . . . I *do*. I don't think Vic is a liar and he's never been the kind to get himself in serious trouble with the law. But he is now, no question. The problem is I don't think he realizes just how much trouble he's in. He seems to think that if he just keeps his own counsel and persists in his statements of innocence the system will take care of him. Partly that's my fault because I've been saying the system is to be trusted when I knew better. Know better. There are plenty of times when I've seen the system not only explode in my face but hit the wrong target. It's supposed to protect the weak, but sometimes it doesn't even protect the strong. Or at least those perceived as strong."

"You mean to tell me you're a full-fledged high-falutin' judge and you can't get Victor cleared of this awful thing? Hell, go to the Supreme Court!"

"It's not the Supreme Court that I'm worrying about and no, *I* can't get Victor cleared. Our system was put together by a group of practical men who became temporary idealists. Sometimes I think they distrusted everyone . . . and especially individuals with power. I'll give you a lecture . . . the Fourteenth Amendment says that no state shall deprive any person of life, liberty, or property without due process of law, which is all very fine except that you can play that sort of by ear. If this thing ever gets as far as a courtroom I hate to think what a half-smart prosecutor can do with the evidence he already has. He's going to do his best to convince the jury that here's a rich kid because he lives in a nice neighborhood. We know better, but the jury won't be invited to look at my bank account. They will be told this rich kid is peddling dope just for kicks and would sell the stuff to their own kids."

"Can't Victor just tell them he didn't have anything to do with it?"

"He can. But who's going to believe him when so much of the evidence is against him? He can plead his innocence all the way to the penitentiary."

"How about the judge? Won't he see the truth of it and let him off?"

"Not if a jury says he's guilty. That's part of the system. You choose a team of twelve amateurs and ask them to referee a complicated game played by two skillful professionals who are out to win no matter what the rules. They are the defense and the prosecuting lawyers. And any judge or lawyer will tell you there is no predicting what a jury will do."

"I hate to see you worrying so."

"Nathan Wolfmann, and there isn't any better, is officially in charge, but I just can't sit on my hands and wait. So I'm going to do a lot of leg work starting as of right now."

Hickock knew he was thinking out loud when he said, "If we start out with the absolute conviction that Victor is innocent then there must be a key somewhere that will tell us more than Victor knows himself. Maybe the reason he was in that crummy motel is important . . . since he doesn't know how he wound up with so much cocaine we have to find out. There are several things I'd like to know. With all the pushers operating in this city how come the narcotics squad made only one bust on Saturday night which happened to be Victor? Was that just coincidence? And how did Boris Estervan find out Victor was in jail when he refused to talk to anyone, let alone say his own name?"

Hickock had expected John Exeter's office to be unusual but he was not prepared for the miniature building which sheltered his legal enterprise. It was located in a part of the city's downtown that had fallen into nearly total disrepair and had then been rejuvenated by people like Exeter who preferred the old to the new and were not afraid of urban rot.

There were six employees on the first floor of Exeter's tiny building and they were all black. "They understand people in trouble better than whites," Exeter explained, "and people in trouble are my business. Now to what circumstance do I owe the honor of this visit? We're not accustomed to receiving such distinguished individuals."

Exeter pulled at his beard, took a deep drag at his cigarette, and smashed it into an overfilled ashtray. He blinked at the morning light through his grimy glasses and stared at a window so long unwashed it appeared nearly opaque. The feeble light illuminated Exeter's wild hair in such a way that Hickock thought he might have posed as one of the biblical saints.

Exeter closed his eyes as if in deep meditation and said, "I can't imagine what you're doing here in my humble bailiwick, Julian. May I call you that since there's no bench between us? Are you just slumming or writing an article for *Judicature*? If so, I can offer you tons of research material that's gathering dust in this very building. We're all gathering dust down here, Julian. I hope you'll decide it's the dust of sages not ages."

Exeter puffed his cheeks and blew at the very real dust on his desk, but succeeded only in ruffling some yellowed papers.

"This is where the poor people come," he continued. "Why I tend to trust them is moot, because I learned long ago that it's foolish to do so. Thieves, prostitutes, pimps, muggers, drunks, junkies, pushers, and pickpockets rarely cross my palm with silver, but I defend them anyway. For the pittance the city pays me to see that they get a squarer deal than they might receive without my help and a certain unexplainable and unfortunate compulsion on my part to defend the foolish and improvident, I'm condemned to this outpost in the social wilderness. Enough of eloquence. Now what the hell can I do for you?"

Hickock noted the framed diploma on the wall which attested that one John Hancock Exeter had graduated magna cum laude from Harvard Law School. He also observed that the glass protecting the document was as smudged as the window. "Would you like a cup of tea?" Exeter was saying. "We could lace it with a little gin."

Hickock said it was a bit early in the day for him and added, "I'm here unofficially. I'm here because I'm afraid my knowledge of the street is limited. I know it's unforgivable in a judge, but I think the majority of us robed solons are handicapped in the same way."

Exeter lit another cigarette and blew smoke at the ceiling. "We never hear apologies for anything around here. I find it very refreshing." He took a deep drag of smoke and coughed. "My cancer proceeds."

"Could I ask you a few questions?"

Exeter glanced at the large railroad-style clock on the wall. His eyes followed the swinging pedulum for a moment. "In twenty-eight minutes, unless you decide otherwise, we are due to meet in your court and knock things around. I take it you're anxious to learn something you'd just as soon not discuss there."

"Do you know anything about a place called the Green Shutter Inn?"

"Sure. It's a junkie hang-out. I would say it's not the place to take the family for Thanksgiving dinner."

"Who owns it?"

"Mort Cheniskie. He lives in Carson City and operates a string of small motels."

"Would he be in the narcotics trade?"

"I doubt it. Strangely enough, he's not money hungry. His passion is fishing . . . ties his own flies, that sort of thing. If you're looking for some gambling action of a very mediocre caliber I understand you can find it at the Green Shutter . . . but that's hearsay."

"Do a lot of young people go there for what might be a different sort of action? Say people of college age?"

"I wouldn't think so. This is a new era, Julian, if you are not already aware of it. The kids don't need motels these days. They do it right out in the open."

Hickock stood up. He tried to smile. He was grasping at straws and he knew it, and the realization hardly encouraged him. "Thanks a lot," he said. "See you in court."

"Is that all you came down here for?"

"Yup." Hickock hesitated. "One more thing . . . maybe . . ." He could not recall when he had been so uncomfortable in front of another man. It seemed that John Exeter's keen eyes were boring a hole right through him. "Will you be talking to any prostitutes this morning?" Usually, Hickock knew, Exeter visited briefly with each of his clients before they actually appeared in court. He had long been on a first-name basis with the veterans and to the neophytes he soon became a father image.

"I think there are about five on the docket. One of them has her own lawyer."

"Would you ask them if they . . . or maybe someone they know . . . was at the Green Shutter Inn early Saturday night? And if by any chance one of them was, arrange for me to talk with her?"

"Consider it done."

En route to his chambers Hickock passed the Public Safety Building and found that he could not resist an impulse to talk with McReady. McReady saw things in black and white, a habit forbidden to a conscientious judge. McReady gave the impression he knew exactly where he stood on everything he thought and did; life must be simple for him. Now this morning when Hickock would don his black robe he knew that all he heard and saw must be taken into consideration, a mental rope trick which presumably just might produce a wise opinion. And still there was always the chance that a gray viewpoint created a gray solution that quite as easily could be hypocritical.

A possible way to have the charge against Victor dismissed . . . there was the case of the *U.S. v. Williams*—the Fifth Circuit Court, 1981. Maybe there was something there? Would the exclusionary rule apply when Victor had to appear in court? If someone like McReady and his partner could be found to have violated the Fourth Amendment then their case, like so many others, could be thrown out the courthouse window. If it could be proved that the evidence had been obtained under the slightest impropriety then McReady and company would not have been acting in good faith.

All right . . . what kind of authority did McReady have to search Victor's room? Still, if he had acted in the *reasonable* though mistaken belief that he was authorized then the evidence would be admitted by the court. Unless one could convince the judge otherwise.

Should he recommend to Nathan Wolfmann that he bring a motion to suppress the evidence, which in turn might even lead to a charge of false arrest? Damn the police, bunch of ignorant rednecks, bullies, breaking in on innocent citizens whenever they pleased. McReady was typical, he thought, as he remembered his sandy complexion and cold blue eyes. Was it possible that McReady was protecting someone who had paid him off and he had inadvertently chosen Victor as a pigeon? He had heard about such arrangements which in many cities had proved very profitable for narcotics officers . . .

Just before he reached the door to McReady's office Hickock came to a sudden halt. He was astonished at his willingness to trim the facts to suit his wishful thinking. The law was for other people if one of your own was involved. The whole world was wrong if the threat struck close to home. Some judge. Some magistrate. Some guardian of legal equity. Like Victor said, trust the system or get out of it. No special, privileged middle ground. Except this was his *son* . . .

McReady appeared rested and to Hickock's surprise went out of his way to seem cordial. "I know what you're here for, judge. Nate Wolfmann is coming to see me at ten. I understand our Mr. Raleigh is your son and I'm very sorry to hear it. It's hard to tell what our kids are up to these days. One of my sons went to Milwaukee last year and found Jesus. We haven't heard from him since.

"One question, lieutenant. Did you make any other narcotics busts on Saturday night?"

"No . . ."

"Then how come you made just the one? How did you find out that the so-called Mr. Raleigh was at the Green Shutter Inn and in that particular room?"

"Simple. We got a tip. It happens and when it does we

follow through, even though most of the time it turns out to be a false alarm. People get mad at each other and think up ways to put one another out of circulation."

"Who gave you the tip?"

"Some woman. Naturally she didn't give her name."

"It was a telephone call?"

"Yessir."

Hickock thought a moment. The vague suspicion that had been troubling him ever since the previous morning became impossible to dismiss. "The woman who called," he said, hoping he was not putting a suggestion in McReady's memory, "do you . . . was it your impression that she had some kind of an accent?"

"She was no foreigner, that's for sure. Well, come to think of it, she did have sort of a southern accent. You know how those broads sound."

"Yes," Hickock said dryly, "I think I do."

Hickock could hardly wait to arrive at his chambers. He passed Lucinda without pausing and went directly to the telephone. He dialed the number at 1011 and let it ring a long time before he was convinced there would be no answer.

He pressed a button on his desk intercom and heard Lucinda's cheerful, "Yes, Your Honor?"

"Dig down in your files of three or four years ago and see if you can come up with anything on a case I heard involving child abuse." The less Lucinda knew at the moment, the better.

He called Nathan Wolfmann, who said he was just leaving to have a talk with McReady. "I think I know at least a part of the answer," he said. "We can be mighty blind sometimes when our kids are concerned. To begin with, I think we have to find my new housekeeper."

They were meeting in the large room next to Boris Estervan's personal sanctum, a space he had always been pleased to designate as the board room. Here on rare occasions the executives of the Rosa Corporation met although the president, Rosa, had never been near the premises; nor had she ever expressed the slightest desire to view the operational center of the enterprise. Boris Estervan was content with Rosa's conviction that a woman should serve as president of the menu and nothing else. He had also been long persuaded that he who would move swiftly and efficiently must do so alone, and now, as always, he regretted even the necessary intrusion of others in his affairs.

They sat around the small mahogany table which had been Estervan's single extravagance in furnishing his headquarters. In contrast the chairs were secondhand and reflected the general paucity of style in furnishings. Whatever physical comforts were available at headquarters were meaningless to Estervan. His sensibilities about such things had calcified after nearly a lifetime of survival, and his tempers whether good or bad were not affected by his surroundings. He used the offices of the Rosa Corporation simply as a tax deduction and a point of collection for the various monies taken in by his scattered establishments. Once in his hands and carefully counted, not even his brother Leo knew what happened to the small canvas bags of dollars delivered biweekly by the different couriers.

Leo was present at this meeting, his bulk looming like a tethered balloon at the far end of the table. His presence was ignored as always and as he expected it to be. Never in his memory could Leo recall having been asked for his opinion. Today Martin Delgado, who was retained by the corporation but was not an officer, was doing his best to soothe Boris Estervan's fulminating impatience.

Today Estervan was becoming more insistent than ever about the influence Judge Hickock had on his affairs. The man had become a prickly thorn in his nearly impregnable hide. Hickock's ever-present intrusion on his personal welfare and his business plans had become a choleric obsession reflected in the ever higher screeching of his voice. The mere thought of Judge Hickock was so distracting it produced a strange overabundance of saliva in his mouth and often caused him to ramble.

Now he pointed one of his stubby fingers at Martin Delgado and said, "You're trying to tell me to hold my water? For Christ's sake I been waitin' one whole month for that judge to make up his mind! What kind of justice is this we got in this country? Can you sue a judge for procrastinatin'? What the hell goes with the man he can't say something by now? Here we spend the last hour yakking about going into the videotape business which we know we got to do or die, and what difference does it make what we decide to do? If that idiot judge keeps me out of circulation for a couple of years we might as well bag the whole corporation. We got at least ten adult theaters we'll have to shut down if that new antiporno bill gets through the legislature; we got five hundred jukeboxes still scattered around the state which are about as useless as tits on a bull. They don't produce like they should any more. They're out and video games are in and we got to buy some and set them up in our locations before somebody else does. We got to put in our orders now and we got to find some sucker to buy the jukes. Who's going to do all this if I'm making license plates?"

Boris jerked is head in the general direction of his brother.

"You think he's going to handle stuff like that and come up with the right answers? Last year the Rosa Corporation grossed one million seven hundred and twenty-six thousand which is better than a kick in the ass, but this year we got to do a lot better on account of that goddamn movie with those girls and all this rigamarole with the trial and all. Leo, he don't understand bottom line at all so if you want to get paid your lawyer's fee you better keep me around to do it."

"There's just so much I can do, Boris. Hickock has a lot of problems of his own right now and I would like to think that eventually he'll come around to seeing things our way."

"What do you mean, *like to think?* You got to lean on him a lot harder. Goddamnit, the man has got to listen to reason or be eliminated—"

"Watch your language, please, Boris."

"I'll say anything I want to say around here. What the hell am I paying you for I sometimes wonder? A while back you sat in that same chair diddling around with your gold pencil just like you're doing right now and you were saying it is not to worry Boris, the jury is going to see things our way. Only it didn't work that way and I suppose if I wind up in the can you'll drop by once in a while to say not to worry again? Am I right in believing that once Hickock says what's going to happen to me he is not about to change his mind?"

"Yes. But we can always take the whole case to appeals court and it is very possible they might take a different view—"

"Very possible? *Might?* I don't want to take chances on no appeals court. The time to reason with Hickock is right now, *before* he commits himself. And if something happens to him now we got two good solid choices. We can work for a retrial with a judge who's not so sticky or we'll have a chance and the time to cook up some new evidence and get the whole thing thrown out. And we got to make a decision on this right now."

Delgado stood up. Estervan asked him where the hell he thought he was going.

"I'm not sure what you mean by something happening to Julian Hickock and I don't want to know. I have already leaned on him as you describe it, far harder than good sense would advise. I value the Rosa Corporation as a client. But no amount of money is going to get me or my firm mixed up in violence and if that's the way you insist on proceeding I hope you fail. Since you appear to be convinced my advice is useless to you and your own efforts are in constant opposition to mine my services are obviously superfluous. If you change your mind and abandon your bullyboy schemes you'll find me in my office. Good day."

Delgado took a handkerchief from his breast pocket, patted at the tiny globules of sweat that had accumulated across his forehead and down the sides of his nose. He secured the middle button of his suit coat and walked without pause to the door. It made a firm *chunk* as he closed it behind him. The sound of its closing fell hard on the silence he left behind him.

Boris Estervan frowned and looked down the length of the table at his brother. "How about that? You ever hear so many fancy words?"

"He's a lawyer. He's got to use them. They get that stuff in school."

Estervan sighed and said that they had just saved themselves a bundle. There was no way the Rosa Corporation was going to pay lawyers who ran out when things got rough. "He reminds me of a guy I knew in the army," Estervan said as if the memory afforded him hidden pleasures. "As far as he was concerned unless you were in the army you couldn't be taught right from left. Any navy guy and especially any civilian was like a dumb animal. You had to lead him to food and water. That's the way he felt right while he was dying beside me on Omaha Beach. He kept saying it was the fault of the goddamned navy. Martin is like that. If you aren't a lawyer you got no right to be wandering around in the world all by yourself. I say I got shot in the neck on Omaha Beach because I was looking after other people instead of myself. And I don't have to have a thing like that happen to me twice."

Estervan sat in silence for a long time. He watched his

brother take a packet of gum from his shirt pocket and apply his heavy fingers to the task of removing the wrapper. He saw him roll the stick of gum into a cylinder with great care and stuff it in his mouth, then begin to chew slowly, his jaw revolving in a figure eight pattern, his lips making occasional little smacking noises.

Estervan eyed his brother with more than his usual disapproval. "Do you have to chew that junk?"

"Yeah. It's good for the digestion. Want some?"

"No. The only thing that will improve my digestion is to get that Hickock to forget about us."

"There might be a way to arrange that."

"Sure. Just call him up and offer him a trip around the world with his girlfriend all expenses paid. A six months' cruise. I already thought of that."

"Maybe he could take a permanent vacation."

"If I follow you I don't like it. Martin is right about one thing. No violence on our part—"

"Maybe it wouldn't be on our part. Maybe we don't know about it. We're surprised as hell to read about it in the paper and very sorry such a thing happened."

"No way. The minute you get mixed up with a professional he's got you by the balls forever. Forget it."

"I'm not talkin' about no professional. But I been thinkin' about that little hooker lately, the one who was mixed up with the Hickock kid. She never went into no details with me why she hates the old man so, but she does. And I would not be too surprised that if she was given some encouragement she might do something about it . . ."

"Why didn't you bring this up before?"

"You told me not to get any ideas on my own. Remember?"

Estervan grunted. He placed his hands on the mahogany table and began to twist his fingers between each other, massaging and intertwining them as if the steady variety of movement would aid his meditation. "It sounds to me like we would be right back risking what Delgado calls a conspiracy charge."

"Why? You don't even know the woman. You never even seen her."

"Yeah, but you have."

"So what? Yeah, I saw her at a party . . . maybe four, five years ago? Can I help it if she suddenly flips and loses her temper? I'm nowheres near her when she does anything. I'm in my own place watching TV. I'm lotsa places and I'll have somebody with me to prove it."

"What makes you think she'll do anything?"

"I can't guarantee, but he's sure not her favorite citizen. And she's a tough little bitch. Who knows? I say it's worth a try . . ."

"What kind of money are we talking about?"

"Maybe zero. I got some leverage on her."

Estervan ceased manipulating his fingers and brought one thumb up to his teeth. He gnawed on the tip of it while his eyes roved uncertainly across the ceiling, around the walls, and finally halted on his brother. He took his thumb away from his teeth and made a flicking gesture toward him. "Okay," he said slowly, "why don't you see what you can do . . ."

Chapter Nineteen

As he had so often lately Hickock waged a silent war to keep himself awake. For too long he had averaged barely more than five hours sleep a night and he knew the strain was beginning to tell. Yet in his mind he was duty bound to see this thing with Victor through to the end or at least until he dropped in his tracks.

Now looking down from the bench of his own superior courtroom as both parties to a divorce case revealed matters to relative strangers that they would hardly touch on to their best friends, Hickock found that he already missed the no-nonsense, fast-action of Butch Goldstein's lower court. And he was impatient with the well-groomed lawyers of the husband and wife as they shuffled through piles of papers containing financial data. How insignificant in comparison with the disappearance of Wanda Usher a.k.a. Raleigh. Finding her had become his dedication ever since that night last month when he was lying in bed rereading Slocum's *Voyage Around the World*. He had just confirmed his belief that Captain Slocum was the escape artist of all time when he heard a light tapping on his bedroom door. He heard Victor say, "May I come in?"

Since they had exchanged only the most necessary sentences for several days Hickock had not been at all sure what to expect.

Victor stood at the end of the bed, his arms folded across his chest. He seemed very uncomfortable, shifting his weight frequently from one foot to another, and once trying the smile that was so reminiscent of his mother. He stared at the fireplace, a heritage from the days when the long ago former owners of 1011 were accustomed to such amenities in their bedrooms. He asked, "Do you ever use this fireplace?"

"No. I'm not even sure if it will draw smoke. I guess I've always been afraid to try."

"How long have you lived here at 1011?"

"We bought the place the year before you were born. It was falling to pieces but it was cheap. We figured on an expanding family and the next year there you were."

"Did it cost a lot of money to fix it up?"

"We did it little by little so it was not too painful. Now I don't really know what to do about the place. It's a relic of a lifestyle that's gone forever and I don't fancy kicking around in it all by my lonesome. Sally is gone and I suppose you'll soon be on your way . . ."

Hickock remembered that a silence fell between them until Victor said, "Maybe you're wondering why I came in here?"

"I must say you have my complete attention. I doubt you've been in this bedroom since you were a very small boy."

"I've been doing some thinking . . ." Victor kept his eyes fixed on the carpeted floor and Hickock saw that he was doing his special fading-away trick again, which usually indicated that what he was about to say might not be pleasing to the listener.

"I guess Nellie-Mae had better come back soon and knock down the cobwebs," Victor said.

"Do you see one down there on the floor?"

"You never know where you'll find a spider at work. They're industrious insects." Victor seemed to experiment with a half-smile.

"I find your concern for the activities of our local spiders very interesting. Now would you mind telling me what is really on your mind?"

"I don't want you to think I don't appreciate this house . . . after all, it is the Hickock home and has been for almost a generation and . . . well, I've been with people lately who never had a home except jail. Never in their lives. It's kind of scary just thinking what that must be like. Dad, what I'm trying to say is, I want you to know I appreciate this place very much."

"That's the second time you've called me dad in a week. I'm pleased . . ."

"Well, you are my father."

Where-oh-where is this conversation leading, Hickock asked himself. He pulled off his half-eyeglasses, inserted a bookmark in the Slocum volume and placed it on his night table.

"Am I keeping you awake?" Victor asked.

"No. Why don't you make yourself comfortable there on the end of the bed? An old judge once told me that people rarely become combative if they are both sitting down. By the way, you made no comment on the fettucini we had for dinner."

"Great."

The smile again. Dolores lived on. "As long as I can read the labels on the can I can't miss."

"What I really came to see you about—"

"Will you please sit down?"

Victor lowered himself to the end of the bed and said haltingly, "Well, like I said, I love this place, dad. I don't want to even think about some other family living here. But I want to get away from it."

"That's fairly normal. But may I suggest you finish college first?"

"I want to get away now. Maybe I could go back east and stay with Sally until this dope thing is settled."

"You can't. Technically you're out on bail. You're remanded to my custody and if you should leave without my permission even for a movie it would be illegal."

"Can't you fix that?"

"Look who's talking. No, I can't fix that."

Victor shoved himself up from the bed and started pacing the room. Hickock saw that he was angry yet he was sure that his anger was not directed at himself.

"I'm not guilty, absolutely not guilty."

"You may have to prove that in a court, but not in this bedroom."

"You told me from the beginning that if there was some new evidence . . . something the police didn't know about or anything else that might help my case . . . then maybe I wouldn't have to go to court at all?"

"Roughly that's correct. But you'd have to appear in court even to have your case dismissed. The law's not something you bump into on a stairway or on the sidewalk and say, Oh I'm sorry and that's the end of it. The law accepts apologies but it can't forget it's been violated—"

"You mean there really is a chance I might go to prison?"

"I'm afraid so . . ."

During the next long silence Hickock had struggled to maintain some kind of order among his thoughts and hadn't succeeded too well. The complexities of the divorce case now before him were relatively simple, almost a respite. The case was barely underway before it deteriorated into a series of accusations and counter-charges founded on an inherently sad situation, but there were moments when Hickock thought the whole affair might be better set to music by Gilbert and Sullivan. Apparently there was no record of infidelities or of physical or even mental violence or even the age-old problem of two people trying to make do with only enough money for one. This husband and this wife, supposedly joined together forever, had endured each other for thirty years. They were both well-educated, well-groomed, well-spoken individuals who lived in one of the city's finest neighborhoods. But they had become bored with each other, or outgrown each other, and what had once been mutual tolerance and presumably affection had now become open hostility. Hickock thought it was almost unbearably sad when elderly people had nothing left to share but the failures they saw in each other. It took extraordinary courage for most people to admit that with the accumulation of years they might change so much they bore almost no resemblance to the original editions. Why couldn't they remember their good times together and be content to let their ghosts separate with dignity?

Now the husband's lawyer was scribbling figures on a blackboard opposite the witness box and asking his client to verify the sums produced by his minor real estate investments and the five dry-cleaning establishments he had worked all of his mature life to make successful. And sooner or later, Hickock knew, the wife's lawyer would be claiming that whatever the total might be, half of it belonged to his client because had she not been there right at his side all the time? Which, of course, would be true.

Hickock rubbed at his eyes while his thoughts went back again to the night Victor had come to his bedroom. He had told Victor that if he had anything new to offer in his defense, for the love of God to come out with it.

"Do you know why I was at the Green Shutter Inn?" Victor had asked.

"I've certainly been wondering."

"I went there because of a girl."

"May I ask who the girl was?"

"I went there to be with Wanda."

"That does not come as a complete surprise to me . . . is that why she hasn't come back to work?"

"I don't know. I tried to keep her name out of this because she once had some trouble with the police and she's still on probation . . . well, I thought I might make a lot of trouble for her—"

"I assume she was actually there with you in the room."

"Yes. But she left while I was still sleeping."

"Why did she leave?"

"That's what bugs me. Maybe she knew or saw the police were coming and took off . . . but she didn't go home to her landlady. I checked that."

"*I* should have checked that. What about the cocaine?"

"I was in the room waiting for her to arrive. I went into the bathroom and fooled around for a few minutes. I remember that, but I can't remember if I looked inside the cabinet. Maybe I did, maybe I didn't."

"Do you think you would have seen the cocaine if you had looked inside?"

"Of course."

"Well, it's clear someone left that stuff in the room before you got there. I had McReady check the names of the three occupants before you signed in. Two were false names with addresses that don't exist. The third was a farmer from South Dakota who was registered with his wife. Not likely candidates."

Victor placed his hands on the mantelpiece and bowed his head between his arms. He kept silence and Hickock was certain he knew why.

"All right, son. We'll start to find Wanda in the morning. . . ."

Now it was weeks later and Wanda had still not been found. On the basis of promised new evidence he had obtained a stay of Victor's trial and a continuance of his custody to himself, but the situation could not be prolonged much longer. There were already some sharp remarks floating through the Public Safety Building, the police department, and even among the people in the courts suggesting that it was very unlikely Judge Hickock's son would ever come to trial. Thus far the media had kept their distance, but proof they were closing in was embodied in one

Larry Constable who had called Lucinda for an appointment this very morning. Constable was a local television commentator with a very long nose for anything askew in the public offices. Once he was on the trail the newspapers would close in for the kill. And no matter how wrong they might prove to be the media tended to resist the bother of making retractions. The wounds of yesterday's news were of little interest to them. And a former judge who lost an election was easily forgotten . . . Where *was* Wanda Usher? Time was growing uncomfortably short and the district attorney's office, including Mr. Terry Undergood, who was hardly a Hickock fan, had taken a particular interest in Victor's case . . .

Hickock directed his attention back to the husband, who was squirming unhappily in the witness box. His ultra-conservative dress suggested that he was the sort of man who abhorred discussing his personal resources with strangers, let alone in a public courtroom, but his wife's laywer left him no escape.

Hickock glanced at the wife, who was wearing long black gloves and a funereal suit ornamented by a single golden brooch. She had no lips, he noticed, at least for the time being. Instead she offered the world a thin crease above her determined chin, and Hickock found himself speculating on how long it must have been since that grim aperture which served as her mouth had offered anyone a kiss. She was sitting very erect and alert in her chair at the attorney's table and if there was either remorse, doubt, or sadness in her bearing then Hickock could not detect it.

The husband seemed mostly bewildered. If Hickock had not missed some important details while his thoughts were distracted then the husband was telling the truth. It was apparent that he wanted done with the whole business. Thus far he had exhibited neither anxiety nor anger at the changes enveloping his established lifestyle. He seemed to express a weariness, as if his exertions in meeting the traditional male standards of the good provider had finally taken more than their usual toll. Hickock had the sudden inexplicable notion that the man might not have much longer to live. In contrast the energies of his no longer beloved were apparent and targeted on the present squabble.

At eleven o'clock Hickock declared his court would recess for half an hour. He wanted to divert what he realized was his growing prejudice against the wife, whose performance in the witness box was anything but sympathetic. Now it seemed that she would only be satisfied with four thousand a month in alimony payments in addition to her half of the community property. Since the husband's gross income per month was three thousand Hickock was having difficulty foreseeing how such payments could be made. He interrupted the wife's long list of requirements she needed to survive in a heartless world and asked how she expected her husband to live even if he could dig up the extra thousand.

"That's his problem, Your Honor," she answered crisply.

Before he could restrain himself Hickock peered at her over his half-eyes and said, "You are wrong, madame. It is just as much your mutual problem as your community property. So far you have given this court the impression that you intend to share only the profits and none of the losses of your partnership. This is not a time for vengeance, but of trying to discover some reasonable way of living for both of you. While this court is in recess I suggest you consult with your attorney to that prospect. And if you fail to come up with figures that are acceptable to your husband as well as logical to this court then I will set my own and I doubt if that will please you."

Hickock got up and heard the rustle of those in the courtroom complying with the bailiff's "All please rise." He made a quick exit through the mahogany doorway directly behind his bench and wondered as he had many times before why no one had ever made a cuckoo clock using a judge in his flowing robe popping in and out of the little door rather than a bird. He might appear on the hour declaring "moot-moot" and the performance would not be too inconsistent with his own. Like a cuckoo he was obliged to keep his opinions to himself except at specified times. His private impression of the immediate proceedings must forever remain secret from the husband and wife now dickering in his courtroom and from all others who brought their troubles there. For he had always thought there should be a small and subtle admixture of fear as a part of such justice as he was able to dispense. The ancient Chinese knew that lawsuits would increase to an intolerable amount if people were not to a degree wary of their tribunals. They believed that all who came before them should be treated without pity and a conscientious magistrate would be at pains to discourage them from having anything to do with the law courts. Every argument since the beginning of history began with two humans who believed they were absolutely right. And since humans everywhere were prone to disagree the only way to prevent perpetual avalanches of lawsuits was to convince people a judge might be unsympathetic . . .

The mahogany door led directly to Hickock's chambers. Passing Lucinda he asked, "Any news?" It was not necessary to specify what sort of news he was waiting for; he had asked the same question for the past two weeks. A character who called himself "Mickey" although his real name was Manfred had been recommended by John Exeter as a man with more local street knowledge and contacts than anyone he knew. Mickey was a five-time loser, a burglar, and a thief currently on parole, and Hickock had been forced to obligate himself to Mickey's parole officer before he was allowed to frequent places where he might find or hear news of Wanda. Mickey was to call Lucinda during court hours or the house the moment he had her located. He would then receive a five-hundred-dollar reward.

Lucinda shook her head. "No news." Lucinda was a study in remorse these days, he thought, and her apologies were strewn around his chambers daily. Since the disappearance of her job applicant she had almost accomplished the act of disappearance herself.

Hickock warned himself that the man called Mickey could have been lying about his efforts all along. It was very possible that his nightly activities when he was supposed to be searching every possible area Wanda might be found were all in his imagination. He claimed to have seen Wanda once—during the early evening in a Pay-and-Save store. Yet Mickey's eyes were bad and he said that by the time he was convinced he had found Wanda she became lost in the crowd. Still, his description of Wanda was remarkably detailed and resembled her in many ways.

Lucinda said in her new subdued tone, "Mr. Delgado called. He said that unless you could give him an early date on the Estervan sentencing he would be unable to maintain credibility with his client."

"Does that mean he's going to be fired?"

"I don't know." She handed him a slip of paper. "I wrote it all down so I would be sure to get it right."

Hickock glanced at the paper and shaped it quickly into the form of an airplane. "What a pity. If he calls again tell him I am deliberating between an old-fashioned hanging or a firing squad. More importantly get hold of John Exeter. Tell him Mickey's services are terminated as of now. Call Wanda Usher's probation officer again and ask if she has heard from her charge within the past few days. I know what she will say but we have to cover all the bases. Also ask Exeter if he has a different number for Margo St. James and her COYOTE organization. I've called there at least twenty times and there's been no answer."

"What's this COYOTE business?"

"Sort of a loose organization of professional hookers. I'm hoping they might have some ideas on how we could find our friend."

"Somehow I'm having trouble relating wild dogs to prostitutes."

"COYOTE . . . call off your old-tired ethics. And don't be so literal. The outfit is actually trying to make things a little easier for the girls although there's going to have to be a considerable change in our national hypocrisy level before they stand a chance of succeeding."

"My, my. You are a liberal thinker this morning, judge."

"More so every day." He nodded toward the doorway to his courtroom. "And people like that woman in there who is making a career out of a divorce are driving me to it."

Hickock continued into his office, seized the telephone and punched Jean Pomeroy's office number. His spirits rose the moment he heard her voice.

"Greetings. This is your judge speaking. I am in dire need of a faith in human nature renewal. Do you know where I can find one?"

"Yes. Just remember that I love you. Remember that although I don't see much of you lately I'm yours to command."

"What happened to women's liberation?"

"Who needs it? I'm paid the same as the other architects at this yard and I have you . . . except I would be a little more sure of my claim if I could have you over for dinner tonight. Do you think we'll ever be able to have a choice so we can say 'your place or mine' like other people who have affairs?"

"I hope so. But tonight I've got to meet some hookers."

Hickock smiled as he listened to the sudden silence on the other end of the line. It was broken only by the distant rapping of a rivet hammer somewhere in the shipyard. Then Jean said, "You *did* say hookers? that was plural, wasn't it?"

"Right. The expert sleuth I hired to find Wanda is getting nowhere. I'm going to have a go at it."

"Well, bully for you. Hoist your quarantine flag when you come by my place again. Just don't get arrested for lewd conduct."

"The police estimate there are about two-hundred working whores in this city. One of them must know where Wanda is."

"It sounds like you're in for a long career. I may be too old for you by the time you find her. And what makes you so sure she's gone back to her old ways?"

"I don't know for sure. It's just a hunch. People who've been in trouble often go back to where it all started. Anyway, there's not much time left and I'm pretty sure the key to the whole thing is Wanda."

"I love you, Julian. Please be careful."

"Give me five nights to see what I can come up with. If I don't make any progress then I'll have to think of something else."

"How is Victor taking all this? I hope he appreciates your efforts—oops, sorry, that was a catty thing to say and I should go wash out my mouth with soap and water."

"As a matter of fact he's mellowing. He said the next time I talked to you to say hello for him."

"I hope you're not just wishing."

"I got him into this so it's up to me to get him out—"

"There you go blaming yourself again. Somehow, love, I have got to get you out of that habit."

"I hired Wanda."

"Did that mean he had to shack up with her? Nuts."

"Are we going to have our first fight?"

"Yes. You have to stop worrying about the trouble other people make for themselves. Otherwise, you're perfect. By the way, if you're going to be such a swinger how about swinging by my place when your research is over?"

"It could be late. You'll be asleep."

"I'll wake up."

"We have a date."

"My mother would not understand. I'm not even sure my father would. But I do. Goodbye, darling."

When he reentered his courtroom Hickock was still thinking that he was among the most fortunate of men.

Chapter Twenty

Since she had moved in with Nancy there was no more of that dawn patrol stuff like slogging off to work at 1011 Maple Avenue. Phooey. This being back in the life even sort of halfway was good for the spirit if nothing else. Most of the people Nancy knew were newcomers, but they were real and they thought the same way you do.

Wanda lit a cigarette. She was smoking all the time these days. It was truly amazing how she had changed her habits once she even got near the old life. She was going to have to kick it though on account of the baby. Starting tomorrow—no nothin.' No, she wasn't really altogether with it back in the life, you better believe. Too risky. Never mind the probation officer. She was too overworked anyway and certainly she could never find little ol' Wanda even if she was right under her nose. Which she almost was. Turning a few tricks here and there might have been all right under ordinary circumstances, but there would absolutely be no physical contact with johns until long after the baby was born. Who needed that part of the life? One thing was for sure. Nobody was ever going to call Wanda Usher Raleigh an unfit mother again.

No question it would have been dull going here if Nancy was not such a dreamboat. She slept all morning, which naturally she had to because she worked the hotels mainly and they were usually late-hour appointments. Guys from conventions and such seemed to throw their watches away once they realized they were like foreigners in town and nobody back home would know what they were up to. And anyway it was a good idea to be off the streets before midnight. You were too conspicuous and then there was always the chance of being mugged by some overeager jerk, or just beat up by some creep.

Afternoons the two of you just sat around yakking or

watching television or both. Dumb programs they had on the box mostly for dumb women. How could any intelligent person swallow that crap? The evening shows were better, but it was still lonesome in the apartment when Nancy left about eight o'clock to check the action. But not little Wanda. She stayed right here . . . out of sight out of mind as they say, just waiting for that big day eight months from now. All confirmed. No period last week. Missed completely. First time ever.

Now there was just waiting and thinking and really not minding at all because it was going to be some event. This here child was going to be all golden. Take his father. Then take his mother. Mix the two and what do you get? A solid gold kid.

He was going to be perfect because he was conceived at the right time of day with Mercury in the ascendant and Libra in the serving position. It said right in the paper that such was the situation and the Pay-and-Save had a whole bunch of astrological magazines which said the same thing. It was just neat to think about all that and then try to figure out from what the horoscope said about whether it would be a boy or a girl. Victor? Victoria? Maybe it would be better to choose some name that had nothing whatsoever to do with the kid's background. That was Nancy's idea. Just put it all behind you and have the kid and be sure to get a good doctor, a real gynecologist and not one of those public health creeps. Go for checkups. Hit the vitamins. No booze, no grass, no cigarettes . . . well, no more than ten a day or something like that.

She looked at the cigarette pack which was on top of the TV set next to a copy of *Cosmopolitan*. Raleigh was such a nice name for the baby to have. Nancy said there was a story in *Cosmopolitan* all about the influences of names on children. After all, what could you do with a name like Usher? Grow up to hustle in some theater?

The problem was to keep from going stir crazy during the long wait. Nancy's apartment had an extra bedroom, but when she wanted to entertain it was pretty hard to get out of the way. And that hard rock she played all the time on the radio was not exactly what you would call a lullaby. Still, there was no good reason to bitch. The roof didn't leak and lots of people came by who knew Sam. Sometimes it was like old home week. And nobody tried to hassle you back to work once they understood. That was nice. They said you should get extra food stamps.

She is going to be a mother, Nancy would say, and there you were being treated like Joan of Arc or somebody like that. People made sure not to bump into you and gave you the best place to sit if there was any crowding and girls who were just new to the life and usually didn't know from bananas about being mothers wanted to know if you felt anything kicking yet. Can you believe the little darlings? After only a month you are supposed to feel some kind of a football game going on in your belly?

It was fun explaining the gestation period to those people who did not know nothing really because ever since they left home and got into the life they had been trying to avoid getting knocked up. Since Nancy's place was sort of an unofficial headquarters for many of the street people there was a lot of explaining to do. And that passed some of the time, telling how they could take all the money and all the jewels in the world and pile them a mile high and say look here Wanda which would you rather have, all that or one baby, and your answer would come out like lightning from a thunderstorm. Zowie! Hooray for our side . . .

Wanda sat in the big armchair watching television and drinking a diet cola out of a can. She was slumped far down in the chair, almost prone. Her head was bent forward and her knees just blocked off the bottom third of the television screen. She did not care. It was a game program and she considered people who would shout and giggle on one of those shows as not worth looking at. Give me kings and queens, she thought. No peasants, please.

She had maintained her position for some time because she could watch her stomach during the commercials and imagine how her profile would look like from the same angle a few months from now. And now and then she would pass her hand across her belly ever so gently; there would not be anything yet to feel, of course, but it was sort of fun to go through the motions . . . sort of a undress rehearsal. In other words just sitting here not giving a damn about anything except the baby, all sprawled out in nothing but the Jap kimono Sam gave you to celebrate him making you his main lady, barefoot by God just like you spent the first fifteen years of your life and the way all people should be like nature meant them, not a damn thing on under the kimono but little ol' Wanda's skin all rubbed down with Nancy's fancypants body lotion which she swore to God would make your skin all over like a baby's ass, creamy dreamy smelling stuff that was supposed to work its way down into the pores like it showed in those big enlargements of the human epidermis on the TV commercial. So soothing just like the jingle those beautiful girls who were whispering about it said. They all looked like debutantes those girls who got jobs in commercials. They didn't have a pimple to share between six of them, but probably they were just faking they were debutantes. The guys though, unless they were selling beer, all looked like fags.

Wanda shifted her weight and spread her legs wide. It was always stuffy in Nancy's apartment and she wanted to let what air there was circulate around her thighs. Just think, in two hundred and forty days there Wanda would be with her legs spread apart again while some really good doctor, a genuine gynecologist like she had seen last week, would be pulling out—hey, there you have it. If *it* was going to be a boy then he would have to go to some university where he would learn to talk like Victor who had no trouble getting his verbs in the right place and like that. You could tell a gentleman sixteen miles away, just by the way he talked. And he didn't use profanity.

If it was a girl then her mom would start right out as soon as she could hack it working in the life. Return of the thoroughbred. How about that for a TV special? She would do as many tricks a night as there would be around and if there was any business in the afternoon she would knock off a few of them too. Fast money. Big money at the end of the week. And maybe outlaw it, work without a pimp, and keep it all. And all the while stashing most of that money away in like a savings and loan which paid so much interest. So when the time came the kid could make a choice on what university he or she wanted to attend. Maybe back east somewhere with the real dudes? Who knew?

Last week mom goes to this Dr. Wagenberger who gives with the official word. Wagenberger! What a name. "Wanda," says he, "you are a bingo. Your urine test is positive." And Nancy says he is not no quack and many of the snobs who live out there near where Judge Hickock's house is use this particular man. Nancy got his name from one of her regular clients who also lives out that way and likes a little strange once in a while. Okay, Dr. Wagenberger, all systems go like in a spaceship. Here is the best little mother in the world. *You better believe.*

Wanda tipped the can of diet cola vertically and finished swallowing the trickle of remaining liquid stuff. As she took the can away from her mouth the last few drops splashed down in the cleavage between her breasts, and as she mopped at herself with a corner of her kimono she wondered if she should breast feed this baby or go the bottle route like with Deidre. Some people said though that if you did it the natural way you could wreck your tits. All right. So wreck 'em. This kid was going to get the very best of *everything*.

She decided to make a trip to Nancy's bathroom, which was populated with dolls—like there must be fifty or maybe seventy. All kinds, little ones and big ones and even foreign dolls in fancy dress. Nancy said they made her feel better. Nancy was a fairy godmother with a heart as big as the moon but she was not just a little nuts.

Wanda's thoughts about the dolls were interrupted by the sound of someone in the front room. Nancy must have found an early john.

She went to the mirror and studied her face for a moment. Give Nancy time to take him to her room because some johns get highly nervous and split when a third person is involved. And rightly. There were girls who worked in pairs and while one was bouncing him around the mulberry bush the other one was rolling him. But not in this place, you better believe.

She paused in her inspection and listened. There was someone talking in the front room. She shrugged off a strange feeling of uneasiness and, grimacing at the mirror, wondered if her eyes had that sparkling look because of the baby? Pardon my saying so folks, but they were beautiful eyes. And the mouth? Wide, maybe a little too big, but containing a collection of pearly whites to even match Victor's . . . She called out, "Nancy . . . ?"

No answer. What was going on here? She called again and thought she heard something move in the front room, but there was no answer. Of course, you nut. You forgot the TV is still on.

She shook her head and started for the front room.

When she entered it she saw Leo Estervan, standing in the middle of it, holding his wallet in one hand.

She caught her breath. "How the hell did you get in here?"

"Don't tell me you aren't open for business."

"No I'm *not*. The door was locked."

He held up a plastic credit card, then slipped it in his wallet. "Not if I have one of these and you have an old-fashioned lock. You must slip this in between the door and the jamb and work around where the lock bolt is for a minute and slide it back and there you are. A course you got to know what you're doin'."

"Get the hell out of here."

Leo advanced smiling, then reached out suddenly, grabbed both her wrists and held them firmly.

"Let go of me."

He looked her up and down. "I wouldn't mind having a little piece of you, know that? You got a lot there to recommend. And we got a lot in common. But I don't like to mix business with pleasure."

She tried to twist away from him, but he pushed her backward toward the couch and shoved her down on it. He raised his hand to slap at her, then apparently changed his mind. "You gonna sit there like a nice girl or do you want another spankin'? You want to do everything I say or you want to be a cripple for life?"

Wanda could not find her voice. Oh God, Nancy . . . please come home . . .

She managed to whisper, "What do you want?"

"Your cooperation."

"What do you mean?"

Leo settled his bulk on the arm of the couch. He reached far out with his long arm and turned off the television set. He brought back the pack of cigarettes and held it in front of her. "Want a smoke?"

She took a cigarette from the pack and put it between her lips.

He reached to the TV set again and brought back a book of matches. He lit her cigarette, blew out the match and tossed it on the floor. "Now," he said, "you all nice and comfortable?"

She took a long drag at the cigarette. "You give me the willies."

"How would you like to go back to Clark?"

"I wouldn't."

"Right. You already graduated. But don't pout like that. I don't like pouting women. The only reason right now that you can get yourself sent back to Clark is if I tell a few people you were with the Hickock kid when he got busted. Is that clear?"

Wanda bit her lower lip. She could not remember ever being so scared—this ape was the worst . . .

"Now listen to me, Wanda," she heard him saying as if, she thought, he was on one planet and she was on some other, "I been to a lot of trouble to find out about your beef with Judge Hickock. I get the whole picture and I sure think you got a bum rap. It's funny how sometimes things work out, I mean here we are me and you both having the same opinion of that sonofabitch. Ever think when you were working for him you might be doing the world a favor if you turned the tables and put him away? Like for example if he ate or drank something that didn't agree with him, or he tripped and fell down the stairs, or maybe some other accident like car run over him. I'll bet when you were locked up in Clark ideas like that come to you now and again . . . right?"

"You got no right to bust in here like this—"

"Would you rather have a caller from the vice squad?"

Leo pushed himself off the arm of the couch and ambled to the window. He stood looking down at the street below and after a while he sighed heavily. "Wanda . . . people like you get a bum deal every time and the only cure for it is to go to some foreign country and start a new life. You stick around here you wind up back in the can sooner or later. You know that. No way are you going to stay out of it because the man is against you and so is everybody else."

When she saw him turn around to look at her she realized she had lost an opportunity. She could have hit him over the head with something when he was looking down at the street. Knock him out, call the police, say he was a burglar, or tried to rape her. Nuts. The police would laugh their heads off. The only protection for a whore was a pimp. And the ape was right. Nobody was on her side except Nancy and a few people in the life.

"What I am saying—" Leo smiled "—is that you ought to go far away from here. Like Europe, y'know? Or like you could go off to Hong Kong or some such place and get yourself a rich Chinaman to throw his money at you. They go crazy for white girls."

"What are you getting at?" she asked, trying to sound confident. If it wasn't for maybe endangering the baby she was sure she would find some way to get up and kick this ape in the balls. "I got a lot of things to do tonight and my friend will be home any minute—"

"No, she won't. She's working the Plaza and there's no action. From the looks of the customers she'll be hustlin' quite a while. You don't appreciate me, Wanda. I take a great interest in everything you and your friend do and for the next forty-eight hours I'm going to take more."

"What's this forty-eight hours stuff?"

"That's how long you have to do yourself and the world a great big favor. You still got a key to the Hickock house and if you lost it I'll get you one. You're going to drop by there and see to it the judge has an accident. Like what kind? That's up to you. Just be sure he can't go to work, like never."

"Why are you so interested in the judge?"

"I'm public-spirited . . . I think he's a disgrace to the bench . . . Now, to help you get ready for this public service let me lay out a few ground rules. One—don't try to leave town until after the accident. If you do your friend Nancy is the one who will have an accident and a bad one. Two—you don't know who I am now and you're never gonna know, no matter who asks you. Unless you want to spend the rest of your life in a wheelchair. Three, when you get the job done go to the Wanderer Travel Agency on Twenty-first and Third Avenue right next to the Metropolitan Bank. They got an open ticket in your name to any place in the world and five thousand dollars to pay for it. You can keep the change. Any questions?"

Chapter Twenty-one

Hickock found it difficult not to see himself as an intruder. Maybe, he thought, he was already marked as someone to be avoided. During his second night on the streets he began to recognize many of the habitues of each district. And he thought that at the very least it was an education for any citizen; whether a judge or otherwise a part of the community he would learn how rigidly the neighborhoods spotted through every large city retained their individuality. At Fourteenth and Virginia, a known area for prostitutes, the same people drank beer in the same tavern every night—and they usually occupied the same places in relation to each other. On Second and Spencer, and area populated mainly by Orientals, there was a poolhall where the same players could be observed at the same tables every night. Hickock wondered what would happen if a total stranger walked in and asked to join the game.

Likewise the street women he had so far observed were apparently on relatively fixed stations. Even with his limited experience he found that he recognized several and he knew they recognized him because they quickened rather than slowed their passing. He decided it was because they could not place him and that made them wary. In a matter of hours he had established that he was not a customer and it was obvious they were puzzled. He was big like so many policemen, but some well-developed instinct told them he was not a direct threat. Then what was he? A social worker? A freak? These days a man dressed like Hickock did not walk the same areas of the city streets at night and alone unless he had something very special on his mind.

On this second night he had met only a Ginger and a Mary. He found that he might walk for an hour without seeing any prospects and then meet two or three the next hour. The encounters usually began with an exchange of "hi's" followed by a slowing of pace, a glide to a halt, and then a pretense of looking in a handbag. Stopping for more than a few seconds could be trouble because it was an open invitation to "loitering," but once a conversation had been established there was an excuse for staying on target.

The chatting sequence seemed to be fairly standard regardless of location. After the "hi's" there was a silence while the girl sized up the customer—in this case me. Hickock smiled. He marvelled at their speed of decision. Too long a delay risked an immediate arrest for soliciting if they were talking to the wrong man. And yet they must advance the situation or risk a good customer shying away.

Hickock had done his best to present a promising appearance. He wore a tie and his best business suit. He carried an umbrella. He wanted to look like a man who could be serious about offering a street woman a hundred dollars in exchange for some simple information.

After the mutual appraisal there was usually some remark about the weather although a few had cut without delay to the standard question . . . "You interested in having a little party?"

He remembered a girl named Stella who seemed more intelligent than the majority of her sisters. She had begun somewhat differently. She was a large raw-boned woman with more age on her than the others he had met and he wondered if her low and seductive voice was natural or simply worn for the occasion. "Hi there, buster. What's your real name?"

"Julian."

"Now that's a nice name. Don't think I've ever heard it before. You just out for a little constitutional?"

"You might say that."

"There's nothing like a little exercise in the evening, know what I mean, Julian? It keeps the corpuscles running around all through your body."

Hickock noted the alacrity with which she had obtained, remembered, and used his name.

"Me," she continued, "I like my evening stroll. At least a few blocks anyway although I'm always worrying about getting mugged. But then I only live around the block. Maybe you'd be interested in escorting me home?"

At this point Hickock knew he was supposed to ask how

much and the bargaining would begin. Most of the girls he had talked with became visibly shaken when he refused to take his cue and offered his own proposition. "If you want to make some real money take me to a girl who might be someone you know. I don't want to make any trouble for her and I have an important message for her."

Usually he gave them the name "Wanda" and watched their eyes. While it was difficult to be certain in the poor light he was almost convinced that so far none of the girls had displayed any sign of recognition. He tried the full name "Wanda Usher" and then "Wanda Raleigh" a few times without any better results and even a physical description failed to generate interest. Once the girls realized he was not in a buying mood they wasted no time in departing. He was beginning to believe that he was frequenting the wrong areas, or the women were all fine actresses, or they were at least convinced he was one of the vice squad.

Tonight he had seen three women whose faces were familiar to him from the previous night. They passed him without so much as a glance and he was even more discouraged. If he could have gone direct to the police and asked for professional guidance maybe Wanda would have been found by now. But to involve the police would be to frighten Wanda and as soon as McReady heard about the search, which he certainly would if it became known that a judge was being escorted through their private jungle, then he would do everything he could to tighten his case. Nor would it go down well with the newspapers or the state officials if a superior court judge was discovered using police officers to prove his son's innocence.

Tonight he resolved to change his tactics and explore a different area. He would not have supposed that Wanda would work the streets surrounding the big hotels (they were too heavily patrolled), but he thought it worth a try. He found an old convention badge in his dresser drawer at 1011 and pinned it on his lapel. "National Conference of Trial Lawyers," and around the edges—"Atlanta." His name was printed in black letters across the center, and he now had trouble remembering he had ever been to Atlanta, let alone when.

Just before ten when he planned to start his patrol of the neighboring streets he stopped in the bar of the Plaza, one of the city's better hotels. He intended to order a single straight whiskey and refrain from swallowing long enough to give his breath the tang of an honest conventioneer. It was like hunting, he thought. You put on all the trappings and proceed to the blind. Then hope for the birds.

Hickock had to smile at finding himself bound for a hotel bar; any hotel, because he hated the places. The light was always bad and the smoke-laden air was always worse. The furnishing was depressing, the prices outrageous and the peanuts if there were any were moldy and as sticky as the tabletops. The drinks were so weak they guaranteed sobriety for all but the most susceptible, and the muzak, permanently, it seemed, grooved to the theme from "A Man and a Woman," was unavoidable. No matter how much money had been spent on the decor he found the simple little cabin of the *Freedom* a damn sight more comforting.

He had never been in the bar at the Plaza and he intended to be in the place only a few minutes, then it would be "off to work," as he had come to think of his searching.

After passing through the bright lobby he entered the bar and tried to avoid stumbling over empty chairs as he crossed to the bar itself. As far as he could see in the subdued light there were only a few people in the room, for which he was grateful. As a reasonably well-acquainted resident of the city it was doubtful if he would meet any other locals (they did their socializing in clubs or homes), but there was always the chance one of them might be meeting visiting firemen at the Plaza. Then it could be inevitable that someone would ask what was Julian Hickock doing prowling the Plaza bar alone. He had not prepared even a lame explanation.

He passed a couple who were arguing in none too modulated tones and a table of four men who were apparently ranchers or Texans or both since their ten-gallon hats were stacked on a spare chair. They were talking money, which Hickock thought may or may not have accounted for their total indifference to the rather primly dressed young woman who sat by herself at the bar.

Hickock went directly to the next stool and sat down. Their eyes met momentarily, they exchanged the slightest of smiles, and Hickock ordered a scotch on the rocks. He decided not to rush things and leave for the streets as fast as he had planned. When his drink arrived he picked it up and made a circular motion with his hand to swirl the ice around. He turned, caught the woman's eyes again and raised the glass slightly. He was certain he saw a smile play around her lips and he thought she could easily have passed as a school teacher, the type who might be working on her master's. While she certainly did not appear to be the sort of woman he was searching for, there was something about her bearing that suggested she was not just waiting for a friend. Her drink for one thing; it looked like orange juice, although of course it could be a screwdriver. No wedding ring. Her eyes did not flinch, and now he was fairly certain he was looking at a working woman.

"My name is Julian," he said wondering at his new boldness. "What's yours?"

"Nancy."

She hesitated and he saw that she was studying his convention badge.

She said, "You're a lawyer?"

"Right."

"Here on a convention?"

"How could you guess?"

"Twenty-twenty eyesight. Staying here at the Plaza?"

"No."

"Don't like it?"

"It looks better by the minute."

He raised his glass again and he saw her smile. This time, he thought, the game conditions were different and he would play by the rules of the other side. Maybe during the past encounters he had been premature; sometimes he had rejected their usual invitation before they had a chance to offer it and had been overanxious in asking about Wanda before they had enough time to ease their normal suspicions.

"Do you live here, Nancy?"

"Sure. Born and raised right here. But I've traveled a lot. I been to Europe twice. Don't like it. Too many foreigners." She laughed.

Well, she's opening up, Hickock thought. He was learning. Obviously this was a better approach even though it was going to take more time.

"How come you don't have a southern accent?" she asked, looking directly at her image in the long mirror behind the bar. She touched gently at her bangs, which Hickock thought was at least partly responsible for her schoolmarm look.

"Why should I have a southern accent?"

"Your badge. It says Atlanta. You don't have a Georgia accent."

"Can you tell one southern accent from another?"

"Sure."

"Did you live in the south?"

"No. Are you going to be in the city for long?"

"Just until tomorrow. The convention is over then."

He thought he saw her smile, but there was something else in her eyes. He sensed that she was laughing at him, which made him uncomfortable. Here was no ordinary hooker, if indeed she was one. For a moment he was reminded of a technicality based on custom. Once this woman began to bargain she could be arrested for soliciting while he, a male who had made the initial advance, would not be.

"What are your plans for the next hour or so?" she asked.

There it was. The invitation as formal as if it were engraved on finest bond. RSVP.

"I'm sort of loose. What about you?"

"The same."

"What kind of money are we talking about?"

"You put up a hundred before we leave the bar. The rest is up to you."

"Things aren't cheap in this city."

"You get what you pay for."

"It's just possible I might want to invest considerably more than your average."

"If it's for something kinky, forget it—"

"Nothing like that. But I would have three hundred for the person who can lead me to a girl named Wanda."

"Really?"

Had the rhythm of her breathing changed? Hickock saw her reach for her glass, caress it gently and develop a sudden interest in the contents. "Julian," she said finally, "did anyone ever tell you that you're one damned poor liar?"

"Why should they?"

"Because a light just went on in my brain and I put a few things together. There's no lawyers' convention in this city. When there is I'll know it because I keep track of such events. Right now we have the Association of Dental Equipment Manufacturers, the International Society of Pump Engineers, and the Audubon Society. That's all. Now you go around wearing that badge which says Julian in big letters and pretending you're someone from out of town. Why?"

"I'm afraid I'm not with you."

"Yes, you are. You're Judge Hickock. What is this? You running me down or something? Is this some kind of an ABSCAM thing? How did you know where to find me? I got a right to know."

The schoolmarm had vanished very suddenly. Her eyes told him that he was now facing a very tough woman. "I assure you this was purely a chance meeting, I've never seen or heard of you before and I have no intention of making any trouble for you. I am not working for the police. All I want to do is have a talk with Wanda Usher or Wanda Raleigh or whatever name she's using these days on a private matter. You must know her because she must have told you about me."

"It's possible."

"Do you know where she is?"

"What if I did?"

Hickock reached into his jacket and pulled out an envelope. He placed it carefully between their drinks. "There's three hundred dollars inside that envelope. It's yours if you can take me to Wanda."

She pushed the envelope away. "Stuff it, judge. What kind of a person do you think I am?"

"All right. Since you seem to be trying to protect Wanda you must be her friend. You must also know that Wanda needs all the help she can get."

"That's for damn sure."

Hickock tried not to hold his breath during the long silence that followed. Nancy, if that was her real name, was obviously having a serious debate within herself while she tried to appear indifferent. The longer she kept her silence, he decided, the better.

He watched carefully as she picked up her drink and went through the motions of sipping at it. She opened her purse and after some prolonged fumbling she found a small mirror. She brought it out, manipulated it until it reflected what little light was available and studied her image. She ran her tongue around her lip once, then touched at some imperfection she pretended to see in an eyelash. She put the mirror away, snapped the purse shut and looked directly at him. Finally she said, "Why should I believe you? You're the guy who took her kid away. You ruined her life."

"It's certainly possible I made a mistake. I've done a lot of thinking about it recently and now I'd like to make some amends—"

"She hates you."

"I'd like a try at fixing that."

Another silence. She passed her fingers across her brow, ruffling her bangs. "I gotta think. I'll make a phone call. Wait for me."

She slipped off the stool and was gone before Hickock could stop her. As he paid the barman he wondered if he would ever see her again. Or Wanda.

Wanda couldn't remember such a sense of anticipation. It started as soon as that big ape had left and she could feel it building until now she was even forgetting about the baby for a few minutes. The old Wanda who was nothing but a collection of skin and bones was going to start life all over again. Hey, what choice was there?

Right away after the ape left she started thinking, mostly the same old thoughts she had nursed for three years at Clark, but now she also thought about the gun she had discovered in Judge Hickock's drawer . . . it seemed a hundred years ago. Maybe she shouldn't actually kill him . . . just maybe let him have it in the leg or arm or some such place like it was on TV when the person who was shot just fell back and grabbed for his shoulder. Whatever . . . at least now you would be doing it for the baby, you might say . . .

Picture this. You are in China or Europe or somewhere and Victoria or Victor is all grown up and going to the best school there is. Even speaks another language. Can add and subtract and read books like crazy. A budding scientist or something. Maybe twenty years have gone by and the two of you come back for a visit to see how things are in the old town. Nobody even remembers a girl named Wanda Usher Raleigh and of course Victoria or Victor don't know nothing about her either. Because ever since they can remember you have been Madame Got-Rocks. My God, would it be impossible that she could have boy and girl *twins*? Hallelujah! Imagine all three of you coming back.

She reached down and turned off the television set, and

thought about the big man who had just left. A real bad news individual, for sure. Every once in a while his type used to show up in the old life but then there was Sam around to look after you, although even Sam might have thought twice about taking on this goon. Well, you survive in this world, she thought, the best you could . . .

She was reviewing what she knew of the Hickock household habits when the telephone rang. She moved toward it reluctantly. She was concentrating on Victor Hickock, who would probably be in his room or asleep by now. The judge would be sitting in his big leather chair in the living room reading, or maybe he would have already gone up to bed. Maybe the thing to do was go out to the house tomorrow during the day and hide in the basement until tomorrow night. There shouldn't be anybody home all day.

She answered the telephone with a soft "hello." It might be one of Nancy's johns or some prospect who read her ad for Escort Services in the yellow pages of the phone book.

"Wanda. It's Nancy."

"Well, hi! This is a surprise—"

"You can say that again. Guess who I got in tow. You never will. Judge Hickock. He wants to talk to you."

Wanda caught her breath, her heart began to pound. I don't believe this, she told herself. I am not ready for this. Her thoughts somersaulted and flipped like the gymnasts she'd seen on TV this very night. God, are you lookin' down at me, man? You trying to tease me? "Where are you?" she asked.

"At one of the pay phones in the lobby of the Plaza. I stalled him off for a few minutes. He's in the bar and probably guesses I'm calling you."

"Wait a minute. I gotta think. I don't believe this. Don't tell me he was looking for a trick."

"No. He's looking for *you*."

"Well, I don't want to see him."

"That's what I thought. Don't worry. I'll get rid of him."

"Wait a minute . . ." Wanda tried to catch at her spinning thoughts. Maybe here was a chance that wouldn't come along again in a hundred years. Or a thousand. Tonight, right now, she knew *exactly where the judge was*. "Listen, hon," she said, "do you think you could play him along for another half-hour? Y'know, keep him right there in the hotel or at least within reach for another thirty minutes."

"I don't know much about handling a guy who isn't horny, but I'll sure give it a try."

"It's quarter after ten now. You can turn him loose at quarter to eleven. Okay?"

Nancy promised to do her best and said she would wait for Wanda's explanation until she got back to the apartment. Wanda slammed down the phone and ran to her little room. She flipped a skirt and sweater out of the closet and slipped quickly into her pantyhose. She had always prided herself on the speed with which she dressed and undressed; now she was out to set a record. In four minutes by her still new watch she was fully dressed and running for the door, purse in hand. Survive, survive . . .

She rushed down the two flights of stairs and fast-walked to the taxi stand on the corner. She pulled open the door of the first cab in line and said breathlessly, "1011 Maple Avenue."

Chapter Twenty-two

Hickock had been heartened and somewhat surprised when Nancy returned to the bar the first time. She was smiling warmly and had suggested they have another drink while they were waiting for Wanda. It seemed she was willing to meet with him as long as it could be at the hotel. Nancy explained she would have to get dressed since she had been asleep. Also she lived far away so they would have to allow time for her to get a taxi. "So give her a half-hour and she'll be here," Nancy said.

Nancy asked if she could have an orange juice and he ordered one for himself. Their conversation, he now recalled, had not been exactly sprightly. Nancy wanted to know why he wanted to see Wanda so badly and he saw no reason to tell her about Victor. Never mind if she already knew. Old-style pride kept trying to look the other way and certainly did not invite strangers to the scene of disgrace.

Nancy was equally close-mouthed about her current activities but she was careful to explain that Wanda now lived on the outskirts of the city ". . . way out in the boondocks so nobody could accuse her of associating with people like me." Nancy was also careful to explain that Wanda was scared silly of violating her probation and was being an extremely good girl. She was trying to rehabilitate herself in every way she could and about to go to work for an insurance company. So said Nancy.

Nancy had kept looking at her watch and when a half-hour had passed she said she could not imagine what was taking Wanda so long and she would go make another call to hurry her up.

That was the last Hickock had seen of her.

He waited a full hour before he would allow himself to admit that he had been deliberately abandoned. Nancy's second phone call, he now realized, was an excuse to leave him dangling and he should have had the sense to follow her. You'd make a lousy cop, he told himself.

He made a final check of every possible place in the lobby Nancy might be, then looked through the coffee shop, the gift shop, the main dining room, and took a final turn through the bar. He asked the two clerks at the front desk if they had seen a woman of Nancy's description using one of the phonebooths on the opposite side of the lobby. One clerk said he thought he might have seen her but he could not be sure. Hickock described Wanda. Both clerks regarded him cynically and said they had not seen anyone fitting his description.

So close and yet so far, Hickock thought as he decided there would be little point in pursuing his planned patrol of the area on this night. He would return tomorrow night and every night until he met up with Nancy once again. Did she really know Wanda or was she just going through the motions in the hope of somehow getting part of his reward? But if that were so, why had she disappeared?

As she paid off the taxi driver and added a generous tip, she thought the old Wanda was back in charge now. It also occurred to her that she had not planned how she was going to get away from 1011 after it was all over. Well, never mind. She had not planned this night or what was about to happen either. She had only thought about it, not really believing it would ever really come to pass; just like there was never no predicting how life was going to turn out. Like why hadn't she thrown away the key to 1011? It was still in her purse right where she dropped it the very last time she left the place. That meant something, didn't it? Like it was meant to be, y'know?

It was planning with the old bean that made the cab driver let you off at the corner rather than right in front of 1011. Why make any more show than absolutely necessary, and of course the way to get away was to walk away, slow and easylike, the old ho stroll even, and then take the bus back to Nancy's—

Except maybe the buses didn't run all night? And hey, what happens if Victor is there and hears that gun go off? You haven't planned this out at all, Wanda girl. You're in too big a hurry because that ape has got you scared half-crazy. What you will have to do is make a *fast* exit, not a slow one. There will be a loud bang and you beat it *fast*. Get the kitchen door all unlocked beforehand and hightail it through the garden in back of the house and down the alley. By the time Victor wakes up and gets his wits about him you'll be long gone. By the time he gets himself unconfused you'll be six blocks away and halfway to China. Don't get panicky and forget to take the gun with you. Stash it in one of those garbage cans in the alley—no, don't . . . take it all the way to the corner of Hyde where the bus stop is and heave it in the bushes by the tennis court. For sure no one will find it there in a jillion years.

For a moment she stood looking up at 1011. The big house was dark. She walked a little way farther until she could see the window of Victor's room. Dark. He must have gone to sleep early. Or maybe he was away to a movie or playing basketball at the university or whatever they did nights out there.

She avoided the cement front walk that led to the porch and moved silently along the grass. She took off her shoes and tiptoed up the wooden front steps and across the porch. She very carefully inserted the key in the door and felt an exhilarating excitement. Now was the time she had dreamed about for so long . . . Like a cat, she thought.

She closed a door behind her without the slightest sound, and moved across the front hall like floating on air, she decided, then moved right on out through the dining room and the pantry just like the lights were full on and into the kitchen and straight to the back door. Which, for God's sake, was not locked anyway. How about that?

Now the cat lady goes back along the same route which you done a hundred times as president of the local mop-and-bucket brigade. Back to the front hall as easy as molasses out of a jar. Maybe the newspapers would be interested in the life story of the cat woman after it happened. Or *People* magazine? And she could be on one of the TV shows being interviewed about how she could move up the stairway without a light. Who needs it when you know every step of the way. Right past the photographs that you knew were on the wall because you could reach across the stairs from the rail and feel them . . .

All right . . . here at the top of the stairs, take it very cool along the balcony because the door to Victor's room is right there and thank God this is an old house with real heavy doors instead of those modern gimcrack plywood doors that you could hear everything going on if you were on the other side.

She paused on the balcony and looked down at the front hall, where a splash of light from the street lamp outlined the big grandfather clock and the coat rack. By bending down and craning her neck slightly she found she could see into the shadows of the living room.

She moved on across the balcony, passing the room she knew was the daughter's and then Nellie-Mae's room. Next was a guest room and finally at the end of the balcony—Hickock's bedroom. The master bedroom . . . yass, massa, this here cotton-pickin' kid is finally goin' to get even . . .

She slipped through the doorway and discovered the street lamp made a twilight all through the room. She went directly to the bureau and with great care slid the top righthand drawer open. Not a sound. She reached far back, found the gun, withdrew it. There was a clicking sound when she closed the drawer and she caught her breath in sudden fear. Her scalp tingled as she stood motionless. Finally when she decided the noise had been so slight it could not possibly have been heard more than a few feet away she drew a breath again. You watch it from now on, cat lady, and don't be moving around knocking over furniture like a elephant.

Hickock parked his car in the small oval of ground which terminated the driveway behind the house. The garage had originally been designed for two cars, but vehicles had less beam then and if both his car and Victor's pickup were inside the occupants were trapped. The big relatively modern car doors could not be opened more than a few inches. As a consequence the garage itself had fallen into disuse; it made little sense to protect Hickock's rusting and asthmatic Chevrolet from the elements while Victor's pickup, which he had brought to glistening perfection, remained outside.

Victor had stubbornly declined the use of the garage, saying that he did not wish to usurp the privileges of the owner of the house so many times that the subject was no longer a point of contention. Now Hickock stood in the starlight between the two machines and marvelled at the overwhelming influence four wheels and an engine had on young Americans. First came the car and only then could life proceed.

He smiled at the pickup and saw that the hood was polished so diligently it even picked up the light from the stars. And he thought that if his son devoted the same number of hours to his studies as he did to his "ancient iron" he could conquer the whole academic world.

Thinking about his son, Hickock walked around the side of the house, his shoes crunching rhythmically against the driveway gravel. He could no longer postpone the inevitable. Victor's preliminary hearing was due on Friday and this was already Tuesday. On the following Monday morning his trial was scheduled before Judge Harold Bonesteel, a man as harsh as his name. Hickock had met him once very briefly and had been impressed with his forthrightness, but he had since discovered the man was inclined to go strictly by the book. In view of all the elements it had seemed best not to risk a jury trial; now Hickock was not so sure. There was just so much damning evidence against Victor and nothing but a lack of a past record working for him. With a by-the-book judge a past record, or lack of it, did not carry as much weight as it might with someone else.

Likewise, Estervan, he thought as he mounted the steps to the porch, took out his keys, and unlocked the front door. If Bonesteel had heard the case Estervan would have long ago been bound for prison and with a maximum sentence under the law. Right or wrong there would have been no waffling about his fate and perhaps that was the best way. Of *course* Estervan had procured an obscene film and of *course* he had offended the morals of the community. But then again, who set those morals? And who could say that by stuffing Estervan into a prison all such activities would stop . . . or even be discouraged? Enough. Concentrate on Victor . . .

Hickock turned on the hall light and went to the grandfather clock. He opened the glass door and pulled on the chains which activated the clock's mechanism until they were at the top limit of their run. He checked the elaborately tooled hands of the clock against his wristwatch. They disagreed and the discovery somehow made him uncomfortable. The big clock read eleven-twenty-five, his wristwatch read eleven-seventeen. A perfect excuse, he decided, to call Jean.

He pulled down his tie and opened his shirt collar as he went to the telephone stand at the foot of the stairway. He dialed Jean's number and while it was ringing he glanced up at the balcony. Victor had obviously gone to bed early since there was not a sound from his room. Or a light. It occurred to him that they should agree to leave a light on somewhere in the living room or perhaps up on the balcony. It was a dreary sensation coming home to a dark and nearly empty old house.

When he heard her sleepy voice he said, "What time is it?"

"*You*. You've been out with your hookers again."

"Right. And I think I made some progress."

"I'm still having trouble adjusting to your project."

"But it was like getting a fish all the way to deck level and then losing it. I'll have to try again. You sound like you were asleep."

"Aren't all decent citizens in bed at this hour?"

"Well at least with someone . . . which is better than I can say for myself."

"Judge! You're becoming downright bawdy. Is some of your research rubbing off on you?"

"Probably. And why not? Maybe I could do with a little broadening of my horizons."

"Nuts. If I ever met a man who can look at any subject from sixteen different angles, you're it. I love you the way you are, and that's a declarative statement."

"With that message under my pillow I'll sleep like a babe. Put the same under yours, and please tell me the exact time."

"Why are you so interested in the exact time?"

"Because my watch and the front hall clock don't agree and a man who can't tell right from wrong has more than just ulcers to contend with. His conscience, if he has one, starts spinning like a bad compass and he doesn't know which way to turn next—"

"*Okay*. It's eleven-twenty-one."

"Thanks. Go back to sleep."

"Now I'll probably dream about you."

"Good. I foresee the time when you won't have to."

"I'll pack my hope chest."

After he hung up he reset his wristwatch and then the big clock. There was no specific reason why accurate time seemed so important tonight and there was no guarantee that the fancy electronic clock beside Jean's bed agreed with WWV at the National Observatory, Big Ben, or Greenwich. Which meant, he thought as he made for the kitchen, it would be unwise to take a star fix using any of the local chronometers. But at least he now knew for certain that the timepieces were in agreement and somehow that it made him feel a little better. The mixture of scotch and orange juice at the Plaza bar had not exactly improved the situation in his already nervous stomach and agreement among clocks along with a glass of milk might give at least the illusion of normalcy. Right now he'd settle for a little illusion.

He took a clean glass from the pantry and turned on the kitchen light. He crossed the kitchen to the refrigerator, took a container of milk, and filled the glass. As he sipped at the glass he leaned back against the sink and it occurred to him that even if he was lucky enough to find Wanda he was running a very long chance that she might just shrug her shoulders and say, tough luck, judge. Why should she do anything else? If he could somehow arrange an occasional visit with her daughter maybe he could persuade her to testify in Victor's defense . . . except the social agency people were very sticky about letting outlawed parents anywhere near adopted children. Still, possibly under the circumstances, they might relent . . . Damnit, there had to be *some* way to pry Victor loose from this felony charge before the system had no choice but to lock him up . . .

He finished the milk, rinsed out the glass, and put it in the dishwasher. He yawned mightily as he went to the kitchen door. When they had first bought 1011, he remembered, they had never bothered locking the kitchen door or the front one for that matter, and that had been only a relatively short time ago. Twenty years. But life in the nation had changed since then and there was no reason to welcome a burglar to the hearth.

He was annoyed to find the door unlocked. Didn't Victor ever think of anything but his damned pickup? There you go, he thought, condemning Vic on discovered evidence that might have nothing to do with him. Some judge.

He locked the door, crossed the kitchen, and turned out the light. He made his way in darkness through the pantry and across the dining room. He turned out the hall light and started up the stairs, unbuttoning his shirt as he climbed.

As he mounted the fourth step he heard a voice calling to him softly, "Stop right there."

Startled, he looked up and sought in the twilight for the source of the voice. Then suddenly he realized he was staring at the muzzle of a gun . . . his *own* gun . . .

"Turn around slowly."

He recognized Wanda's voice even as he felt the cold metal of the gun against the base of his scalp. "Don't make a sound," she whispered, "or I'll . . . I'll blow the top of your head off. Now start back down."

As Hickock moved back down, his thoughts spun with the realization that Wanda might well be capable of pulling the trigger. He tried to remember if there were any cartridges in the barrel, or had the gun been cocked, forcing one shell into the barrel?

At the bottom step he reached out and felt with his foot for the floor. He sensed that one misstep might aggravate this woman and any quick movement might damn well be his last. Incredible . . . this was not really happening—

"Turn left."

It was happening.

As they moved slowly into the deeper darkness of the hall he felt the gun again—this time prodding at his spine.

"Keep going until you get to the basement door," she whispered, and he noticed that her voice was hoarser and more anxious now. "Open the door. Turn on the light at the head of the stairs and start down slow. Don't look back or make a sound or I swear I'll do it."

There was a trick the police were taught, he remembered . . . a way to disarm an attacker when approached from behind . . . you made a quick pivot of your upper body, extending an arm . . . somewhere between hand and elbow you would contact the gun and knock it from the attacker's hand before they had a chance to pull the trigger . . .

Sure . . . and the attacker should cooperate by maintaining just the right distance behind and should hold the gun at just the right level for everything to go like the practice sessions, but he had only *seen* it practiced in the police school—

"Wanda—"

"Shut up!"

There was a desperate quality in her voice. She could be high on something. But there had to be some way of getting to her . . . He opened the door and reached inside for the light switch. It seemed miles down the old wooden steps to the oblong of light at the bottom.

"Go down three steps and stop. Don't look around."

He did, and after a moment heard the door shut behind her. He could hear her breathing rapidly.

"Wanda, you're a smart girl. Too smart for this. This is insanity . . . you know that. Think what you're doing—"

"I am. Keep going to the bottom. Turn right and go to the storeroom, keep your eyes straight ahead."

He started down the steps as slowly as he dared, trying to stall but not provoke.

"Wanda, listen to me." He blinked at the two bare bulbs hanging from the overhead beams and tried to rally his fractured thoughts. "I'll do whatever you ask if you'll put down that gun."

"Can you give me back my daughter?"

"Give me a chance to try."

"You didn't give me no chance. Keep going for the storeroom and when you get inside close the door after you."

Hickock halted at the door to the storeroom. He saw there were two cases of wine at the back of the room which he had utterly forgotten. They had been there since Dolores's time . . . put away one Christmas . . . "Why do you want me to go in here?" he asked as calmly as he could manage.

"Because I don't want to see your face when you die . . ."

He took a half-step forward. He could move into the room, and close the door and hit the floor. It was a flimsy door, not like the rest in 1011. Maybe she would shoot straight ahead and the bullet would pass over his prone body. And maybe she would fire several times at various angles.

Or he could turn now, tackle her low and hope for the best. If he was quick enough . . .

There was one other chance. A slim one.

"Wanda, listen to some reason. What will you get out of this except a temporary feeling of revenge? At the very least you'll go away for the rest of your life. You'll certainly never see your daughter again—"

"Maybe I don't need to, judge. I got what I need right inside me. All safe and sound tucked away."

"What do you mean?"

"Too bad you didn't live to be a grandpappy, judge. Your precious son done it to me. We done it together. Ain't that something to chew on? I wanted to be sure you knew about it before you checked out. Now git in there."

It has to be now, he thought. Right now.

He turned his head very slowly, keeping the rest of his body rigid.

He turned his head until out of the corner of his left eye he saw the gun. His gun. It was aimed directly at his shoulders.

His gun . . . the left side . . . *the safety lever was pushed up . . . tight in place. She didn't know guns . . .* But she might learn damn fast once she pulled the trigger and nothing happened . . .

He began a step toward the storeroom, then bent double, turned, grabbed her and twisted the gun away from her hand and threw it toward the storeroom. It clattered across the cement and came to rest against the wine cases.

She struggled violently for a moment, then suddenly went limp and began to sob incoherently.

And as her anger seemed to dissipate, so also did his fury. She was, after all, so small, this whimpering creature who had tried to kill him with a gun on safety. She'd made a mess of it, just as she had of everything else important in her life. Tears had smeared her wet cheeks with mascara. Her hair was tousled and fell across her eyes making her look more like a broken doll than a killer.

He heard her murmur, "Please don't hurt me," and he wondered how he could tell this girl without sounding disgustingly smug that he had never in his life known the need to hurt anyone.

When they returned to the front hall from the basement Hickock roused Victor with a shouting of his name. He came sleepy-eyed to the balcony rail and was understandably confused when he saw Wanda in her disarrayed state, his father's arm firmly holding one of hers.

Hickock nudged Wanda into the living room, turned on the light and told her to sit on the window seat. Victor, wearing a bathrobe over his pajama bottoms, joined them almost immediately. "What's going *on?*"

Hickock suddenly felt the need to sit down. Somehow he had wrenched his back.

"Let me say," Hickock replied grumpily, "that I do not entirely trust this young lady." He eased himself into his big leather chair and added, "I'm getting too old for this sort of thing."

For a moment he debated having Victor call the police, then changed his mind. He had gone to a great deal of effort to find Wanda, and here she was in a very handy location. There were some very important questions he wanted to ask before the police took all of her attention . . .

Almost an hour later the grandfather clock in the hallway emitted a single discreet bong and Hickock marvelled at the swift passage of time as well as his inability to obtain straight answers from Wanda. It was as if she still held him hostage now with an invisible gun at his back. Whether she understood her remaining power or not was impossible to determine, for she appeared remorseful and had said over and over again that she was sorry for what she had done and that she hoped both Hickock and Victor would forgive her. There were times when she became almost incoherent again as she rubbed at her red eyes and kept repeating something about a man who was going to cripple her for life or worse if she failed to do what he said.

"Who was the man?"

"I don't know," she insisted.

"Why should he choose you?"

"Because he knew I worked for you. He wanted you dead."

"Why?"

There had yet to be a satisfactory answer to that just as Hickock had yet to conceive of a practical plan for Wanda's immediate future. And the more he inquired the more complex a possible solution became.

He sensed that Wanda's natural stubbornness was strengthening. She was beginning to feel again that she was not helpless, and he thought, she was sort of like an alleycat, still spitting and full of fight.

"I'll remind you once more," he said, "that you can be charged with assault with a deadly weapon on one count and with the intent to commit murder on a second count. Those are, to put it mildly, serious felonies and could send you away for years. You would be an old woman when you got out—"

"Is that where you want Victor's baby born? In prison?"

"How do we know you're pregnant?"

"Call Dr. Wagenberger. His office is right near here and he saw me last week."

"How do we know Victor is the father?"

She managed a smile. "Because I picked him. And the dates are right for the Green Shutter. And besides I wouldn't go to bed with nobody else. Not when I wanted to get knocked up." She glanced at Victor. "I wanted the best baby any man can make and I chose him just like they do a stallion down in

Tennessee. You breed big and strong, Judge, and that's the way my baby's gonna be."

There was a long silence. Sooner or later, Hickock thought, he would have to notify the police—the system demanded it—but there were some very personal reasons to postpone that action. For one thing the police would want to know why he had been so long in calling them and he had yet to think of a believable explanation.

He thought of another tack. "Wanda . . . your fingerprints are on that gun down in the basement. When I tell the police you tried to kill me they can easily prove it."

"You won't call the police."

"What makes you think I won't?"

She looked straight at Victor, who met her eyes and then looked at the floor. "You been in jail now, Vic. You like it? You want your own kid born in one?"

Victor said, "Dad, this is my problem. I'd like you to let me try and take care of it?"

"It's *not* your problem. She made an attempt to commit murder and nearly succeeded."

Wanda said, "If you call the police I'll tell them I just came here to collect my back pay and you tried to rape me. I'll say I did it in self-defense."

"You know they won't believe you—"

"Why not? Isn't my word as good as yours?"

"No. And you know it isn't. That's the way the system goes and fair or not, right now I'm damn glad of it."

He noticed that her eyes had changed now. They appeared to be filled with contempt, as if he had actually tried to attack her.

"Wanda," he said patiently reminding himself that she could easily twist reality to her own fancies, "I understand your anger about your daughter, but what have we done since then except try to help you?"

She appeared at least momentarily to consider his challenge, then sniffled and asked for a tissue. Victor moved quickly to the bookcase and took down a box of tissues, crossed the room to Wanda and standing before her offered the box.

As she took one and then another to wipe at her eyes and cheeks, Hickock began to realize that something was happening to her. Once again her eyes seemed to be changing. The defiance seemed to go out of her, her shoulders slumped. She looked up at Victor. Her eyes followed him as he left her and returned to his position by the fireplace. She seemed fascinated by him. She appeared to be almost worshipful of him and Hickock found this made him uncomfortable.

There followed a long period when only the faint tick-tocking of the clock disturbed the silence. Then very suddenly Wanda inhaled in such a deep and audible manner it was as if she had been starving for air. And she said uncertainly, "Well . . . I guess there is something you two oughta know. I guess maybe . . . I don't know how to say it . . . but being called unfit mother sort of made me flip for a long time. Y'know what I mean? I mean you can't tell just by lookin' that I got a baby inside me now, but *I* know there's somebody in there and I want her or him not to be alone like I almost always have been. If she's a girl I want her to have a chance to dream some and have some of her dreams come true. *Not* like me. There are certain people who just can't get it all together, and I guess I'm one. We screw up . . . even with the best intentions . . . I don't know . . . it just happens . . . and then it happens again, y'know what I mean? No matter how we try not to screw up, we manage . . . Can I have a glass of water?"

Victor left the room in his bare feet and while he was gone Hickock continued to watch Wanda's eyes. She changes like a chameleon, he thought. She was several persons all in one. Her eyes were still wet and red but she was no longer weeping . . . if anything, he thought, she almost seemed to be enjoying herself, maybe once more exchanging reality for the illusion that things were as she would like to see them . . .

Hickock shifted position in his chair and felt a sharp pain in his back. Damnit. He was getting too old to wrestle—with Wanda or anyone else.

When Victor returned from the kitchen and handed a glass of water to her, Hickock saw the suggestion of a worshipful look repeated in Wanda's eyes. He heard her sigh and thank Victor and decided it was a good moment to ask her, "Wanda, do you have any ideas about how that cocaine happened to be in the motel room?"

She shrugged her shoulders and shook her head. "Why should I? You think I had something to do with it, don't you? You think all of us screwups are alike . . . we make trouble for ourselves? Well, maybe you're right. That's why I want a kid so much because with her or him I can start out life all over again . . . like in a new package. I mean, sometimes it is to laugh, like there are scads of kids running around in real schools and not getting in no trouble of any kind . . . sometimes even if their parents are the kind who just sit around watching the box and drinking beer or beating each other up or just wishing they were dead. What's happening is that they got another life goin' for them right under their noses. I mean, if we can throw away the package we're living in right this minute then I figure we'll be all right, understand? Like reborn. Understand? And I guess in my screwy way that's part of what I been tryin' to do . . ."

She looked over her shoulder at the dark street beyond the window and then turned back into the room. She glanced at Victor an instant, then looked Hickock straight in the eye. "If you'll help me get into this new life . . . I'll help you."

"Dad," Victor said quietly, "I'll pay for whatever she needs. I'll earn the money or sell the pickup, or something . . ."

Hickock had suddenly forgotten the pain in his back . . . because now he was sure he saw something entirely new in Wanda's eyes. He hardly dared hope, though, for easy confirmation.

Wanda took another deep breath and said quietly, "I put those balloons in the bathroom . . . and I was the one called the police."

Hickock waited a moment while he tried to control his excitement. "Will you testify to that?"

"Yes."

Hickock pushed himself to his feet and stifled an involuntary groan. He went across the room to Wanda and stood looking down at her. He bent down, hesitated a moment, then surprised himself by kissing the top of her head.

Later they sat in the kitchen drinking coffee and saying very little while they waited for Lieutenant McReady. Hickock had wanted him particularly to make the arrest, and was relieved to find him still at work. He told McReady that considering the hour he was now convinced he was telling the truth when he said he rarely had a chance to go home. He invited McReady to come to 1011 and in less than half an hour he appeared on the front porch. "You want my partner to come in too?" McReady asked with a nod toward his car. "If he's not really needed he'd just as soon grab a wink of sleep while he's waiting."

"No. I doubt if you'll have any problems."

Feeling the pain in his back again, and wincing slightly, he took McReady back to the kitchen then and introduced him to Wanda. He explained as simply as he could that here was the Mrs. Raleigh of the Green Shutter Inn and that she would tell him her own story.

McReady accepted Wanda's offer of a cup of coffee and sat down next to Victor. In the harsh light of the kitchen Hickock decided that McReady looked like an eroded gargoyle—only his buck teeth still stood as ramparts to a rubbery face that appeared to be near total collapse. "I been in these clothes for thirty-six hours," he said, rubbing at the bristles on his chin. "I guarantee you that between the junkies and peddlers I got my own Disneyland. Nothing surprises me any more."

Hickock was pleased with the way McReady accepted the presence of Wanda in his house. Obviously bone-tired, he made a few notes and explained that in order to clear Victor it would be necessary to book Wanda for possession of a controlled substance. Since she was still on probation she would probably be "sent away for a spell."

"How *long* is a spell?" Wanda asked quickly.

McReady glanced at Hickock, pulled at the drapery of skin around his jaw and said, "That depends on whoever is the judge. Now you take a fellow like Bonesteel—"

Hickock interrupted. "I promise you it won't be me," he said. The less said about Bonesteel at this time the better, he thought, or anything about Wanda's attempt with the gun.

McReady inquired then about the cause of Hickock's obvious back pain and was told it was really nothing—probably just age.

It was three o'clock before McReady said he would have to go before he fell asleep where he sat. He told Wanda that if she promised to be a lady he would take her out to the car without handcuffs. "Anything else we can do for you this morning, Your Honor?"

Hickock shook his head, followed them to the front door and let them out to the porch. As McReady took Wanda's arm and started for the steps he halted a moment and looked over his shoulder. And in the light from the street lamp Hickock had the distinct notion that he was being surveyed from head to toe.

There was obvious suspicion in the eyes he now saw focused on him.

"Better take care of that bad back, sir," McReady said.

"Yes*sir.* I'll do that."

Looking after them, Hickock thought that a good cop is one who does not ask more than he actually needs to know.

Chapter Twenty-three

Hickock decided that he had better stop by and see Doc Heath and ask him why a slight injury to his back should have caused him to feel like the Hunchback of Notre Dame for nearly two weeks. Still, the back had provided some benefits; he had received a great deal of sympathetic attention from Jean, who had not pressed him for details on how his injury had been acquired, but made broad hints that his research of the lower depths had perhaps been too much for him. Lucinda clucked around his chambers with nearly perpetual pots of tea (a mixed blessing), and he had a handy excuse for stealing a bit more time on the Estervan case.

Best of all was the return of Nellie-Mae, who insisted there had been enough troubles at 1011 in her absence and no hospital could hold her. Her presence was now heralded by the heady aroma of sausages and grits floating up the staircase, along the balcony and into Hickock's bedroom as he chose his tie for the day. In spite of the sparkling morning, which he had observed with so much pleasure as he paused to thank God for another day, he supposed that something solemn was in order.

He flipped through his ties, most of which dated from Dolores's time and a few even from his postgraduate days. A pompous purple? No. A dignified green . . . possibly. How about a celebrative red and white? Certainly not. Sober as a judge, he mused, and pulled away a dark blue knit. Because of his black robe, about the only way a judge could visually relay his mood for the day was via his necktie.

At last Estervan and company would be in his court at ten this morning to learn of their future, and he wanted at least an illusion that everything including his decision was exactly right.

Sometimes, he thought as he descended the stairway and

checked his watch against the grandfather clock, the main reason he kept 1011 instead of getting rid of such an anachronistic home-sweet-home was to please Nellie-Mae. When the time came that Victor would take off on his own, as it certainly would, what then? Long ago the saying was—"take a wife." Okay, but if the prospect of marrying Jean Pomeroy was too ridiculous because of the generation gap then what was the alternative? Better to take a course in advanced curmudgeonry and die a bachelor? The local widows he knew were permanently wedded to ghosts and the divorcees were mostly still chewing contentedly on their resentments—and with those fat generalizations, he thought, he would now start the day by putting something more palatable under his belt.

Victor was already seated, and to Hickock's surprise, rose when he entered the dining room. He smiled at his heaping plate of hominy and said that Nellie-Mae had returned just in time. His appetite had also returned ever since Judge Bonesteel had cleared him. "Hominy," he said this morning, "is the finest filler known to man."

Nellie-Mae came through the pantry bringing a second tureen of hot grits for Hickock. She sat down between them and said she felt so much better out of the hospital she had about decided to take a long vacation, "maybe a tour of Europe. You all got along fine without me around here. I feel unneeded."

"Wrong," Hickock said. "Another week of that slumgullion Vic and I were making do with and we would have been at each other's throats."

"As it is we seem to understand each other better," Victor said.

"It's been a very valuable experience getting along without you," Hickock added. "Vic understands that I can't cook and I understand that not even my son is perfect. You'd better stay home."

They laughed, and later when they met in the oval of the driveway Victor had said how grateful he was for a father who would stand by him. And Hickock had thought that he was as close to being at peace with himself as he had been in a very long time. Driving to the courthouse he hoped that someday the right time would come when he could explain to Victor how agonizing it was for an ordinary man like his father to pass down judgment on another human.

As Hickock drove toward the courthouse the glass of the city's center glistened in the sunlit morning. And beyond the last fringes of the city to the southwest, some forty miles removed, a young woman who insisted her name was Wanda Usher Raleigh was admitted to the superintendent's office of the Clark Treatment Center for Women. Her welcome was cool. Miss Pope said, "Well, well. I thought you were never coming back here."

Wanda shrugged and tried to smile. As she looked around the office and saw the exercise quadrangle beyond Miss Pope's window, she sighed. It all looked as if she had never left.

She watched Miss Pope scanning the sheaf of papers the female deputy from the sheriff's office had brought with her from the county jail. "It says here you're pregnant, Wanda. Don't you think at all? Didn't you ever hear of the pill? What's the matter with you anyway? I suppose you'll never know the father."

"Oh yes I do."

"Hmph. That's a switch. Is that why you call yourself Raleigh now? Are you married?"

"No. But Mr. Raleigh and I have an understanding."

"That's convenient. Okay, Wanda, I'm afraid we can't put you in your old room. It's occupied. You'll be over in the south wing . . . Number 9. Behave yourself and you'll be out in six months. Just in time to have your baby. And let's hope you won't break parole *again* . . . I suppose you'll apply for public assistance?"

"No. That won't be necessary. What I can't handle the baby's father will. He's a man of his word. A real gentleman." Wanda hesitated. "And Miss Pope. If you still have that drafting class can I get back in it? Maybe I can't learn it all in six months, but it's a start for when I get out and this time I'll really concentrate."

"We'll see what we can do."

As always when the inevitable day came that Hickock was obliged to place his signature to a sentence he was troubled. And as always he now wondered if he was the right man for the job . . . Now on this otherwise sprightly morning he chewed thoughtfully on the horn of his glasses while he riffled through the sheaf of papers before him. Lucinda had typed the final draft of his opinion on the Estervan case, and he hoped it reflected at least some honest wisdom. The sentences he had finally determined were on separate pieces of paper.

Looking back, Hickock was appalled at how long he had agonized over his decision; too much of the six weeks, he realized, had been procrastination, not deliberation. It was now when the morning cut a sharp rectangle across his desk that he longed to be a Brandeis, a Frankfurter or a Holmes. Some much brainier brain than mine, he thought, should be resolving the future of Boris Estervan and Martin Chisolm, who directed the film, and Tony Arbutto, who procured the juvenile girls. It was going to be a very controversial series of sentences. No one, not the Moral Majority and not the ACLU was going to be satisfied. Their representatives were already gathering along with the media outside the courtroom.

Sentencing the defendants who were directly involved in the filming had been relatively easy. Two years for Chisolm with a chance at probation after one year. Tony Arbutto, who had been either careless or stupid or both in finding the girls, would pay more heavily. Three years. Why? There was some chance, although by no means any certainty, that such a heavy sentence might discourage other procurers who were cynical enough to identify themselves as agents from doing the same thing.

According to the judgment of the jury they had violated the law. Once that had been established the sentencing should have been automatic, but Hickock had decided that in this case there were no real victims. To suggest that the two girls who performed before Estervan's cameras must have had their morals corrupted was ridiculous since their records proved they had happily abandoned any recognizable moral code at about age fourteen.

The news media riding a sudden holier-than-thou mood and encouraged by a confused legislature who were on the verge of passing an obscenity law that was so all-encompassing it amounted to covert censorship of every art and communication including the printed word, had suddenly charged to the rescue of the two supposedly innocent maidens. There had been photos, cartoons, and stirring prose depicting Estervan as an arch villain. A caricature on the editorial page of the city's paper featured Hickock leaning far out from his bench and regarding the girls' cleavage with an unmistakable leer. The caption was: "Tut-tut, my dears, it's all in fun." He had not been amused.

From what he could gather in his daily rounds Hickock had become convinced the public would like to see Estervan strung up by the thumbs or even his neck. Those who held that the accused had not committed anything more than a misdemeanor were no more than a handful. Because of the publicity Hickock thought that this was hardly the best time for any pronouncement of sentence, but he could not delay any longer. Today, on Friday the seventh of the month, all but Estervan would be taken away by the sheriff's officers, processed through the county jail, and within a few days transported to the State Penitentiary. While they were hardly the sort of men Hickock would have chosen as regular companions, he knew his mouth would sour when he looked down from the height of his bench and declared their future. He took no pleasure in the realization that he was giving them less than the maximum punishment allowed by the law. They were not going to learn anything in prison and certainly not contribute anything to society. Roughly, he had calculated their incarceration would cost the taxpayers at least one hundred thousand dollars plus the amount of taxes they might have paid if they were making money in the real world.

As for Estervan, Hickock thought, uneasy lies the head that wears the crown. For the jury had found him technically as guilty as the others. He had not been present during the filming of the girls, nor was there any solid proof that he had prior knowledge that they were underage. Yet he was the captain of his ship. He was also an unsavory character in a nasty business and he stood to profit by whatever his henchmen produced.

But then, as always, there was the other side. Estervan was well past middle age and the notion that any of his habits, or activities, would be changed because of a year or two in prison was just not realistic. The system said that he was guilty of wrongdoing, but the fact was he had actually done nothing. And if the law was not supposed to demand vengeance must it then demand that Estervan be punished for something he had not done?

The final decision was there on the top of his otherwise clear desk.

Boris Estervan, for violation of Criminal Code 9 Section 2, (employment of minors for pornographic photography), two years in the State Penitentiary—suspended.

Yes, he hardly needed to remind himself, Estervan was a lousy human being . . . a man who had tried to bribe him, to intimidate him with phone calls to his lady. But he had neither been indicted nor convicted of those acts. The press would howl that Julian Hickock was the worst kind of a bleeding heart judge, and they might even hint that he had been paid off. If they carried the condemning on long enough and loud enough his defeat in the coming election would be almost a certainty. Good. There would be a lot of wounded Hickock pride scattered about, but at least the distress involved in making decisions like this would be over. And maybe, he thought, he should never have been allowed to put on a black robe, since a stubborn honesty and a law degree from a middle-rate college were all he had to offer.

Hello to equity and farewell to rancor, he thought. Maybe his critics would feel somewhat appeased when they heard the balance of Estervan's sentence. He would not have to spend even a day behind bars, but his purse was going to suffer a severe puncture. First he must pay a fifty-thousand-dollar fine to the state and all legal expenses created by the actions of his case. Martin Delgado would like that. Next he had one year to perform four hundred hours of public service, the nature of which to be designated by his parole authority, or (his choice)—exhibit only film available through the regular commercial distributors in his theaters for the next two years.

For the last time Hickock asked himself if the restriction on Estervan's choice of films amounted to a form of censorship. And he concluded that if it was censorship, it was at least admissible. His decree would not affect the right of the public to see what they wanted, since there were other theaters where the so-called pornographic films were available.

Hickock glanced at his watch. He took off his glasses and rubbed at the bridge of his nose. It was nine-forty-five. In fifteen minutes, according to schedule, he would make his cuckoo-clock entrance to his courtroom. But this morning he would enter with as much dignity as he could muster because Estervan and Chisolm and Arbutto would all be watching for even a slight indication of his decision. For them this was no ordinary day, and villains or not they deserved whatever sense of majesty the law provided.

Imagine, he thought, what the result would be if an ordinary citizen said to another, "I am going to put you in chains for two years." Depending on the available weapons someone would certainly be injured. Yet because of a black robe he was reasonably certain the accused of this morning would take their sentences without physical protest and probably without a sound.

Now, unasked, Wanda suddenly intruded on his thought. He tried to remember how she had reacted when he had pronounced her unfit and ordered her daughter to be taken into custody. But he could not recall her behavior . . . too many faces, too many eyes unbelieving, too many despairs revealed. Perhaps it was a good thing that they all eventually melted into one, although at the crucial time of trial they had been overwhelmingly singular to him. Maybe it was instinctive self-protection as it must be sometimes for doctors . . . concentrate on the case at hand but don't dwell on it when it's over, or risk going out of your mind.

He could not reverse Wanda's original sentence now, but if she were to come before him again under the same charge he thought he might look at her differently. Did that mean that if the judge dared to doubt himself he could have been wrong? If so, where was the forgiveness for such error?

He ran his fingers through his hair, angry at himself for such useless brooding. He picked up the phone and punched Jean Pomeroy's number.

"Hello. I called for no real reason except to tell you how very much I need you at fifty-six minutes past nine on this particular morning."

"Good. Then you haven't been thinking about throwing me away."

"Not likely. At this time tomorrow morning we'll be sailing and I need a crew. You're elected."

"My sleeping bag is rolled around a bottle of burgundy. Ready to go, sir."

"Would you mind if Vic came along?"

"Will he mind if I do?"

"I don't think so. I told him you gave me life and he understood."

A pause. "Likewise."

They said a quick goodbye and Hickock rose. He went to the clothes locker by the door and took out his black robe. He slipped into it easily, conscious as always that the mere action caused something very complex to occur within him. Now, almost instantaneously he became another man. For he had always known that here within this simple black fabric might be hidden the true sovereignty of the law. Here, slipped on like another skin, was a mere human suddenly elevated to deal with life and death and misery and joy. The "Your Honor" fitted now, if not for the ordinary man protected within then for the robe itself as the symbol of civilization.

Hickock took a final glance out the window because the sight of the real world of sky and clouds helped place his courtroom in perspective and gave him a sense of permanence; it was easier to believe the dramas of good and evil he witnessed from his perch had been performed since the earliest tribal elders sat in the shade of trees and heard the same arguments. The thieves and pimps and murderers, the harlots, the rapists, the drunkards, the wife beaters, the derelicts and the lechers, the borrowers and the lenders, the schemers, the exploiters, the rascals and the bullies—nothing among them was new, and so in a sense nothing was changed.

Nothing in ten thousand years.

Except now perhaps, there was the hope that a man in the right place might contribute a minuscule stone to the bulwark of his society. If a man believed in the rule of law, and was fortunate enough to serve it, he could also believe that his own small role might help speed by at least a fraction the long march forward from revenge and barbarism.

No doubt about it, Hickock thought as he ascended the bench. He was a lucky man.